Tam.. Cohen is a freelance journalist ... with her partner and three teenage child... Her first novel was the acclaimed *The Mistress's Revenge*. Her third novel, *Someone Else's Wedding*, is out now in Doubleday hardback. Follow the author at @mstamarcohen.

Praise for *The Mistress's Revenge*:

'Deftly plotted and bleakly funny, with a devious twist of an ending, this is a dark tale of love gone wrong'
Marie Claire

'Gasp in recognition at this cracking tale, narrated by a woman scorned . . . Sister, we've all been there'
Grazia

'Dark, often funny, sometimes unnerving'
Woman & Home

'This book is *Fatal Attraction* with a twist and will grip you from the beginning to end'
Prima

'Hell hath no fury like a woman scorned'
Essentials

Also by Tamar Cohen

THE MISTRESS'S REVENGE

and published by Black Swan

The War of the Wives

Tamar Cohen

BLACK SWAN

Tamar Cohen has asserted her right under the Copyright, Designs and Patents
Act 1988 to be identified as the author of this work.

This book is a work of fiction and, except in the case of historical fact, any
resemblance to actual persons, living or dead, is purely coincidental.

A CIP catalogue record for this book
is available from the British Library.

Addresses for Random House Group Ltd companies outside the UK
can be found at: www.randomhouse.co.uk
The Random House Group Ltd Reg. No. 954009

The Random House Group Limited supports the Forest Stewardship Council®
(FSC®), the leading international forest-certification organisation. Our books
carrying the FSC label are printed on FSC®-certified paper. FSC is the only
forest-certification scheme supported by the leading environmental organisations,
including Greenpeace. Our paper procurement policy can be found at
www.randomhouse.co.uk/environment

Typeset in 11/14 pt Sabon by Falcon Oast Graphic Art Ltd.
Printed and bound by CPI Group (UK) Ltd, Croydon, CR0 4YY.

2 4 6 8 10 9 7 5 3 1

MIX
Paper from
responsible sources
FSC® C016897
FSC
www.fsc.org

For Billie, with all my love

PROLOGUE

When those who were present look back on Simon Busfield's funeral – which they still do, although less harshly as time goes on – they might disagree on the peripherals: who was standing where, whether the sun flung dark shadows like nets over the guests, or whether the clouds muffled the light before it fell. But on the basic facts, they are unanimous: the two women facing each other, dressed in black, the grown-up children who encircled them like a ring of barbed wire, all sombre clothes and sharp-edged grief, the outrageous claim that momentarily hung solid in the air before mushrooming over the proceedings like an atomic cloud.

By the time that cloud finally dispersed, a great many things had changed. It is a question of perspective whether those changes have proved to be entirely for the worse. Still, it is the moment itself that matters, not the ripples that came after it; the moment when Lottie Busfield, trailing her daughter behind her like a wheel-on suitcase, came face to face with Selina Busfield, the grieving survivor of a twenty-eight-year marriage, outside the crematorium.

Two wives. One husband. You can see how that might be awkward.

But then again, not technically wives any longer.

Widows. Two widows.

Part One

DENIAL

1

SELINA

Flora is perched on the kitchen table, her big blue eyes following me around the room. She has just finished a very long-winded story about a party she and Ryan went to where Ryan was the only person who refused to wear fancy dress. Ryan thinks fancy dress is 'gay', apparently. Give me strength! I maintain a diplomatic silence. I've discovered that's the best way of dealing with the matter of my daughter's inappropriate boyfriend. If I were to voice an opinion – that he has all the charm of a dead haddock, for instance – she'd go back to giving me the sanitized PR version of Ryan – the Dear Leader version, as Simon calls it – like she did in the beginning when it became obvious what Simon and I thought of him. At least this way I get to hear the truth, even if the price is that I have to swallow my own tongue at times.

So I nod, and murmur appreciatively, and start wondering – oh, the guilt – how soon I'll be able to switch her off.

That's the problem with Skyping. You can never get away. There's some old friend or family member on the screen on your table, or the arm of the sofa, and you've had a lovely chat, but you're now running out of things to talk about, and because they can see everything that's going on, you can't invent a saucepan boiling over, or a ring at the door, or any of the normal things that end a conversation. So there's an awkward pause while you come up with something else to say and try to stop yourself thinking about the million and one things you really ought to be getting on with.

The other problem with Skyping is – and I know this makes me sound as if I come from the Jurassic era – that you can *see* the other person. The other day, I was thinking about how Simon and I never Skype, even though he's always away. Of course, that's partly to do with us both being so ridiculously busy, but really, I realized, it's more to do with the business of sitting there *looking* at each other. Even though we've been married all these years, it made us both uncomfortable the couple of times we tried it. It's so *intimate*. When we first got together we used to spend hours sitting across from each other in cafés and pubs, playing with each other's feet under the table while we put the world to rights, but what couple who've been married nearly thirty years still gaze into each other's eyes when they talk? There's something unnatural about it. Awkward. I found myself focusing on the collar of his shirt, or the wayward lock of hair he kept smoothing back with his hand.

I don't actually *want* to be able to see the people I'm talking to. It's distracting. While Flora launches into yet another long-winded story, I'm looking at her frizz of hair and thinking (yet again) how much better it would look if she had it cut. Nothing extreme. Just a little bit of shaping. And I'm looking at her desk in the architectural firm where she works as a PA and noticing, with a bit of a wince, that she has some kind of cuddly toy on there (no doubt bought by Ryan in a petrol station somewhere), and I'm looking at her clothes and wanting to cut through her story and shout 'Colour block!' or 'Texture!' or 'Layering!' or any of the other stupid things overbearing mothers want to say to their grown-up daughters but don't dare. It's a kind of maternal Tourette's, I suppose.

Instead I tell her I have to be getting to the gym. This isn't technically a lie. I do have a class. Flora doesn't need to know it doesn't actually start for another hour and a half. Then we have that awkward Skype goodbye moment where neither of us wants to be the first to click on Disconnect. Silly, isn't it? It ought to be a straightforward technological act. Lean forward, press, gone. Yet it feels like an emotional rejection.

At the gym, I try to concentrate.

'Into the Half Moon. And ho-old . . .'

Jawohl! While my body obediently contorts itself as instructed by the new rather Germanic instructor of Hatha Yoga (Advanced, Wednesdays), my mind keeps itself busy.

1. Book Pierre's for Book Club Christmas Lunch (just let them *try* to tell me there aren't any tables left, in *September*!).

2. Research printers for Simon's study. Criminal, those ink-cartridge prices . . .

3. Ring round for history tutor recommendations. Surely one of the other mothers must know someone, preferably someone who doesn't smell of wee like the last one.

Starting to ache now. I shoot a glance at the mirror that runs the length of the studio wall in front of me, surreptitiously comparing myself with the rest of the class.

Body straight, arm stretched. Not bad, as long as you overlook the slight sheen on my forehead. So unforgiving, those overhead lights, even after two sessions of Botox and a discreet dermal filler (not that I'd ever admit *those* to anyone). But when you consider I probably have a good ten years on most of the women here, I think I'm doing OK. Not that I like to think in terms of age. So counter-productive. And so bloody depressing!

4. Call Lorenzo and make sure he has the revised flight times. Oh, and get him to stack the firewood in the main living room. Not much use to us outside the back door. Not with Simon's back. Which reminds me . . .

5. Make appointment with chiropractor.

6. Email that friend of Hettie's about the Cricket Club fundraising quiz questions. No soap opera questions this time, please God!

7. Send out Tweet about the Book Club Lunch. Mustn't forget!

Ouch. I don't actually gasp out loud, but my arms are starting to feel the strain. Sadist, this instructor. Some of the other women have already collapsed in a heap on their mats. Stamina. That's the thing. You can have a twenty-five-year-old body, but if you have no stamina, you might as well give up.

'And straight into the upward-facing dog.'

In my head I heard Josh's voice mutter, '*You're* an upward-facing dog,' and I can't help smiling. Internally, obviously. Such a worry, that boy, even at seventeen, but he can still make me laugh. The other day I asked him to unload the dishwasher, and he muttered under his breath, '*You're* a dishwasher,' and we both looked at each other crossly and then laughed like drains. Not funny in the slightest,

14

now I think about it, but somehow it was at the time.

'Come on, ladies, stretch those necks, lengthen those backs.'

The instructor has very muscly calves, I notice as I stretch and lengthen like crazy. (Even at fifty-one I retain a ridiculous compunction to please. I can criticize the instructor till the cows come home, but it doesn't stop me craving her approval. Go figure, as my friend Hettie would say.) She makes her rounds of the class, tucking in chins and pulling back shoulders. She could be a pretty girl if it wasn't for those calves, but I don't think men really like that kind of thing, do they? All that gristle. It's so important to know where to draw the line. I think so, anyway. I know I'm probably not best qualified to know what men want, having been married for so long, but you don't have to be actively engaged in the business of men to appreciate what they do and don't like. It's like our villa in Tuscany – I'm not looking to sell it, but I still like to know what's happening in the Italian property market. It's just a question of being prepared for every eventuality. I know there are some people who believe being prepared spoils things, takes away from the spontaneity of life. The same people who love surprise parties, probably. Personally, I can't think of anything worse. What if you had on a dress you'd always loathed, one of those 'fat dresses', as Flora calls them, that you throw on those mornings when you wake up feeling the size of a house? (I don't actually have a fat dress myself, although I do have a couple of pairs of good quality leggings I reserve for that time of the month.) What if the person organizing the party forgot to invite the most important people or, worse, invited people you couldn't stand?

After the exercise class, I get out my Emergency Repair Kit. Little travel-sized jars into which I've decanted some essential toiletries. There's something very therapeutic about the ritual of applying nice-smelling stuff on fresh cotton-wool pads. It feels *useful*. Practical. When I look at my reflection in the mirror of the Chelsea health club (*not* a cliché, whatever Simon may say – just convenient, and really not so very expensive when you work out how much use I get out of it. Not like Hettie, who jokes that when she was a member she used to pay £2,000 a year for a sauna and a half-leg wax), I make sure to do it piecemeal fashion. Hair, eyebrows, upper arms. Anatomical fragments. After forty-five, you don't really want to go looking at things as a whole. That's one thing I've learned. Now I'm fifty-one, I'm finding out about the places inside yourself where you can tuck doubts away like unopened bank letters. The trick is to break everything down into its constituent parts and work though them systematically. I like to look in the health-club mirror and focus on the positives – overall shape, level of fitness, a general sense of purpose – rather than the areas where I can't compete, like youthful complexion and cut-away shoulders.

In the changing room afterwards a woman compliments me on my cardigan. It's a new powder-blue one I'm rather pleased with so I ought to feel gratified, but something about this woman bothers me. Her nails, when she puts out her hand to stroke the soft cashmere, are all broken with bits of ragged flesh around them, a bit like Josh's. *What kind of person chews their own skin?* I used to ask Josh as a boy. *Are you a cannibal?* The thing he never seemed to get is that people judge a lot about a person by the state of his or her nails. Of course, he used to argue that those were the very people whose opinion he least cared about, but he'd be surprised how important those kind of things can be. My own mother taught me early on that there are few challenges in life that can't be faced more easily secure in the knowledge of the possession of well-manicured hands and matching underwear. 'It's about self-esteem,' I tried to tell Josh. 'That boost that comes from knowing yourself to be . . . in order.' *In order!* I made him sound like a lavatory! No wonder he looked at me as if I was bonkers.

'You always look immaculate,' says the woman in the changing room. 'It puts me to shame. I feel like a complete *mess* in comparison.'

Oh Lord. Clearly what I should do at this point is to disagree warmly, or say something self-deprecating, but the truth is she *does* look a mess. She has on one of those flesh-coloured thermal tops that make people look as though their upper half is encased in a surgical bandage, and a pair of faded black multi-pack-style knickers. I don't mean to be unkind, but obviously she has money or she wouldn't be here in the first place, so presumably she has a selection of clothes, and it seems bizarre that she must have *chosen* to wear that top, weighing up its relative merits this morning against some other less offensive item before deciding in its favour. So I say, 'Nonsense, you look perfectly nice.'

Which, as everyone knows, roughly translates as 'Oh dear God.' The woman backs off sharpish after that, and I feel like giving myself a good slap. All the way home in my zippy little Fiat 500 with the red leather trim that usually cheers me up, I feel cross and out of sorts. 'Kindness costs nothing,' I used to drum into my three children as they were growing up. Oh hypocrisy, thy name is Selina Busfield!

On reflection, I should have made the cardigan situation into some kind of joke, only I'm so useless at jokes. Simon once told a dinner-table of guests that I don't have a 'talent for humour'. I was in the kitchen preparing the dessert at the time and he was holding court, rather drunkenly. He didn't know I could hear him. 'Selina has many talents, but humour isn't one of them,' he said.

I never told him I'd overheard. But it hurt. Those kind of throwaway remarks always do. What was that wartime slogan? Careless talk costs lives. Someone should remind Simon of that from time to time. Of how much can ride on a careless comment.

The journey home takes an age. The roads are already being dug up and repaired in preparation for the Olympics, even though it's still nearly two years away. Waste of money, if you ask me. All those new state-of-the-art stadiums. What will we do with them when it's over? Pay our gas bills with them? Prop up the euro with them? Use them to sort out the bogging mess the universities have got themselves into?

A couple stroll past as I am idling at a junction. They have their arms draped across each other's backs, hands plunged deep in each other's back pockets. They are laughing at something on a mobile phone, their faces tilted together, and I feel this sudden whoosh of longing. To be so included in someone else's world. As I watch the X of their arms against their backs recede into the distance I suddenly feel like bursting into tears, which is most unlike me.

As I cross the river and approach the wide leafy avenues

of Barnes, my bad humour persists, prompting me to notice all the irritating details I usually blot right out – the CCTV cameras sprouting like alien fruit from telegraph poles and lampposts, the custom-built timber-clad huts that house the wheelie bins. (In Barnes, plastic is practically illegal. Christmas mornings are filled with the outraged wails of children who've been bought tasteful wooden toys instead of the garish coloured ones they covet from the television ads.) Funny how, even after twenty-seven years in our home, I still navigate my way around these streets according to the properties we saw when we were house-hunting all those years ago. *This road had that one that was deceptively spacious inside, but no garden to speak of; down there is that one that smelt like someone had died in it.* Of course, there are the inevitable pangs of regrets also. *Who could guess that street would become so desirable? If only I hadn't let Simon talk me out of taking on that structural work!*

Turning into our road, I have the strongest urge to talk to Simon. Not for any gooey reason, but because he is the only person I ever want to talk to in moods like this. As my husband it's his job to listen to the failings of my day, and then to poo-poo them – Clause 593 in the Married Couples' Charter! I don't have to pretend with Simon that everything is hunky dory. There's always a degree of pretence with other people, isn't there? How could there not be?

But Simon is AWOL somewhere in the Middle East. Not in his apartment in Dubai, I don't think, but somewhere else to do with this new contract. He's not due back until tomorrow night. Anyway he'd think it was odd if I rang him out of the blue in the middle of one of his trips. We don't have that kind of marriage. Thank God! Not like Hettie and Ian, who call each other ten times a day to talk about absolutely nothing at all. *This train is so crowded! I was boxed in at the supermarket car park! I drank three espressos and now I feel like the Duracell bunny!* Blah blah blah. And always finishing with an 'I love you.' So unnecessary. Love is like any other commodity. The more you flaunt it, the less value it has. The real trick is to make the other person *feel* loved (Clause 594!). I always make Simon one of his favourite meals after he's been away – roast lamb or beef, Yorkshire pudding, the works. There's a joint waiting in the fridge downstairs ready for tomorrow night. What greater expression of affection is there than cooking for someone? Words are just words. It's *doing* that counts.

Simon would be shocked if I tried to track him down. He's constantly marvelling at how self-sufficient I am. 'Selina doesn't even notice if I'm there or not' is his regular joke. Bloody good thing too, seeing as he spends half his life away from me. Dubai, for goodness' sake! Even after all this time I still can't quite get over it. Why couldn't it have been Spain or South Africa – somewhere with a bit of culture or beauty? At least he's used to it now, being there on his own, but I still feel a bit guilty. I did *try* to like it, but I knew as soon as I got there it wasn't for me. Ghastly place, I've never felt heat like it. And the dust! When we drove out of the airport, there were all these cars around literally covered in the stuff. I assumed they'd been abandoned there for years, but Simon said they'd probably only been parked there a few weeks. I haven't set foot back there in nearly twenty years. Can it really be so long? It's horrible how time compresses itself these days like one of those zip files on my computer, all the hours stuffed inside like duck down into a pillow.

I haven't really got a leg to stand on when it comes to him spending so much time away, but there are times, like now, when I long to be able to just pick up the phone without even thinking, without having anything in particular to say. He rings me, of course, between meetings or from a bar (so irritating that there's still no signal in his apartment), but by then I've always forgotten why I wanted to speak to him so urgently in the first place. Quite often, in fact, he catches me at an inopportune moment – in the middle of a Cancer Research fundraiser meeting, or taking my mother shopping in the ghastly new retail park – and I end up being curt and snappish, quite forgetting how much I've been wanting to hear his voice. It's the little things that are often lost between us, the minutiae from which intimacy is stitched. Sometimes I feel a bit sad about it – all those trivial moments that have slipped through the cracks between the floorboards of our marriage.

I decide to phone Felix instead. My older son has spent a lifetime filling in for his AWOL father, but increasingly he's becoming first choice. I know that's an awful admission and he'll probably end up in therapy for life, but there's something about the way Felix says 'Hola, Madre' that instantly calms me and reminds me how much I have to be proud of: my beautiful six-bedroom home, my three largely on-the-rails children, my fundraising work, my size-twelve figure, my legendary pavlova (well, what's the point in being coy?), my patronage of struggling artists, my newly rationalized wardrobe, my never-missed twice-weekly visits to my mother at the marvellous residential home I almost killed myself researching, my competent skiing, my law degree (well, one year of it anyway), my olive oil made from our own olives from the trees around our Tuscan villa and given out at Christmas with our own distinctive, specially designed (by Josh) labels, my discovery of just the right white for our bedroom walls, my vegetable garden.

Felix doesn't answer. He must be busy with work. I have to admit I don't have much idea what he actually does for a living. Something creative, I know that much – something to do with film. He seems to spend a lot of time in meetings (at ridiculous hours of the night) in various Soho bars and restaurants, and it certainly seems to be lucrative enough – Shoreditch lofts don't come cheap these days (not like thirty years ago when they couldn't give them away). I remember us all trooping off to Wardour Street last year to see that film he'd made. We were ushered into a private viewing room with plush, purple-velvet seats set so far apart we practically had to yell to hear one another. The film was short, barely half an hour long (*thank God*, said Simon later), and consisted of a couple arguing in various locations around London. The arguments always started off with something completely random, like the man accusing the woman of sighing loudly, and her denying it. Then they'd escalate to full-on shouting matches during which the woman kept saying she'd 'settled' by entering into the relationship. I didn't entirely understand it, but you could tell it showed promise, although Josh said, 'If I'd wanted to listen to people arguing with each other I'd have hung around the girls' changing rooms at school.' Flora, bless her, tried to be tactful, but put her foot in it by asking, 'Why was it all filmed at night?' Felix was quite touchy about it. Apparently the dark quality is all to do with mood. Who knew? Which is another one of Hettie's sayings.

Back home again, I feel at a bit of a loose end. Walter, our ancient arthritic Miniature Schnauzer, waddles painfully over to greet me, and I manage a distracted pat, then sit down heavily on the bottom step of the elegant curved staircase that first made me fall in love with this house. Can it really be nearly three decades ago? I run my fingers absently along the wall. So glad I stuck to my guns about the plum colour, when Simon was so set on grey.

'Have you lost the use of your legs?'

Oh my!

It's a funny thing about having nearly grown children – especially ones with older siblings who've already left home – you're always forgetting they're there. So Josh's face looming upside down as he bends over me from the step above gives me a jolt.

'Just taking off my shoes,' I tell him, although it's patently obvious I'm doing no such thing. It's just as well Josh exists in a separate time/space dimension where nothing that isn't directly related to his own physical or, on the odd occasion, emotional needs actually registers.

'Did you warm up the cottage pie I left for you?' I ask.

'Nah. Couldn't be bothered. Had some toast.'

I close my eyes and count to ten in my head. Then I heave myself to my feet and make my way into the kitchen. Yep, still there! On the work-surface where I left it lies a carefully written list of instructions. ('Turn oven on. 180. Far left knob, not middle knob which is timer,' etc., etc.) Next to it, the unblemished mashed-potato face of the cottage pie smirks up at me.

'Just goin' out, yeah?'

Question, or statement of fact? It might be either.

Statement, I decide, and attempt to protest, more because it's expected than out of any great conviction.

'Joshua, it's a Tuesday night. You have mocks in two weeks for which you haven't done a jot of work. You were out all weekend—'

'Whoa!' Josh raises his hands, mock-surrender style, and shuffles around amiably, pulling on his thin nylon jacket. 'Nah worries. I know all that. That's why I'll be back in an hour or so. Just need to see a mate about something.'

'One of your estate friends, I suppose.'

I hate the way 'estate' has become an adjective in my vocabulary. I know it makes me sound like a terrible snob, but in my defence I don't mean it that way. I'm genuinely glad Josh is socially grounded and can mix with all sorts of different people. It's just that it seems so wilfully stubborn of him to hang out with the kids from the estate two roads away when there are so many interesting people at his own school. One of his classmates even has a recording contract, for goodness' sake! Not that Josh sees it that way. I once overheard him tell Felix, 'Mum thinks my friends from school don't take as many drugs as the other lot. What she doesn't realize is they take just as many drugs, only they pay twice as much for them! What's so great about that?' I took it with a pinch of salt, though. Younger brothers – always trying to impress.

'I really would prefer you to stay home tonight.'

'Yeah, I will. Promise. Just as soon as I finish this thing I gotta do quickly.'

I stare at his retreating back as he makes his way out of the kitchen, narrow shoulders adolescently hunched in his hooded jacket. There's something about men's backs,

I always think, that makes them appear so vulnerable.

'Am I invisible?' I call after him. 'Mute? Do I even exist?'

I'm not being entirely facetious either. More and more, I find myself wondering if I exist outside of my children's need for me. Rather, I know I exist, as an amoeba or mould exists. But existing with purpose. That's the thing.

Alone, I move aimlessly around the kitchen, eyeing with disapproval the five-ring range (with inbuilt electric griddle) and the industrial stainless-steel fridge that Simon bought from a famous 1980s pop singer who lives two doors away and which shows every finger mark. Really, what's the point of a five-ring range when I'm on my own half the time? Or a titanium Kenwood mixer? Or a set of heavy copper-bottomed saucepans big enough to cater for a dinner party of sixteen? What, when you come down to it, is the point of *me*?

I don't often go in for this kind of mawkishness. Normally I regard self-pity as a needless indulgence, like scented bin-liners, but today I feel disquieted. Sitting down at the enormous blond-wood table that dominates one end of the open-plan kitchen-diner we had built on to the back of the house, I retrieve my iPhone from my handbag and call Simon's number. Yes, I know it's stupid, but maybe, just this once, I might get him between meetings or just getting up or just going to bed. (I've long since stopped tracking his progress through the time zones. Let the silly bugger muddle up his own body clock!) No chance. His phone immediately diverts to his voicemail service, a sign that he's either busy, sleeping or in transit, the three states that between them account for 99.9 recurring per cent of Simon's life.

'You're so lucky with Simon,' Hettie is always telling me, making him sound like a used car bought randomly through the classifieds with which anything could have gone wrong but miraculously hasn't. 'He hasn't slowed down like so many men our age have. He isn't defeated.' I never tell her that sometimes I'd quite like him to slow down a little. Just so I don't always feel like I'm in second place.

There I go again, with the self-pity! I jump up and stride over to the 'everything drawer', which is on the right-hand side of the deep, white custom-built storage unit that occupies the far wall of the kitchen-diner. The 'everything drawer' is where odds and ends and miscellaneous items end up, a planned oasis of chaos amid my otherwise strictly disciplined kitchen. Rummaging around, I pull out my diary. Eureka! A week before my period is due. I feel a twinge of relief at being able to slap a 'hormonal' label on my weird mood. Also, to be completely honest, at my age there's a certain relief that there is to *be* another period. Troublesome though they are, these days there is always that slight pang when each one ends. Might it be the last? There really is no way of telling. No one rings a bell to warn you it's the last stop. Like so many important life events, you don't know it has happened until it is already over. A long time ago, pre-Simon, I went to an end-of-pier palm reader while on a hen-party weekend. 'You'll have one all-consuming love of your life,' the old woman told me, before frowning and peering closer, holding my hand up to the light. 'Oh, looks like you've already had it,' she said. Well, naturally everyone else found it hysterical but I was secretly appalled. Can such things really come and go without you even noticing?

Much later, while I'm in bed doing my Duty Reading for my book club – the most *dreary* collection of short stories (why does literature have to be so depressing? As if life wasn't depressing enough?) – I hear the front door slam. Josh is home, my signal to turn the light off. I fall asleep listening to the familiar crash and clatter of my younger son in the kitchen preparing himself another round of toast, or heating up one of those awful Pot Noodle things he always makes me bulk-buy.

Some time afterwards, I'm awoken by the phone ringing. Sluggish with sleep, I vaguely register that it's the house phone. Who rings on the house phone, for goodness' sake?

'Mrs Busfield? Mrs Selina Busfield?'

My head still fogged with dreams, I think it must be Simon, calling inconsiderately from Abu Dhabi or Qatar or wherever place he's gone, miscalculating the time difference, as he's done before.

'This is Detective Inspector Bowles from the Metropolitan Police, Mrs Busfield.'

A polite voice, but devoid of warmth, as if the inside has been scooped out and discarded like a Hallowe'en pumpkin.

But the landline? Why would anyone be ringing on the landline?

'Mrs Busfield, we're outside your house. Can you let us in?'

'But what—'

'The front door, Mrs Busfield. Please?'

The hollow voice is firm, and I find myself obediently slipping my arms into my new waffle bathrobe. From long-ingrained habit I make a quick detour into the en

27

suite bathroom to run a comb through my hair. The familiarity of the action wards off the panic I can feel bubbling up inside me. *Keep things normal. That's the key. Don't think about what a policeman at the door in the middle of the night might mean. That way everyone will be safe.* Glancing into the mirror, I'm reassured at how calm and ordinary I look, although my eyes are those of someone I don't altogether recognize.

Opening the front door takes time. The alarm has to be deactivated (the day and month of Felix's birthday. Mustn't panic and mess it up), top and bottom bolts drawn, chain taken off its latch. Amazing that Josh remembered to do all that last night for once. All my nagging must be paying off! I don't rush. If I can control the opening of the door, I can control whatever is coming next. *Thump, thump, thump.* How loud my heart sounds.

Detective Inspector Bowles is a pointy-faced man with that sort of hair that changes from blond to ginger like a two-tone suit, depending on the light. He is wearing a rather hideous thigh-length black leather jacket with a wide elasticated band around the bottom, and a camel-coloured scarf that blends so seamlessly into his freckles it makes him seem like he's naked under his jacket. With him is a heavy-set young woman in a police uniform who introduces herself with a name I instantly forget.

'Mrs Busfield?'

What if I don't let them in? Then they won't be able to say whatever it is they're here to say. But of course my years of social conditioning kick in.

'Come in,' I say, and hate myself for minding that Josh has left his trainers strewn messily on the floor at the foot of the stairs. Who thinks about mess at a time like this?

Instinctively, I lead them into the kitchen rather than the living room. I've watched enough TV detective programmes to know bad news comes to people perched stiffly on the edge of sofas, not casually arranged around a blond-wood table in a warm family kitchen. I'll be safe here because of the dentist reminders pinned to that awful monolithic fridge by circular jolly-coloured magnets, and the remains of a Pot Noodle next to the sink. All this is protection against something bad having happened to Flora, or Simon. Or Felix.

'Is your husband here, Mrs Busfield?'

The gingery policeman sits opposite me, turning his mobile phone around between the fingers of his right hand. A fidgeter.

'No, he's away. Saudi Arabia somewhere. Or Bahrain.' In my nervousness it comes out sounding like brain.

The woman, who is sitting at the end of the table, glances away at this point, seeming to find something intensely interesting about the all-singing, all-dancing espresso machine Simon bought but which neither of us has ever managed to master. She has thick orange foundation which stops at her jaw, making her neck appear to belong to someone else.

'Is there something wrong?'

Idiot! As if there might yet exist the possibility of there being nothing wrong, of two strange police officers dropping in at 3.42 a.m. for a random social visit.

The ginger policeman clears his throat slightly. He's obviously the designated spokesman.

'I'm sorry to tell you, Mrs Busfield, that a man's body was found in the Thames near Limehouse earlier tonight. Your husband's wallet was in his pocket.'

Limehouse? The panic that has been bubbling in the pit of my stomach like simmering stock is washed away by a tide of relief. A mistake then. Simon is abroad. In the Middle East somewhere. He isn't in Limehouse. Where is Limehouse anyway? It is some other Simon. Some other poor woman's husband.

'I'm afraid you're wrong, Detective.' My voice is calm and authoritative. Someone used to dealing with crises. Someone used to clearing up muddles. The kind of voice a police officer can respect. 'My husband is several thousand miles away on business.'

'I very much hope you're right, Mrs Busfield,' the policeman replies, although he sounds as if he very much believes I'm not. 'But we need to make sure. I know this must be extremely hard for you, but perhaps you could pop upstairs and get dressed and come with us to make an identification. Is there anyone you'd like to call to come with you?'

I shake my head and get heavily to my feet. Denial fits around my skull like a crash helmet. *Not him. Limehouse. The idea!* At the bottom of the stairs, I pause to pick up Josh's trainers. That boy! How often do I have to tell him?

I'm conscious of my composure, my purposeful walk. The two police officers must be grateful not to be dealing with the type of woman who gets hysterical and falls apart.

Entering my bedroom, done out in its shades of white and ivory, I look at the bed. The duvet is thrown carelessly aside and the plump feather pillow is still softly dented like a mound of just-started basmati rice. *Oh!* I feel a sudden sharp sense of loss for the woman who raised her head from the pillow (can it really be just minutes ago?) and fumbled for the phone, her thoughts full of sleep and time zones.

Completely calm, I sit down on the edge of the bed, immoveable, inscrutable, sphinx-like. A woman in control. Moments later I'm surprised by a commotion at the bedroom door. Josh bursts in, and it's a shock to see his normally unruffled, practically catatonic expression replaced by wide-eyed panic.

'What?' he yells, and his seventeen-year-old voice breaks, exposing the child's squawk hiding underneath like new skin. His big boy-man's hands are on my shoulders and he's shaking me, quite roughly. 'Mum! What? *What?*'

I haven't seen him like this for an awfully long time. Nakedly afraid. Not for years, I suppose. It's quite awkward really. He'll be embarrassed afterwards, I'm sure. Poor Josh.

I summon my maternal impulses and try to formulate some kind of verbal reassurance, more from habit than anything else. There is a sudden and terrible silence.

That's when I realize I've been screaming – an awful, high-pitched reedy wail that, now I've stopped, is notice-able only by its absence.

2

LOTTIE

My head is wedged into a stranger's armpit, I swear to God. It's my own fault for squeezing on to this crowded Tube instead of waiting for the next one like I'd normally do. After two years back in London you'd think I'd have learned by now. The armpit in question belongs to a man in a grey shiny suit with short black gelled hair, who is listening to his iPod on full blast. The bass tones shudder right through me, though he obviously believes himself to be in his own hermetically sealed little world. Silly, to be in such a rush just because Simon's coming home. I ought to be a bit more blasé about it by now.

Already, the thought of Simon is making me forget about work and about the lovely but inept temporary receptionist head office lumbered me with all day. She's hardly older than Sadie, no joke, and has clearly never come across the concept of VAT before. Still, I must try to put all that out of my mind. I'll try to concentrate on my Happy Place. That's better. *Dappled sunlight, cool water.*

My sister Jules reckons it's because of the constant separations that I still get a thrill from seeing Simon, even after all these years. 'Your relationship is nothing but partings and reunions, it's bound to be passionate,' she says. Of course, she's exaggerating. And of course, she's jealous, seeing as she's been single for two years now and claims the hole has closed right over like an ear piercing.

'It'd take a fucking pneumatic drill to get through that,' she says. She can be so disgusting sometimes. Simon claims that's why she's into all this New Agey stuff. 'Wise move on her part. Focus on the mind and soul, give up on the body,' he said, even though there's nothing wrong with Jules's body. She just has her own style. We had a big row after he said that. I hate anyone criticizing either of my sisters. I know I do it all the time, but that's different. The way I see it, when you love someone, you can say pretty much anything. I think so anyway. Love excuses a lot.

I suppose Jules is right in a way, about the separations. It must be the same with soldiers and their wives. But she's wrong about it being the partings and reunions that are the main thing. Since we've moved back to the UK and I've begun to feel more settled, it's the bit in between, the anticipation, that's the best. Even after all this time, I still love the build-up to seeing him again. Occasionally – and I don't like to admit this – the reality can be a bit of an anticlimax. Sadie and I are such a tight little unit when he's away. We fight like cat and dog, but we function together. All that changes when Simon is home. After he's been back a while, there's usually a bit of a dip while we readjust to the reality of each other – the bristles left in the sink after he's shaved, the pressure of proper mealtimes again, when Sadie and I are happy with a sandwich and a yoghurt in front of the TV, the guilt that I'm spending time with him instead of working on my illustrations, or vice versa. But the anticipation of him being back? Now that is something else.

Crowded on the 106 from Finsbury Park station, I glare at a woman at the back of the bus who has spread her stuff over two seats. Some days that kind of thing makes me want to scream, but today I try to let it wash over me and focus instead on the letter G. I've been stuck on G for days. It's such a funny shape – a sweeping curve with a little straight bit on the end, like it doesn't really have the confidence to be completely one thing or the other. I've got to get past it though – Mari's already extended our dead-line until the middle of October.

I find myself imagining (*again!*) how much more I'd be able to get done if I didn't have to work in the hotel and could spend all day instead in the newly installed studio-cum-office-cum-jumped-up-shed in the garden at home. Incredible now to think of all those years living in the sun-shine with nothing more pressing to do than read the next chapter of my book and track down the latest new restaurant; all those years I could have spent drawing, but hardly ever did. What did I do with all that time? Did the sun just burn it all away? No point regretting it now, I suppose. Who knows, maybe this book – an alphabetized fantasy story and my third collaboration with Mari – will be the one that actually makes us some money! Everyone knows it's easier and less painful to get rich from selling a kidney than illustrating children's books, but you have to dream, don't you?

I dive into the corner shop near the bus stop for some eggs for Sadie's dinner and a celebration bottle of wine. As usual, I dither for a while in the wine aisle. Lucky Simon isn't here. My inability to make even the smallest decision unaided drives him up the wall. 'Next you'll be asking me whether or not you want to go to the loo,' he said the other week when we went to a party and I made him decide which shoes I should wear. Most of the time I think he quite likes being needed, but sometimes I suspect it gets on his nerves. I suppose when you spend your working life making decisions, you must long for the occasional break. I went to see a counsellor about it once, my indecisiveness. At thirty-eight it's embarrassing. She said, 'Ask yourself what's the worst that could happen if you make the wrong choice.' I try it now. *What's the worst thing that can happen if I choose a naff bottle of wine?* But I don't really see the point in that approach. It's so negative. Why would you want to go through life focusing on the worst things that might happen?

In the end I splash out on an £11.99 bottle – the most expensive in the shop. I have a pang of guilt at the counter when I think about the unpaid TV licence, but hey, you only live once. (Unless, like Jules, you believe we live an infinite number of times, but not necessarily in the same bodily form. Good. Maybe I'll be taller next time. With boobs!) 'Simon's on his way,' I tell Mr Patel at the checkout, who goes through the usual pantomime of being heartbroken that I'm married, while Mrs Patel rolls her eyes and does her Sudoku.

On the short walk home, I juggle my shopping bags so that I can try Simon's number again. Still switched off! It's quite often off or out of signal in the Middle East, but it ought to be back on again now, surely?

If you'd told me when I first started art school that I'd end up with someone who works as a property developer, even an 'international' property developer (how amusing my sisters always found that phrase – *my brother-in-law, the international property developer*), I'd never have believed it. Painter, singer – that's the kind of person I thought I'd be with. Not that it's what Simon imagined for himself either. You don't do a history of art degree thinking, 'Oh, I think one day I'll go and build some hotels in the desert.' The way I see it, most of us fall into things, don't we? Simon 'fell into' what he does after getting a job on a property magazine. It sounded exciting, I suppose – travel, money, sunshine.

Then I fell into Simon.

'Completely crazy,' was my parents' verdict when I said I was flying halfway across the world to live with a man I'd only known a few months. I didn't dare tell them I was already pregnant by that time.

Looking around now at the grey London street, it seems weird to think that other world still exists, that even now there are people lounging on luxurious cream-cushioned beds on white-sand beaches being waited on by men in spotless white uniforms, or walking barefoot through marble-lobbied apartments, relishing the feeling of cool stone against the soles of their feet. Funny how it's always those things you remember, and not the gridlocked cars or the stink of the drains in the summertime. Memory is a slut, as my other sister, Emma, is fond of saying.

I can still remember flying into Dubai for the first time all those years ago. (How brave that younger me was – I wonder where all that courage went? Now I can't even buy a bottle of wine on my own!) A few weeks, that's what I told myself on the plane over. Just a few weeks, to make up my mind about Simon and about the baby. I had no intention of staying. Whenever I'd dreamed of foreign travel it was of the tropical jungles of South America, Africa, South-east Asia. I'd never pictured deserts where the only things growing were gold-plated hotels. But the lifestyle was so seductive, and love can be a jungle of its own. Weeks turned into months, and months into years, time trickling through my fingers like water in a palm-shaped swimming pool, no joke.

It's different, time here and time there. Here you're always aware of how little time there is, how much there is to do in it. There you never noticed time – until it was gone.

I try Simon's phone again, even though I know I'll get the same 'switched off' message. I ought to be used to it now, but it still frustrates me, that sense of Simon being out of reach, even after all these years of separations. It was the separations that finally forced the move back here. Dubai can be fun, but not for a woman on her own with a child, as I was for half the time.

Every Christmas when Sadie and I used to come back to Derbyshire to stay with Emma and her kids (so weird leaving Simon behind to work, even though Christmas isn't at all the same there and he always says it's a load of commercialist crap anyway), I'd wonder why I stayed out there. I'd all but stopped doing anything creative. That hot wind – like spending your life inside a hair dryer – saps your motivation. Simon seemed to be spending half his life in London anyway, so why not base ourselves back here? At least I'd be able to work again, and Sadie would get a different perspective, away from that crappy little international school. Ironic to think now I actually believed the change might make her less difficult (not difficult, *challenging* – Jules says I must change my mind-set), although I try not to complain too much to Simon about that. He was so set against us moving back here.

We knew the cost would be crippling – keeping up the rent on his apartment in Dubai as well as buying a flat in London was never going to be easy, and of course the property market going tits up over there hasn't exactly helped. I don't want to risk an 'I told you so' by moaning about Sadie's moods.

Now we've been back nearly two years it's as if those fourteen years abroad never happened, like new skin forming over a cut so you can't tell it was ever there. Even Sadie, who lived there all her life, is struggling to believe it was anything but a dream. It's amazing how quickly she's adapted to being in London – the clothes, the way she speaks. Such chameleons, children. The only thing I miss about Dubai is the money. It's hard to get used to worrying about finances after years of it all coming so easily. Even with my job at the hotel, we're still struggling. It doesn't help that neither Simon nor I have the saving gene. As soon as we get money, we spend it. There was that blow-out party for Simon's fiftieth back in Dubai. And the flat here cost a lot more than we'd planned to spend, but as soon as I saw the height of the rooms and the cornicing on the living-room ceiling, I fell in love with it. And then there was the outside studio . . .

No. I'm not going to think about money now. 'Whenever a negative thought occurs, you have to pluck it out of your head, like plucking an eyebrow,' Jules told me the other week. Blimey, I'd have no eyebrows left! I'd be like Anya at work and have to paint them on.

Ours is one of those schizophrenic London streets where big old Victorian villas that have been carved up into flats butt up against low-rise blocks and boxy sixties-built houses with mean little windows and concreted front yards. Sometimes when I turn on to the wide path that leads to our front door (*still* boarded up, even though the burglary was months ago now. We must call the free-holders again to complain. A job for Simon), I imagine how it would be to own the whole house instead of just the ground floor. A century or so ago, the whole thing would have belonged to just one family. The top-floor flat, where that new young couple have just moved in, would have once been the servants' quarters. Strange to think of all that history, literally sitting on your shoulders. That's something you don't get in Dubai amid the soaring steel towers and the bland apartment complexes.

Still, no time for all that today. The communal hall is scruffy and littered with flyers for fast-food outlets and Indian takeaways. There's a pile of mail on the bottom step of the carpeted staircase that leads to the upper three storeys, but I don't bother going through it. The only things we ever get through the post are bills, and I can do without any more of those tonight. Anything to do with money sends me into a spin, always has done. Before I met Simon, when I was still in art college, I managed to get into so much trouble my bank manager made me cut up my credit cards in front of him. I remember struggling to keep a straight face. It was just like being back at school and being hauled in front of the headmaster. That was in the days when bank managers were real people, not computers, or underpaid minions in a call centre in Glasgow or Delhi or somewhere. Simon's not much better than me at the money side of things, but at least he takes care of the joint account, as well as his own. I only have to manage mine, but even that seems to be beyond me sometimes. Usually we muddle along, but every now and then Simon will say, 'Time to tighten your belt.' (I hate it when he uses that expression – it makes him sound so *ancient*!) At the moment we're in a 'tighten your belt' phase. I'm *useless* at tightening my belt. We both are, really.

The door to our flat is at the back of the communal entrance, to the left of the staircase. Inside, the narrow hallway is in darkness, which means Sadie isn't home yet, which makes me both anxious and relieved. Anxious because it's six thirty and she bloody well ought to be home, or at least have let me know where she is (she's only sixteen – not twenty-six, as she'd like to think). But also relieved I'm spared having to tiptoe around her moods. Hopefully by the time she gets back, Simon will be here. She never acts up in quite the same way when he's around. There's something about mothers and daughters, isn't there? Sadie is a daddy's girl, through and through.

When I switch on the light, there's a sudden explosion of colour, like fireworks, not just because of the burnt-orange-painted walls, but also the mishmash of paintings, a few by me but most of them done by Sadie as she was growing up, and the photos and silly postcards from travelling friends and from exhibitions we've seen over the years. The floor is bare wooden boards, but there's a long, thin, rather threadbare rug on the floor in multicoloured stripes. 'Your hall is the colour of happy,' Emma's youngest once said when she came to visit. I've never forgotten that. The colour of happy.

I drop the shopping and rush through to the bathroom at the back of the flat, intending to have a quick shower, but of course I stay in there way longer than I should, slathering myself in gorgeous-smelling bath stuff which reminds me again of my sister Emma, whose bathroom shelves are crammed with expensive, unopened bath oils and body lotions she's been given for Christmas and birthdays but is waiting for an 'occasion' to use. She also has a set of 'best' cutlery, for Christ's sake. 'What if you get run over by a bus tomorrow?' I ask her. 'Before you get a chance to use all your stuff.' She doesn't get it though. She just says, 'If I got run over by a bus, it'd be just my luck.' I love Emma dearly but I hope to God I never end up like her. Three gorgeous kids and an adoring if not wildly exciting husband, and yet she still won't allow herself to be happy – always holding back on the things that give her pleasure, always looking for downsides.

When Simon's away I never think about my body, but now I stroke it all over as if I'm rediscovering it all over again. Hello, little pot belly! Hello, newly shaved legs! Always the thrill of imagining my hands are his hands, feeling what he will be feeling. Such a shock to remember I'm a physical presence, after two weeks of living solely inside my own head.

When the water starts running lukewarm, I wrap myself up in a towel and dart into our bedroom, hoping no one is watching. Our bedroom looks out across our section of the back garden, now dominated by our all-singing-all-dancing outside studio. In the summer it's fine because the trees planted against the fence at the end shield us from the row of houses behind, but it's September and the leaves are starting to thin out, and I'm suddenly a bit paranoid, us being on the ground floor and everything. The room has a massively high ceiling, which is what I love about our flat, but it isn't huge, and the king-sized bed takes up most of the floor space. I finally got round to changing the sheets last night, which has to be my least favourite job. Try wrestling a cover on to a king-sized duvet when you're only five foot one! Now, flinging myself back against the newly laundered pillowcases, I'm glad I made the effort. There's something so restorative about clean sheets. And these are my favourites – bright fuschia with yellow block-printed flowers. It's like sleeping in a Warhol print. From here I get a perfect view of the painting on the far wall – a nude of me done by an art-school friend, which Simon insisted on bringing back from Dubai. Sadie used to love that painting – 'Mummy being *rude*,' she used to say. Now, of course, she just thinks it's tacky.

My handbag is on the mattress beside me, and a little frisson of guilt passes through me as I retrieve the small package. *Ta-dah!* New knickers! I bought them on my lunchbreak today. I know I shouldn't have (the TV licence!) but I just couldn't resist. At least it's only under-wear, not a new pair of shoes or a dress or anything. There's something about putting on a new pair of knickers, especially silky black ones with pink spots and a pink bow at the back that come wrapped in tissue paper from a shop that definitely *isn't* M&S, that makes you feel instantly sexy, which is just as well because Simon and I have a lot of catching up to do!

It's not really about sex though – well, not just about sex. Whenever Simon comes home after being away, I almost feel like I have to reclaim him. I know that sounds mad (when I told Jules she said it was 'sick'), but I can't help it. I don't feel relaxed until we've been to bed and I've taken him back, so to speak, like a dog marking its territory. Sometimes I think it's to do with me being so young when we first met. I hadn't long got out of that adolescent stage of writing my name in books or anything else I could get my hands on. (I've noticed Sadie does it too, always very neatly, unlike her usual writing. I think it's a girl thing.) As I was the youngest of three sisters, there wasn't much in our house that hadn't already been claimed with someone else's name, so it seemed extra important to me. I even had a special pen I used – a fine-tipped blue ink-pen – and I'd practise my writing in rough beforehand, to make sure I got it right. Maybe that's what I'm doing with Simon – writing my name on him all over again. I hope he's not knackered out, like he sometimes is when he gets home from a stint away. I *hate* that. It reminds me of the fifteen-year age gap, which is one of those things like pensions and life insurance that I can't bear thinking about.

'You'll wind up being his carer,' my mum charmingly pointed out when I rang to confess we'd got married on a beach in Goa, with just a couple of newly made friends for witnesses. That was another thing that bothered my mum. 'Why couldn't you get married in a church like normal people?'

I did try to explain how Simon had been engaged once to a woman who'd made such a song and dance about the bloody wedding that he'd been put off them for life. That's partly why he was so relieved to meet me, because I've never really been one of those Big White Meringue Dress kind of girls. While I've always loved owning nice things, I never wanted to own a husband, not even a nice one. Being bridesmaid at both my sisters' weddings was quite enough for me, thank you very much, especially as Jules's wedding ended in divorce within eighteen months – she was still paying off the loan for the dress when she was signing the bloody divorce papers. I can't think of anything worse than stressing about seating plans and whether the bridesmaids' flowers match the groom's cummerbund. We probably wouldn't have bothered to get married at all if we hadn't living in Dubai, where you really don't want to go having a baby out of wedlock.

Now Sadie's older, of course, I can understand why Mum worried so much. When your children are younger you think you want to raise them to make their own choices, but gradually you realize what you really mean is the *right* choices, *your* choices.

I wish Mum had lived long enough to see how happy we've been, Simon and I. Not that we haven't had our bad patches, and some spectacular rows – especially in the beginning when I was so insecure about him being away all the time and needed constant confirmation that he wasn't about to go looking for someone else whenever he got lonely. But on the whole we've been happy and it upsets me that Mum never got to see it. Sometimes I wonder if that's the thing you miss most when someone dies, not so much the person themselves as the things they'll never now know about you and what's happened in your life. The you they'll never meet.

Every now and then it does cross my mind that Simon and I might get married all over again back here, in a proper church wedding. I'd love a big party with all our friends and my dad and sisters, and Sadie of course, but it isn't a big deal. When we first met, Simon loved how unconventional I was about things like that compared to his ex-fiancée. Selina. Even her *name* is prissy! Apparently she was totally insecure and status driven, and incredibly possessive. I'll never understand how he ended up with someone like that. Even though he finished with her years before we got together, I've always made a point of being everything I imagine she isn't – even though I admit sometimes I've had to bite my lip a bit.

Like about him getting that new contract just after we'd moved back to London, which means he now spends just as much time away as before. I can't really complain, seeing as he only took it to pay for the move and because the market in Dubai was so crap, and as *Seleeeeena* would obviously have thrown a hissy fit about something like that, I had to try to take it in my stride. Well, mostly.

Anyway, the one good thing about him going away is him coming back! He should be here any minute!

My phone rings while I'm cracking the eggs into the pan. I've got Adele playing at top volume so I have to strain to hear what the unfamiliar voice is saying.

'Lottie? It's Chris.'

'Chris who?'

I'm already cursing myself for answering. All I want to do is get this bloody Spanish tortilla out of the way for Sadie. (When is she ever going to grow out of this vegetarian phase? And where the hell is she, anyway?) Simon and I will get a takeaway or something later. (Sometimes I wish I was the kind of woman who could throw together a lovely home-cooked welcoming meal, but fuck that for a game of soldiers at the end of an eight-hour shift! Anyway Simon doesn't mind. He calls me his undomestic goddess. 'Just as well she's good in bed or I'd have to chuck her,' he joked the last time I attempted to cook dinner for friends – a risotto that looked and tasted like wallpaper paste.)

My impatience must be obvious, because the voice on

the other end of the phone goes all tight and thin like a skewer.

'Griffiths,' he replies. 'You remember?'

'Oh my *God*!'

I'm so surprised that it comes out as a kind of squawk. What the fuckity fuck does Chris Griffiths want? I haven't seen him in aeons. I start babbling like a complete lunatic to cover my embarrassment, as I always do, but he butts in, and his voice is now all tight and awkward. All of a sudden I have a vivid image of him standing in the doorway of my old flat, shifting his weight nervously from foot to foot, and I feel sorry for him. He was always so socially uncomfortable.

'I found your sister, Emma, through Facebook of all things,' he said, making Facebook sound like something from Mars. 'She messaged me your number. I just wanted to say how sorry I am. About Simon, I mean.'

The phone is tucked uncomfortably under my chin, and I'm conscious of the oil still spluttering angrily in the pan. I think about turning the sound down, but my iPod dock is out of reach on the table, balancing on a pile of Sadie's schoolbooks. The place is a tip. Funny how when you live with mess you don't notice it, but then something unusual will happen that shifts you out of your normal perspective, like an old boyfriend phoning out of the blue, and all of a sudden you're seeing the things you don't normally see. Like the empty pizza boxes on the chair, and all the stuff for the recycling heaped on top of the wooden counter next to the sink.

'What do you mean?'

It's the weirdest thing, I start to have this tingling feeling, like an anaesthetic working its way through my body.

Chris's voice, when he replies, is even more awkward than before, if that's even possible. 'Our old boss at the property mag Simon and I worked on all those years ago sent an email round this morning saying Simon was ... Well, he had ... you know ... died. I know we didn't part on the best terms, but I really was ... that is to say, I really am ... terribly sorry.'

The oil is crackling ferociously now and I turn it down absently while my brain tries to sort out what's been said. Obviously there's been a horrible mistake, but that awful word *died* is bouncing around my skull, making it impossible to focus.

'I don't have a clue what you're on about.'

Is it some sort of sick joke? Chris Griffiths was always on the odd side. I try to see how it could be funny, but there's a horrible black shape forming in the back of my mind and the tingling is getting worse.

'Simon's on his way home. He'll be here any minute. He's been away.'

But my mind keeps replaying the 'this phone is currently switched off' message I've been getting every time I try to call.

'He quite often has his phone off when he's away,' I add unnecessarily, wishing Chris Griffiths would just go away so that I can get rid of this bloody black cloud mushrooming in my mind.

'Look, Lottie, I don't know what's going on. If I've made a mistake I'm really sorry and embarrassed, but the email was very specific. It even included information about the funeral tomorrow. Oh God, this is just so awful.'

'Well, why don't you get straight back to whoever sent that horrible email, and find out exactly what they're playing at? It's obviously a mix-up, or some stupid joke, but tell them to get their bloody facts right next time.'

As I press the Off button on the phone, I'm suddenly aware of a sticky warmth in my right hand. Then clear liquid begins trickling through my fingers. I gaze transfixed at the remains of the egg I've been holding in my palm.

Oh God. Oh God Oh God Oh God. There's now a pool of yellow-stained albumen on the wooden kitchen floor. If I focus on that, I can block out any other thoughts.

Where's my asthma inhaler? Where is it? Thank God. *Press and gulp. Breathe. Breathe.*

I need to talk to someone. I need to hear a reassuring voice tell me that Simon is where he should be, doing what he should be doing. But even as I'm scrolling madly through my phone contacts, I'm realizing that there's no one. Simon's working life in Dubai is pretty much a solo operation so there are no work colleagues I can call, and all our friends here are ones we've made together. Like most men, Simon's useless at keeping in touch with people from way back, and his parents are both dead, so no help there. I can feel a ball of panic building inside me. If I stay here, staring at the mess of egg on the floor, I'm going to explode.

In desperation I ring Jules, although if she starts spouting any of that self-help-book crap I'll hang up, I swear to God.

'Oh fuck, babes, that's awful.' My sister's voice is squeaky with shock and indignation. 'Don't worry, Chris Griffiths always did have a screw loose. I'm sure Simon will walk through the door any minute. You've just got to have faith, hun.'

I'm glad now that I called. Of course it's a mistake. I'm

so stupid sometimes, always jumping in when I should hold back and analyse a little more.

'I do have faith,' I say, not wanting to tell her about the black shape at the back of my skull or the hammering of my heart in my chest. 'I'd know if something had happened to Simon. I'd know deep down.'

'Absolutely, babes. There's such an *amazing* connection between the two of you, something would have told you if he'd . . . *gone*. Just keep those positive thoughts going.'

All of a sudden there's a beeping noise. Another call coming in. Simon – finally! My heart jumps right into my mouth and I cut Jules off without a word.

'Hello?' I shout. 'Simon?'

But the voice isn't the one I'm longing for.

'Sorry, no. It's Chris again.'

His voice has always sounded like that. Nervous and trembly. I mustn't start reading anything into it. It's the way he's always been.

'Look, Lottie, I don't know how to tell you this. I wish to God I didn't have to. But I've spoken to Bill, who sent the email. He says there's definitely no mistake. I'm so sorry, but it seems Simon really is . . . God, this is so horrible. He really is . . . dead.'

My head is shaking, even before he has finished speaking. Stupid. Chris Griffiths was always stupid, and always, always jealous of Simon. He never forgave him for all that business. Trust him to get the wrong end of the stick. Trust him to get it all wrong.

'I'd know. The police would have told me. Someone has to identify a body. Someone has to arrange a funeral. You're talking rubbish. I don't know why you're talking such rubbish. I would have been told.'

Chris makes a noise that's halfway between a groan and a cry, and for some reason it makes me hate him.

'I'll forward you the funeral details. What's your email?'

To my astonishment, I hear my own voice obediently trotting out my email address quite as if there isn't a fucking great tsunami churning everything up inside me, turning me liquid.

'I'll send it now. Oh God, Lottie, please believe how sorry—'

But Chris's sympathy is lying in the puddle of egg, and now I'm on my knees, watching the yolk seep into the denim of my jeans and trying to close my thoughts down one by one so I don't have to think about what he's said. 'He's wrong,' I repeat like a mantra. 'He's wrong, he's wrong, he's wrong.' Simon is on his way back from Dubai. Even now he's in a taxi somewhere, getting closer. He's probably had the driver's entire life story already – so maddening, that compulsion to get perfect strangers to open up.

I have no idea how long I remain like that, but at some point the doorbell rings and I fall into Jules's arms on the doorstep, almost sending us both crashing to the floor. 'He's wrong,' I tell her. 'He's wrong, he's wrong, he's wrong.'

And now Jules is logging on to my emails, bright-red hair falling over her eyes, and opening up the one from Chris Griffiths. And there's a funeral notice and the name Simon Busfield jumps out like something in a horror film. There's also a newspaper snippet. Fragments embed themselves in my fogged mind like shrapnel. 'Drowned . . . Police still investigating . . .'

I'm making a noise like cattle make when they're scared,

and now Sadie is coming in and Jules is trying to explain to her what is happening and why her mother is lowing like a cow. I watch as my daughter's face, which is Simon's face, crumples in on itself and now I'm staring at the bony ridge of her back through her T-shirt as she bends double over the rug, shoulders heaving, retching. 'It's a mistake,' I tell her, as Jules runs to get a cloth, but deep down I know it isn't. And all of a sudden I'm running through the flat like a mad thing looking for Simon in every room. In the studio in the garden, I fall to the pine-boarded floor and curl up like a broken thing. Finally I allow the black shape to overwhelm me. I'm waiting for Simon to come and find me and tell me that everything will be OK.

He doesn't come.

3

SELINA

∽

The thing about grief is it doesn't exempt you from normal life as you somehow imagine it should.

There are moments when I feel my insides going into spasm as if someone is grabbing hold of my guts and twisting. Then the next moment I'm putting out the bins, or answering the door to the gas-meter man, or plucking a stray hair from my chin, or taking Walter for a walk, or any of the other myriad tedious chores that make up my daily life.

'You're so incredible, the way you just get on with things,' Hettie said when she walked in just now and found me emptying the glasses from the top shelf of the dishwasher.

For heaven's sake, who does she think is going to do it? The dishwasher fairies? Hettie is my closest friend – it's inconceivable to me that she can't tell from looking at my face that barely ten minutes ago I was curled up over there in the corner of the kitchen, rocking back and forth on the Chinese black-slate hand-cut floor tiles and wailing like a banshee.

It's been six days since Simon's death (funny how I can

say 'death' or 'since he died', but not 'dead'. Never 'dead'.
It's something about that word and how it sounds, the
dreadful finality of that one harsh syllable with its thudding
'd' at the end), and I don't even recognize my own life any
more. I mean, obviously it's still my life – my friends are still
my friends, my children are still my children, but it's as if
someone has taken my life and rotated it ninety degrees so
it's all fractionally and eerily different, like when you get out
of a lift you always take one floor too early.

'I don't really have a choice,' I tell Hettie. 'When it
comes to getting on with things, I mean.'

'Yes, but lots of other women would be in *bits* on the
day of their husband's funeral. No one would blame you
in the slightest if you were a complete *basketcase*!'

I don't know how I'd have managed without Hettie
these last six days, but now I can't help wondering if she
isn't a tiny bit disappointed about how well I'm coping,
outwardly at least. Not that she wants to see me falling
apart or anything, but I suppose there's something a bit
spoil-sporty about a stoic widow on the day of her
husband's funeral. *Widow!* The word slices right through
me. I've always loved being a wife, loved being introduced
as Simon's wife. In the early days, when he was still working on the magazine, I used to ring the office sometimes
even if I knew he was out, just to say to the secretary, 'Tell
him it's his wife,' just for an excuse to say the word. How
can I bear a lifetime of being a widow instead?

'Ian will be here in an hour or so,' Hettie says. 'I wanted
to come early. To give you support.'

I notice that Hettie's brown eyes have dark-red rings
around them as if she's been wearing too-tight ski goggles.
It's not surprising she's taking it so badly. She and Ian have

been our oldest friends since university days. Yet somehow it seems to me that Hettie is wearing her mourning like a badge and her red-ringed eyes feel like a rebuke. I have the maddest urge suddenly to turn myself inside out so that Hettie can see what I'm really feeling. Like that awful building in Paris with all the internal pipework on the outside. I want to reach inside myself and pull out a random handful of grief and thrust it under her nose. *See?* I'd say. *See now?*

Instead I say, 'Thanks, darling, I appreciate it.'

'How are the children?'

Always the children. I'm so sick of being asked about the bloody children. It's as if people think that my concern as a mother will somehow transcend my grief as a wife. No, not as a wife. As a widow. *Bugger the children*, I feel like saying. *Bugger their needs. What about me?*

Of course, I say nothing of the sort.

'Oh, you know,' I tell Hettie. 'They're managing in different ways.'

As if on cue, there's the sound of a key scrabbling in the front-door lock, followed by Flora's anxious voice.

'Mum? I'm here. Where are you, Mummy?'

What's left of my heart sinks a little. I'm barely coping with my own grief, how can I be expected to deal with my daughter's as well? Especially when there's so much of it, spilling out of her like an overfilled cup.

Flora arrives in her usual breathless rush. Immediately she launches herself at me, enveloping me in a tight hug, so that my face is pressed into her hair. My heart softens at the sight of her, but the hug goes on just a little too long. She has always been so tactile, Flora, so unboundaried when it comes to other people's personal space.

Eventually I escape.

'New dress?' I ask, just for something to say. Flora is clad in billowing layers of black. She's clearly been aiming for Helena Bonham Carter, but somehow it looks as though she's wearing a burka instead.

'Yes. Do you like it? Do I look OK?'

Always the constant need for my approval. For goodness' sake, she's twenty-one years old!

'It's fine, darling,' I say. *Perfectly nice, I said to the woman in the gym in that other life.*

'You look lovely,' she tells me, and all of a sudden I think I might burst into tears. Other people's kindness is so hard to take at the moment. It's true, though, I've taken particular care over how I look today, selecting a slim, knee-length black dress with a deep V-neckline that Simon always liked.

'You're the classiest woman in the world,' he'd say whenever I wore it. I never told him that just once it would have been nice to be the sexiest woman, or the most beautiful woman. There's something a bit mealy-mouthed about classy, isn't there? Something not quite from the heart.

I've teamed the dress with a pair of slate-grey mid-heel suede shoes. There's always the temptation to go higher, but who knows how long I'll be on my feet? All that meeting and greeting and keening and weeping and rending of garments that'll be expected of me.

Oh God, I can't do it. I can't . . . No. Mustn't panic. Just take it one step at a time. Leave the house, get Felix to pick up Mother, arrive at the cemetery. That's better. Baby steps. Don't think of the thing as a whole, of what it all means. It's a series of stages, that's all, one after the other, until it's over.

Getting ready this morning, I sat at my dressing table and dried my hair smooth with a flat paddle brush as I always do. It's second nature to me now, that blow-drying, brushing routine, and I do it without thinking. But halfway through, I stopped for a moment and looked at my reflection and all of a sudden I felt disgusted with myself. Who was this woman preening herself in the mirror on the morning of her husband's funeral? And more than that, what was it all for now that he's gone? All the preparations and the potions and the sit-ups and the miracle anti-ageing creams – what use are they now there's no one to come up behind me and put a big warm hand on my shoulder and say, 'I don't deserve you. I really don't.'

You'd have thought, wouldn't you, that the worst thing about having a husband who dies (*not dead, mustn't say dead*) is trying to find a moment in the day when his death *isn't* what you think about? But actually it hasn't been like that. I'm so used to his absences that all week I've been having to remind myself again and again that he's gone and that I won't be hearing his key in the lock and the thud of his case on the hall parquet. 'He's gone,' I keep repeating to myself like a mantra. 'He's gone.' It's as if I have to keep making myself feel that pain, just to prove that it's real, like moving a wrist to make sure it's actually sprained.

Already I worry about forgetting his face. Ridiculous when our whole marriage has been full of absences. I stare at photographs as if cramming for an exam, trying to commit him to memory before it's too late. But it's already too late.

When Flora compliments me on how I look, I'm aware of Hettie's red-ringed eyes as she leans against the granite worktop and I get that feeling again of being judged. Not on how I look but how much I'm grieving. Now that I'm a Widow, not a Wife, does it count against me that I've taken such care over getting ready? Can love and loss really be measured in lipstick and styling mousse?

'Is Ryan with you?'

I try to make my voice natural, but as always it tightens a bit when I pronounce Flora's fiancé's name.

Flora doesn't seem to notice. 'He'll be in in a second. He's just pre-setting the sat nav ready for the funeral. He doesn't want to leave anything to chance.'

She stumbles on the word 'funeral' and her wide, pale-blue eyes begin to water. My heart constricts but I stop myself moving towards her. I need to keep myself together in order to face what's coming. I can't fall apart now.

A nervous cough announces Ryan's arrival and I try to arrange my features into what I hope resembles a smile before turning to greet him. Despite my best intentions, I find myself appalled all over again at Flora's choice of suitor with his slightly shiny suit and pasty complexion, hinting of over-boiled vegetables and holidays in Wales.

'Sorry for your boss,' he mumbles.

What?

I gawp at him, uncomprehending, before it dawns on me that of course he said 'loss', not 'boss'.

'Thank you, Ryan,' I manage.

I can see that Ryan is trying to be sympathetic, it's just that sometimes it seems to me that he attempts emotions like someone else might attempt a particularly ambitious roulade.

Thankfully the awkwardness is interrupted by Josh ambling in wearing a pair of novelty boxers with a clover print and the message 'Lucky Pants', and an old grey T-shirt. He has the barely-conscious look of someone fresh out of bed and still half asleep.

'*Joshee!*'

Flora, all this time silently weeping, leaps to her feet and flings her arms around her younger brother. Taken aback by the ambush, Josh stands frozen to the spot, patting her stiffly on the back while making exaggerated expressions of wide-eyed strangulated alarm over her shoulder. Eventually he pulls away and turns to Hettie.

'All right, Bossman?'

At the use of his childhood nickname for her, Hettie instantly bursts into tears, her face cracking apart like a poppadom, and I get the impression she's been waiting for an excuse to cry, as you do sometimes. *But surely it's me who should be crying?* It must be hard for her, watching the children suffer like this. She's known them since birth, after all. Hettie's own daughter, Hannah, used to splash naked with Flora and Josh in a paddling pool right here in the garden. And now he's to be fatherless, this boy who once asked her, aged five, for a tie for Christmas so that he could be like his dad. It's insupportable. Yet it must be supported.

My voice, when it comes out, is gruffer than I intended.

'Joshua, we have to leave in half an hour. You promised you'd be ready on time. Couldn't you have made an effort, today of all days?'

Josh is bearing the brunt of my irritation, but really it's Ryan I'm cross with, with his suit and his sat nav and his eyes that never quite meet mine, and therefore Flora by implication for bringing him. And Hettie. All that judging. When did grief become a competition, I'd like to know?

But no, that's not it either. Really, underneath it all, I'm angry with Simon. All our married life we've planned and negotiated jointly, sitting down at the beginning of each month with our diaries, synchronizing and compromising – well, as much as is ever possible when one partner spends half his life working away.

Our family life is controlled by schedules and computerized 'to do' lists. When the kids were younger I used three different-coloured felt pens to plot their activities on the family calendar that always hangs on the back of the kitchen door. Felix was red, Flora pink (such a cliché, I know) and Josh blue. 'Cricket Club!' screamed the red pen. 'Drama!', 'Debating!' The blues were mostly about playdates: 'sleepover at Michael's', 'football party'. For two memorable years, there was a steady succession of blue 'trumpet lesson' markings, and we were all relieved when these were replaced with '5-a-side training', also in blue. I remember Flora once standing in front of the calendar, eyeing the lack of pink marks amid the sea of red and blue and saying sadly, 'I don't do much, do I?' How dreadful I'd felt, because of course she was right. If only she hadn't insisted on giving up ballet. If only she'd stuck at the tennis. Stupidly, I'd tried to make up for the disparity by writing Flora's activities in bigger letters, as if that was going to fool anyone! And now all this planning ahead, all these *contingencies* have been for nothing. Because this thing, this biggest of things, is the one I never allowed for.

Josh looks up at me from his heaped bowl of cereal with his hazel eyes with their ridiculous black lashes above cheeks still randomly (and mortifyingly to him) freckled, and whoosh! What was a rush of anger becomes a rush of love, so intense I have to look away. My feelings are like that at the moment, turning on a dime. For the past six days and nights, since Life As We Know It was ended by the ringing of the phone in the middle of the night, Josh and I have skirted around each other like tongue-tied teenagers, both of us silenced by the memory of that scene in my bedroom with Josh's wild face and his hands on my shoulders and my own dismembered howling voice. Embarrassing now to think of it. I ought really to talk to Josh about how it has affected him, that horrible night. I ought to set aside my own grief to concentrate on his, as I used to set aside my own meal in order to cut his up first. Yet somehow I can't. Grief has made me selfish.

'According to my mate Tom-Tom, it should take exactly eight minutes to drive to the cemetery,' Ryan informs us. 'Best leave twenty, to be on the safe side. Flo has been operating on half speed all week, haven't you, doll?'

Ugh! I can't work out what I hate more, that awful 'Flo' or the 'doll' self-consciously tacked on to his insipid Hounslow tones like a slogan badge.

'I wouldn't worry,' says Josh, affable as ever. 'I've been operating on half speed for years.'

Again that burning rush of love, mixed with worry. It's the day of his father's funeral – shouldn't Josh be showing some sort of emotion? Just how deeply is he burying things?

Still, at least he was spared what came after that scene in the bedroom. That's one relief – that I made Hettie come round to the house rather than take Josh with me. He protested, but I was so right to leave him. My memories of that night are disjointed, like fragments of a vase that's been broken and then stuck back together all wrong. I remember going into that place in East London somewhere with those two police officers who'd come to the door here. I'd known them less than an hour yet already I felt locked into some bizarre love-hate relationship with them. What's the name of that thing kidnap victims get where they form attachments with their captors? Stockholm Syndrome. I couldn't bear to look at them, yet equally I couldn't bear the idea of being separated from them.

The place we went to was strip-lit from above so everyone's faces looked greenish-white.

'This isn't him.'

I didn't even need to look at the figure under the plastic sheet. (Plastic! For the man who hunted down the finest Egyptian cotton.) The left hand was uncovered, so puffy and wrinkly, and I could see straightaway from the ring on his wedding finger – a much gaudier gold than Simon's – that it wasn't him. I was engulfed with relief, but also with anger. All that worry, all that shock. And now all for nothing.

'You haven't looked at his face.'

This new non-uniform policewoman had met us at the door. She was gentle and polite, but there was something about her imitation leather handbag (quilted, for goodness' sake!) with its gold chain strap that bothered me, and the way her pointy, low-heeled shoes clicked like a metronome as we walked down the interminable corridor.

'I don't need to see his face. That isn't his ring. And he wouldn't be in the East End. He *loathed* the East End.'

I shouldn't have said that, I realize. Who knows where that policewoman is from. People can be sensitive about things like that. But she was very patient, explaining that because of the shape of the river, something about how it makes a U-bend around Limehouse, bodies can wash up there from miles away. 'It's a trapping point,' she said. The phrase still makes me shudder. The ring could have become discoloured in the water, she said. She had an explanation for everything.

'I understand this is very hard, Mrs Busfield, but we do need you to look at his face.'

Hard? Really? You think so? I shouldn't have been there. I wanted to be back home in bed. I didn't want to see his face. If I didn't see his face, it wouldn't be him. But the policewoman had wispy bits of blonde hair that escaped from her ponytail and made me realize how young she was. No older than Felix.

She reached out for a corner of the sheet and folded it back as solicitously as if she was loosening the covers around a sleeping baby. Her gentleness caught in my throat like dust.

That face. His face and yet not his face. The colour of it. Was it really possible for skin to be that colour? My husband and yet so manifestly not my husband.

I closed my eyes so I couldn't see any more and was reminded how, as toddlers, my children would think that closing their eyes made them invisible to the world. If I shut it out, maybe it wouldn't be happening.

'It's not his ring,' I said.

But that was days ago, and now Hettie is looking at me strangely, her brown eyes brimming with concern in her lightly tanned face, like that chocolate fountain someone bought Flora for Christmas when she was already way too old for such things. I know Hettie is desperate to be help-ful, to be included, but how can she possibly understand about the shoes or the gold chain on the policewoman's bag, or the colour of Simon's face? What can I say to her about this strange new world of probate applications and forensic post mortems and interim death certificates, and police and more police, and how when they say 'accident' the word 'suicide' hisses in the background. It's as though, without any warning, I've crossed the platform and climbed on to a completely different train where no one else can follow. And I have no idea where it's going or how to get off.

Oh my God! He's here! Simon. He's here. Arms around my shoulders, face nuzzling my neck, breath warming my cheek. My whole body collapses into him.

'Hello, Madre.'

Not Simon then. Of course not. Stupid woman! But still I allow myself to linger there a moment, leaning back against Felix with my eyes closed, head tucked under the slightly cleft chin which is his father's chin.

Freeing myself, I glance at my oldest child, who is now leaning back against the work surface, picking absently at his narrow, well-cut jacket, blond hair falling across his face and hiding it from view.

'New suit, darling?'

'Only the best for Pa,' says Felix.

I look more closely. He looks well, Felix. Taller than Simon, he's slimmer than he used to be. Sleeker even. But his face has that pinched expression I recognize from the playground years, on those occasions when things wouldn't go his way and he couldn't work out what to do about it. It's hard to be a mother sometimes, having to deal with all your children's previous selves, as well as the people they are now. What's the name of that mental illness? Multiple Personality Disorder. That's what we mothers have, except by proxy. When I look at Felix I see the successful, attractive young man he is now, but also the argumentative teenager and the highly strung ten-year-old. It's exhausting keeping track of them all.

'Petra's going to meet us at the crematorium,' Felix says. He sniffs and wipes the back of his hand lightly over his nose.

Oh. Petra. I feel guilty that I haven't even thought about Felix's girlfriend. Such a sweet girl really. Within limits.

'Her parents are coming too.'

Her parents! Oh, now that is really too much. How did Simon's funeral become a public event? We might as well have sold tickets! I don't even know Petra's bloody parents. I've only met them a couple of times. There was that awful dinner where Petra's father tried to engage Simon in conversation about politics. The Single European Currency, I think. *Currency*, for God's sake! Simon was drunk. He can be such a bore when he's drunk. *Could* be such a bore, I mean. Oh God. He started some argument about being opposed to the euro on aesthetic grounds. Because the euro's so ugly, I think he meant. I know he used a pretentious phrase like 'aesthetic integrity' because I remember Petra's father freezing in that way people do when they're not sure if they're being made fun of. Afterwards I called him puerile. Simon, I mean.

Oh God, to think I'll never be angry with him again. We'll never again stand in the detritus of some dinner party or other and bicker about something one of us said or didn't say, or else laugh about what someone else said, or didn't say. No one to share that after-the-party post mortem. *Did you see how much he was drinking? What possessed her to choose that dress?* Instead of Simon I now have Ryan, and Petra's parents. What are they doing here, anyway? What are they to me? Or Simon?

Am I to have no control at all left to me? It's one of the things Simon always loved about me, how I kept everything in order. Of course, when he was cross, he'd accuse me of being over-controlling – *anally retentive*, he said more than once – but really he *liked* the way I organized our social life with the precision of keyhole heart surgery. It gave a structure to our lives, and structure underpins everything. And now his death has taken that away. Suddenly people pop in unannounced, and stay far too long. My home with its beautiful minimal lines is crammed with flowers I don't want. Someone even sent carnations, for goodness' sake! So lovely of them obviously, but carnations! I hate the way I'm expected to smile gratefully and run around finding yet another vase when all I want to do is cram them into the nearest bin. And now it seems the funeral is also being taken out of my hands, hijacked by people I haven't invited and relatives we haven't seen in years, insisting on reading dreary eulogies – Auden, Tennyson or, God forbid, something they've made up themselves.

Things are slipping away from me, and I haven't the faintest idea how to get them back.

4

LOTTIE

Fuckity fuckity fuck.

He's here. No, don't let him be here. If he's here it'll be real, and it's not real. It's not. It's not. *Tra la la!*

From the living-room window, I watch Chris Griffiths pull up in his car ready to take us to Simon's funeral. There. I said it. Funeral. *Funeral funeral funeral funeral.* Preposterous word, preposterous idea. I'm wearing the clothes Jules laid out for me on the bed after she shoved me gently into the bathroom this morning, with strict instructions to shower and wash my hair. It was a relief to be told what to do, to be a child again. But now I'm not so sure.

'I look like shit,' I say, staring down at the long black dress with the clumpy black boots and the black mohair shrug.

'Well, I still think it's fucking ridiculous for you to be going,' says Jules, who is wearing a black jacket I haven't seen before with an ostrich feather trim. Her hair, in the early-morning light, looks the colour of blood. 'You're not in any state to do this. Wait until you're feeling a bit more together and we've got to the bottom of what's been going on.'

'I can't wait. What if it's true? I can't miss his funeral. We've been through this.'

'Well, then leave Sadie behind. I'll look after her.'

'She *wants* to come. Have you ever tried stopping Sadie from doing something she wants to do?'

Jules knows I have a point, but she's still reluctant to give way, even though I can tell she also doesn't want to risk me getting hysterical again. All through the long night while we've tried – all right, while my sisters have tried – and failed to find out any more about what happened to Simon, Jules has been arguing against us turning up at the time and place stated in the funeral notice Chris Griffiths sent over.

'We have to talk to the police first. There's obviously been some kind of hideous mix-up. You don't organize a funeral without telling the wife and child. Simon's probably still in Dubai, or Saudi, or whatever godforsaken place he's working in these days.'

But it was already late by the time she started trying. Phone call after phone call – '*My brother-in-law is missing . . .*' But no one seemed to know anything, and the people who might know were nowhere to be found.

Emma fared no better from the ramshackle kitchen of her sprawling semi in Derbyshire. 'Ring back in the morning,' she was told time and time again. 'Someone will be able to help you in the morning.'

But now it *is* morning, and there's no time to wait for hours on the phone, being passed from department to department. From the window, I see Chris Griffiths opening his car door. *Stop there. Don't come any nearer. I don't want you to come.*

Jules isn't going to let me go without a fight. 'I just don't know what good can come of it, babes. Whatever's happened to Simon, if the worst really has come to the worst (and I don't for a minute believe it has), you don't need a formal funeral to remember him. We can have a ceremony of our own here in the garden. We can bury something symbolic and think about him – just you, me and Sadie – and don't forget Emma said she and Ben and the kids could be here by three o'clock. You just have to say the word – you know how she hates to feel excluded. We can let off balloons with little messages tied to them.'

Sadie has walked in while Jules is talking and now she makes a snorting sound. 'Balloons,' she says. 'What are we – five?'

Through the fog in my head, I register that Sadie is wearing a microscopic black skirt over black tights, a baggy jumper and sheepskin boots. She looks awful. Her face, when I can finally focus on it, is the colour of lychee flesh, and there are purple smudges around her eyes. Normally, my daughter buries her emotions as deep as she can, thinking it a sign of weakness to show what she's feeling, but now they are etched on the surface, red and raw on her skin like a fresh tattoo. I want to stay strong for her sake, but instead I'm dissolving at the sight of her, throwing my arms around her neck and clinging on to her jumper as if it might stop me falling. I feel her turn rigid and I grip on tighter. Her thin shoulders feel as fragile as chicken bones and I worry I will snap her.

'Sadie!' I know I'm being pathetic, but can't stop myself. 'What are we going to do?'

She wriggles away, furious.

'He's not dead!' she shouts, just as the doorbell rings. 'It's a mistake.'

She's right, of course. He's not dead. He can't be dead. Someone would have told me. I must calm down. I must give myself time to think.

I really don't want to see Chris Griffiths. I'm in no fit state to meet anyone, let alone someone I haven't seen for eighteen years. Oh God, he's even brought his *wife*. I vaguely remember Jules telling me he was married after she got off the phone to him for the fourth time last night (or was it the fifth?). By then I was in bits and he was feeling so responsible he apparently insisted on coming here to pick us up and drive us to the funeral. I didn't think he'd bring his bloody wife though, all sensible hair and shapeless black trousers. She's got some kind of backpack with her in place of a handbag and she's standing behind him pointlessly fiddling with the buckle. My eyes are so swollen with crying I feel like I'm looking at her from two slits. Two piggy little slits.

He looks so different. How on earth could I ever have found him handsome? His face is all puffy and doughy. What did Jules say he does now? Some kind of tutoring?

I have a sudden flashback to Chris as he was in his late twenties when we had our short-lived romance. He was always so intense, I remember that. 'I think I love you,' he told me on our second or third date. Such a shock, and so excruciatingly embarrassing. I didn't know what to say. I was only twenty and not remotely interested in anything serious (ironic really when you consider what happened next). I only went out with him in the first place because I hadn't long moved down to London from Derbyshire and was still impressed by anyone with a flat and a grown-up job. So I was already looking for an escape plan the night we went to a pub in Soho and bumped into Simon.

'Busfield! I don't believe it – I haven't seen him in years,' Chris said that night, glancing over at a big fair-haired man sitting reading at a table. 'Bit of a knob. We worked on a property magazine together – until he left to go into property himself. Somewhere in the Middle East, I think. Probably made a fortune.'

Oh God, Simon. That first meeting of eyes. His leg brushing against mine as we squeezed an extra two seats around his table. The heat searing through where our bodies touched. Chris sensed something was up. Well, a blind, deaf mute would have been able to sense something was up. I remember shrugging Chris's arm off when he tried to drape it over my shoulders. 'How's your fiancée?' he asked Simon, pointedly. 'Selina, isn't it?' I dug my nails into my palms waiting for the reply, and practically expired with relief when the reply came, 'Oh, we broke up. I've been single for ages.'

He can't be dead. Can't. I'd know. I'd just know. We had that kind of connection. There was that time I was having lunch in a beach-side bar in Dubai and I had the strangest feeling something was wrong. And when I called him, he was standing by the wreckage of his car on the E311 waiting to be towed. 'How did you know about the accident?' he kept saying. So I'd know now if there was something wrong. Something has happened to the flight, some sort of delay. He's back home in our apartment in Dubai, leaning back in the cane armchair, his feet up on the stool, reading a book with the aircon humming softly. There's some completely rational explanation. I must just be calm and breathe. It will all be all right.

Chris didn't take it well, of course. My going off with Simon. 'So you've been seduced by his money,' he said, hurt making him bitter. 'I expected more from you, I must say.' My arguments that I wouldn't care if Simon didn't have a bean went unheard. Chris didn't want to accept it had anything to do with him so he made it all about Simon. I was relieved when we lost touch. And now here he is in my multicoloured hallway. Where Simon should be.

'I can't believe it,' says Chris, and his eyes keep flicking from me to the floor. 'After all this time . . . under these circumstances.'

His wife is called Karen apparently. She shakes my hand as if we're sealing a business deal. My hand in hers feels limp, like it belongs to someone else.

The back seat of Chris's Volvo is covered in dog hairs.

'We have two Labbies,' Karen says. 'They're supposed to stay in the boot but they're always jumping over.'

I am wedged between Sadie and Jules. The feathers of my sister's jacket keep getting up my nose. I can't breathe and keep my hand clenched around my asthma inhaler. 'It's a mistake,' I say out loud, as if repeating Sadie's words can make them true. 'It's a mistake.'

Nothing feels real. Simon can't be dead.

But if he isn't dead, whose funeral are we going to?

SELINA

'Josh, you're sitting on my dress!'

Flora has foregone the pleasures of Ryan's Ford Mondeo to ride in the funeral car with her younger brother and me, but I almost wish she hadn't. I long for silence in which to roll out my thoughts like newly laid turf. But she wants to talk.

'It isn't right, is it? This dress, I mean. I knew it the minute Ryan saw it this morning and said, "Never mind, Flo. No one expects you to look like a supermodel at your dad's funeral."'

'It's fine,' I say.

For a few moments there's a blissful hush.

Then: 'Josh, you're good at science. Where do you think energy goes when you die? Dad had such massive energy, didn't he? Where is it now?'

Josh shrugs and looks uncomfortable.

'Flora, darling,' I say. 'Please. Not now.'

When we pile out in the crematorium car park, there's a gentle grey drizzle coming down. The leaves have already started falling from the trees and lie sodden on the tarmac in desolate brown and orange clumps of mulch. There's a short path leading to the crematorium and up ahead I can see the knot of mourners already gathered, their faces turned towards us with anticipation, like vultures waiting. I want to run away.

'Are they expecting us to do something?' says Felix, eyeing them with distrust. 'Are we the entertainment?'

He has driven here separately in his beloved powder-blue left-hand-drive vintage Merc, after picking up my mother from her residential home. The two of them are inching their way across the car park, and something inside me pings as it always does when I see my mother after an absence and have to readjust my mental image to this new horrible reality.

'She refused to bring her zimmer,' Felix hisses. 'Said it wasn't "appropriate".'

As usual, my mother is immaculately dressed – black woollen dress, black and green checked jacket over the top. Everything stylish – until you look at the shoes. A sour taste comes into my mouth at the sight of those bulbous misshapen feet crammed into the only footwear that can accommodate them – specially made black leather and Velcro monstrosities that strain to stay fastened. As a child, I adored trying on her shoes. I remember a pair of pale-pink satin ones she wore for going out that I coveted. They were what I imagined being an adult was about. Mystery, glamour, parties. Now look at her. I can't bear it.

'Josh,' I whisper, 'stick to Granny's side like glue or she'll hit the decks.'

I step forward to give my mother a hug. 'Hello, Mummy. Are you OK?'

'Well, it's me who should be asking you that, surely?'

As we embrace, I can feel my mother's hands – turned to claws by the arthritis that is mangling her body just as surely as the recently diagnosed dementia mangles her mind (two-pronged attack – double whammy) – alighting on my shoulder blades.

'You've lost weight,' she says, as I knew she would. Her cloudy blue eyes look at me with pity, but her voice is sharp. She has forgotten lately how to moderate her tone of voice according to the situation in which she finds herself. Empathy, one of the last emotional skills my children acquired, seems to be the first my mother is losing.

'I know these things are very difficult, my darling,' she continues, still in that uncompromising tone. 'But I know you'll cope. You've always been a coper.'

A coper. But Mummy, what if I don't want to be a coper any more?

Felix is staring rudely at the black-clad mourners up ahead by the crematorium.

'We'd better get a move on,' he says. 'The Undead are getting restless.'

Deep breaths. Yoga breathing. What's it called? Pranayama. The Germanic instructor of Hatha Yoga (Advanced, Wednesdays) shortens it to Pran, which drives me mad. 'Let's focus on our Pran,' she says. Ridiculous woman.

As we approach the crowd, I avert my eyes from the noticeboard by the side of the path, which displays a photo of Simon next to an order of service. I can see people arranging their expressions into what they imagine to be Mourning Faces: eyes slightly downcast, lips pressed together as if there is too much to say and no words to say it. I should know, I've done it often enough myself at other funerals. Other people's bereavements. As unfathomable as other people's marriages.

As we make our way through, small smiles stamped on to our faces, I'm bowed by a crushing weight of emptiness. Can emptiness be weighty? I have no idea. All I know is that, far from being an absence, the emptiness bears down on me like a tumorous mass. I look down at my legs, with the ladder-resistant 15-dernier tights and the slate-grey suede shoes, and marvel at the way they keep moving, one in front of the other, without any apparent instruction from me. What an awesome thing the human body is – except when it's floating face-down in the Thames, eyes open, peering into nothingness.

The vicar is standing by the steps. I have a sudden urge to turn around and head back the way we've come. *Don't make me talk to him. I don't want to talk to him.*

He moves forward to meet me, hand outstretched. 'Mrs Busfield. So very, very sorry.'

He starts talking to me about the service. I don't want to hear. I am looking at his mouth moving but seeing only the mole on the side of his jaw. It has two hairs growing out of it. Would it be so painful to pluck those two hairs? Or is it the vanity he objects to? Is vanity ungodly? I suppose it must be.

'Aaaaaaaaaaaaaaaargh!'

The scream is ear-splitting. Horrible. Like an animal at night. Everyone whirls around to see where it's coming from. There's a small knot of people around the notice-board. One appears to be kneeling down on the damp tarmac, amid the sodden leaves. She's the one screaming. For heaven's sake, what a racket!

'Who are they?' Felix is angry, I can tell.

'I've no idea,' I reply. 'Never seen them before.'

Then I look closer. There's something about the man . . . something vaguely familiar. Oh Lord! I remember now – it's someone Simon used to work with before he and I were married. But that must be nearly thirty years ago. What on earth is he doing here?

'Chris Griffiths,' I say out loud. It just comes to me. 'He was a staff writer on that property magazine Dad worked on donkeys' years ago. He used to write long, pompous pieces that nobody ever read.'

The few times we met he had been intense and dis-missive. 'But what do you *do*?' he wanted to know. 'What are your ambitions?' To be a wife and mother clearly didn't impress. I couldn't stand him. I had no idea Simon had kept in touch with him. He's never mentioned him in all this time. But who are those strange women with him?

And why is that one on the floor? What is this? Open house for nutters?

The screaming has stopped and the woman is being helped to her feet. She looks to be in her twenties with masses of black hair. That 'I'm-so-ditsy' corkscrew look I never could abide. It seems to me that women only cultivate 'big personality' hair when they have too little personality themselves. How dull must one be to be defined by one's hair? There's a younger, pretty girl with her, and a woman with awful red hair and some kind of bizarre ruff affair going on around her throat. Oh, and there's a fourth woman, behind them, a bit mousy. I don't recognize any of them. I just want them all to leave. Up until now I've been distracted, but suddenly my grief catches up with me, swelling up inside me like a balloon, squeezing my breath out in shallow gasps.

Oh dear God, the woman with all the curly hair is heading straight towards me. Now she's closer I can see she's older than I thought. Attractive, in spite of her manic expression, but mid thirties. Late thirties even. Certainly too old to be dressed like a student. What in heaven's name does she want? Hang on, it's not me she's making for, after all, it's the vicar. Oh please, let her not be about to make a scene. That's all I need.

LOTTIE

It's the photograph that does it. Simon's picture – black and white, a professional shot. When the hell did he have that done? I've never seen it before. He's wearing a suit

DENIAL

and he looks corporate and unsmiling, but the instant I see it, I know it's real. His photo makes it real. This whole nightmare is real. And I'm screaming. I can't help it. And I'm on my knees on the wet path. Oh my God, I can't breathe. Air. I need air. Someone (Sadie? Jules?) closes my fingers around my inhaler. *Press and gulp. Press and gulp. Breathe. Breathe.* 'That's right. You're doing fine.'

No! Tra la la! This isn't happening. I need to find someone to sort it out. This can't be happening to me. To us. *Press and gulp.*

There! Over there! The vicar. That's who I need to speak to. That's who'll know what's going on.

Chris is trying to stop me, his hand on my arm, but I shake him off. I don't want him touching me with his pudgy, white, marshmallow-soft hands. He has to leave me alone. And I'm hurrying down the path towards the vicar. He's talking to a woman who looks like she ought to be at a village garden party. Highlighted blonde hair. Court shoes, for fuck's sake. Who *are* these people? Why are they here? What have they got to do with Simon? Where are all our friends, the familiar faces from all the dinners and holidays and weddings and parties over the years?

Now I've reached the vicar. Thank God! He'll be able to help me. He'll tell me it's a misunderstanding. He'll explain. I have my hands on his arms and I'm clinging on for dear life.

'Is something the—'

I cut him off. 'What's happened to Simon?' I ask. 'Why have you done all of this without telling me?'

My voice goes all squeaky at the end because my

pounding heart is cutting off oxygen to my head. *Press and gulp. Press and gulp. Breathe, breathe.*

The vicar, his eyes wide behind thick glasses, takes a step back and almost stumbles under my weight.

'But who are you?' he asks. There's a mole near his mouth that looks like an insect. 'What is your relationship to the deceased?'

'*I'm his wife.*'

SELINA

When I hear the word 'wife', I stop feeling angry with the woman and feel sorry for her instead.

How mortified she's going to be when she realizes what a terrible mistake she's made! I'm embarrassed for her, but suddenly grateful for the distraction – the attention being deflected from me for a few moments. I look away, out of delicacy, as the vicar says, 'I'm afraid there's been some mix-up. You see, this lady here is Simon's wife. *This* is Mrs Busfield.'

I look back now, ready to see her horrified face, but instead I catch the eye of the girl just behind her. Wham! My insides turn to stone. The eyes are his eyes. The face is his face.

I don't understand.

LOTTIE

I don't understand.

Why is he saying that's his wife? That *old* woman with her lacquered hair and pearl earrings. This is all a nightmare. I'm trapped in a nightmare. Will someone please tell me what's going on?

In desperation I look at the young men on either side of her. I've no clue who they are. But isn't there something about the older one? Something slightly familiar about the chin?

Press and gulp. Press and gulp. Breathe. Breathe.

SELINA

I'm not looking at the girl now. That's better. *Just focus on the woman*, who is staring at Felix as if he has grown another head. But the boulder inside me is growing bigger.

'I'm Mrs Busfield,' I say, and my voice sounds like a stranger's. 'Selina Busfield.'

Now the woman turns to me, and her mouth is a circle. And she's staring, staring, staring. And now she's on the ground, and the woman with the ghastly red hair is pressing something against her mouth, and she's making a horrible croaking sound, and I won't look at the girl with Simon's eyes. Won't. Won't. But now the girl is standing right in front of me so I can't avoid her, and her face – his face – is red and scrunched up and she's screaming, for heaven's sake.

'You can't be his wife!' she's yelling. Her finger, pointing at me, is shaking, the skin around the nail ragged and ugly. 'You can't be. *She* is! My mother! Because I'm his daughter.'

The boulder inside me becomes a bomb that explodes me into a million pieces.

Bang!

I am destroyed.

5

SELINA

∽

Simon now lives with his face to the wall. Every photo of him in the house is turned around so his nose is pressed against the cold plaster. Unable to see what's going on. Out of the picture. Ignored.

How he'd hate that.

The turned-around photos are just one of the things that have changed in the five days since the French Farce Funeral, as Felix has named it. But really everything has changed. How could it not? The ironic thing is that before all this happened, when everything was normal, change was something I craved. Ever since I turned fifty I've been conscious of a lack somewhere, a space needing to be filled, a building horror of the sameness of my life. And now, of course, I crave nothing more than to go back to how things were, back to boring, back to normal.

Amazing, though, how life goes on. Even when one is quite certain it simply cannot. Even after that scene out-side the crematorium, the world didn't end. The drizzle continued to come down, covering the scene in a misty grey film, the birds continued to sing. My lungs remem-bered to take in air, my heart continued to beat.

There is a particular quality of silence that always follows a bombshell. As if the world is teetering on the edge between what was known before and this new altered reality. I was looking at the woman on the floor, and I was feeling nothing. Zilch. Void. Then all of a sudden, whoosh, this great gush of something bitter came up through me and for one awful moment I thought I was about to be sick. Right there. Can you imagine? Instead, I made a sort of moaning noise and it was as if someone had depressed the Pause button, because everyone else came to life then. Even though my mind felt completely disconnected, I was vaguely aware of a sort of frenzy building around me. Whispers spreading like a forest fire. *Did you see? Have you heard?*

All a bit of a blur after that. The woman was led away by her red-haired friend. She didn't want to go, but seemed not to have the strength to resist. The girl who wore Simon's eyes like borrowed jewels followed, making great gulping sobs like you do when you're trying very hard to stop yourself crying out loud. I became aware of my own children around me. 'What just happened?' Flora kept asking. In complete shock still, obviously. And again, 'What happened?'

Josh wasn't much better. 'I don't fucking believe this,' he said, over and over. Felix was silent but his fingers gripping my arm were tight as a vice.

Remarkable, when you think about it, that the funeral went ahead as planned. It was as if by collective, unspoken consent we all agreed to put on hold what had just happened. I allowed myself to be guided into the crematorium, taking my mother's arm because it gave me some sense of purpose. She was so confused, poor old thing. I think the general atmosphere of barely suppressed panic set off her dementia and she kept asking, 'But who was that little girl, the one with all the hair?' (*Little girl? Ha! Facing forty, more like!*) 'She seemed so *hungry*!' No one had the energy to suggest she might mean angry.

Incredibly, I sat through the whole service without once screaming or frothing at the mouth, or falling to the floor in a faint. I even listened to some of it. I think my mind froze as a way of self-preservation, like bodies are supposed to do sometimes, shutting themselves down when faced with physical trauma. The boys both got up and gave their readings as if on autopilot. Only when we were walking out of the crematorium did that surreal scene begin to sink in. The children glanced over at me with eyebrows raised over scared, reddened eyes. *Did that really happen?* the eyebrows asked. *Can that really be real?*

I half expected to find them waiting outside, the awful dark-haired woman and the girl, but instead there was just Chris Griffiths, pasty-faced and anxious. When I'd known him before, all those years ago, he'd had a sort of baby-faced prettiness, but now the rounded cheeks have slipped southwards into jowls and a receding hairline has carved channels of flesh into both temples.

'They're in the car,' he said. I didn't ask who 'they' were.

'I just need to get this straight,' he continued. The pomposity of him! I've just been told my husband's a bigamist and *he* has to get things straight. 'You were married to him for all those years?' he asked me. 'Since I knew you? But at the same time he was also married to her?'

Firing questions at me, as if he had a right.

I couldn't speak. Well, it's hard to formulate words

when your body lies scattered around the car park in a million pieces. So it was Hettie and Ian who asked questions of our own. How long had Chris known *her*?

'Lottie, you mean? She was my girlfriend for a while, years ago. Until I introduced her to Simon.'

Simon had told them both he was single, Chris explained. My bleeding heart ripped right open then, at that cruellest word 'single'. Lottie had been 'bowled over'. That was the term he used. *Bowled over*. As if she was a skittle!

Things had got 'strained' after that, Chris went on. There was some kind of trouble.

'I loved her, that was the problem,' he said, and his usually pallid face flushed red. 'I'd allowed myself to imagine a future with her, you see. That's when you're done for, don't you agree? When you let yourself think in terms of the future?'

I didn't want to listen, but he wouldn't shut up. It was as if he was desperate to talk about it.

He'd kept in touch with them for a little while, he said, even after she moved out to Dubai. (*She was there – with him!*) Well, not exactly in touch, but 'abreast of their movements', right up until the daughter was born a few months later. (*A few months! It figures!*) That's when he'd let go.

'There has to be a point, doesn't there?' he asked me. 'Where one lets go.

'Now I feel dreadful,' he told us all, his bland features twisted with misery. 'It's my fault they came today. But the fact is, you must see she deserved to be here. Eighteen years isn't nothing, you know. After all, they were his family too.'

Family? That screaming woman? That scrunch-faced girl?

My insides caved in like an avalanche.

'Take me home,' I whispered to Felix. 'I want to go home.'

And he, white-faced, lips closed tight as a mussel, for once did as he was asked.

And home is where I've been for the last five days, turning photos to the wall, hiding all reminders. I slump on the sofa like boil-in-the-bag rice. The police keep dropping in. They had to make investigations, of course, after the funeral. They had to question that woman, find out what was real and what wasn't. Turns out it's all true, what she said, but really I knew it was true the moment I set eyes on that girl. She lived with him in Dubai for all those years, the woman. The apartment I thought he lived in alone was actually their family home. All that time I worried about him being lonely thousands of miles away, he was there with her and their daughter. *Did he phone me, when they were out, from rooms lined with photos of their faces? Did he email me from under an umbrella on the beach while the two of them cavorted in the sea in front of him?*

Two years ago they moved back to the UK and bought a flat in a bohemian part of North London, apparently. The policewoman who came said the woman was in a terrible state. 'She had no idea he was married,' the policewoman said. 'All those years? Can you imagine?' Then she realized. 'Oh,' she said. 'I'm sorry . . .'

So many questions, the police have. If Simon wasn't with *her* the night he died, and wasn't with me either, who was he with? I shrug when they ask me. *How would I know when I clearly didn't know anything about him at all? I'm only the widow. I'm the last person you should be asking.*

It hasn't only been police. The phone hasn't stopped ringing – friends, family, people I've never heard of. Everyone wants to chip in with their bit of information – 'It always struck me as odd . . .', 'Now it all falls into place . . .'. All desperate to be part of the freakshow attraction my life has become, to write themselves into my story. I hear their voices talking into the answer machine on the home phone but I don't take their calls. I put my mobile in a drawer where I can't read the messages.

Because as long as I can't see or hear anything, I don't have to face any of it. And if I don't face any of it, I can deny it ever happened. All of it.

There was no funeral. There was no woman screaming on the floor, no girl wearing a dead man's face. There was no death. There was no Simon. I had no husband.

It never happened.

LOTTIE

He wouldn't do that to me. No way. I know he wouldn't. He wouldn't be capable of lying like that, for so long. I knew him inside out, no joke. I always knew when he was lying. He loved me so much. We loved each other so much. I believe in love. I absolutely do. I have to. If you don't believe in love, you might as well give up on life. There's been a mistake. Any minute now something is going to come up that will explain it all. Any minute now I'll hear his voice on my phone. 'Didn't think I'd leave you, did you, Baby?'

I'm wearing his T-shirt. It's dark green with 'BRAZIL'

emblazoned across the front and a picture of the Brazilian flag. He bought it in Dubai one year when Brazil were playing in the World Cup. It wasn't his favourite or anything, but he wore it the last weekend he was here to go running in. When I fished it out of the dirty washing basket, it still smelt of him. But now, after five or six days, it's starting to smell of me as well, and soon I'll have to find another one, sniffing through the dirty washing on my hands and knees.

The bed is full of crumpled bits of paper – the notes he used to leave hidden around our bedroom for me to find when he was away to reassure me when I was feeling insecure. Silly how his absences, the separate self he kept hidden from me like an embarrassing suit, were somehow redeemed by these scraps of paper, scrawled over with his familiar looping handwriting.

'I love you,' he wrote. 'You are the pulse of my life.'

I know I should get up. 'You'll get bedsores if you stay there much longer,' Jules told me this morning. She's been staying here since it happened. Apparently Emma was here too for a couple of days, although I barely remember it. I have no energy. It might be something to do with the pills, I suppose. My bedroom looks like a hospital, so many little boxes with long complicated names and bumpy foil packets. Antidepressants, beta blockers, plus the herbal sleeping pills Jules insists on buying which I take like sweeties. Some of them you're not supposed to touch with your fingers. You have to press the end of the tube and a tiny pill drops into your mouth. There's something very satisfying about it. I do it again and again. When we got back from the *thing* (can't say the 'f' word), apparently I was in such a state of hysteria that the GP had to be called out to write a prescription on the spot. I didn't even know GPs came out any more. And now I exist in a permanent state of sedation, which suits me very well.

The police have been here. A policewoman with psoriasis on her wrists came and swept the pill packets to one side so she could perch on the edge of my bed to talk to me. Jules was here, too, leaning against the wall. She insisted on opening the curtains, even though I didn't want her to. The room looked like someone had died in it.

The policewoman was young but she had a kind face and she kept saying things like 'I know this will be hard for you to hear' and 'I'm really sorry to have to tell you this'. I expect they're trained in this sort of stuff and given stock phrases to learn, but I felt sorry for her really, having to sit there and say those things. She talked about another family, and she mentioned a house in Barnes and twenty-eight years. I zoned out. Jules has been trying to learn to meditate (without success – surprise, surprise) and I've listened to a few of her CDs, so while the policewoman was talking I used the visualization techniques I remembered. You have to think of your Happy Place. Mine was a holiday we had in Tuscany a couple of years ago, in a beautiful villa belonging to a friend of Simon's. I focused on that while the policewoman talked on and on, and Jules shook her head in outrage. The smell of the pine trees, the dappled sunlight on the vine-covered terrace, cool water trickling through my fingers as I floated face-down on a bright yellow lilo in the green-tiled pool. Eventually the policewoman went away.

Every now and then Sadie comes in and my drugged heart flops over. My baby looks lost. Her beautiful face is all shadows and angles. I drag myself up to a sitting position and hold out my arms, but she stands stiffly by the door, looking disgusted, as if the place smells. Which it probably does.

It hurts to look at my daughter. Ever since she was a baby and her navy-blue eyes turned almond-shaped and green and the dent in her cheek graduated from a slight dip to a dimple, she has been the image of her father. Even strangers in the street used to comment on it. 'The daddy has strong genes,' old ladies in Dubai would say approvingly, looking from Simon to Sadie and then back again. Both had the same pronounced teardrop shape between nose and upper lip (it has a name, I know it does, but I can never remember it). 'It's my fingerprint on your face,' Simon would tell Sadie, pressing his finger into the soft groove of skin so like his own.

I haven't spoken to Sadie properly about what happened at the crematorium. I know I should, and I will, very soon, I promise. But if I talk to her about it, it's real, and I can't bear it to be real.

Even so, I occasionally allow myself to revisit it, hoping to propel events down a different channel by the sheer strength of my will and force a different outcome. In my revised memories the photograph turns out to be of a different Simon Busfield, not *my* Simon; the vicar explains there's been a mix-up, he isn't dead at all; the awful blonde woman with her Tory-wife clothes is just an acquaintance, she's not his—

I can't go any further. I can't say the word. Quick, clang the memory shut. Take another pill. Block it out.

What's the worst that can happen when the worst that can happen has already happened?

Part Two

ANGER

6

SELINA

I hate her. I hate her. I hate her.
I hate him. I hate him. I hate him.

LOTTIE

I hate her. I hate her. I hate her.
I loved him. I loved him. I loved him.
I hate myself. I hate myself. I hate myself.

7

SELINA

∽

When Simon and I were first married, before he took the job in Dubai, I instituted a Sunday-night stock-taking ritual. We'd sit down together with a bottle of wine and look back on the things we'd achieved over the week, and set some goals for the week ahead. Not big things. Manageable. I'd read it in a magazine somewhere, one of those 'be your own life coach'-type features, and though Simon always groaned about doing it, I thought it was very useful. It stopped us from drifting. So let's do a stock-taking exercise now, a week after the funeral.

1. My husband drowned. The official view is drunken accident, but obviously they suspect suicide.

2. An inquest was called and then immediately adjourned (*now you see it, now you don't*). Apparently that's normal in 'cases like this'.

3. My husband turns out to have another wife. We're still trying to find out if it was legal. (*On a beach, f*or goodness' sake!)

4. He has fathered a child.

5. He lived with this 'other family' for seventeen years.

6. They never knew we existed.

7. We never knew they existed.
8. My whole adult life has been a lie.
9. I hate him.
10. I hate him, I hate him, I hate him.

There, now. I feel so much better.

You've got to laugh. Or else you'd die.

'I know how angry you must be feeling,' Hettie says, over a cup of tea and a smoked-salmon sandwich she insisted on making, even though she knows I won't eat it.

'I doubt it,' I reply.

My anger is a living thing, throbbing inside me, growing and growing. I see through its eyes, it's inside my thoughts, my veins, my marrow. Sometimes I think it'll grow so big it'll end up choking me. Hettie doesn't know how that works. Hettie thinks anger is in your head. She thinks it's contained. She doesn't understand how your heart can pump it around your body so it gets into every single cell, every hair follicle, every pore. My glands secrete it, I sweat it, I cry it, I mix it with bits of food in my mouth and swallow it down. Hettie doesn't know any of that.

'Selina, Simon loved you. He did. Despite being a twat of the highest order. You have to keep hold of that thought.'

She doesn't get it.

'People who love you don't lie to you for nearly twenty years,' I tell her. 'People who love you don't publicly humiliate you.'

The humiliation is the worst thing, the idea that everyone now knows that my life – the life I've spent thirty years building up piece by careful piece – has been a sham. A stupid, Farrow & Ball-painted façade of a life. A timber-clad structure of a life hiding an ugly plastic wheelie bin inside. Even the best of marriages aren't betrayal-proof, I know that. But for the betrayal to be so public! It's like when you unwrap a present in front of a big group of people, and they're all watching for your reaction. And you have a smile already welded to your face before you've even opened it, because that's what's expected. And then that present turns out to be a mistress and a child, jumping fully formed out of a giant cake. It cannot be borne.

That woman's sister rang here one day. Josh answered the phone. The nerve of her! Ringing me. As if we could have a nice little civilized chat about everything! I refused to go to the phone. But now I'm starting to wonder if I should have spoken to her after all.

'I'm going to invite her here,' I say to Hettie, surprising us both.

'Her? That woman? Why on earth would you do that?' How can I possibly explain?

'Let her come here and see our home, where he was happy. Let her see that family photo on the stairs from Simon's fiftieth. Remember how much fun that was and how Simon made that speech saying he couldn't imagine how his life would have been without me? Let her see the stone outside under the willow tree where he buried Flora's hamster that time. Did I ever tell you he cried? Can you believe that? Over a hamster!'

Hettie is shaking her head. I can see a narrow, tell-tale strip of grey at the temples and parting of her brown wavy hair. We are getting old, my friend and I. Except now I will be getting old alone, a widow.

'I don't think it's a good idea, Sel. You're not in any state to meet her again. Let the lawyers sort it all out. You don't have to see those people again. Put them out of your mind.'

Hettie doesn't know that the woman and the girl are papered on to the inside of my eyelids. She doesn't know that I see them in my sleep.

'I *want* to see her again. I want to know what he saw in her. She's nothing *like* me.'

'Maybe that's the point.'

'Don't be ridiculous,' I say. 'Men have a type. Everyone knows that. Even when they trade the wife in for a younger model, she's always the image of the wife as she was ten or twenty years ago.'

Hettie looks as if she's about to say something, but glances at my face and stays silent.

The thing is, I was Simon's ideal woman. He told me so many times when we first met. Less so as the years went on, I suppose, but that's only to be expected. We had rough times. All marriages do. It did cross my mind that he must have been tempted over the years, with all that time away from home, although I never asked outright. There are some things one would rather not know. And there was that scene, in Tuscany . . . But we dealt with all that. Those occasions were like little leaks and spillages easily mopped up and absorbed back into our relationship. I was his ideal woman. He told me that. On our wedding night when we got back to the honeymoon suite and lay on the monstrous bed, giggling like children. 'Thank God that's over,' he said. And I thought for a moment about the months of preparation and organization, the agonizing over menus and table centres, the relentless whittling down of the guest list. Some of that must have shown in my expression because he said, 'I only mean I'm glad to have you to myself at last. You handled everything so perfectly today, darling. I'm so lucky. I've married my ideal woman.'

So if I was his ideal woman, what on earth was he doing with *her*?

All that unkempt hair, those awful clothes, the way she went to pieces in front of everybody – such histrionics! No class, no shame, no self-control. A child-woman. No figure to speak of. Completely flat-chested, and Simon such a breast man. Shorter than me, paler than me.

Younger than me.

She *must* have known. Must have. What kind of woman lives with a man who's only there half the time, and doesn't suspect anything? It was different for me. We were established. We had our patterns, our understandings. She must have known she was stealing someone else's husband. There would have been some giveaway. He'd never have been able to eradicate us totally from his life. We were everything to him. We were his world. He must have said something. *She must have known!*

'I want her to come,' I tell Hettie. 'And the girl. We need to sort out this bloody mess.'

'How can *you* sort it out?' Hettie wants to know. 'Simon is the one who made it – and he's gone.'

'Exactly! He's gone. But he's left it all behind and some- one has to do it. As usual, it all comes down to me.'

Hettie glances over, then looks down at her tea. She has two red spots in her cheeks.

'You don't have to take responsibility for this,' she says. Her voice is quiet. 'Why not just say "to hell with it"? We could go on holiday somewhere, the two of us. Somewhere far away from all this mess. Leave it all behind.'

For a brief moment I allow myself to imagine it. Hettie

and me thousands of miles away. The sun warming my face. No reminders of the husband who wasn't mine, the life that wasn't real. I imagine sleeping properly, which I haven't done in nearly two weeks. Sleeping on a soft-cushioned lounger by a crystal-clear turquoise pool, sleeping in a rope hammock under a spreading cypress tree, sleeping in crisp white cotton hotel sheets.

Impossible! The weight of my grief and anger crushes the fantasy to dust. Because of Simon, and that woman, I can have no rest, no respite from the images that run like a slideshow through my head. Because of them I am stuck in this awful limbo where I cannot grieve, yet neither can I slip my old life back on like a pair of familiar slippers. I've taken to striding around the house, from room to room, without any purpose, just knowing that if I stay in one place my head will explode like a piñata. Trapped indoors, I lug my rage around like one of those strap-on bellies designed to show men how pregnancy feels. But equally I'm too ashamed to go out. Imagine how people will laugh! *There she is, the woman whose husband was married to someone else. What an idiot she must be.*

'Why do you care so much what other people think?' Josh asked me yesterday.

He was exasperated, I think, by my endless pacing. My poor boy doesn't know how to react. His father turns out to be not the person he was supposed to be, and his mother has gone quite mad.

You'd think he might at least be enjoying not having me always nagging him about work, and asking where he's going and where he's been, sniffing the air around him like a specially trained police dog as soon as he walks through the door. But instead he seems lost.

'I'm off,' he'll say, and hover in the doorway, expectant.

'Right,' I say. 'Have a nice time.'

I have no energy to remind him how many days of revision time remain before his exams, or to point out the spot on his neck that wouldn't be there if he ate a healthier diet, or that a Duke of Edinburgh Award would look better on his personal statement than 'Hanging Around on the Common Smoking Dope with My Mates'. Now that I'm a widow, I have no time to be a mother.

Flora is finding it very hard, dealing with the new version of me. She's stayed here a couple of nights, announcing on her arrival that she has come 'to help out'. But instead she spends the time following me from room to room, shaking her head and asking, 'Why? I still don't understand why.' I tell her if she does ever understand it, I hope she'll let me know. She wants me to be strong for her. She wants me to explain. But how do you explain what cannot be explained?

Felix isn't much better. He sits at the table drumming his fingers, then leaps to his feet to go rifling through the desk drawers in Simon's study or through the pockets of his suit jackets still hanging in his closet. Looking, always looking, for the clue he's sure we've missed, the key that will take us back to the thing that we have lost.

Felix met that policeman the other day, the one who came here that first night. He walked into the living room to find him sitting here, asking me more questions I couldn't answer about Simon's movements on the night he died.

'This is Detective Inspector Bowles,' I said, wishing Felix wasn't wearing the pork-pie hat he's taken an unaccountable liking to recently. I know such things are back in fashion now, but looking through that policeman's narrow eyes, I can see how it might seem . . . foppish. Policemen are judgemental like that, I should imagine.

'I'm sorry for your troubles,' said DI Bowles, shaking Felix's hand gingerly as if he might have one of those joke-shop electric-shock things concealed in his palm.

Felix looked cross.

'Troubles? What am I, Northern Ireland?'

We all laughed, although we knew he hadn't meant it to be funny.

'I've been telling DI Bowles that your father would never have committed suicide,' I said to Felix. 'It would go against everything he believed in. There has to be another explanation.'

'Rest assured, we're considering every angle, Mrs Busfield,' said the policeman.

'I'll certainly sleep more soundly tonight then,' said Felix, so rudely that I had to apologize for him after he'd gone.

They're waiting for something from me, my children, but I don't have anything to give them.

Last night I tried to force myself out of myself. Josh had his laptop on the kitchen table, and his Facebook page was open. I glimpsed a long column of condolence messages written in that teenage gobbledegook they all use:

Prayin 4 u an yr pops

Sendin u big luv babes

All with a liberal sprinkling of sad-face icons and crying-face icons.

Maybe I should start using icons instead of speech. Maybe I should get an angry-face icon and plaster it over my own face so there's no need for words at all.

'It's lovely so many of your friends are sending you messages,' I said in an approximation of motherly concern.

He looked at me as if I was crazy. 'I don't even know most of those people. I have 759 friends on Facebook, Mum. How could I possibly know them all?'

'But it must be nice to know they're all thinking of you, regardless?'

He shrugged. 'Not really. They do it because that's what people do. It's a format, like in *The X Factor*, where they start playing that sad music to let you know this is the Sad Bit. Except the Sad Bit is me.'

'Who are you calling a Sad Bit?' I joked. He didn't laugh.

I think Simon's death is only now beginning to sink in with Josh. At first he was distracted by the novelty of grief – he tried it out tentatively as if he was sampling a particularly spicy dish. But now the novelty has worn off and he's confronted for the first time by the terrible permanence of it. Modern life is so full of second chances. Young people resit exams again and again until they get the results they want, they switch careers and girlfriends at the drop of a hat. Josh has never before been faced with something irreversible and he's finding the brutal finality hard to take.

'Mum, I wanted to ask you something,' he said last night, pretending to concentrate so intently on his laptop that I knew this had to be something important, and suddenly I guessed exactly what he was going to say. *Please no*, I begged him in my head. *Please don't let us have to talk about it.* But it was no use.

'Did Dad fall into the river, or did he . . .? Was it . . .?'

His misery was so palpable, I finished his question for him, in spite of myself.

'Deliberate?'

He nodded, eyes still glued to the screen.

'I don't know,' I told him, and it was the truth. If anyone had asked me two weeks ago what were the chances of Simon – greedy-for-everything, life-guzzling Simon – committing suicide, I'd have said there was more likelihood of hell freezing over. But that was before I discovered that the man I thought I was married to had been abducted and replaced by an alien.

Suicide though. When that old university friend of his killed himself a couple of years ago, Simon was angrier than I'd ever seen him. 'What about his kids?' he demanded. 'I don't care how bad things are. You don't do that to your kids.'

Useless to try to argue the case for mental illness or depression. Simon's position was unchangeable – unless the man was in a straitjacket, he was able to make choices, and only a coward chooses that way.

'The police now seem to think he was somewhere near Southwark on the night he died,' I told Josh. 'They made enquiries all along the river and found a barman in a pub near Borough Market who thinks he recognized him, and a woman who claims she saw someone who looked like him later on by Southwark Bridge. There might have been someone with him but she couldn't be sure. He looked drunk, the woman said. There was a lot of alcohol in his system apparently. So he could have . . .'

'I think someone pushed him.'

I stared at Josh, surprised.

'He's not an idiot,' Josh went on. 'He wouldn't fall in,

or jump in. And I know he'd never have hurt himself. Remember the fuss he used to make about having to go to the dentist? I think someone pushed him. Probably this guy he might have been with, or maybe he saw something. A robbery or something. Or maybe some nutter came along – you know how many weirdos there are.'

I was about to protest, but changed my mind. It's no more far-fetched than anything else that has happened. No harder to believe than my husband being a bigamist, my children having a half-sister. Me inviting my husband's mistress to my house.

I ask Hettie to call Chris Griffiths for me, to get a message to that woman and her daughter, asking them to come. I suppose I could have called the police instead – I know they've been liaising with her as well, asking what she knows about Simon's death. But I don't want to involve them. It's embarrassing enough, my new Jeremy Kyle life, without that.

Now that I've decided to meet her again, *that woman*, I'm filled with impatience. I'll get Carmela in for a whole day's cleaning beforehand. Carmela has given us a wide birth over the last two weeks, out of some misguided South American notion of respect, I imagine. Grief, it seems, is blind to dust and smudge marks and dried mud on carpets. I'll make a list of things for her to do. And I'll make canapés or a cake. I'll even turn the photographs back around. Let her see, that woman, what she is up against. Let her understand that though she may have tempted him to stray, then held on to him with whatever emotional threats she used, he would always have come back. I was here first. This was his home.

*

She's coming on Monday. I'll bet she is! I bet she can't wait to see where he lived, how much he was worth. I bet she thinks she's entitled. Why else would she have married him?

She's going to get a shock. I've been Googling for the past two days – 'weddings in Goa', 'weddings on the beach', 'marriage-wrecking bitch weddings'. It's surprising what you can find on the internet, I'm discovering. I've never been a big fan up until now – there are always so many better things to be doing with my time than sitting indoors glued to a screen. But now I can see the appeal. No wonder Josh spends his life on his computer.

I've been going on infidelity sites as well. Who knew there would be so many? All those pseudonyms – HitByATruck, ShatteredInside, LiedTo4Years. All those broken hearts. Thousands of them, hundreds of thousands. I don't write anything on there myself. Quite apart from the fact that I don't know how – all that registering and logging in – there's also the pride factor. I won't let him turn me into the type of person who pours out her heart to faceless strangers. But I lurk. I do lurk. They're the only ones who have any idea what it's like inside my head, these people I've never met. Their lives have been gutted and filleted too, just like mine.

I was reading a thread last night – that's what they're called, those strings of messages replying to a post (I'm getting good at it now, the jargon of betrayal) – started by a woman calling herself Blindsided23 (presumably there were already another twenty-two Blindsideds before her – who'd have thought?). She'd been married for thirty-eight years and believed she had the strongest marriage of anyone she knew, until she went on the home computer last week, just after her husband had been using it, and found herself logged into an email account she didn't even know existed. The inbox was empty but when she clicked on 'Sent' there was one message there. The subject was: *100 Reasons Why I Love You*. The recipient wasn't her.

How do you recover from that?

How do I recover from this?

Baby steps. That's right. Baby steps.

Going to see Joe Haynes this morning is a baby step. Before that bitch – that *skank*, as they say on some of the infidelity sites – comes here on Monday, I need to know exactly where I stand legally and financially, so a visit to Simon's solicitor is in order. Once I'd made the appointment, I felt much better, as if I was taking back control. I wrote it carefully in my diary: *Joe Haynes: 11.30 a.m.* Seeing it written down comforted me.

Getting ready to go out, I spend a long time in front of the mirror applying my make-up and arranging my features just so, like a top chef plating a particularly complicated dish. I look like someone impersonating myself. It's the first time I've left the house since the funeral and as I hurry to the car I have the feeling that all the neighbours are gathered at their upstairs windows, watching. The Walk of Shame, Josh called it at breakfast.

Driving into town, I find myself going over and over past events as I've done a thousand times since the funeral, trying to reconstruct the timeline of my life against the backdrop of what I now know.

Had he already met her by the time of Felix's fifth birthday, when we built a mini version of Neverland in the back garden and forty-five little boys rampaged around stuffing themselves with green pasta and green cake with green icing until three of them were sick? After they'd gone, Felix fell asleep in his Captain Hook costume with his sword still in his hand and his mouth smudged green as if he was spouting mould and Simon and I stood watching him, his arm draped over my shoulders. 'You do love me, don't you?' Simon asked me then, out of the blue. 'You know I do,' I replied. 'I wish you'd say it more,' he said. And I remember feeling a guilty thrill of power – that he was wanting more, and I was holding back (I meted out my 'I love you's like a teacher's grudging praise). 'We can do this, can't we?' he said then as we watched our sleeping child. 'We can go the distance?' And the question shocked me because it had never occurred to me that we might not.

Or is that completely true?

Unbidden there comes a memory of a sun-soaked afternoon on the terrace in Tuscany a few years later, and Simon setting down his wine glass with a sound that was heavier than anything I'd heard before, and saying, 'I've got something to tell you.'

No. Not going to think of that now. That's one of the worst side effects of what has happened, that it's opened up the crack for memories I'd thought safely shut away.

Joe Haynes's office is in a Georgian house, uneasily sandwiched between modern blocks on a quiet road a few streets north of Oxford Street. I've been here once before, but many years ago, and Joe and his wife have attended parties at our house over the years. They were at the funeral, of course. More witnesses to the Public Shaming of Selina Busfield.

Joe's office is a mess, with files piled up on the sagging sofa by the window, and ring-marks on the polished wooden desk behind which he sits, slumped in an old-fashioned leather chair. His eyes, behind their glasses, are horribly magnified. Josh used to draw people like that, with eyes ten times too big for their faces. I have a Moleskine notepad open on the desk in front of me, in which I've written a list of questions neatly in blue ink. I am prepared.

'Such a wretched business,' Joe is saying. 'I was so very shocked.'

Not as shocked as me, I want to say, but don't. I'm finding it hard these days to judge what is and isn't appropriate to voice out loud.

There's an awkward silence while we both smile small pretend smiles and gaze around the room. I can tell Joe is building up to tell me something. He keeps glancing over and then opening his mouth as if he's about to say something, then looking away again. So when he finally does speak, the sound startles us both.

'Selina, I know you've had to cope with . . . well, certain shocking revelations recently.'

I keep my eyes firmly fixed on his. Whatever he has to say, I'm not going to make it any easier for him.

'I hope what I'm about to say won't add greatly to your grief.'

Here, Joe removes his glasses and leans back in his leather chair, wiping the lenses with a scrap of pale-blue cloth extracted from the top drawer of his desk. His scalp, where it shows between the thinning grey hair, is the pink of freshly boiled lobster.

'The thing is, Selina, Simon obviously loved you and the children very much, that goes without saying.'

'Does it?'

'Er, does it what?'

'Go without saying. Does it go without saying that Simon loved us very much? Even though he led a completely double life and lied to us all for years.'

'Well, dear, these things are difficult, to be sure, but . . .'

'Carry on.'

'What?'

'Carry on with what you were going to say about Simon, but perhaps you could leave the emotional context out this time, OK?'

Joe looks a bit taken aback by the phrase 'emotional context'. When I've spoken to him in the past it's been about holidays just taken or the prospect of an Indian summer, or the National Theatre's latest Shakespeare production. '*Emotional context*' is a whole new language.

'Well, the thing is, Selina, in the light of Simon's, ahem, unusual domestic situation . . .'

'You mean his whore and her daughter?'

Funny to see a fully grown man blushing like an embarrassed child. All these years I've spent trying to make people feel comfortable, I never realized how pleasurable being uncompromising could be. There's a savage thrill to be had from watching Joe's composure slipping like a comedy toupee. He clears his throat.

'The fact is, to get straight down to it then, that Simon made a will some years ago that superseded the earlier one that you might be more familiar with.'

Aha! There. He's said it. What I've been hoping against hope he wouldn't say, ever since the funeral, when I looked beyond that woman's stupid ringlets at the girl's face which was Simon's face. All of a sudden I can't bear it. The knowledge that Simon came here on his own, and sat in this same cushioned chair where I'm sitting now, heavy with all the secrets he was keeping from me, to make another will. One that will take things away from our children that ought to be theirs.

Oh, it isn't about the things themselves, not about stuff ... No, that's not true. It *is* about things. Things matter. Stuff matters. What was that American book Hettie lent me once when Simon and I were going through a tricky patch? You had to identify your own love language, the currency by which you gauge the emotional temperature of your relationship. Mine was gifts. Things. *Stuff.* People talk about being materialistic as if it's something awful, but what does material mean? Solid, visible, touchable. Why would you set store by something that disappears into thin air as soon as your back is turned? Only things are tangible. Things are the commitment, not sentiment.

'Don't be alarmed,' Joe says. 'You and the children are amply provided for, of course. You remember you made that will to reduce your inheritance-tax obligations, which split the house in half, so you have your half, and the inheritance tax on Simon's share won't become payable until you either sell the property or, erm, pass away. The, erm, other party will also keep her flat and contents, and the remainder of the estate will be split in half between you both. Simon's accountant or financial advisor will give you details of the actual figures.'

Half!

It's like a punch to the stomach. *Half.* For a marriage that lasted more than half a lifetime? The humiliation tastes like bile in the back of my throat. Not to take precedence, even after nearly thirty years. I struggle to maintain my composure.

'What exactly does "estate" mean?' I ask.

'Well, obviously we're talking about any remaining assets. In this case, the various stocks and shares, and of course the house in Tuscany.'

The shock feels like something sharp and metal and poison-tipped.

The villa in Tuscany. Terracotta tiles and wooden shutters and views over rolling hills and children's bathing suits draped over railings, drying in the afternoon sun. Wine-mellowed laughter floating on the warm breeze.

That first glimpse of it, in the estate agent's window a week after our wedding, while we were in Florence playing that favourite honeymooners' game, 'Imagine We Were Buying a House Here'. Lingering while we perused the sun-bleached photographs, exclaiming over the gulf between what money could buy in London and in rural Italy (even the swankiest part, as Tuscany already was by then).

'Let's go and see this one, just for a laugh,' Simon said, pointing to a honey-coloured stone building with a vine-clad central tower and arched widows with fitted wooden shutters, and a vast flagstoned terrace with a loggia leading off it, from which the Tuscan countryside fell away in every direction. *Why not? What fun!* So we went, and of course we fell in love with it, despite the damp in the bathrooms and the rotten state of the woodwork around the French windows. 'I knew we shouldn't have gone,' I told him, when we had to tear ourselves away, watching the dream-house grow smaller in the wing mirrors of our hire car.

And then the surprise. I'll never forget Simon's expression when he came bounding up the stairs eighteen months later, right after Felix was born, when I was still in that shell-shocked new-mother phase, lying in bed, wondering what had hit me. His smile threatened to burst right out of his face.

'I bought something,' he said, climbing into bed with me, fully clothed. 'As a celebration.'

I stared at his empty hands, his unbulging pockets.

'It's obviously very small.'

'On the contrary. It's *huge*!'

The room could barely contain his delight as he produced from his inside pocket the crumpled particulars of the house. *Our* house.

'I couldn't believe it was still for sale.' He always talked so fast when he was excited, as if someone might stop him at any minute, his words tripping over each other like children in a sack race. 'It was even reduced because the condition has got worse. I had to buy it. It would have been rude not to!'

So typical of him to plunge right in, without consulting me about whether we could afford it. In hindsight, his gesture seems like the act of a megalomaniac, but at the time I thought it romantic (*stupid, stupid, stupid*), even though the restoration dragged on for months, years even. Finding the right person to oversee the repairs, making sure nothing we did breached the million and one bits of Italian red tape, sourcing replacement antique wood for the door frames, choosing the right colour green tiles for the pool we had put in at the side of the house. So exhausting, even with a part-time nanny for Felix. And now it's to be half hers. That money-grabbing *tart* will be in my

112

kitchen, cooking at the range I had specially made. The sullen daughter will be sunning her sallow skin on the teak loungers I spotted in a reclamation yard just outside Sienna. It cannot be borne.

'He can't do that,' I tell Joe. 'Not the Italian house. That was mine. That was ours. It belongs to our family. He can't.'

Joe looks at me sadly through his magnified eyes, then tactfully looks away again.

'I'm so very sorry,' he says, and he sounds as if he is genuinely regretful. 'The Italian house was in Simon's sole name and therefore it counts as part and parcel of the estate.'

I keep my eyes on him, steady, but something is churning in the pit of my stomach.

'You knew.'

Why didn't it occur to me before? Of course he knew. This Joe Haynes, family man – with his photographs of grandchildren on his desk, and his lunch in a clear plastic tub on the shelf behind him, no doubt prepared by his wife before he left for work – sat right where he is sitting now and listened to my husband make provisions for his mistress.

'I didn't ask questions, Selina.' Joe is clearly uneasy at finding himself in so morally ambiguous a situation. He starts straightening a pile of papers in front of him, lining up the edges just so. 'I didn't know the exact nature of his relationship with this other woman. You must understand that Simon was a client, as well as a friend. It's not my job to make moral judgements about my clients. My job is to carry out my clients' instructions. Nothing more.'

As if that makes it all right! As if your job gives you the

113

right to shrug off your conscience like a too-heavy bag!
I'm struggling to keep control over my anger, which is
turning liquid inside me. My jaw is clenched tight, back
teeth grinding together.

'He didn't talk about her then?'

Amazingly, my voice sounds calm, but my overlong
nails dig into my palms. The momentary stab of pain is
welcome. Normally I have my nails done every fortnight,
but like everything else, that has slipped by the wayside.
Now I relish their sharpness, as they make indentations
into my flesh.

Joe Haynes shakes his head. The pouches of his cheeks
sag over the collar of his checked shirt. 'As I say, I didn't
ask many questions, Selina. I felt it best to know as little
as possible.'

That's when I lose it, realizing that Joe didn't want to
ask because he didn't want to be an accessory to Simon's
crimes – whether the legal one of bigamy or the moral one
of infidelity.

'And you didn't think about me? You didn't think about
our children? You've been in our house, Joe. You must
have known it wasn't right.'

There's a moment after I finish speaking when my voice
reverberates shrilly in the air, and we both look at one
another. Then Joe Haynes removes his glasses once again,
and his eyes, when they look into mine, are huge with a
pity I don't want.

'I'm sorry, Selina. I'm a lawyer. I don't deal in rights and
wrongs, just in procedure and consequences.'

Soon after that I leave, unable to stay in this room
where my husband came and made arrangements that
didn't include me and signed his secrets in fast-drying

black ink. But all the rest of the day, as my jaw clenches and my stomach churns and images of happy times in the house in Italy flash in front of my eyes (always sun-kissed, of course, never the days when the rain turned the honey-coloured stone to sludge-brown and the swimming pool to a dank puddle and the children, bored, watched endless videos and loudly wished to be back home), I think of what Joe said, about not dealing in rights and wrongs.

Is it really possible to choose? Can one really decide to abstain from right and wrong, like turning down a third drink or sticking on a round of cards? Might other people be looking at what Simon did and thinking, 'He might not have done things by the book but I won't pass judgement'? Who are these people? Who am I?

Who was he?

8

LOTTIE

A War Council Meeting.

That's how Jules billed it in the email she sent to me and Emma. *General Trumpington requests the company of Admiral Shithead on Saturday 2 October, for a meeting of the War Council at War Council HQ, aka Brigadier Fartface's kitchen.*

She was trying to cheer me up, of course, using the names we haven't called each other since we were children, still living back home in Derbyshire. In those days the War Councils tended to be about the girl who hadn't invited Emma to her party, or the boy who had asked Jules for her number then never called her.

Not about the husband who was married to someone else.

Jules has been staying with me for nearly a week now. She says she was owed lots of holiday from her high-powered job which I can never quite fathom (what does a Resources Manager do anyway?), but I suspect she might be taking unpaid leave. She's kept things together for me at home, dealt with the police and Sadie's school, and even managed to track down Simon's solicitor. She spent ages on the phone yesterday and came off fuming.

'He kept referring to *her* as Mrs Busfield. I said as far as I'm concerned there's only one Mrs Busfield and that's my sister!'

Then she started trying to talk to me about estates and flats and probate, but I couldn't listen. I shut down my thoughts and went to that place in my mind where Simon is still alive and none of this is real.

'*She*'s got a fucking great mansion in Chelsea!' Jules said loudly, bursting through my fantasies.

Jules is prone to exaggeration. Family trait, actually. I know it's Barnes, not Chelsea. Not that it makes much difference. Jules tried to phone her one day. The other woman (not *wife*, not that). She got her number from the internet and spoke to one of the sons. She wouldn't come to the phone, apparently. Refused. Jules was furious (*'Thinks she's so superior – bitch!'*), but it didn't surprise me. I could see she was the superior type. We've built up a pretty good idea of what she's like from hints the police have dropped and from what Chris Griffiths told us ('neurotic' was his word), but really it only reinforces what I already knew just by looking at her at the funeral.

Emma arrived at lunchtime today, for the War Council. She got Ben to look after the kids for once and came on the train. He insisted she upgrade to first class for an extra tenner, and by the time she rolled off at St Pancras she'd already downed two large gin and tonics. When I opened the front door to let her in, she promptly burst into tears, even though she'd seen me just a few days ago.

Now she's sitting opposite me on one of the kitchen chairs and banging her hand down so hard on the table that the half-empty bottle of champagne in the middle is shaking all over the place.

'Uptight!' Emma screeches. 'You can spot it a mile away!'

Emma's round cheeks are flushed from the alcohol and from the curry she and Jules and Sadie have just consumed (I picked at some rice – I do a lot of picking these days). The fringe she painstakingly straightens each morning has turned damp and frizzy. She rarely goes away without her family – the three children so inconveniently far apart in age – and when she does, she often goes over the top as if unable to regulate her own behaviour once freed from the constrictions of being a wife and a mother.

She's looking at the photo on Jules's laptop that came up when Jules Googled 'Selina Busfield'. She's at some charity fundraiser ball wearing a long, satin, baby-blue dress with her hair in a neat French pleat. She's carrying a cream-coloured clutch bag. I've never understood women who carry clutch bags. Why aren't they always losing them?

'She's got "ball-breaker" stamped all over her,' Emma elaborates, demonstrating on her own pink forehead where such a label would go. 'No wonder he was too scared to leave her. Who wouldn't be?'

This is the story my sisters have decided on. Simon was miserable in his marriage, he met me and saw a way out, but she wouldn't let him leave. He was weak. She was a monster. He pulled on the chain. She yanked him back.

I swear to God, I don't recognize my husband in the picture they are painting.

Sadie comes in and Emma pulls her down on to her lap. Miraculously Sadie allows herself to be held. Ridiculous to be jealous of my own sister. Sadie looks awful. Her skin is stretched so tightly across her face it looks as if her cheek-bones will bust clear though it.

Sadie never got used to missing her father, though you'd think the absences would have got easier over the years. All those tantrums she threw because Dad wasn't there to hep with her science project like he'd promised (I was useless, of course. What's a circuit? I asked. What's refraction? What's frictional force?), all the school plays where she scanned the audience and I watched her face fall when she realized the person sitting next to me wasn't him, all those nights when she woke up from a nightmare and called to him. 'No,' she'd cry when I arrived, wild-haired and sleepy-eyed, by her bedside. 'Not you, not you.'

'Come on, more words,' Jules says.

My oldest sister is standing by the kitchen counter on which she has propped a whiteboard pilfered from my studio. Along the top of the board she has written, in red felt-pen, MILITARY STRATEGY. The rest of the board is filled with the disjointed words and phrases we've been throwing out, like 'money-grabbing' and 'status-driven' and 'Bitch from Hell', all radiating from the one word in a box in the very centre: HER! Jules calls this a Mind Map. Apparently being a Resources Manager gives you 'whiteboard experience'.

Jules has a man's tie around her head. Emma and I are also wearing ties properly knotted around our necks. Jules bought them in the charity shop earlier on. She said the War Council should be formally dressed.

'You're all drunk,' Sadie observes. She is fiddling with the voodoo doll key ring Emma brought me as a present. It has long blonde hair. There's another doll as well, a man, but I refused to let them stick pins in it. 'He's not

119

here to defend himself,' I told them. Emma tried to insist, but stopped when I started to cry. I know they call Simon all the names under the sun when I'm out of the room, but I don't want to hear them

'Horrible shoes!' shouts Emma.

'Oooh, yes, awful shoes,' agrees Jules. '*Court* shoes.' She writes it down, underlining the word 'court' as if it's particularly telling.

'What I don't understand,' says Emma, who has already fallen off her chair once this evening, and is leaning dangerously to the left under Sadie's weight, 'is how this is a strategy.'

Jules looks back at the board. 'Profiling the enemy,' she says. 'How else do you mount a military campaign?'

I put my head down on the table. The alcohol inside my system is mixing with the pills the doctor gave me in a not unpleasant way. If I close my eyes now I just see black, rather than Simon's face, which is what I see the rest of the time, floating in front of my vision, always out of reach.

'Look!' I hear Sadie say. 'Mum's not crying!'

Three sets of eyes swivel towards me, verifying the miracle. But that, of course, sets me off, and tears start rolling down my face again.

'That's it. You're not going,' says Emma from underneath Sadie. 'You're not going to give that witch the satisfaction of seeing you cry.'

'She has to go.' Jules is leaning over me and giving me a crushing hug from behind. The end of the tie around her head tickles my cheek and her alcohol-soaked breath is warm against my ear. 'She has to find out what's been going on.'

'The police already told her . . .' Emma again.

'No, she has to hear it for herself. From the horse's mouth.'

Which, for some reason, my sisters find unaccountably hilarious.

'Horse!' they shrill. 'Write it down!'

'I wish *I* could go,' says Emma, convinced as always that she is missing out. 'Maybe I could throw a sickie on Monday. It's not as if anyone will come into the shop anyway. Who buys jewellery on a Monday?'

'Oh, Ben and the kids will accept a sick note from your doctor, will they?'

Jules is still upset that I won't let her come with me to that woman's house. She doesn't think I'll be able to cope on my own.

'I still can't believe she wouldn't even come to the phone,' she says, and we all know which 'she' she is talking about. 'The cow.'

She scrawls 'cow' on the whiteboard.

Both my big sisters think I will fall apart without them to protect me from the hidden slights and digs that only they see. They might be right, but all the same, they don't understand. They're filled with fury on my behalf, but it's directed as much at Simon as at her, and it's not tempered with grief. They hardly knew Simon – with all those years away, how could they? The grief they feel is for me, not for him. Grief once removed.

I can't let them come because they'll make it be his fault as well as hers, and I can't survive it being his fault, I swear to God.

She's the one. It has to be her.

'Horse *and* cow?'

I am sitting up now and squinting through my tears at

the words on the whiteboard – descriptions of her hair, her shoes, her face. Suddenly, an image of Selina Busfield (how that sticks in my throat, his name, my name, Sadie's name, purloined by someone else, someone who is nothing to do with me) flashes crystal-clear into my drink-addled mind and a wave of fury almost drowns me.

If it wasn't for her, Simon would be alive. I know it. I deliberately haven't listened when the police have talked about how he died, but now it's blindingly clear. She was behind it, with her prissy clothes and her tight-lipped smile. She made his life untenable.

The pills in my system make it hard to think. My brain is sluggish with the effort, but now another thought is slowly taking shape behind the cotton-wool cloud of my mind.

Maybe she did it.

Why not? Simon would never have chosen to leave me and Sadie. He loved us too much to be careless with his own safety. Maybe she found out about us. Maybe she had him killed rather than risk losing him, or rather losing his money!

I test this theory on my sisters. They do not seem convinced, but Jules obligingly writes 'murderer?' on the board.

I make my excuses and go to bed. It's quarter to eleven – the latest I've managed to stay up since this whole nightmare began. I have some stronger sleeping pills Emma brought. Jules was furious with her for giving them to me. She said grief is a natural process that needs to be worked through. Emma said cancer is a natural process but you still need all the drugs you can get. I love the pills. I love them with my whole heart. Because of them, I don't have to lie awake night after night reliving the funeral, I don't have to see that woman's face in my dreams. Jules tells me I can empty my mind without the drugs. 'Imagine yourself taking all the crap out of your head as if you're unpacking a supermarket bag,' she says. I've tried, I really have – out with the worries about money, out with the thoughts of that woman and the children who are his children and the ugly nylon thread of lies that sews us all together. But it never works. Only the pills work, allowing me a few precious hours of nothingness. And best of all, when I wake up there's a time-lapse before my mind catches up with my body, and for that brief moment, Simon isn't dead. He's still on his way home, forever suspended in the act of coming back to me.

Before I go to sleep, I arrange one of the pillows lengthways down the bed on Simon's side so that in the night it feels like someone is there. I should be used to sleeping alone, but now I find that cruel expanse of empty sheet impossible to bear.

The sound of my phone ringing forces my heavy eyelids open. My brain, already surrendered to sleep, struggles to adjust. There's no number on the screen, just the word 'Call', which is what always came up when Simon rang from overseas.

'Hello?' I say, with my pharmaceutically thickened voice.

There's no reply, but the line breathes with someone else's silence.

'Simon?' My befogged mind tries to make connections. 'Simon? Is that you?'

The silence continues, though I know someone is there. *Speak*, I urge him. *Please speak*. Then there's a click and the line is dead.

When I wake up the next morning, my fingers are still curled around my phone and, for one brief pill-groggy moment, I mistake it for my husband's hand.

9

SELINA

∽

Carmela has just left. The house reeks of cleaning fluid.

When I sat down last night and made a list of things I wanted her to do, I had to go over on to a second sheet of paper, there were so many. I got up extra early to help her or it would never all have got done. When Josh finally emerged from his pit of a room I was outside in the garden washing out the kitchen bin with a bucket of water mixed with a few drops of bleach.

'What the fuck are you doing?' he asked.

I hate it when he swears, but when I tell him so he just says, 'Don't you think, on the scale of things, my language comes quite low down your list of problems?'

He has a point.

It's fair to say Josh wasn't impressed when I told him I'd invited that woman to the house. And he seemed particularly concerned about the daughter.

'Is *wassername* coming as well?' he asked in the studiedly casual way that usually means something.

'I expect so,' I told him. 'They'll want to come and have a good nose around, price up the furniture, see how much he was worth.'

'But the furniture's not theirs".'

'No. But they don't know that yet. They probably think they've won the bloody Lottery.'

'They didn't look like they were celebrating. At the funeral. They looked . . . you know . . . like *us*.'

Josh didn't mean to be inconsiderate, I know, but he has no idea how much that 'like us' hurt.

'They're nothing like us,' I told him.

The thought of her coming to the house makes me feel sick and yet at the same time I can't wait.

This thing that's happened to me. This ghastly, terrible, unfathomable thing, sets me apart from everyone. Yes, there are women who've lost their husbands, and there are also women whose husbands have been unfaithful. But to experience the two at once. In such a way. No one could comprehend.

But this woman, this ridiculous, unprincipled, conniving woman who has caused all this agony, is also the only person who can possibly make sense of it. She is part of it, which makes her connected to me in a way that Hettie, who I've been friends with for most of my life, can't be.

Josh appears now in the doorway of the living room, where I am rearranging the cushions so that they are square-on. Carmela will insist on putting them in a diamond formation, lined up against the sofa backs like After Eight mints. I've given up telling her I don't like it. Now I just wait for her to leave and do it myself. Much simpler that way.

'You sittin' in here?'

I look up at my son in surprise. Since when did Josh express an interest in anything beyond his own physical and emotional needs? Since when did he care where visitors sat?

'Why wouldn't we?'

Josh shrugs. 'Bit formal, innit? Wouldn't they feel more comfortable in the kitchen or the den?'

I cast an eye around the room, with its two mink-coloured sofas facing each other across the cut-glass coffee table. On the floor, there's a huge Persian rug in shades of butter-yellow, cream and grey. Is it too formal? Too intimidating?

Good.

My phone beeps while I am straightening up the black and white photograph on the wall. It's of Simon and me on our wedding day. We are shockingly young. I've been staring at Simon's face as he smiles down into the eyes of the bride I once was, looking for some indication of what his older self would be capable of, but I find none. We are shiny with excitement.

Great News! reads my text. *You are eligible for a £3,500 loan, which can be delivered straight into your bank account within TEN minutes!*

I've had four texts like this already this morning, and three calls. Last night, when I checked my emails, there were 127 spam messages. Something has happened, but I don't know what. Why am I getting offers of loans from people I don't know? Why did an accident helpline call me this morning and offer to help me with my claim? What prompted a sexual-health clinic in Essex to email me to confirm an appointment? Since when have I been interested in safaris in Kenya, or Nile cruises?

I don't understand, I don't understand.

Since Simon died, the world has gone crazy and I have no control.

HE HAS TO COME BACK!

The sound of the doorbell makes both Josh and me jump. We catch each other's eye and I see my own wariness reflected back at me. So she's come, has she? I half expected her not to. Her type – the type who falls apart in public – is not renowned for keeping to arrangements.

Now that she's here, I wish to God she wasn't. What possessed me to invite her? And the girl? Why have I chosen to heap indignity upon indignity, insult upon insult? What kind of masochist am I?

The doorbell again.

Josh makes a 'Well?' gesture, but I don't move. He glares at me, then turns on his heel to let them in. I check my reflection in the mirror over the mantelpiece, even though it's less than an hour since I got ready. I took extra care with my appearance today. My hair is piled up in a loose ponytail and I'm wearing a tunic top in the softest camel-coloured suede over wide cream trousers. The overall look is casual but expensive. Classy. I want her to see who I am, and why who I am was what Simon wanted. But now, listening to Josh opening the front door, I'm having doubts. Is this really me, this beige woman in the mirror? Is this who I am?

There are voices in the hallway and then Josh pushes open the living-room door. I slide quickly into the nearest sofa, so that I can see them coming in. It puts one at an advantage, I think, to be already seated. Armies do that in battle, I believe. Dig in their position and turn to face the oncoming enemy.

The girl comes in first. Again that shock of seeing his eyes in her face, the sudden involuntary clench of the heart. Now that her face isn't screwed up and pink with shouting, I can see that she's really very striking, with long glossy dark hair, delicate features and high, wide cheekbones. She's much taller than her mother and reed thin in the way some teenage girls are – not Flora, of course, but some – and she's wearing a black jumper over a frayed denim mini-skirt, with thick black tights on her pipecleaner-long legs. If it wasn't for the sullen, set expression, she might be quite beautiful.

I focus on the girl for a long time, partly because of the shock of seeing Simon's features replicated back, but mostly to avoid having to look at *her*.

I wish she hadn't come.

Finally, when the silence grows so pointed it becomes like another presence in the room, I take a deep breath and gird my abdominal muscles, like they teach you in Pilates to provide a core of strength, and turn my eyes towards her.

Oh, how could he?

All that hair, so much of it, taking up so much space in my home. Baggy, blue and white stripy T-shirt over narrow jeans tucked into flat, clumpy black leather boots. Tiny body, like a child's – how on earth does it support the weight of all that hair? Brown eyes far too big for her face. Bright-red lipstick to match red earrings. So out of place here in the muted colours of my living room.

I make a gesture, not trusting myself to speak, and they sit down on the sofa opposite, while Josh positions himself next to me. We face each other like chess pieces.

My core muscles are still clenched, holding me upright. I am a rock. I can do this.

I look at her hands. They are tiny, soft. Young. There's

a plain gold ring on the fourth finger of her left hand, inset with three tiny diamonds.

I stare at the ring while my heart grates like Parmesan cheese. And stare, and stare.

LOTTIE

I'm not looking at it. I refuse to look at it.

Jules primed me before we left. She said to watch out for her mind games and she was right.

The wedding photograph is on the wall behind her head, straight in front of me. Amazing coincidence, *I don't think!*

If I don't look at it, I'll be OK. That's right. Look around the room. The off-white walls, the pale yellow fringed lamps, the fireplace with the ornamental log basket which clearly never gets used. Not a home – a show-house. The row of wellies in the porch when we came in (that expensive make, naturally), the polished parquet flooring in the entrance hall expanding out to the rooms on either side and stretching ahead, the sweeping staircase with its gleaming balustrade, the ornate antique chandelier in the centre of the hallway ceiling, reflecting the colours of the stained glass in the door so that the whole hallway danced with light, the one liver-coloured 'statement' wall, the inescapable stench of Eau de Money.

The boy is so ill at ease, sitting there not knowing where to look. Simon's son. My heart dissolves as I look at him. There's something about boys, isn't there? Everything is on the surface. When you come from a family of girls, you notice the difference.

But her.

How could he?

Those clothes. Can that top really be suede? Who would wear something like that? Someone who doesn't work, that's who. Someone who has nothing better to do with their time than shop and have their nails done. I'm looking at her nails now. Yes, I thought so. She has one of those immobile faces. Botox. You can always tell. No expression, no warmth. Her eyes are chilly blue, the perfectly applied make-up emphasizing the colour. She must have spent all day getting ready. Pathetic.

I'm not going to look at the photograph. I'll look at the rug, a huge velvet-soft Persian thing. Must have cost a fortune. I'll look at the coffee table. Glass – could have been sculpted from ice. I'll look at the over-stuffed bland sofas. I'll look anywhere except at that photo.

Too late.

But oh, how young he is. *How am I to bear it?* The breath stops inside me, though I had a big puff on my inhaler just before I came inside. This Simon that I never saw, never knew. This boy-man with his dreams painted on his face. That beautiful face. She had all that, this woman. She had the gift of him when he was, what, twenty? Twenty-five? She didn't deserve it. Look at what she's made of it. This mausoleum of a house. No wonder he always said that coming back to me, wherever in the world I was, was coming home.

The silence in the room is deafening. The woman is staring at my hands. I clench them so she can no longer see where, over the last week, I have bitten the skin around my fingers until it bleeds. She won't judge me. I won't let her.

SELINA

∾

'Wanna cup of tea?'

In the end it is Josh who shatters the silence. Offering to make tea? What a day this is for firsts! All of a sudden I'm anxious for him to leave the room. I want to be alone with this other woman, this *Lottie*.

'Excellent idea,' I say. 'Why don't you take . . . with you to help?'

I make a gesture with my hand even though I know her name is Sadie. The police told me that much. But somehow I can't say it. If I say it, it's acknowledging her, acknowledging *their* child.

Josh's face flushes deep red. Unlike him to be so awkward. I glance again at the girl. She is undeniably attractive. But related. He knows that. (I won't say *sister*. I will never say *sister*.)

'My laptop is in the kitchen,' I tell him. 'You could go on YooHoo or something.'

Why did I say that? I know perfectly well it's called YouTube. Why am I deliberately making myself sound so much older than I am? Because I want her to see how old *he* was. We were old together. We had a history together. That's something she hasn't got. That's something she'll never have.

Josh's blush intensifies. 'Oh my days! YooHoo? For God's sake, Mum.'

132

He is standing by the door, stiff with embarrassment, arms wooden by his sides. 'Do you want . . . ?'

He is looking at the girl, yet not looking at her. Focusing his eyes on a spot behind her head.

She shrugs. Clearly she doesn't want.

'Good idea.' The other woman seems similarly keen for them to go. 'Go on, Sadie, give Josh a hand.'

My insides freeze when I hear her say my son's name. She doesn't have the right. *My* children, *my* home, *my* husband.

Anger bunches inside me like a fist.

LOTTIE

I force myself to use the son's name – he introduced himself at the door, it would have been so rude not to – but it sounds grating and wrong.

I'm glad when he and Sadie disappear, although I know she'll hate me for it. He seems a nice boy. Or man? How old is he anyway? My mind, sluggish with happy pills, struggles to remember.

'How old . . . ?' I ask. It's the first time either of us has directly acknowledged the other.

'Seventeen.'

Her voice is so sharp and clipped you might almost cut yourself on it. No wonder Simon was desperate for softness and warmth and somewhere he could be himself.

'He was born in February 1993.'

'But that's not possible. I met Simon in March 1992.'

Her smile is thin like a paper-cut and I realize she must

have worked all this out already. Why didn't I? What have I been doing?

'Yes. Touching, isn't it? My wonderful, loving husband must have gone out picking up women and then come home to me to conceive our third child.'

How dare she? *Picking up women?* As if I was one of many, as if I didn't matter.

'It wasn't like that.' My voice is trembling. I mustn't cry in front of this woman. 'We didn't go looking for each other. It was love at first sight. It just happened.'

'"Love at first sight", was it? How romantic!' She's almost spitting. 'And how romantic was it all those months later, when he left you and your baby and came home here? To me? To us?'

I'm not prepared for this. I haven't thought it through. Whenever my sisters have tried to get me to put things in chronological order I've refused to listen. I don't want to think about the dates, or the lies he must have told.

He was so excited about us having a baby. Together we found out about the logistics of giving birth in Dubai. It never ever felt like he'd done it before. But then he hadn't, I suppose, not there. I was young and stupidly fearless, but he still fussed about me. How would I cope in the heat? Would the medical care be good enough? When it got near the end, he hired that woman to look after me and the baby, what was her name now? Amirah, that's right.

And after the birth, he took three whole weeks off work. We'd never spent so much time together in one stretch. We'd lie in bed in our apartment just gazing at our daughter. 'She's so beautiful.' I still remember his face as he said that, as if no other man had ever had a daughter before. And when he finally went back to work, leaving Amirah in charge, it was as if he was being ripped from us like sticky tape.

And yet he came straight from us to here. To her. And said nothing. It can't be true. It's impossible that it's true. Suddenly I am flooded with hatred for the woman telling me these things. It's her fault, all of it. She should have let him go. She must have known.

'Did it never strike you as odd,' I ask her, 'that he was always away? That he was never here for Christmas?'

Surprise makes her plastic face suddenly animated.

'Of course he was here for Christmas!' she says, her eyes wide. 'He missed a couple of years, but the rest of the time he was with us. Where else would he be?'

'No,' I tell her. 'You're lying.'

But instantly I know she isn't. All those years where he'd drop me and Sadie at the airport a few days before Christmas, weighed down with presents for my sisters and nieces, and I'd feel guilty imagining him slogging away at the office in Dubai or on some dusty building site while we were celebrating, because work in the Middle East doesn't stop for Christmas. And instead he must have followed on, flying back to London that same day or the next on a flight of his own. To be here, with them.

It can't be possible. It can't be.

SELINA

∽

Ha! She didn't know! She thought he spent Christmas somewhere else. The thrill of watching her face and seeing the realization dawn. The silly bitch! Did she really think he wouldn't be here for Christmas? All the little traditions we had – opening a bottle of champagne to drink while decorating the tree, listening to Frank Sinatra's Christmas album, wrapping presents for the kids' stockings, even after they were fully grown. He must have told her he was staying in Dubai to work. Oh, it's priceless!

'He loved Christmas,' I say, relishing the look on her face. 'We'd usually have a houseful of guests. Lots of silly games, walks across the common, that sort of thing. Real family time.'

She flinches as if someone has struck her. Then her red-painted mouth sets into a line.

'It's amazing, seeing as he was having such a wonderful *family* Christmas and everything, that he always found time to phone me for an hour at a stretch – or more.'

What is she talking about? He couldn't have done that. He wouldn't have time to do that.

Then I think a bit harder. On Christmas morning he'd always drive over to pick my mother up, while I stayed behind to prepare the food. Could he have pulled in by the side of the road somewhere? Pretended he was calling her from Dubai? Or what about the evenings where we'd all be flaked out on the sofas in the den and he'd appear with his coat on. 'Just taking Walter for a stroll, to clear my head.' Could he really have left us, sitting by the fire with the lights twinkling on the tree and the presents piled in corners, and gone to phone his mistress? (Not his wife, never his wife.)

'Tea's ready.'

Josh and the girl appear, carrying mugs. The girl puts hers down straight on to the glass table, and when I push two coasters towards her, she looks embarrassed.

'Sorry,' she mumbles, sliding them under the mugs. It's the first thing I have heard her say today.

My brain is still reeling from the Christmas thing, but the presence of the two teenagers inhibits me from saying more. I wish they'd go away.

We all sip our tea awkwardly until, surprisingly, the girl breaks the silence.

'Where's that?' She is looking at a photograph of Flora, Felix and Josh in a heavy silver frame on the far windowsill. They are sitting on the terrace of the house in Tuscany, their smiles white against their deep summer tans.

'Italy,' Josh mumbles.

'We have a house there,' I say, and I'm gratified to see how the woman's face changes, the triumphant expression she's had since the comment about Simon calling her on Christmas Day replaced by confusion. That's another thing she didn't know!

'But isn't that . . . ?' The girl is looking at her mother askance, and suddenly a horrible thought is occurring to me. They couldn't . . . He wouldn't . . .

'We've been there,' the woman says, and her voice is flat. 'Simon said it belonged to a friend of his.'

No. It's not true. They can't have been there. Lorenzo would have said something. He'd never have stood for it . . . Or would he? He's Italian, after all, and a man. How much of a stretch is it to imagine him getting the place ready for Signor Busfield and his 'other lady', particularly if Signor Busfield made it worth his while? I start thinking about the holidays we've had there recently. Might I really have spent long summers drying myself on towels that woman had also used, eating off the same plates? Oh God, have we slept in the same bed? That carved four-poster Simon came across in an antiques market near Florence and had delivered by lorry, which cost more than the bed itself? Could he have slept with her on the embroidered Egyptian cotton sheets I had sent over from that shop in Fulham?

'It's not possible,' I say. 'That's *my* house. He wouldn't have . . .'

LOTTIE

Oh wouldn't he? Not feeling quite so superior now, are you? Now you know I've been there, to your precious villa with the terracotta tiles and the cool green swimming pool with the deep end fashioned out of rocks so it looks like it's growing right out of the Italian countryside.

But, oh, to think it was hers all along. My Happy Place. I simply can't bear it. Although, hang on a moment, if it belonged to Simon, wouldn't it be just as much mine as hers? He was my husband just as much as he was hers.

Or was he?

All week long, I've tried not to listen to what Jules and Emma have been saying about my wedding, and whether or not it was legal. 'Simon was my *husband*,' I shrieked at them. 'We were *married*.'

He organized the wedding and it was just how we'd wanted it to be. On a beautiful white sand beach, as the sun dipped into the sea. I wore a white halter-necked dress and a garland of white flowers in my hair, and my feet were bare and covered by the shallow surf. Simon wore a cream linen suit with the trousers rolled up and a white T-shirt underneath, and he cried when he put the ring on my finger. There was a minister who took the service. There was paperwork. My surname changed from Carling to Busfield. It was real.

'I'm going to see Simon's lawyer next week,' I tell her. 'To find out where we stand.'

'I've already been, so you might as well save yourself the bother,' the woman says, her voice newly enamelled.

Then she gives her papercut-smile.

'It wasn't legal, you know,' she says, her mug of tea halfway to her lips. 'Your little Indian wedding on the beach. You have to have lived there thirty days for it to be legal. Joe, the lawyer, told me.'

I feel dizzy, the room sways in front of my eyes. I'm married. I've been married for seventeen years. It's part of who I am. I'm a wife. A widow. We had paperwork. It was all stamped. For seventeen years I've been filling in forms as Mrs Busfield. If the wedding wasn't legal, who have I been for the last seventeen years? If the wedding wasn't legal, Sadie would be illegitimate. If the wedding wasn't legal, we might be left with nothing, Sadie and I. This woman might claim our flat – the ornate cornices, the garden studio, the foot-high skirting boards. It's not true. I won't think about it. It *was* legal. We were married.

I was a wife.

SELINA

She's thinking about the money. I can see it in her face. She might as well have pound signs in her eyes. That took the wind out of her sails – finding out she wasn't really married after all. Well, what did she expect? On a beach, for goodness' sake!

The girl makes a sort of gasping sound. I've almost forgotten they're here, her and Josh. I suppose it wasn't very kind to say that in front of her, about her parents not being married, but I can't be held responsible for that. Blame her father. Blame her mother.

'You'll be all right though.' Josh is looking, stricken, at the girl. 'He made a will and you get half. So you'll be all right.'

Oh bugger! Why on earth did I tell him about the will? I know he's just trying to make them feel better, but what the hell is Josh thinking of? They would have found out sooner or later, of course, but not now. Let her sweat for a few days.

'I'm not going to discuss the contents of *my husband*'s will right now, thank you very much, Joshua.'

My voice sounds like my mother's. I hardly recognize myself.

LOTTIE

My husband. Her words are knives. Slash, slash, slash.

No. I won't think about what she just said, about the

wedding. I won't give her the satisfaction of watching me fall apart. Stick to the practicalities, that's what Jules told me. I try to remember what was on the list we drew up in the kitchen before we left. Oh yes, I remember.

'Ashes.'

She looks at me as if I'm mad.

'We want half of his ashes. We have a moral right to them.'

'Don't be ridiculous!'

I can hear the blood pounding in my ears. Ridiculous, is it? To want to remember your own husband in your own way?

'We could give them some, couldn't we?'

The boy, Josh, is obviously embarrassed by his mother. My heart goes out to him as he stumbles over his words. He has a way of scratching behind his ear, nervously, that reminds me so much of Simon.

His mother's eyes widen in exaggerated disbelief – well, as much as the Botox will allow.

'Oh right,' she says and she's almost shouting. 'Let's see. How much would you need? A foot's worth of ashes? Or would a couple of toes' worth be enough? Maybe I could measure you out a *dick* length of *my husband*'s ashes?'

There's a stunned silence. Well! The poor boy looks as if he wants to melt with embarrassment. We exchange a look.

'What d'you want to do?' he asks me in a strangulated voice. 'With the ashes, I mean?'

SELINA

Rings! I've heard it all now, I really have. Even Josh is looking at her as if she's talking in Urdu.

'I've found a place where they fuse ashes with molten glass to make beautiful jewellery. I want to have rings made for Sadie and me.'

It's clearly the first the girl has heard of it.

'Mum!' she hisses. 'That's gross!'

She's right. It's gross. It's ridiculous and gross. Who are these tacky, end-of-pier people that Simon has brought into our lives? They don't belong here, in my living room.

Rings. For goodness' sake!

'Simon's ashes will be ready for collection some time next week, whereupon they'll be coming back here, to his home.'

No need to tell them how I fantasized last night about collecting the ashes and scattering them from a footbridge over the M25, watching as they sprinkled like dandruff on to the passing vehicles, mingling with the mud on truck windscreens, dissolving into grey sludge, like death porridge.

'We intend to bury them under the willow in the garden in a *private* ceremony.'

'You can't! We have rights!'

The woman's whiny voice is cut short by the ringing of my phone.

'No,' I say, pressing 'Answer'. 'I don't want advice on consolidating my debt.'

'What the fuck—' says Josh.

'Someone seems to have signed me up for every bit of

142

spam going,' I tell him, resisting the urge to add 'and don't swear'. I turn to the woman, whose red-lipped mouth is still frozen in a round 'O'. 'I don't suppose you'd know anything about that?'

She glances at her daughter, rolling her eyes as if I'm mad, and then looks away.

'I haven't a clue what you're on about,' she says.

Liar. Liar. Liar.

We glare at each other across the table, and I suddenly want her out. Both of them. Out of my living room, out of my house, my life, my marriage, or at least the memory of it.

'Fuck off,' I hear my mother's voice saying, through my mouth. 'Fuck off out of my house!'

'Mum!' Josh is shocked, I can tell. 'Chill!'

Chill. Of course. How stupid of me. Chill, while my life is slashed to pieces by strangers.

The woman lurches to her feet.

LOTTIE

I didn't want to come anyway. I knew it would be like this. She's mad. Unhinged. Glancing across at Sadie, I see that, like me, she's on the edge of tears.

'Come on,' I tell her, glad now that Jules insisted on waiting for us outside in the car.

I turn back to the woman, to *Selina*.

'It's your fault Simon did what he did,' I say, snatching up my bag from the floor. 'You drove him to it. *You* killed him.'

SELINA

They're gone, but the word 'killed' hangs in the air, and Josh is looking at me as if I'm someone he doesn't know, and Simon is everywhere and nowhere and I hate him, hate him, hate him, and my hatred is a hard lump of gristle that catches in my throat and stops me from breathing.

And no one but me knows it's there.

10

SELINA

～

I'm not proud of what happened. If I close my eyes – not advisable while I'm driving, I suppose – I still hear my shrill voice telling her to fuck off out of my house. In front of the girl, too.

Flora was horrified when she heard about it, but Felix thought it was hilarious.

'I love it,' he said, when Josh finished telling them both about it over dinner last night. 'My mother, the fishwife. Seeing off Lottie Lost the Plotty.'

The children are still all over the place, one minute shrieking with laughter and the next gulping back sobs. I have to keep reminding myself that they're grieving for their father as well as trying to come to terms with what he did.

Flora confided last night that she had assumed mourning would be a 24/7 thing (that was her phrase, '24/7' – so American). She hadn't realized it could slot into your everyday life, instead of the other way around, hadn't known that there's only so much grief a person can take before normality gets in the way, and said she felt consumed by guilt the first time she laughed after Simon died.

It was when the three of them had gone off to register Simon's death. Apparently the woman behind them in the waiting room was talking about how the undertakers had come to fetch her dead mother from the upstairs bedroom but hadn't been able to get the stretcher around the turn in the stairs. 'We've a very sharp turn,' the woman said. 'The sofa had to come through in pieces.' 'You couldn't really do that to your mother though, could you?' her friend said. And that, by all accounts, set all three of my children off. Well, Felix had started at the phrase 'sharp turn', but the other two weren't long in following. And when Flora goes, of course, there's no stopping her. The boys used to take such pleasure in goading her into hysterics at inappropriate times.

I told her she didn't need to feel guilty, that Simon wouldn't have wanted her to feel guilty. But even while I was saying it, I realized I felt like a fraud. How on earth can I say what he'd have wanted when I clearly never had the first clue who he was?

Felix was in one of his restless moods. He kept jumping up from the table and disappearing off upstairs. He hardly touched his food because he was talking ten to the dozen. There's definitely something up with him, I can always tell, but when I asked him, he just said, 'What, something other than having a dead, bigamist father?'

They had such a difficult relationship, Felix and Simon. I suppose it was to do with them being so alike. I remember Felix as a tiny boy, so beautiful with his white-blond hair as it was then, squeezing into the armchair next to Simon, wearing his little checked dressing gown and clutching whichever was his favourite book of the moment, demanding a story. Simon would put down his drink or his paper and start to read, but inevitably he'd begin skipping words or even pages, and Felix would grow ever more anxious.

'No, Daddy. You missed a bit! Go back.'

And Simon, whose mantra was always 'Never go back – onwards, onwards,' would grow instantly bored with the whole exercise.

'Don't take things so seriously,' he'd tell his tightly wound child, snapping the book shut with a disheartening thump. 'Loosen up a bit, Felix. Life is an adventure to be enjoyed, not an ordeal to be endured.'

Of course, to Felix at four, or six, or eight, such sentiments meant nothing. Just another excuse for his father to remain out of reach.

Felix tried to quiz Josh about the girl, but Josh didn't want to talk about it.

'She's nice, I s'pose,' he said.

Flora went very quiet then. 'It's weird, having a sister,' she said.

A sister! I lost my temper then. It seems to be happening all the time nowadays. I'll call her later to apologize. It was that word that did it. *Sister*. It's insupportable to think your children might have relatives who are not related to you. I have a vivid memory of Flora as a young girl, sandwiched between brothers and so desperate for a sister she fashioned one out of cardboard and carted it around with her from room to room, insisting on it having its own seat at the dinner table until it became so spattered with grease and bits of food I made her get rid of it. Poor Flora, always grasping for intimacy. I shouldn't have got cross. I'll ring her when I get home.

*

147

I'm on my way to meet Simon's financial adviser, Greg Ronaldson. When he called yesterday and suggested we should meet, I was still a bit shaken up by the scene with that woman. But there was something about his voice that I found very soothing. I don't normally like financial people – probably a throwback to my mother insisting it's bad taste to discuss money – but I found myself almost enjoying talking to Greg Ronaldson. I've never met him but I know Simon used to like him.

I'm wearing black today, as befits a widow – or at least Number One Widow, as Felix jokingly called me last night in a flash of gallows humour. Slim black trousers tucked into high-heeled black boots, a long slash-necked black tunic. Out of long-ingrained habit I've thrown a khaki jacket over the top though, automatically adhering to my mother's dictum that straight black is too draining for a woman over thirty-five. Widows' weeds, they're called, aren't they, the clothes we women wear to mourn our dead?

The lift of the Mayfair building in which Greg Ronaldson's office is housed is hideously brightly lit. The mirrored wall reveals a trail of horrors. First an unsightly clump of mascara clinging to the upper lashes of my right eye, then, on closer scrutiny, a criss-cross of fine lines in the corner like the skin of an over-roasted chicken. Finally, as I break my own rule and step back to take a look at the overall picture, I see that my face is sagging like an old sofa.

Old, old, old.

Before Simon's death, I never allowed myself to think of age, except in terms of how to beat it, but since sitting opposite that woman and seeing the wedding ring on her smooth thirty-something hand, I haven't been able to shake off the feeling of things shutting down around and within me. I read something once that has stayed with me – an interview with an actress of a certain age who was lamenting how her looks had been lost so gradually she hadn't even noticed them going. 'Why didn't anyone tell me at the time that this was my last day of being beautiful?' she asked the interviewer. 'Why didn't anyone say, "This is the last day men will pass you in the street and look twice," so that I could mark it in some way, or at least remember it?' At the time I didn't think I'd ever read anything so cruel, but still I hadn't really believed it would ever happen to me. Foolish woman that I am, I really thought that a combination of good genes and expensive skincare would exempt me. But Simon's death and his mistress's unlined hands have triggered a landslide of self-doubt.

Of course, even if Simon hadn't died, I'd still have had to face getting older, but there's something about being half of a couple that protects you somehow, isn't there? As if partnership doubles your capacity to withstand decrepitude.

'Selina? I'm Greg.'

The man who takes my hand outside the lift is broad and powerfully built. His dark hair is long at the front, with threads of silver at the temples. He looks, despite his expensive suit and light, even tan, like someone who'd be far happier outside than stuck behind a desk. There's an air of barely suppressed energy about him and my hand tingles in his.

He leads the way into a square office, with glass on two sides through which mansion buildings and office blocks bask in the sharp autumn sunshine. There's a wide desk at one end, but he indicates for me to sit down in one of the two black leather armchairs by the windows.

For a second or two we look at each other in silence, while I prepare myself for the inevitable 'I'm sorry about your husband' speech.

Instead he says, not taking his eyes from mine, 'You must be finding this very hard.'

I am momentarily blinded by tears. Oh dear God, what is wrong with me? When did I turn into the kind of woman who cries in front of strangers? It's the surprise of it, that's all – of someone being concerned about me, rather than about Simon or the children or the mess he left us.

Greg Ronaldson's thick-lashed eyes are grey and accentuated by his tan. He's not classically handsome, absolutely not, with that slightly crooked nose, and the gold filling that glints in the back of his mouth when he smiles, as he does often, but he is rude with life. Behind the sympathy in his gaze, there's something else, a kind of appraisal, and I feel the stirrings of something inside me long forgotten.

The fact is that since Simon's death, even at the funeral, I've become aware of a certain amount of, well, testosterone wafting my way where I'm pretty certain none existed before. Men I've known for years and who've never evinced the slightest hint of sexual attraction press my hand just a moment longer than necessary or catch my eye in a meaningful way. Even Joe Haynes, in his late sixties and married for over forty years, looked at me once or twice in a way that didn't feel exactly lawyerly. Hettie says there's some research about widows giving off pheromones that make them suddenly irresistible to men. Looking at Greg now, I wonder if she might be right.

'As you know, I was Simon's financial adviser as well as his friend,' Greg tells me, his eyes still trained on mine. 'I asked you to come in so I could give you an idea of his financial position.'

I can't be sure, but I think I detect a slight hesitation in his words. I sit up straight, alert. Then my phone rings. Damn.

'No,' I bark down the invisible line. 'I am *not* interested in an off-plan apartment complex in Marbella.'

I turn my phone off, embarrassed.

'It's a long story,' I say in answer to Greg's raised eyebrows.

He nods, like someone used to long stories. Then he speaks.

'I didn't have access to all of Simon's accounts until Joseph Haynes contacted me and asked me to look into it all. The fact is, Selina, things were complicated.'

I give a harsh, unattractive laugh that I immediately regret. *Complicated*. I'll say.

I'm reflecting on the complicatedness of things and on why Greg saying my name should have such a physical effect, warmth pooling suddenly in the pit of my stomach, when he continues: 'Simon made a lot of money, but he was sailing very close to the wind. There was the upkeep of your house in Barnes, the house in Italy, your children's school fees for all those years, the rent on the apartment in Dubai, the constant travelling back and forth. All that he could have just about sustained, but then on top of that he incurred . . . other expenses.'

I look at him, determined not to make it easy.

'The flat in London he bought for the other party.'

'You mean his whore.'

I see from Greg's eyes that the word takes him by surprise, but he continues as if I haven't spoken.

'I don't know how much of this you're aware of, but he didn't have the ready cash for a deposit, so he released equity from your own home in Barnes.'

It's the first time I've ever understood what people mean when they talk about the blood rushing to one's head. *My home?* Our family home? Used to buy a place for *that woman?*

'How could he? It's mine. I'd have to have been informed.'

But apparently, because we split the house down the middle in some inheritance-tax loophole, technically I only own half the house and Simon was free to do what he wanted with his own half. Which was to take out a mortgage on it to cover the equity he released in order to buy his mistress a flat.

'He'd raised funds against the equity on that property by remortgaging it several times,' Greg said. 'But whatever he was trying to do, it clearly didn't work, because the mortgage on that flat is three months in arrears.'

I stare at him like an imbecile while I try to take in this latest fact, prodding it gingerly in my mind like something suspect in a salad. But eventually my feelings come into focus. I'm elated. ELATED. Sod the money. I still have my half and the house in Italy. What matters is what *she* doesn't have. She doesn't have Simon and now she doesn't even have his money. All those years she's been inveigling herself into his affections in the expectation of being

152

provided for, and all for what? NOTHING! NADA! BIG FAT ZILCH! If I was the kind of woman who knew how to dance a jig, I'd be dancing one now.

But it seems Greg hasn't finished.

'Then he put up the rest of his half of your house as security against the mortgage of the new one.'

I'm not following. I'm normally very good at financial matters. I handle all the finances to do with the day-to-day running of our lives. I respect money. You know where you are with it. It's not open to interpretation like so many other things. I'm not one of those people who pretend to think it, in itself, is something vulgar. But I can't seem to get my head around what Greg is telling me.

'So half of my house is either mortgaged or used to guarantee that woman's mortgage?'

Greg nods. 'I think he'd always been reassured by the fact that there was an endowment attached to the mortgage which would pay out in the event of his death. I'm afraid I've just learned that the endowment won't pay out if the insured commits s— Takes his own life.'

I feel my face burning, as if I myself am being judged.

'He didn't.' My voice is sharp. 'He wouldn't . . . The inquest will prove that.'

'Of course.' Greg's grey eyes gaze straight into mine. There's sympathy there, but not, I'm relieved to see, pity.

'The inquest will show it was an accident,' I repeat with a confidence I don't feel. The inquest, as we both know, was adjourned as soon as it was opened. The police say it could be months until we know what happened.

Greg stands up and walks over to the desk to pick up a

sheaf of papers. Seated back in his chair, he leans forward to put a hand on my knee. He means it as a reassuring gesture, but there's a jolt of electricity where he touches me.

'I'm afraid there are also certain . . . discrepancies in Simon's accounts.'

'Pardon?'

Greg does a thing with his mouth where he presses his lips together as if physically stopping himself from speaking until he's completely decided what to say. It feels as if all the nerve endings in my body are concentrated in that part of my knee where his hand rests.

'As I said, his accounts are complicated. But I've been going through everything and there are large sums of money – really very large – that have been going out quite regularly to an offshore account I've had no luck in tracing. Do you have any idea, Selina, what that account might be?'

He's holding out a sheet of paper. My eyes follow his finger to a row of numbers that seem to be doing a sort of Mexican wave across the page. I'm struggling here. Really struggling. My house is at risk because of that woman, and now there's a mystery account that he's been sending money to. It has to be something to do with her. Building up a nice, fat nest-egg with my children's inheritance, a gold-plated shag-pad! Rage sweeps through me, white-hot.

'I don't recognize it,' I tell Greg. 'But no doubt it's to do with *her*. Oh, she saw him coming, all right. She must have thought all her birthdays and Christmases had come at once.'

Greg leans back in his chair and gazes at me, nodding

slightly. 'I presume you know that Simon sold all his shares?'

What? I stare at him, uncomprehending. No, I don't believe it. Now this really is going too far. Even before we met, Simon had a portfolio of shares that he had inherited from his father. Stocks and shares are something Simon has always done, like supporting Arsenal and flossing his teeth. He wouldn't have got rid of them. I know he wouldn't.

'You're mistaken,' I say, knowing even as I speak, that he isn't.

'I'm sorry,' Greg tells me, seeing my expression. 'This must all be coming as a bit of a shock.'

I'm feeling cold suddenly, shivery, though the autumn sun is flooding through the plate-glass windows of Greg's office, the Venetian blind throwing a slanted grid of shadows across our faces. The walls seem to be moving on their own and I'm struggling to separate what is real from what isn't.

No shares. A mortgage on the house. Money haemorrhaging from Simon's account. Thank God for the house in Italy. I can't ever go back there, of course, knowing that he took her there, that they swam in my pool, slept in my bed. I'll sell it – or at least my half of it – to make sure my home is secure.

'It's not good news on the Italian house either,' Greg says, as if he can read my mind.

Well, I know it's not good news. I've already lost ownership of half of it.

'The fact is that Simon mortgaged that too. Up to the hilt, actually. There's a bit of equity left in it, but I'm afraid that'll be swallowed up in the various taxes you have to pay to sell a property in Italy. I hate to tell you this, Selina. I can see you've been through an awful lot recently, but the truth of the matter is your husband was broke.'

Broke. The word bounces around my head, rebounding off the surfaces, and it's as if there's a five-second delay between Greg Ronaldson speaking and me being able to make any coherent sense of what he's saying. *Broke*.

Simon always had money. It's one of the things that defined him, like being tall and having green eyes. The very first time I set eyes on him at that student party in Bristol, I knew that here was a man of substance. What a relief it was to find him. Ah, I remember thinking to myself, here he is, finally. The fact that he was in his final year of his history of art degree and I'd only just started the second year of my law course didn't really bother me. Oh, I knew I was clever enough to finish – my teachers always told me that – but I just didn't have a burning ambition to. I could have stayed on at university when he moved to London the following summer, but really, what would have been the point? I remember drawing up a list with Hettie of all the things we looked for in an ideal man, and Simon pretty much ticked all the boxes, so why would I wait? I think somewhere in the back of my mind I'd always expected to have to choose between money and love, and it seemed such a stroke of luck to have found both.

And now it seems I was wrong on both counts.

I'm conscious of heat on my leg and see Greg has replaced his hand. There's panic rising inside me. Broke. No shares. No house in Tuscany. No comfortable life. The phrases pass through my mind like a PowerPoint presentation.

156

A memory comes to me of that time, a few weeks ago, during one of my twice-weekly visits to my mother's nursing home.

'Is everything all right with your husband?' my mother asked, and I remember being irritated by that phrase 'your husband'. I knew it was probably the creeping memory loss, but there was something dismissive about it, as if she couldn't be bothered to remember Simon's name, after all these years.

'Everything's fine, thank you, Mummy,' I said sharply. 'Why do you ask?'

'Because he was here a couple of days ago, asking to borrow some money.'

At the time I assumed it was the dementia talking and gently corrected her. 'You mean he was asking if you needed to borrow some money?'

My mother was profoundly offended. 'Certainly not,' she snapped. 'I've never borrowed money in my life and I'm not about to start now.'

Later, Simon and I laughed about it. 'I did drop in on her while I was passing,' Simon said, 'but we didn't talk about money. Although we might have discussed Monet . . .'

Monet? Pompous git!

That conversation with Simon plays through my mind now as I try to remember whether he appeared particularly preoccupied before he died. Did he give any signal of being weighed down by financial worries? Was there something I should have picked up on? I can't remember anything, but then he has proved himself to be a black belt in compartmentalizing. How else could he have lived a double life all these years? If he could

157

successfully hide from me another home-life with a second family, how hard would it have been for him to disguise a few money problems?

Greg still has his hand on my leg but I won't look at him. I can't risk seeing pity in his eyes.

'I understand you must be reeling, Selina, but here's something else . . .'

Something else? Isn't this enough?

'There were also a couple of large payments into Simon's account in the last year, but again I can't trace the source. Have you any idea where these might have come from?' He holds another sheet of numbers under my nose and points to a couple of ringed entries.

'So there *is* money, then?' I say hopefully.

He shakes his head. 'I'm afraid even these amounts were swallowed up by the size of Simon's debts. I just . . . well, I'm worried about where this money might have come from. I heard reports, you see, Selina.'

'Reports?'

'Well, rumours really, I suppose, that Simon might have been involved in a business venture that wasn't quite . . . above board. Brokering a huge development project with the Arab authorities, claiming to be acting independently, but really being funded by other people. Very unpleasant people, by all accounts – the kind of people who wouldn't have looked good on paper, if you know what I mean. Taking backhanders from both sides.'

'What do you mean, "wouldn't have looked good on paper"?'

'What I'm saying is their money might not come from sources that are completely legal – which is why they'd need a legitimate frontman.'

'Someone like Simon?'

'Perhaps.'

I don't have a clue what he's talking about. illegal sources, legitimate frontmen. What world is that? The Simon he's describing isn't anyone I recognize.

'He wouldn't,' I say. But immediately I'm not sure. How would I know what this unknown Simon would do? 'He wouldn't risk his reputation like that.'

'You're probably right.' Greg sets the papers down on a glass-topped side table. 'It was just something I heard.'

Though I'm still struggling to take in what I've just learned, I can feel the panic bubbling up inside me and my heart thudding against my ribcage and I wonder if Greg can hear it, too.

'You still have your half of the house,' he tells me, trying to be kind. 'And the other half too, unless the, er, other party defaults completely on her mortgage.'

And now I can't bear it. She's responsible for all this. Her. *Lottie*. She tricked him into being with her by getting pregnant, then proceeded to bleed him dry. He's clearly been siphoning off money to give to her, maybe even getting involved in something dodgy – never a clever thing to do in the Middle East, for goodness' sake – just to keep supporting her. My children's inheritance, my own quality of life – squandered, lavished, wasted. And as if that's not enough, now it seems my home is linked to hers, the two of us tied grotesquely together in some hideous three-legged race.

It's too much. Simply too much.

'And what happens if she doesn't? Keep up her payments, I mean.'

Greg looks at me steadily, and I'm aware that I'm breathing noisily – short, shallow pants like a dog.

'I'm sorry to say, Selina, that if the other Mrs Busfield' – *no, no, no* – 'loses her house, there's a very good chance you will lose yours, too.'

11

LOTTIE

How dare she?

Really, how dare she?

Phoning here, accusing me of – well, what exactly? Offshore bank accounts, dodgy business deals, mortgages, stocks and shares. My head is about to explode with her madness, I swear to God. She's obviously unhinged – it makes me wonder what Simon must have had to put up with over the years.

My heart is racing and I fumble for my asthma inhaler. *Press and Gulp. Breathe, breathe.* I mustn't allow myself to get upset, the GP told me when I went to see her yesterday. I must protect myself.

I can hear Jules on the phone in the other room, still talking to that woman. Thank God she was standing right by me when she called. I don't know what I'd have done if she hadn't snatched the phone off me. I could hear myself growing hysterical.

'You're mad,' I kept shouting. 'Crazy!'

Now Jules is trying to work out what the witch is on about.

'I don't know why it's come as such a shock,' I can hear

her saying. 'My sister could have told you he was broke. They've been skint for the last two years.'

Pause. And now, 'Oh, might you have to go and get an actual job, now? Poor thing, my heart bleeds for you.'

The woman is obviously repeating the same mad allegations, because Jules is sounding properly angry now.

'What account? Oh my God, you have totally lost it!'

I pick up my sketch book. Maybe drawing will calm me. I'm on to H now. H for Horrid, H for Hellish, H for Harridan.

Jules appears in the doorway of the living room, her pink flushed face clashing horribly with her bright red hair.

'You won't believe what she's accusing you of now. Squirrelling off a fortune from Simon into a secret bank account – making him go into debt, driving him to a life of crime!'

Laughable really, the idea of me having a pile of money banked somewhere. If Simon was sending money to anyone, it would be her. Maybe he was paying her off, bit by bit. Building up a fund so that she'd finally let him go. That'd make sense.

Breathe, breathe. I mustn't think about that now.

I've taken two anti-anxiety pills and I'm lying back on the sofa, propped up against cushions, waiting for them to take effect. I must just stay calm.

Jules comes in and drops into the beanbag on the floor by my feet. I'm glad she's here. I feel safer when she's around. Protected.

'Hun, you're going to have to start thinking about money, you know,' she says.

I close my eyes. I know my sisters talked a lot about this

over the course of the War Council weekend – the tricky question of my finances, or lack of them. But I don't want to think about it. Having to think about money just reminds me all over again that Simon isn't here to look after those sorts of things.

'I'll work more hours,' I tell Jules dully. 'I'll cover the mortgage.'

She smiles then. 'And if you don't, you'll always have the satisfaction of knowing the witch will lose her house as well.'

That's one thing Jules has managed to find out – that Simon used the house in Barnes to guarantee the mortgage on my flat. It's almost funny, when you think about it.

But Jules has her serious expression on again, her head cocked to one side as she looks up at me through her bright-red fringe, as if she's weighing something up.

'There's something else,' she says suddenly, as if she's come to a decision in her head. 'Emma didn't want to tell you, but I think you need to know.'

While she's speaking, I'm tracing a letter H with my pencil, going over and over the lines until there's a groove in the paper.

'Well, the thing is, I spoke to someone about your legal position – a lawyer friend of mine.'

I don't want to listen to this. I focus on the dress Jules is wearing – a wrap-over one in black and white stripes. If you look too long, the stripes start to blur together like an optical illusion.

'Lottie, you need to hear this. It seems the witch is right. Your wedding – the wedding on the beach. It wasn't legally binding.'

Tra la la. I don't have to listen. The same rubbish

that woman was spouting. I can choose not to hear it.

'And because your wedding wasn't legal, it means you weren't legally Simon's wife, which means you don't have the same legal rights. And don't even get me started on what might have happened if the Dubai authorities had realized you weren't really married when you had Sadie.'

I start filling in the trunk of my H with soft black pencil. *Tra la la.* My fingers zigzag furiously across the page.

'Lottie, because you weren't legally married to Simon, you're not exempt from inheritance tax. Are you listening to me, babes? Lottie? Are you listening?'

'I'm going for a bath,' I tell her, cutting her off short. 'I've been dreaming of a bath all day.'

It's true, all through the interminable afternoon on the hotel reception I've been longing for the moment when I could get home, lock the bathroom door and immerse myself in warm water, thinking of nothing.

My sisters think I'm mad, going back to work so soon. But they have no idea of the things grief can do to a heart when there's too much time to think. Sadie was desperate to get back to sixth form – she's only just started and she was worried about falling behind – and for the first two days after Jules went back to work, when I was left alone in the flat for the first time, I just sat in a corner of the living room, rocking, or else ran through the rooms frantically searching for something I couldn't explain – the door that led back to the life I used to have.

Simon is everywhere. Since the night when I listened to his breath on the phone, I've also twice heard his footsteps coming down the garden path. But when I fling the door open, no one is there. Sadie comes home to find me stretched out like a rag on the hallway floor, wrung out with grief.

'I need to come back to work,' I told Anya, the Slovenian (Slovakian?) hotel assistant manager.

When I went in that first day, the girls on the desk tried to be nice, but they're so young. They seem to think death is something shameful and not to be talked about. They gave me a card with a sad-looking teddy on it and failed to meet my eyes. A couple of the cleaners who heard what'd happened grasped my hand across the reception desk and said things about time healing everything and the importance of keeping busy.

When Anya called me in for a 'chat' at the end of the second day, I didn't have the faintest idea what she wanted. I remember sitting there across her desk and staring at her eyebrows. Funny how I'd never looked at them properly before – they're painted arches that sit high up on her forehead like upside-down smiles.

'Are you sure you don't need to take more time?' she asked. 'Take another week off. Although four days of that would have to be unpaid, I'm afraid.'

Unpaid – that figures. I thought of home, with the empty rooms and the closing-in walls, and shook my head.

'That's fine,' said Anya. 'We only want to help you. But Lottie –' she tapped her long fingernails on her desk – the fingernails were purple with little pictures on them, rainbows and starbursts, and made a loud clicking sound on the laminated surface, 'we have to remember that this is a special place. Our clients come here to feel pampered and looked after. So, happy face!'

She put a hand up to both sides of her mouth and pushed each corner upwards with a purple-painted fingernail to demonstrate.

When Jules came round later that night and I told her

that story, it was the first time I'd laughed in days. '*Happy face*' we kept screeching at each other, pushing up our mouths in grotesque clownish smiles. But once I started laughing, I couldn't stop. I literally laughed till I cried. No wonder Jules is looking at me now as if she's worried I might break.

I leave her in the living room while I dash to the bathroom and start the taps running, pouring in a few drops of jasmine bath oil. I don't try to analyse it, this need to lose myself under the water. 'Doesn't it make you feel weird?' Emma asked once, when she was still here. 'Being in water, after the way Simon died?' I suppose it should, but it doesn't. I won't let myself delve into how Simon died. I don't think I could survive it. That preposterous notion of suicide.

On my way to the airing cupboard to grab a towel, I find Sadie standing outside her bedroom door.

'Another bath?' She makes it sound like an accusation.

I look at my daughter. She wears her misery wrapped around her like a shroud. I know I should try harder to break through to her. We need to talk about what happened at that house in Barnes, and I suppose I will have to talk to her about the money and the wedding that wasn't. But those are things I don't want to think about right now. My own grief is so all encompassing there isn't room for anything else, or for anyone else's. Surely she's old enough to understand?

'It helps me,' I say. 'Having a bath, I mean. It helps me not to feel.'

Sadie looks scathing. 'Lucky you,' she says. 'I wish *my* feelings could be washed away in six inches of water.'

'That's not what I—'

Bam. Sadie is gone, slamming her bedroom door behind her. I'm reminded of an action film we watched together once, when she was little, where a huge boulder closes over the mouth of a cave, sealing up the people inside. She was terrified by that at the time, the idea of being entombed. But that's what her closed door brings to mind now. As hot water gushes into the bath, I hesitate in the hallway, contemplating knocking on her door to explain what I meant, but I'm just too tired. What's the point in trying to get Sadie to share her emotions when I'm having so much trouble dealing with my own?

I select a towel and open up the bathroom door. The hot, jasmine-scented steam rises up to meet me like a friend.

When I emerge, nearly an hour later, Jules is still here. When not obliged to be at work, my sisters are clearly keeping me under observation. Lottie Watch. Jules reporting back to Emma on my changing moods. It's touching, but sooner or later I'm going to have to get used to being by myself.

'I think Sadie's got a boyfriend,' Jules whispers, as I flop down on to the sofa next to her. 'She was talking to someone for ages while you were in the bath.'

A boyfriend? I suppose it's not inconceivable, but she hasn't mentioned anyone. Not that she'd talk about it to me. Terrible to admit that I feel a pang of jealousy at the idea that my daughter might have someone to comfort her. I imagine her leaning into this mystery boy at the bus stop or on a park bench, experiencing that blissful surrender that comes from having someone's arms around you and allowing your problems to be absorbed through their coat, their clothes, their skin. What kind of a terrible mother is jealous of her own daughter?

A text comes through from Emma. *Go to Twitter and look up @BarnesBookworm.* I've never been able to fathom Twitter. All tweeting this and hashtag that. But Jules knows exactly what to do. She opens my laptop and within a few clicks she's called up a webpage on the screen. There's a picture in the top right of the page. It's her. *Wife, mother, booklover and Barnes dweller*, reads the blurb. *Fount of all knowledge regarding the comings and goings of the Second Wednesday Reading Club.*

'Look – her most recent tweet is on the day Simon died,' says Jules, pointing to a column down the left-hand side.

Crisp autumn morning in Richmond Park, read the message dated that day. *Aquamarine sky and golden leaves. Good to be alive.*

'Aquamarine!' Jules exclaims at exactly the same moment as I say, 'Good to be alive?'

We gape at each other, mouths open.

'Of all the pretentious . . . ' says Jules.

'You couldn't make it up,' I say.

We scroll down through the other messages – or tweets, as Jules keeps insisting I call them – drinking them in greedily. They're a mixture of the practical – *The Red Lion, Wed 11th August, 8pm. We'll be discussing McEwan's Solar. Wine will be drunk!* – and the personal – *Nipped out for a paper and a loaf of sourdough, came home with a new pair of shoes. How does that happen?*

'Ha!' Jules retorts regularly.

'Have you seen this one?' I rejoinder.

There isn't a single mention of Simon. There isn't a single reference to their life together or her hopes or dreams. She's like a hologram of a person, this Selina Busfield, this @BarnesBookworm, a shiny surface without depth or substance.

'He couldn't have been happy with someone like that,' I insist to Jules.

She puts a hand on my arm. 'I don't think people necessarily stay together because of happiness, babe,' she says.

Eventually, Jules goes home to her garden flat in Kentish Town. I've been willing her to leave so that I can be alone to think, but the minute she's gone I miss her and want her back again. I hate the silence, hate hearing the sound of my own breathing. There's a thick rope of grief coiled inside me, pressing painfully on my heart.

Sadie is in the bathroom, brushing her teeth. The door to her bedroom is open and as I walk past, I see her phone charging up on the floor just inside. I remember what Jules said about a boyfriend. I shouldn't. I know I shouldn't. But I want to know if she's all right. I am her mother, after all. I need to feel included. Alert to sounds in the bathroom, I quickly scroll through the menu until I come to her list of recent calls. Next to today's date, there's just one name:

Josh.

Part Three

BARGAINING

BARGAINING

12

SELINA

∽

'Something looks weird.'

Josh is staring at the blank wall in the living room as if it might at any moment perform some sort of magic trick.

'That's because I've taken the wedding photograph down. I have no wish to be reminded of the biggest mistake I ever made every time I walk into the room.'

I catch sight of Josh's face and guilt flushes through me. I shouldn't have said that. I'm an awful mother.

'I don't mean that, darling. Ignore me.'

I try to settle down on the sofa, but can't relax. My mind is filled with images from last night. It still doesn't seem real. That wasn't me, that woman. I don't do that.

And yet the unfamiliar ache in my thigh muscles tells me that it was, and I do.

Impossible to believe it's only twenty-four hours since he called. I was sitting on the sofa in the den.

'Selina, it's Greg here.'

How ridiculous, that pounding in my chest, as if I was sixteen again. And yet as soon as I heard his voice, I realized I'd been expecting him to call.

'I was wondering if maybe you'd like to have lunch one day. You're bound to have some questions, after all, about that stuff I threw at you the other day.'

And I, foolish woman that I am, played right along with it.

'Yes, I do. Have questions, I mean. When were you thinking of?'

There was a pause then, and I could almost feel the energy crackling down the phone.

'Today?'

The old Selina would have been horrified. The old Selina knew that there are rules to be adhered to when it comes to social arrangements, acceptable time-frames within which to operate. The old Selina was an idiot.

'Today is perfect,' I said.

I told myself it was all about business, and even wrote down a list of questions to ask, sitting at the kitchen table with a carefully sharpened pencil. But who was I kidding? If I'd really thought it was just business I wouldn't have agonized so long over what to wear or booked a taxi in case I drank too much to drive home. God, my heart is hammering away just thinking about it now! How I walked into the restaurant and he stood up to meet me, and gave me a kiss on the cheek and muttered, 'Fuck, you're gorgeous.' Not classy, but gorgeous. I think I knew right then that I was going to sleep with him.

Impossible to say how much of it was because of who he is – those grey eyes, that sense of aliveness, the way he says something pompous, then adds, 'and now you think I'm a complete wanker' – and how much was because of wanting to get back at Simon. *If I do this, we'll be even*, I reasoned with myself, watching Greg over the lunch table.

If I do this, I'll regain some control. I just wanted to feel some of what Simon had all that time, the vicious thrill of being wanted by someone *other*, touched by someone *other*. I wanted to get my own back for the financial chaos, for the panic that freezes me inside when I start to think about a future without money.

My being with Greg was the first step towards levelling the scores with Simon, I thought, for that woman and her daughter, for the life that wasn't real.

But of course it wasn't just about Simon.

The lunch was strained. With all that electricity zinging between us how could it have been anything else? I ordered salmon, then realized as it came to the table, all anaemic pink flesh and slimy grey skin, that I didn't actually want it. I forced myself to eat half, hoping it wouldn't leave a fishy tang in my mouth. He had the steak, as I guessed he would.

Afterwards we went to a hotel. That was the first time it occurred to me that Greg might, after all, be married.

'Fifteen years.' He was quite proud of it and showed me the ring which he wore on a chain around his neck 'for allergy reasons'. 'We have a very unrestrictive relationship. Do you mind?'

'Not really,' I said. And amazingly, that was the truth. Greg was the trophy-wife type, I decided. I could picture him wearing her on his arm like an expensive watch.

When we fucked (which is the only word, really, to describe what we did in that hotel room), I was half appalled by him and the way his chest hair felt coarse, like coir matting, under my fingers, and half charged with desire. Sex with Simon was so samey by the end –

something we mostly did when it seemed too long since we'd done it last. Oh, it was fine, I suppose. After nearly thirty years you get to know what makes you both tick, and the quickest way of getting there. But looking back on it now, it seems as if sex had become just about the shorthand. We'd got so good at the shortcuts, we'd forgotten the point of the journey. But sex with Greg was quite different. I don't think I knew such positions were possible. Or rather, of course I knew they're possible, but I just hadn't thought them possible for *me*.

I worried that I might feel guilty afterwards, but instead it was gratitude that flooded through me as we lay there in that anonymous hotel bed. I remember running a finger along Greg's surprisingly meaty shoulders that weren't Simon's shoulders, and a line popped into my head: 'from death, comes life'. Is it a poem? Something I read? I've no idea. Normally I haven't got a lot of time for poetry. It's a bit self-indulgent. Like Jungian therapy or something. But yesterday afternoon, in that hotel room, that was what came into my head. And after so many days and nights of my head being filled with Simon and that woman, it was such a relief to think of something else.

In a way, being with Greg gave me back some of myself, pretentious as it sounds. Since Simon's death, it's as if every standard by which I judge myself has been rubbed out, rendering me shapeless and formless, an amoeba in designer clothes. But Greg's fingers on my body shaded me back in, stroke by stroke.

How ridiculous, at my age, to be sitting here hugging the memory of yesterday afternoon to me like a child with a party bag, not daring to open it up for fear that someone else might see. How adolescent I've become.

BARGAINING

I stand up to gaze out through the French windows, noting absently the effects of fast-encroaching winter – the patchy lawn scabbed over with dead brown leaves, not to mention my lovely herb garden, where armies of unseen creatures have made delicate lace of the once healthy mint, and the stooping, wilted basil reproaches me for having failed to dig it up and bring it inside. Now that I can't afford the gardener, the garden has a forlorn air, waiting resignedly outside the back door like a neglected dog.

My eyes fall on my left hand, pressed up against the wooden door frame. There's the white-gold wedding band, on the fourth finger, just where it has always been. How bizarre that my hand still looks the same as it always has done, while everything else in my life is different. How is it possible that I could have looked down at this hand one month ago, or two, when my most pressing concern was whether Josh had completed his A level sociology course-work on time, and it would have looked exactly the same as now, when my husband is dead, my home at risk of repossession, my body so recently touched by someone else.

Idly I twist my wedding ring around my finger, wondering whether, after all these years, it will actually move or remain jammed fast. Ow! At first it's unyielding, but after a few moments of rigorous activity my finger surrenders the ring with only the slightest of protests.

Well! How odd! My hand looks like someone else's. The bottom part of my finger, where the ring was, has the whitish translucence of a freshly boiled egg. I hold it up to the pale autumn light, half expecting to be able to see straight through it, and am surprised to find my finger

177

solid, after all, with just a halo of light surrounding it like a solar eclipse.

The ring feels cold and hard in the palm of my hand. Such a tiny, insignificant thing to have embodied the spirit of a twenty-eight-year marriage. All these years I've worn it, and only now does it strike me as odd that the greatest symbol of marriage should have a gaping hole at its centre. I gaze at it, imagining all those months and hours and minutes compressed into this tiny band of gold. For nearly three decades I've looked after this ring like a holy relic, wearing it around my neck when advanced pregnancy caused my fingers to swell, scrubbing it with soap and a soft toothbrush before dressy events. In my mind it wasn't an item of jewellery but the physical embodiment of my marriage. And yet here it is, just a small nugget of metal sitting in my palm, and, after all, it's my hand that turns out to be the solid thing. Who knew?

Without stopping to think, I pick up the ring between my thumb and forefinger, open up the French doors and fling it out into the garden with as much force as I can muster, watching it arc gracefully over the flagged patio, the lawn and the flowerbed, where last summer we saw that explosion of gladioli and gerberas, before disappearing behind the willow halfway down the garden.

'What are you doing?'

Oh, I've forgotten Josh is here, distracted from his rapt contemplation of the wall by the gust of cold air blowing in through the French doors.

'Nothing,' I say. 'Just getting rid of a dead fly.'

I leave Josh still staring at me and walk self-consciously into the kitchen, wearing my secrets like a set of unfamiliar clothes. Suddenly unseen hands clamp themselves over my eyes from behind. My scream is ear-splitting.

'Chillax, Madre.'

Felix keeps his arms wrapped around me as I slowly turn to face him.

'You gave me a fright,' I say, closing my eyes as if there's a danger of my elder son looking into them and being able to tell what I've been thinking.

'Not doing anything naughty, were you, Madre?'

'Chance would be a fine thing.'

I break away and busy myself at the sink. Where did all those dirty dishes appear from? The house is looking grubby suddenly, I notice, making a mental note to book Carmela for an extra two hours next week, before remembering about the money, and the fact that I don't have any.

Felix is in an odd sort of mood, prowling the perimeter of the kitchen as if marking out his turf.

'The thing is,' he begins, apropos of absolutely nothing, 'just what the fuck was Dad playing at, linking this house with *hers*? I mean, I just don't get it.'

His long legs seem out of sync somehow with the rest of his body as he moves jerkily around the room, picking things up randomly, then putting them down without looking at them.

I'm suddenly reminded of when he was a small child and something wouldn't go quite how he wanted and he'd work himself up into a self-righteous frenzy of rage, heaping justification upon justification to validate his building anger. In the end I stopped trying to talk him out of those emotional crescendos. It was easier to wait on the sidelines for them to blow themselves out.

'I mean, Dad obviously had the *semblance* of an idea

179

about money.' Felix is clearly warming to his theme. 'He would seem to have had the most *basic* clues about how money works. So what the fuck was he playing at, tying our house in with that *parasite*'s? It just doesn't make any fucking sense.'

Indeed it fucking doesn't.

'Just face it, Madre.' Felix's narrow face is suffused with a deep-red flush. 'He really wasn't all that, was he? The wonderful Simon Busfield. Everyone's best friend. Don't make me laugh.'

'That's enough, Felix.'

My voice comes out sharper than I intended, but then old habits die hard. All those years I spent brokering the peace between my dominant husband and my highly strung older son have left their mark.

'Whatever your father was, and whatever he did, he was still your father and he loved you very much.'

'You'd be surprised.'

'I beg your pardon?'

'About love, Madre. You'd be surprised about love.'

What on earth is Felix on about now?

Before I can find out, Josh comes barging in. 'All right, bro?'

The brothers give one another their strange, convoluted greeting which consists of putting fist to fist, shoulder to shoulder and then clasping a hand to an upper arm. What's wrong with a handshake, for goodness' sake?

'I was just congratulating our mother on her great taste in men.'

I feel the heat rising through me. Surely he can't know anything about Greg? Seen potentially through the eyes of my sons, yesterday's episode seems suddenly tawdry and seedy. Please God don't let them find out. I swear I'll never repeat it as long as they don't find out.

Josh starts opening cupboards and then closing them with a bang. He goes to the fridge and spends a long time gazing inside before slamming it shut.

'There's literally nothing to eat,' he says.

Poor Josh. I know he's missing his father, but sometimes I wonder if it's his mother he's missing the most. The mother who used to cram the fridge with homemade quiches and pies and bags of fresh salad and small, round, polystyrene pots of indeterminate oily stuff from the local deli for him to reject in favour of meals that come in powder form, springing synthetically to life with the addition of water. He's nostalgic for the mother who used to berate him for not touching the casserole left in the oven, or for starting a new loaf when yesterday's was still largely untouched. He misses, I think, the days when the kitchen was a place where food was made and stored and consumed, rather than this graveyard of rotting fruit and takeaway boxes.

The sound of my ringtone cuts through my thoughts and I'm glad of the diversion.

'No, I don't want insurance, debt advice, legal representation or discreet cosmetic surgery.'

My anger feels like a release, although Felix is looking at me as if I've altogether lost my mind.

'What the fuck are you talking about?' comes a woman's voice.

It's her! Lottie Lost the Plotty, as Felix calls her. Ringing me. The nerve of it!

'As if you don't know exactly what I'm talking about.

The phone calls, the emails, the endless spam you so charmingly signed me up for.'

There's a pause on the other end of the phone.

'I've told you before, I don't have a clue what you're on about. A woman like you must have loads of enemies. It'll have been one of the others. Anyway, this isn't a social call. I'm ringing to talk about your son, Josh.'

'Josh? What about him?'

Perched on top of the kitchen table, Josh raises his eyebrows and holds his hands up in the air questioningly.

'I want you to give him a message for me. Tell him to leave my daughter alone.'

LOTTIE

That got her attention all right.

I feel a small thrill of triumph as I put down the phone. That Selina Busfield, always so in control. It feels good to have shocked her. I try not to think about how furious Sadie will be when she finds out what I've done – snooping through her phone records, warning Josh off. But surely I'm allowed to look out for her? I'm her mother, for God's sake. I just want what's best for her.

She'll hate me.

He'll hate me.

I hate myself.

He didn't seem such a bad kid, considering his mother. And they were just chatting on the phone. Is there really any harm? Now that I've already made the call, I'm thinking about what Simon would say, if he could see how

I've reacted – or overreacted. The boy is his son, after all.

No, I don't want to think about Simon. But it's too late. I'm lying curled up on the bed that used to be our bed, and Simon's in my head yet again and I can't get him out.

'Aren't you angry with him?' Emma asked me on the phone last night. 'If someone did that to me, I'd never forgive him.' But Emma isn't me; she's harder, stronger – or at least she thinks she is.

I know my sisters think I ought to hate him, but I can't. The worst thing that can happen has already happened, and hating him isn't going to bring him back, or change what he did. All I have are my memories of him, and if I allow them to be corrupted by anger, I'll be left with nothing.

The being a Not-Wife hurts. The being a Not-Widow hurts. I'm not who I thought I was. And he's not who I thought he was. But I still love him. I have to believe in love. Love will out in the end, I'm sure of it. It always does. And Simon believed in love, too. Emma and Jules don't know that it was him who was needier, pushing me again and again to tell him how much I loved him, ringing me up in the middle of the night, explaining, 'I just like to hear you say it.'

At night, when I'm sucked out of sleeping-pill oblivion to lie, open-eyed, staring at the ceiling, I talk to him in my head, trying to bargain him back to life. *If you come back, I'll accept not being married. If you come back, I'll move back to Dubai. If you come back, I'll never force you to make another decision again. Just come back.*

I'm doing it now, though it's the middle of the afternoon.

If you come back, I'll understand about Selina, about the children. If you come back, I won't make a fuss . . .

Who am I kidding? Since when did I not make a fuss?

'You're already eulogizing your relationship,' Jules warned me the other day. 'You've already forgotten how much you used to argue. You're making him into some sort of saint.'

She's wrong. I know he had his faults. You can't live with someone for nearly twenty years without coming across things that make you want to rip out your hair at the roots with frustration. Simon was inclined to repetition, telling the same stories whenever there was a new audience. I used to think I'd scream if I had to listen one more time. 'Not that one again, darling,' I'd groan, hearing an ominously familiar intro. 'We've all heard it already.' '*They* haven't,' he'd say benignly, indicating whatever new quarry was sitting in front of him. Sometimes I'd look at him as if he was a stranger. *Are you boring?* I'd think, panic-stricken. *Have I ended up, after all, with someone dull?*

I used to grow incensed when he'd retire to bed after a long, leisurely Sunday lunch on our balcony in Dubai, to lie in the semi-darkness listening to Leonard Cohen or Neil Young or Chopin with his eyes open and the air-con humming. 'You're hardly ever here as it is,' I'd rage. 'You've no right to absent yourself like this. Sadie misses you.' But what I really meant was I missed him. I couldn't bear for him to choose to be apart from me. Coming across him lying in the gloom, staring into space, I'd be reminded again of his 'otherness' and, worse, of his mortality.

Normally we never discussed the fifteen-year age gap.

Simon was still fit enough for it not to be an issue, and if I ever made a joke about it, he would go quiet and act wounded. Oh, let's be honest, he was inclined to be vain. The incursions of age were a personal affront. 'Is my hair thinning?' he'd ask anxiously, holding a hand mirror up in the bathroom and contorting his torso in an attempt to see the back of his head. 'Will you still love me when I'm bald?'

I was never one to see the point in worrying about the abstract, so I never allowed myself to think about how the future would be with an ageing Simon.

And now there is to be no future at all.

Thwack! I'm pole-axed all over again by the full force of that realization. When will its impact start to lessen? How long before the fact of his not being in the world any more becomes something I already know, rather than a bomb-shell that hits with renewed force each time I think of it afresh?

Not even forty and here I am a single mother, a Not-Quite-Widow, washed up, abandoned.

I mustn't cry. I mustn't give in to that. Jules tells me I mustn't give negative thoughts space in my mind. She brought round a newspaper cutting about a long-haired kitten who loves squashing itself inside jam-jars, illustrated by a photo in which the kitten gazes out serenely from an empty mayonnaise jar. She stuck the photo to the fridge and said every time thoughts of Simon and what he did, and that woman, come into my head I have to replace them with the image of the kitten in the jar. I try it now. It doesn't work.

Trying to shake off my misery, I power up my laptop, thinking I'll check my emails or read the papers or something, but instead I go straight to Twitter. I know I shouldn't keep doing it. What do they call that? Online stalking? But I can't seem to help myself. Much as I loathe her, I feel linked to that woman in a way my sisters could never understand. I click on @BarnesBookworm's profile. Oh my God – she's actually updated it! I double-check the date just to be sure, but it is today's date. *Loving the new Bill Bryson*, reads the most recent tweet. *Putting the smile back on my face after recent events.*

Recent events! I swear to God that's what it says! Who is this woman my husband was married to, who glosses over death and betrayal and bigamy with two words, *recent events*? Has she no feelings at all? Did he mean nothing to her?

I stare and stare at the screen, waiting for her to update again, to write something else, feeling the bizarrest sense of being connected to her by an invisible steel cord stretching through my computer and into hers, but the page doesn't change.

I ought to be at work. I shouldn't have taken the whole day off, but after seeing Greg Ronaldson this morning, I couldn't face going in. He's one of those men who make you feel like a prize heifer in an agricultural show – weighed up, appraised, evaluated. Is that the kind of man I'll be meeting from now on, now that there is no 'husband' to shield me? All through the meeting, while Greg Ronaldson droned on about mortgages and inheritance tax, I was thinking about how Simon was the last man who'll ever look at me and see the twenty-year-old I once was. From now on men who look at me will see just another woman entering stiffly into middle age, like someone who's boarded the wrong bus but has to make the best of it. How will I bear it?

Curled up on my bed, I'm conscious of the big window through which the backs of the houses in the street behind are clearly visible through the thinning branches. When we bought this flat Simon worried about it being on the ground floor and Sadie and I being on our own so much, but it didn't really bother me. I liked being the tough one for once and laughing at his old-lady fears. Now I feel vulnerable. I hear noises in the night that I didn't notice before.

There's a small statue on the windowsill. I'll focus on that instead of thinking of Simon or Greg Ronaldson or @BarnesBookworm. Carved white limestone, the pleasing curved shapes of a couple embracing. I'll look at that, and I won't think about anything else . . .

Sometimes I see Simon. There, I've said it. Ridiculous, isn't it? But I do see him. I'll walk into the living room and there he'll be, lying on the sofa with his head at one end and his feet up on the arm at the other, or I'll find him in the kitchen, pouring two glasses of wine and turning to smile at me. One time I was on the bus going to work and I looked through the window and saw him perched on a house roof wearing a Hawaian shirt with faded jeans and flip-flops, his favourite get-up on lazy winter weekends back in Dubai. I'm going mad, I think, but I don't tell my sisters. They'd only worry.

Greg Ronaldson told me exactly how big the mortgage is on this place. He even wrote it on the back of an envelope with a thick felt-pen just in case I wasn't taking it in. There were so many noughts, I couldn't reach the end of them. How will I pay that many noughts? But if I don't, I'll lose my flat. But if I lose my flat, Selina

Busfield will lose her home ... Losses and gains, gains and losses.

Lying here, curled up on my own, there is only loss.

13

SELINA

∽

Can those really be my legs?

I find I cannot stop staring at them, stretching out in front of me and resting on the footstool in the den, where I'm sitting on the sofa.

I never wear dresses this short. It's just not like me. But then, I find at the moment *I'm* not even like me any more. Wearing this tunic as a dress over tights, instead of over trousers, would never have occurred to the old Selina. But then, neither would meeting a married man for lunch for the second time in a week have occurred to the old Selina. And it's not only the clothes either. When I popped my head around Josh's door to tell him I was going out this morning, he said, 'You've done something.'

It's hard to tell with Josh whether this was a statement, question or an out-and-out accusation. He's been in such a strange mood recently, ever since the phone call from that woman, warning him away from her precious daughter.

'Have I, darling?'

'You look different. Did you do something to your hair?'

189

It's true, my hair does look different now I no longer go to the salon for my fortnightly visit. I can't bear the idea of the twenty-something stylist giving me the 'men are all the same, aren't they?' speech, forcing us into an unwanted and unnatural sisterhood, or having to stare at my own reflection in the mirror for two and a half hours. *Woo hoo! Look at me, I'm the woman whose husband married someone else.* Instead I've started dyeing the roots at home, with a kit I bought in Boots, and my hair is longer and looser. I've also put on a bit of weight, I think, now I no longer go to the gym. Things are softening and filling out.

Greg obviously liked the dress. He kept trying to talk about money – I really think he might believe that secret account is something to do with me! *Ask her*, I kept telling him. *Ask Lottie about that* – but his heart wasn't in it. When he told me he'd met up with her while we shared a plate of sushi at a place near Victoria, I was shocked at the sudden stab of jealousy I felt. Had he fancied her? It's not inconceivable, Simon clearly did, so why not him? For the first time, it occurred to me that Greg is probably quite a few years younger than me. Probably closer to her age than mine. Insecurity seized me by the throat.

So I was actually relieved when he suggested going somewhere afterwards. Grateful even! So often, these days, I feel I don't exist, now everything I defined myself by has gone. Being desired gives me a purpose and makes me real again. Dear God, how pathetic I'm becoming.

I have a sudden flashback to the two of us giggling like schoolchildren in the shower of that cheap hotel room, as the nasty plastic shower curtain plastered itself to our bodies. I can't remember the last time I was in a shower with a curtain. How bizarre it was – that institutional plastic sticking to wet skin.

The facilities were the last thing on our minds when we stumbled into the first hotel we came across. We just wanted a bed and a door that locked. Is that an awful admission? Afterwards, I was quite thrilled by how seedy it was – nylon curtains over windows that refused to open when Greg tried to let in some fresh air. A saucer with three tea bags. Milk powder in pink sachets. Looking back on it now, of course, it seems indescribably tacky.

It's Simon's fault. All of it. Everything that is going wrong with my life. If he hadn't left me in financial melt-down, so I'm practically out of my mind with worry, I wouldn't be so desperate for distraction. If he hadn't betrayed me for seventeen years with a woman thirteen years younger than me, I wouldn't be so desperate for male attention. If he hadn't had a child with her, there'd never have been that scene with Josh after the phone call from Lottie warning him to keep away from her daughter – in front of Felix, too.

Restless, I go to the kitchen table and turn on my laptop. Logging into Twitter, I pause, my fingers hovering over the keys. Hettie was horrified when she found out I'd started tweeting again. 'You do realize, *she*'ll be reading everything you write, don't you? She and her sisters.' What Hettie didn't realize is that's precisely why I'm tweeting again – to show them, show *her*, how unaffected I am by their grubby little goings-on.

Book Club meeting next Wed as usual, I write. *Brush off those short stories, ladies!*

I smile to myself, imagining their faces when they read that and realize that my life is going along perfectly nicely in spite of them, thank you very much! But after I've clicked the 'Tweet' button, I feel myself sagging inside. I'm deliberately making myself sound brittle, but how do I really feel? I spend so much time worrying about the me I present to other people, I seem to have lost track of the me I really am.

Looking around the kitchen, with its sleek wall of cupboards, I find myself wondering if the woman who spent days with a kitchen designer, poring over diagrams, working out the perfect arrangement for the storing of breakfast cereals and copper-bottomed pans, long-handled mops and tins of 'staples', still exists. I feel I no longer belong here. But if not here, in the kitchen I designed and in which I catered for numerous dinner parties, then where?

I jump to my feet and stride out of the room and into the den, where I start rummaging through the drawer in the antique dresser along the back wall. It belonged to Simon's parents and he insisted on keeping it, but I've never liked it. All that dark wood. So out of place in our modernist home.

I'm looking for the wedding photo I shoved in there last week, or was it the week before? Time seems to have lost all meaning.

There. Propping it up against the dresser shelves, I stare into Simon's green eyes, looking for answers. *Did you love me?* I ask the preposterously young man with the lopsided smile who is looking delightedly at his new bride as if he'd just grown her himself, like a prize marrow. *Were you excited to be getting married? Did you look at me and think, 'Yes, there she is, the woman I want to spend my life with'?*

I was sure about him, of course. From the very beginning. It was the being married that mattered, though, just as much as the being married to *him*. When my book group did *Anna Karenina*, we had a heated debate about marriage. There were a couple of women there – divorced, of course – who were scathing about marriage, calling it a contract and saying it devalues romance, but I always loved that side of things, the idea of a contract between people who agree to love each other for the rest of their lives. Where's the lack of romance in that?

And yet . . . There was that scene, wasn't there, on the vine-shaded loggia in Tuscany? 'I need to talk to you,' he said, putting down his wine glass heavily, and I knew instinctively that I didn't want to hear what he was about to say, that it would threaten the contract we'd made. 'We've had a good marriage,' he said, and I remember hating the way he was talking in the past, as if he'd already moved on somewhere. 'You can't leave me.' My voice clear, sure of itself, halting him in his tracks. 'I'm pregnant.'

No. No point in thinking about that now. The past is the past.

Yet still I gaze at the photo – at Young Selina and Young Simon. It strikes me suddenly – how stupid not to think of it before – that I'll never now see how Simon's features will appear in old age, I'll never get to know the end of his story. Grief floods through me as I think of how my lists and my diaries, already filled in six months or a year ahead, gave me the illusion of being in control of the future. Nothing momentous could happen before next June because we're going to Sue and Michael's silver-wedding party in a lovely country house near Chichester. I really did believe – *oh stupid, stupid woman* – that taking out two-year club memberships and five-year bonds was some kind of shield against the unforeseen. Oh, death happened, I knew that – just not to people with seven-year extended warranties.

I need to do something to take my mind off everything – something useful. I can hear Josh coming downstairs with his best friend Lewis, on their way out somewhere. I'm relieved Lewis is here. Josh's friends haven't been round in a while and it feels like a sign that things are getting back to normal.

'Where do you think he is now, your dad?' I hear Lewis ask, as they descend into the hallway. 'Don't get me wrong, I don't believe in God or anything, but it would be pretty weird if we just stopped existing, d'you get me? I think maybe there's some kind of other dimension where all the people just go to chill.'

'That'd be called Heaven then,' says Josh sarcastically.

'Nah, bro,' says Lewis in that fake patois they all seem to use nowadays. 'It's not to do with religion an' shit. It's spiritual.'

The front door opens and then closes again behind them. Smiling to myself, I open the drawer to return the photo, spotting as I do so the large stack of condolence cards that have been sitting there since the funeral. At the time I was in such a state I didn't even register them, just opened up the envelopes like an automaton, looking at them without reading them. Oh well, no time like the present, I suppose. I fetch my reading glasses and carry the cards back to the sofa.

But oh, the *naffness* of them! A mass of embossed silver writing and waxy-looking flowers and sombre, looping letters spelling out 'sympathy' and 'sorry'. Suddenly I'm reminded of Ryan muttering 'Sorry for your loss' and how I thought he said 'Sorry for your boss', and I let out a little snort.

The cards are surprisingly touching. After all these days and weeks building up a picture of Simon the Monster, it's a shock to read about all the kindnesses he did for people. So many moving anecdotes about the kind of man he was. And yet, did any of them really know him? This man who kept hidden another woman, another child, another life?

There's a card from Chris Griffiths that arrived a few days after the funeral in a pale-blue envelope with a puckered, over-licked seal. It's long and rambling and written in a tiny, cramped hand. I set it aside without reading it.

Ah. Finally a card that's a bit more tasteful than the others. That Monet painting – elegantly arching bridge over a river carpeted with lilies and banked by weeping green trees. Good grief, it's from Caroline Howard! I had no idea Simon had kept in touch with his old university girlfriend. How curious.

A lion amongst men, she has written. *I can't believe he's gone*.

I feel a prickle of unease. I haven't thought about Caroline Howard in decades and now this. Hackneyed sentiment spills across the page like cheap perfume. How strange that she should be writing like that after all this time, with such an emotional message. *I can't believe he's gone*. As if she saw him yesterday rather than thirty years ago.

I must tell Hettie. I'm not sure whether she and Ian will even remember Caroline from university days but I need a sounding board, someone to bounce the strange message off, to see if I'm over-reacting. It's about time I spoke to Hettie anyway. I've been putting it off because I don't want to have to tell her about Greg. Not that I'm ashamed. Not really. But he's my secret indulgence, like a long bubble bath or a Cadbury's Creme Egg. Hettie wouldn't approve. No matter what Simon has done, at heart she's still loyal to the idea of him, or rather to the idea of him and me and her and Ian. I can imagine her face when she finds out that Greg's married. Infidelity is anathema to Hettie. Of course, I believed my own marriage was sacrosanct, but Hettie believes *all* marriages to be so. She regards other people's affairs, even people she doesn't know, as a personal threat. Plus, I'm not altogether sure Greg would stand up to public scrutiny. I'm afraid that whatever it is that makes him attractive to me will disappear if Hettie or anyone else finds out and I have to see him through their eyes, like an ancient relic crumbling on exposure to light.

But I need to talk to someone about Caroline Howard, so I pick up my phone.

'Yes, I remember her.' Am I imagining the hesitation in Hettie's voice?

'But don't you think it's odd?' I persist. 'That she'd write to me like that? In those words?'

Hettie is silent.

'Hets?'

'I think,' says Hettie eventually, 'you should probably talk to Ian about it. We'd better come over.'

What? Why on earth would I talk to Ian about Caroline Howard? But Hettie has already cleared the line.

*

Twenty agonizingly long minutes later and they're on my doorstep. Ian is loitering behind Hettie and looking sheepish.

'He didn't want to come, did you, darling?' says Hettie.

Ian shakes his head, looking miserable. For some reason his hangdog expression infuriates me. After everything I've been through these past few weeks – the death, the funeral, the revelations about Simon's double life, the money worries – what right does Ian Palmer have to look as if he's carrying the world on his shoulders?

'If you've something to say to me, Ian,' I say, leading the way into the den, 'I'd rather you just get on with it.'

'I'll pour us a drink, shall I?' says Hettie. She darts off into the kitchen carrying the bottle of white wine she brought with her.

Ian stares after her disappearing back as if he might cry.

'I don't quite know how to say this,' he says, gazing at a spot on the floor by his right foot. His discomfort is tangible, perching on the sofa between us like an uninvited guest.

'Oh, just spit it out, for Christ's sake!'

There's a knot of anxiety sitting heavily in my stomach like undigested steak.

'Well, the thing is, Selina, that years and years ago, when you two hadn't been married very long, Simon told me – and I want you to know I've wished many times since then that he hadn't – that he and Caroline had been, well, had been . . .'

I stare at the red flush sweeping up from his neck over his face. The knot of anxiety hardens inside me as realization sets in.

'Fucking?' I suggest.

197

Ian looks horrified. His hand shoots to his upper lip to urgently stroke a non-existent moustache. Good. Let him suffer. He's telling me this now? Twenty-eight years too late? What does he expect from me, a fucking medal?

'I told him I thought it was ... reprehensible.' *Reprehensible!* What kind of person uses the word reprehensible? How stuffy my friends are, I now realize. 'You and Simon had small children by then, if I remember. He said he felt awful about it and was ending it. He begged me not to tell you or Hettie.'

'He knew I'd have killed him if I'd known,' says Hettie, coming in and plonking three large glasses of wine down on the coffee table. The wine splashes on to the smooth wood.

'Oh my God, Sel! Coasters, I forgot!'

Coasters? Is that really what she thinks of me? Her husband has just told me that Simon was already unfaithful, even at the very beginning, and she thinks I care about coasters?

'Bugger the coasters,' I say.

'I told Hettie about Caroline after the funeral when all that other stuff came out,' Ian says. 'I hated keeping it from her all these years. You know we always tell each other everything.'

Ugh! That look that passes between them. Complicit. As if nothing can threaten them. I shouldn't mind it, but I do. I mind violently. For a second I want to take a baseball bat to the cosy shield they've built up around themselves. 'Not so cosy now!' I'd yell as I smashed it to pieces around them.

'But I'd promised Simon,' Ian continues. 'And it did seem to be all over – a momentary blip.'

The knot in my stomach has become a hard ball, pressing on my lungs, making it difficult to breathe. Wine. That's what I need. I take a long, thirsty gulp. That's better. Can it really be just a few hours since Greg and I shared a bottle of sake over lunch at that Japanese restaurant? Already it seems a different era, and me an entirely different woman. Is there to be no end to the number of Selinas there turn out to be, hiding one inside the other like a never-ending Russian doll?

'Are you OK, Sel?'

Hettie's hand is on my arm and her brown eyes are soft with sympathy, like muscovado sugar.

I shake my head. 'I know I shouldn't be shocked, not after everything else. It's just so . . . disappointing!'

I'm not explaining myself well. The fact is, I've been clinging on to that first near-decade of marriage, the pre-Lottie years, as the one pure thing remaining to me. In my mind I've pegged out those ten unsullied years proudly on the line like clean white sheets. And now in one moment they've been ripped off and stamped into the mud.

Is this never to end, this steady dismantling of my life? Am I to be left with nothing?

'It was all a sham then,' I say. 'All of it.'

'No, no!'

I can't remember the last time I saw Ian so het up.

'Simon adored you. He worshipped you. He was always going on about how lucky he was. You mustn't ever believe his feelings for you weren't completely genuine.'

'So why Caroline Howard? Why the other one – Lottie?'

Ian shrugs. Disquiet radiates from him. 'What can I say? He was Simon. He had that massive appetite for life. I just don't think he knew how to stop himself.'

'Or perhaps he didn't know why he *should* stop himself,' Hettie offers. 'Once he'd got away with it once, he must have thought he could just go on getting away with it.'

Now Hettie and Ian have left. I'm still on the sofa, drinking wine by myself. This new betrayal of Simon's burns like acid in my gut. Was it right, what Hettie said? Is that how it works? Are our moral choices predicated on no deeper level than what can and can't be got away with?

It's true what Ian said about Simon, that he could never say no to himself. His own mother told me much the same thing a few years before she died. 'As a child he always wanted more,' she said of her only son. 'More, more, more. He was never satisfied with what he had. When it comes to the things he loves, Simon can be very greedy.'

A warning, perhaps? Of course, stupid me didn't want to be warned. I was so sure I'd be enough for him, so sure I knew him better than his mother, who still insisted a property developer was just a jumped-up builder and sent him torn-out magazine articles on people who'd retrained in later life as lawyers and architects. Ha!

What do I remember about Caroline Howard? She was one of those slightly intimidating redheads – tall and pale, with long hair that she gathered in a loose plait to the side. She wore sunglasses a lot, I seem to recall. Large ones that hid most of her finely boned face. The only thing I've heard about her since university is that she married someone incredibly rich. A Lord something or other, as far as I remember. He was a lot older than her, by all accounts. Some people at the time said she only married him on the rebound from Simon. It made me feel rather powerful, hearing that, I remember, knowing that I had what other people wanted.

How dare she come back into my life, into my marriage? Simon was done with her. He'd chosen me. Why couldn't she just leave it at that? If he'd never strayed that first time, with her, and opened up that chink in the armour of our marriage, maybe that other one would never have found a way in. At least Lottie hadn't known he was married. Caroline Howard knew exactly what the situation was, that he was now another woman's husband.

Fury mixes with the wine inside my system, propelling me off the sofa and into Simon's study off the main hall. I hardly ever come in here any more. It's too redolent of him. I always expect to find him leaning back in his leather chair, his arms behind his head, long legs stretched out in front of him, listening to music full blast and gazing at nothing.

Flinging myself into the chair behind his large oak desk, I yank open the top drawer and extract the mobile phone I tossed in there after the police handed back that plastic ziplock of Simon's things.

No power. Obviously. The briefest of hunts through his desk locates the charger. That's better. Scrolling through his contacts list is like bringing Simon back to life, and for a moment I'm hit by a powerful wave of loss. So typical of him – always so awful with names, he developed his own system of logging contacts – a first name, accompanied by an identifying description. Anthony (bald), Anthony (banker), Anthony (wanker). Ben (vet), Beverley (ghastly). Reaching the Cs, I find there are four Carolines. Caroline (golfer husband), Caroline (PR), Caroline (travel agent, helpful). The fourth is plain 'Caroline'. Nothing else.

The pain is sudden and crippling.

Naturally she wouldn't need any description. What would he have put? Caroline (whore)? Caroline (husband-stealing bitch)?

Anger bursts inside me like a blood vessel.

Dashing into the hallway, I snatch my own phone from my bag and come back into the study to punch in the number. *She won't get away with it. What was she playing at?*

Listening to the ring tone, I realize that it's quite late. Eleven thirty-five. What do I care? Let her be disturbed. Let her know what it's like not to be able to sleep. Let her be put on the spot in front of her husband or children or whoever else is there, so that her famous alabaster skin turns pink and mottled with embarrassment.

Four rings. Five.

'Hello?'

A deep, cool voice that cuts through the years, as if the last three decades never happened. Only now do I remember how impossibly self-contained Caroline Howard was – always that Pinteresque pause before she spoke. I must be calm. But, oh Lord, I think I might explode with the effort of keeping myself under control.

'This is Selina Busfield here.'

That's right. Composed. Business-like. Not the voice of someone given to histrionics.

There's a pause (of course). Then, 'Ah.'

That's all she has to say? After all this time? After everything she's stolen from me? Just *ah*?

'I need to speak to you about a private matter.' Why do I sound like an officious secretary suddenly? 'So if your husband is present, I suggest you take the phone elsewhere.'

'Don't worry.' The voice on the other end sounds maddeningly amused. 'My husband and I have been separated for five years now. And even if we weren't, he's deaf as a post.'

'I'm afraid this isn't a joking matter. You see, I've just found out you had an affair with my husband.'

What am I hoping for? That she'll exclaim, or gasp, or beg forgiveness?

'I see,' says the former Caroline Howard – now, I remember suddenly, Lady Caroline Yardley.

I close my eyes. It's too much.

'Is that it? Is that all you have to say? *I see*. What kind of a person are you?'

Again a maddening pause.

'Selina, dear, I know this must be a dreadful time for you.' Her voice is measured, but kind. It's the kindness that is the worst thing. 'But you must know this all started a very long time ago.'

'Well, forgive me if my rage is fucking inappropriate, but I've only just found out!'

It feels good, letting rip. Saying what I mean after the effort of trying to stay in control. I continue: 'And when our children were so little as well. Shame on you! Thank God Simon had the sense to call it off!'

What's that noise on the other end? A sigh?

'OK, I think it's time to be very straight here.' Now her tone is less practised. Less patronizing. 'How much honesty do you want, Selina?'

How much honesty? What kind of a question is that?

'Obviously I want the truth,' I say stiffly, doubting it instantly. Do I? Do I really want the truth?

'Very well then,' says Lady Yardley, née Caroline Howard.

'The truth is, Selina, that Simon and I . . . that is to say, your husband and I . . . Goodness, I sound like the Queen suddenly, don't I?'

A peal of laughter follows. I can't believe that woman is actually laughing. Isn't she supposed to be apologizing at this point, or justifying herself?

'Sorry,' she continues. 'Well, the truth is – and I'm trusting this won't come as a complete shock to you, given what you now know about Simon's character. Well, Simon and I, we never really stopped being lovers.'

The leather chair is squishy underneath me, but the walls of Simon's study are coming towards me, and then going back the other way, moving forwards and backwards, forwards and backwards. I feel sick in the bottom of my stomach.

'Never stopped,' I repeat dully.

'Well, when I say never, what I mean is, we stopped, of course. We had periods of years, sometimes several years, when we didn't see each other, when life got in the way. I had my children, of course, and he had his. And his, well, his *other* family.'

The blow catches me unawares. She knew. She knew about that, too. What was I, just another part of the 'life' that kept getting so inconveniently in the way? The last person to be told about anything?

'So you slept together all through my marriage?'

Incredibly, my voice is steady, polite even. I could be requesting formal clarification of something – a driving licence number, or the time of a delayed flight.

'Off and on,' says Lady Yardley. 'Well, obviously more

off than on. And once he was with Lottie it grew more difficult. She was quite demanding, quite high-maintenance.' (*As if I should be flattered by the inference that I, by contrast, am the very model of laissez-faire.*) 'Although we did manage it on occasion. More for old times' sake by the end than anything else. You know, I hope you don't think this is too dreadful of me, but it's such a relief to be talking to you about this, Selina. I miss him so much, you see, and you're the only one who has any idea what I'm going through.'

Oh! The pain of it! The nerve of the woman!

'Don't you dare,' I say.

'Now Selina dear—'

'Don't you dare compare what you're going through to what I'm going through. How could you have any clue what it's like to be me? You weren't married to him. You didn't have his children. You have no clue. Do you understand, *Lady*?'

When I press 'End call' my heart feels as if it will thump a hole right through my chest and my breathing is shallow and uneven.

I have no idea how long I stay seated at the desk in Simon's study staring at my phone. At some point I retrieve the bottle of wine from the kitchen and bring it back to the study, where I sit, gazing around me as if seeing the room for the first time and trying to work out what kind of a person might inhabit it. There's a photo pinned to the noticeboard on one wall of Simon presenting a large cheque to the fundraising director of some charity in Dubai. 'You sanctimonious prick!' I tell it. 'You fuck! You cunt!' I've never said the 'c' word out loud before. For a second I'm dizzy with the power of it.

I feel as if I will burst if I don't tell someone what just happened, but who? Not Greg, probably snuggled up with his oh-so-understanding wife. Not one of the children, who've been through enough. Then who? Who could possibly understand? There is only one person.

LOTTIE

I'm having a dream where Simon is calling to me from inside the television. 'How do I get to you?' I keep asking, jabbing uselessly at the remote. 'How do I get in?'

For a moment I think the ringing tone is part of my dream. 'I'm coming,' I mumble, reaching for my phone. 'Just tell me how.'

Disoriented now, I can't read the name that flashes up on my screen.

'Hello?' My voice is croaky with sleep.

'It's me. Selina.'

Oh. I'm wide awake now. What does she want? Why is she ringing me in the middle of the night?

'I've just had a rather interesting conversation,' she says. Her voice sounds odd.

'So interesting you have to wake me up at one thirty to tell me about it? What's the matter with you? You sound drunk.'

'One thirty?' She sounds surprised, but recovers quickly. 'I talked to an ex-girlfriend of Simon's tonight, someone he went out with before I came along. Caroline Howard, as she was then. *Lady* Yardley now.'

Pah! I make a snorting noise. Trust Simon to have

an aristocrat tucked away somewhere in his past.

Selina seems to appreciate my response. 'It *is* quite preposterous, isn't it? That stupid title? Anyway, the interesting thing is that it transpires he never quite stopped sleeping with her.'

Her voice is brisk and conversational, but I'm confused.

'So he slept with her after he got together with you, you mean?'

'Yes. After he got together with me. Oh, and after he got together with you, too. In fact, he's been sleeping with her off and on for the last thirty years.'

No. Impossible.

And yet not impossible.

From nowhere comes a moan – a horrible noise that sounds like something breaking. Every single part of me wants to tell her that she is wrong, that I know she's making this up as a new way to hurt me. But equally, every single part of me knows it immediately to be the truth. Simon lied to me about so many things. Only Selina Busfield, it seems, tells me what is real.

I close my eyes and gently bang my head against the bedpost, trying to shake loose the image of Simon that has just popped into my mind. He's lying right here, in our bed, propped up on one elbow and looking down into my face.

'You're the only person I can be honest with,' he says, running a fingertip down the bridge of my nose. 'You allow me to be me.'

But who was he, this 'me' I let him be, who slept with other women and then came home and held me clasped to his chest like a prize?

'Oh, oh, oh,' I say, in time to the banging of my head. 'Oh, oh, oh.'

SELINA

I listen to the muffled noises on the end of the line and know exactly what she is doing. It's as if I'm there, watching her head thumping against the wall or the door or wherever she is.

Funny, it should make me feel better, this 'oh, oh, oh-ing'. I ought to feel triumphant. But I don't.

I stay for a few moments, just listening. Then I clear my throat.

'I'm . . . well . . . sorry,' I say.

And, shockingly, I really am.

14

LOTTIE

A snapshot of our bedroom, *my* bedroom:

A bed scattered with photographs and love notes (Simon's looping writing: *I ache for you*), pill packets, tissues, a shirt of Simon's, a phone that doesn't ring, at least not with his voice, a sketchpad, pencils, some drawings of nothing. Three empty mugs, a tear-soaked pillow. The curtain drawn, the air thick with loss. A mirror that reflects a woman who is quite alone.

My husband is dead. But then, he wasn't my husband. Our whole life together was a lie. He's left me broke. No money, no trust.

I believed in love. But the love I believed in wasn't the kind that would carry on sleeping with its university girlfriend, or fail to divorce its first wife. Its only wife.

A Not-Wife, a Not-Widow, in a world where only Widowhood, it seems, is sacred. A nothing.

It's not bearable.

But Sadie? No, I can't think about Sadie, safely two hundred miles away in Leeds, visiting Emma's eldest, Ella, newly installed at university.

I'm so tired of this pain. So tired. I just want it to stop.

I'll pop the pills out of the foil and hold them in my hand. And now I'll open another packet and pop some more. A heap of dazzling whiteness cupped in my palm. There's no harm in holding them. No harm at all.

Just looking and holding.

If I could just get things back to how they were, I'd do everything different.

If I could just go to sleep and wake up as someone else.

If I could just take out my heart, to stop it from hurting. Please make it stop.

15

SELINA

Seven to the left, three to the right. Click, click, click. *What the hell?*

I know it's right. It's got to be right.

'I know the fucking combination!' I'm aware that I'm yelling down the phone to Hettie, but don't seem to be able to stop myself. It doesn't help matters that I'm on my hands and knees in front of the safe, which is bolted to the floor inside a cupboard at the back of Simon's study, and I'm almost sobbing. 'So why won't it bloody well open?'

'Are you sure it's three to the *right*?'

Oh dear, Hettie sounds fed up. We've been on the phone ages and ages and ages while I've tried all the combinations I can think of, and even through my drunken haze I can tell that her patience is growing strained.

'Of course it's the bloody right.' *Mustn't snap at her.* 'Although now you're making me have doubts. Maybe it was 7745, not 7735—'

'For God's sake!' Hettie erupts. 'Why did you have to lock the thing in there in the first place?'

'It was right after the funeral,' I say, injured. 'I wasn't thinking straight.'

'Well, you're still not thinking straight. If you knew the combination then, you must know it now. You just have to stop trying so hard to remember and it'll pop back into your head.'

She's right. I must empty my mind. That's it. Nice and empty.

Blank.

Oh, but it's not *totally* my fault. When I brought Simon's ashes back from the undertaker's a few days after the funeral, I was still all over the place. So it seemed entirely sensible to pop them in the safe until I decided what to do with them. *Pop* – funny word. But now, after nearly a bottle of Pinot Grigio, I've come up with an excellent plan.

'I'm going to mix the ashes with water,' I explain to Hettie now. 'To form a paste that I'll use to daub over his study walls.'

'You what?'

Hettie doesn't sound impressed, so I carefully put her down on the carpet and rattle the dial a few more times in frustration. Nothing. Dejected, I lie down prostrate on the floor, my face pressed into the deep pile rug.

'All for nothing,' I wail. 'Everything's been all for nothing.'

'What's all for nothing?' demands Hettie from the discarded phone.

I think Hettie has had enough. She wants the old Selina back. Ha! We *all* want the old Selina back! All these years we've drifted along so effortlessly on the same wavelength, and now there's this great big chasm between us. Gulf. Ocean. It's like I've been whisked away overnight to a desert island, and all Hettie can do is jump up and down on the shore miming great pantomimes of regret. Hettie misses the me I used to be.

I'm still lying on the rug when Josh comes in from a night out with his friends. How much later? Five minutes? An hour? Two? I sense him hovering in the doorway.

'Tired?' he asks eventually.

'Drunk,' I reply.

'Me too.'

Normally Josh can't get away fast enough when he comes in. He doesn't want me sniffing his breath, asking probing questions. Tonight, though, he sits down on the floor next to me.

'I can't open the safe,' I say from the rug. 'And your dad's in there.'

Josh stares at the small square metal box and I know he's imagining his six-foot-one father squashed into it, like a sleeping bag stuffed into a little pouch.

'Shall I try?' he offers. 'What's the combination?'

And suddenly, just like that, it comes to me. Simon changed the combination just a few months ago, complaining that the original was too hard to remember.

'Our wedding anniversary,' I say. '1504.'

Click, click, click, click.

Josh opens the safe without a problem and pulls out the cardboard box which contains the plastic urn which in turn contains his father. Cardboard and plastic. Who'd have thought a man with such a love of nice things would end up in cardboard and plastic? Maybe I should have done better, but at the time I had more on my mind than leafing through the Urns Catalogue.

'I had to put a seatbelt around it,' I tell Josh now, propped up on my elbow.

'What?'

'Around it.' I gesture towards the box with my free arm. 'Around him.'

'What you on about?'

Oh really. Sometimes it's as if Josh is being deliberately slow.

'When I went to pick up the box from the undertaker, I put it in the passenger seat of the Fiat, but when I turned the very first corner, it slid off. Ploppppppp!'

I sit up to mime an impression of a heavy cardboard box sliding off a car seat.

'So then I had to put the seatbelt around it, and I had the strangest idea that he was sitting next to me. Your father, I mean. Sitting there all belted up in the Fiat – you know how he hated to go anywhere in that Fiat. Pompous ass,' I add as an afterthought.

'That's not very nice,' says Josh sadly. 'Although he was a very pompous ass.'

How funny is that? We both laugh like drains.

'A *fucking* pompous ass,' I say, which sets us both off again.

'What's going on?'

Oh Lord. Flora. I completely forgot she was here.

In fact, she's been here for two days now. I've tried to talk to her about what's going on, why she's not at her own flat in Queen's Park, but she is tight-lipped. They get so defensive, children. She did tell me, though, that she and Ryan haven't been getting along. Apparently Ryan thinks our family is 'grubby'. *Grubby!* The nerve of him! 'He said, "No offence, but your family's a bit grubby, babes."' Flora's impression of her boyfriend – sorry, *fiancé* – was actually very good, although when I laughed at

214

it she clammed right up, frightened of seeming disloyal.

And now she's standing in the doorway of Simon's study in a pink towelling dressing gown. Not looking very happy. Oops!

'I was fast asleep and you woke me up. Why are you lying on the floor, Mum?' She comes into the room to peer at me closer. 'You're drunk, aren't you?'

I pull myself upright again. 'Yes,' I say. 'I believe I am.'

Flora looks hurt, as if Josh and I have been having a wild party down here and haven't invited her.

'Well, you might try to be a bit more considerate. I'm only here because I'm having such a difficult time with Ryan, and what with Dad and everything . . .'

Now Flora is staring at the cardboard box on the floor in front of Josh. Such wide blue eyes she has, my daughter.

'Is that . . . ?' She tries again: 'Don't tell me that's . . .'

'Yeah, Dad,' says Josh.

Abruptly, he crawls behind the box, so he's half hidden, and sticks his hands around the sides.

'Hello, Sausage,' he says. *Oh Lord – he's imitating Simon!* 'Is it wine o'clock? Shall we crack open a bottle?'

It's the funniest thing I've ever, ever heard.

'That's brilliant,' I shriek. 'Make him say something else.'

Flora lunges forward, almost tripping on her outsized fluffy slippers.

'Stop being horrible!' she yells, swooping on the box of ashes. 'That's Daddy in there.'

'Oh my Daddy, my Daddy!' says Josh/Simon in a take-off of Flora's favourite scene from *The Railway Children*.

Flora picks up the box and cradles it awkwardly in her

arms. It's clearly heavier than she thought because she staggers a bit.

'I don't know how you could be so heartless,' she says. 'He may have done some not very nice things, but he is . . . you know . . . *dead*!'

A moment of silence. Josh and I exchange looks. Then the laughter. Gales of laughter.

Flora isn't amused.

'I'm phoning Fee,' she says, setting the box down on Simon's desk with a loud thud and picking up the desk phone. 'He'd hate to see how totally *disrespectful* you're being.'

She looks so young standing there in that silly dressing gown and those silly slippers, with the phone tucked under her chin and a patch of her hair tangled at the back where she's obviously been sleeping on it. I feel a rush of love. I wish . . . I wish . . .

'Petra?' says Flora into the phone. Why does she sound so doubtful?

'Petra? Is that you?'

She stays frozen, listening, for a few moments more, before carefully replacing the receiver.

'How weird,' she says. 'It sounded like Petra was . . . *crying*!'

Flora's not cross any more. The phone call has made her anger fizzle out. *Fizzle is a great word. I can't think why I don't use it more.*

'I know what we need now,' says Josh, jumping up.

Clang, crash. The noise of Josh in the kitchen.

Ah, there he is. He has reappeared in the doorway clutching a bottle of Jack Daniel's and two glass tumblers.

'It was all I could find,' he says.

'You're not going to let him drink that, are you?' Flora shrieks. 'He's only a baby!'

I look at my son. So sad and weary all of a sudden. Not a baby at all. A hundred years old like one of those children they're always featuring in the *Daily Mail* with the syndrome that makes them prematurely aged.

'Got any better ideas?' he asks Flora.

'Yes.' Flora's cheeks are pink like flowers. 'Give it here,' she says, reaching for the bottle. 'I'll drink it myself.'

Boom, boom, boom. What the hell is that? The sudden loud bass sounds make us all jump.

Josh fumbles in his pocket. 'Phone,' he explains to us, before pressing to accept the call. 'Wassup?'

He listens, and suddenly he straightens and reddens, half turning his body away from me and Flora. 'What? . . . You're kidding me.'

I smile conspiratorially at Flora. What teenage angst is this? A two-week relationship on the rocks? A party busted? Someone's lump of weed confiscated?

Josh snaps shut his phone and turns to me and – *oh, my poor boy* – his face is once again the face of the child he is, was – just yesterday.

'That was Sadie,' he says. He's awkward now, his hazel eyes flicking between Flora and me. 'Her mum just tried to kill herself.'

217

16

LOTTIE

So loud! The sound of the television in the corner of the ward is up so high, it hurts my ears. There's a group of women sitting on high stools around some sort of a table and they're practically shouting. Why are they so loud? Every now and then one of them says something the others seem to find hysterically funny and there's whooping and clapping from the audience. Every time I sense a joke coming on, I tense. The women look very orange, although that might just be the set.

I'm so, so tired. I keep dozing off but the noise of the television jerks me awake. So sore, my throat. Swallowing hurts. I gaze at the plastic beaker of water on the bedside table and imagine putting my hand out to pick it up. Impossible. Simply impossible.

My mind is pleasantly empty. Maybe they pumped out my thoughts along with the contents of my stomach. That'd be nice. If it wasn't for the noise, and the burning in the back of my throat, I think I'd be perfectly content.

Propped up on my pillows, I look around at my fellow patients. An ancient woman in the bed opposite, mouth gaping wide like the opening of a paper bag. The hunched

218

shape of a back in the corner bed, shoulders silently heaving under the bedclothes.

Sleepy now. That's better. It's so wonderful not to have that pain inside me any more. Everything's so light and easy. I'd be quite happy, if only Sadie was here . . .

Sadie.

My eyes snap open.

All the time I've been lying here luxuriating in the absence of thought, I've been aware of a shadow at the back of my mind, a dark blur in the corner of my eye. And now I know what it is. Sadie.

Oh my God, oh my God, oh my God.

My poor daughter.

What have I done?

Oh, but surely she'll understand. About loss and long-ing and how it wasn't to do with not loving her enough, but just about loving him too much.

My daughter's lovely face flashes into my mind, shuttered up like a shop-front.

No, she won't understand.

Hahahahaha! One of the orange women has made a joke at the expense of the male guest star and the others are leaning off their stools with laughter. The guest perches stiffly in the middle of the women like Jesus at the Last Supper.

Mustn't drift off. Must think about what I've done. As penance, for Sadie. What do I remember?

Sitting on the bed, thinking how beautiful the pile of pills looked in my hand. A handful of oblivion. A handful of not-hurting. But it wasn't like what they say Simon did. *They're wrong. He wouldn't.* There's a difference, isn't there, between deciding to leave the people you love, and just feeling that it's impossible to stay? I could have borne Simon's death, just about, but it's his *life* that has proved so impossible to bear. The secrets he kept. The mess he made. When you build a life around a person and that person turns out not to exist – what are you left with? A hollow space at your centre. A hole where you ought to be.

I didn't mean to do it though. And when I'd done it, I didn't mean for Sadie to find me. I was going to text Jules to warn her. How did I forget to do that?

Blurry memories come back to me. Vomit pooling on the sheepskin rug next to my bed. Sadie's frightened face. Then Sadie on the phone to the ambulance, remembering to tell them about the road being repaired at the top. Reading the names off the empty pill packets in her clear, young voice.

Oh, I have failed my child.

On the television screen, the male guest is holding up a book he seems to have written. An autobiography. He looks about twelve. What on earth could his life story possibly consist of? The way I see it, you're born, you live and then you die. That would make a short book, wouldn't it? One of the women on the stools looks like a man in drag. I'm tired. I'm drowning in tired. The pillow makes a crackling, plasticky noise when I sink my head back.

I'm awake again now, and the news is on. A picture flashes on the screen of a street crowded with people and police. 'STUDENT PROTESTS BRING MAJOR DISRUPTION' reads the banner headline running in a loop along the bottom of the screen. The newsreader keeps talking about a kettle. Except kettle is a verb. How peculiar. I remember the row when I took Sadie on the anti-Iraq-war protest all those years ago while we were over on a visit. Simon was livid when he saw the photos of her with the CND symbol Jules drew on her face. 'Let her make up her own bloody mind,' he said. I never told him how we hung back at Trafalgar Square and nipped into the National Gallery to use the loo and ended up spending the afternoon there, having tea in the café while the march went on without us. So many things I'll never tell him now.

'Here's your mum. I told you she'd be looking better, didn't I?'

Jules has appeared beside the bed, her red hair and emerald-green coat so out of place in the institutional grey of the ward, like an exotic parrot that has flown in by mistake off the grimy London street. Behind her, head lowered, is Sadie.

I try to sit up. 'Sorry, Sadie.' Is that really my voice? That raspy sound? 'I wasn't thinking straight.'

Sadie shrugs. 'That makes a change then,' she says.

Jules pulls up a chair next to the bed. Her hair is the colour of the bruise on the back of my left hand where the intravenous drip went in. 'Fuck, babes,' she says, squeezing my hand so tightly I feel my fingers will splinter like dry twigs. How brittle I am at the moment. Simon's death has drained the sap right out of me. I look at the television so I can't see the tears in her eyes, her mascara already smudged around her lashes.

'You're gonna be fine,' she tells me. 'You just need time to heal.'

Oh my God, that's all I need. The spiritual big guns.

'I'm coming to stay again,' she says. 'You mustn't be alone after this.'

I picture our little flat with Jules installed on the sofa-bed in the living room, watching everything I do and reporting back to Emma.

'Thanks,' I croak. 'But I think Sadie and I need a bit of time to ourselves.'

Jules looks doubtful, but doesn't say anything.

Behind her, Sadie is still standing up, staring fixedly at the television. Not wanting to look at me.

'Sadie?' I pat the bed next to me, but she doesn't move. 'Please try to understand just a little bit. I was missing your dad so much. It sent me a bit crazy, that's all. I kept imagining I heard him and saw him. I didn't mean to abandon you. It was a moment of weakness.'

Sadie keeps her eyes glued to the screen. 'Why change the habit of a lifetime?' she scoffs.

Jules turns and grabs Sadie's hand. She has that evangelical look in her eyes that makes me dread whatever she is about to say.

'Sades, hun, your father is still alive.' OK, now she has really lost it. 'He lives on inside of you, babes. Love lives on inside of you.'

'Like a tapeworm?' my daughter says.

Sadie and Jules have come to take me home, but first we must wait for the duty psychiatrist. I need assessing, apparently.

'It's like waiting for the fucking Second Coming,' says Jules as the hours tick by on the white plastic ward clock (*so terribly LOUD, that ticking*) and the newscaster on the television disappears and is replaced by a programme where very fat people are made to stand in their under-wear while an average day's food contents are poured into a clear plastic tube in front of them. So humiliating I can hardly watch.

'I'm thinking about going raw,' says Jules, staring at the screen in disgust. 'White bread is the work of the devil.'

Sadie makes a pah-ing sound. 'Death by white bread,' she says. 'It's amazing any of us are still alive.'

If I concentrate on the television screen, I can zone out what Sadie and Jules are saying. The fat woman is now fully dressed and staring at a small salad that has been placed in front of her as if she's never seen one before. 'That's dinner? You can't be serious!' she exclaims to no one in particular.

I try to imagine a life where a salad can evoke such strong feelings. *You should try living my life*, I want to say to the fat woman. *Then you'd have more to get upset about than a salad*. Thinking about my life makes me start to cry.

'Lottie, hun,' Jules is so close she's practically sitting on me, 'that's right, let it all out. I've got broad shoulders. I can take it.'

But that's just it. Jules can't take it. Neither can Emma. They can only try to help me take it.

'It's the salad,' I say, sniffing. 'It's . . . so . . . sad.'

Jules looks slightly alarmed, but carries on squeezing my hand. 'Of course it is, hun,' she says. 'Just terribly sad.'

Finally the psychiatrist arrives. ('We said it was like waiting for the fucking Second Coming,' Jules repeats. He doesn't smile.) The other two are asked to wait outside, as he pulls the plastic cubicle curtain around my bed. I stare at the pink flowers on the curtain, transfixed.

'Are you still having thoughts about hurting yourself?' the psychiatrist wants to know.

I shake my head slowly. It's true. I have hardly any thoughts at all! A big improvement on how things were before, when my thoughts were all jammed together in my head like those students on the news. What was that called again? Kettling. My thoughts were kettled.

'On a scale of one to four, with what frequency would you say you entertain thoughts of suicide, with one being not at all and four being all the time?'

'One,' I say dutifully.

The duty psychiatrist has a beard that looks fake, like he didn't grow it himself, but he seems satisfied with my answer. I'm pleased with myself for getting it right. I tell him that my husband has just died and grief got the better of me. He nods, as if he knows all about grief.

'OK, Mrs Busfield,' he says. 'You're free to go. Just don't do anything silly, hmmm?'

Silly. I mustn't do anything silly. Already I'm feeling a pang of regret about leaving the hospital. I like it here, away from reminders of Simon and echoes of his footsteps outside, with nothing to think about except what's on TV next. I like the routine of it – the tea trolley, the four-hourly checks, the lovely, lovely super-strength painkillers that make you feel so floaty. I even like the smell – industrial-strength bleach with just a faint fleshy under-tone (*unspeakable bodily fluids*). I'm almost sorry to be going home.

The psychiatrist gets up to leave, but as he pulls the curtain back, a nurse appears.

'Can I have a word?' she asks.

Just the one word? I wonder, as they whisper outside. Not much you can say with one word.

I hear the psychiatrist say 'I see,' then he reappears, clutching a computer print-out.

Strange – he's pulling the chair back up to the bed. Did I get them wrong, after all, those questions? He's rubbing his bloodshot eyes. He looks tired. I must help him. I must do better. I'll retake the questionnaire and get it right this time.

'Mrs Busfield, we carried out some blood tests when you first came in, to see what you'd taken.'

I nod, trying to appear alert.

'I'm not sure if this will come as a surprise to you . . . I hope it's not too much of a shock . . . Maybe you knew already?'

He is doing a strange thing, where he has interlocked both his hands under his chin and is rocking gently back and forth.

What on earth is he talking about? I have no clue, but I smile anyway, I hope in an encouraging way. He sighs. A big, drawn-out sigh. Then he continues:

'Mrs Busfield, you're pregnant.'

17

SELINA

∽

Bloody Christmas.

How did I not notice it before?

I must have been deliberately blocking it out because as I walk down Oxford Street to meet Greg, Christmas is all I can see. Christmas trees in shop windows, Christmas lights strung across the traffic, Father Christmas hats on sale at all the kiosks. There's the remnants of old, dirty snow piled in dark corners after last week's deluge, but in the shop displays the fake snow is startlingly white and glistens like crystals. To think I used to love Christmas. Now I loathe it. Vile, hypocritical Christmas. Simon playing Mr Family Man then slipping out to call his mistress.

Normally I'd be in full organizational flow by now, finalizing menus for charity Christmas functions, making appointments for facials and haircuts, working out logistics for getting from one pre-Christmas drinks party to the next.

This year I'm on my way to meet my lover.

Shouldn't I feel happier about it, more excited? I certainly shouldn't feel guilty. Not after everything I've been through. Anyway, I won't sleep with him. I've decided that much. I'm allowed this one lunch, but I absolutely won't, most definitely, sleep with him.

'The sexiest widow in the world,' says Greg, getting to his feet. His eyes travel over me like one of those hand-held airport friskers and I have a sudden reassuring sense of myself.

Ah, so that's who I am then. A sexy widow. Not an ageing woman whose husband betrayed her for years, but an attractive, sexy widow. It's a start.

At the table, Greg leans across to take my hand. He's not looking so good. The skin under his eyes is the colour of raw liver. I fight a small wave of distaste. Everyone has off days, after all.

'I've ordered a bottle of Sauvignon Blanc,' he's saying, but I'm not really listening. Instead I'm looking at his shirt collar, which I know hides the chain on which his wedding ring hangs. He doesn't know that I looked up his wife on Facebook a couple of nights ago. Her profile picture showed the two of them together on a beach somewhere. She looked nice.

'I'm worried for you, Selina,' Greg says. 'About money, I mean.'

I turn my attention back to him. *Concentrate, Selina. Money is important.*

'I'm concerned about the money that disappeared from Simon's account. If he was mixed up in something dodgy, those people are not going to give up their investment easily. It's really important that you trace that mystery account.'

Greg's tone is light as always, but there's a new tightness to it, and his eyes are the colour of slate.

I look down at his hand in mine, the fingers muscular

227

and spiked with black hairs like the nylon bristles of a brush. I'm reminded of being a small girl and pestering my parents for a very expensive doll I'd set my heart on in a toyshop in town. My mother said no, of course, but my father, always a soft touch, eventually gave in. But when I got the doll home, after the first rush of euphoria died down, I realized I didn't really want her. I hated her thick blonde plaits and her ugly pink rosebud mouth. Guilt at having forced my parents to buy her made me feel sick just at the sight of her.

I'm thinking of that doll and about what happens when the forbidden thing you lusted after turns out not to be what you wanted after all, while Greg is talking about the account and the money. Why is he so interested? Simon was his client and his friend, but Greg has no responsibility for him. Is it because of me? Concern for my wellbeing? Or might Greg be more involved in Simon's affairs than he is letting on? If Simon was taking back-handers from crooked developers or from bent officials, mightn't Greg have known about it, or even been part of the deal?

Something occurs to me.

'If Simon was mixed up with dangerous people, might they not have been looking for him?' I ask. I'm talking fast because I'm excited. 'Might they not have done something to him?'

'Like kill him?' asks Greg.

I'm expecting to see his usual amused smile. It *is* ridiculous, after all, the two of us sitting here discussing murder over our £19.95 three-course lunch specials. But Greg's face remains serious, and my own smile feels suddenly inappropriate.

'To be honest, Selina,' he says – this unfamiliarly intense Greg, 'I wouldn't put anything past them. These people are . . . not very nice.'

For a moment I'm giddy with the idea of it. If Simon had upset some people so much they wanted to kill him, it would mean someone pushed him. He didn't decide to jump. He didn't choose to go. If Simon didn't commit suicide, the endowment will pay out and I'll keep my house, but more than that, I'll no longer be the wife whose husband would rather be dead than married to her.

But Greg's sombre expression sobers me up and I stare at him, the dregs of my smile dying on my lips. 'Have they . . . threatened you, these "not very nice" people?'

He shrugs and looks away. 'They've . . . been in touch. They think I know something. Guilt by association.'

'But who are they?' I feel muddled by the wine and by the surreal conversation. 'What are they involved in that makes them so dodgy they'd need to use Simon as a frontman?'

'I don't know,' says Greg crossly, clearly reluctant to discuss it. 'Drugs probably.'

I laugh out loud. Well, I can't help it. Simon was always so evangelically anti-drugs, so enraged when I first came across packs of rolling papers and tobacco stashed away in Josh's bedroom. *He doesn't need this stuff*, he stormed, further angered at being forced into an authoritarian stance that went so much against his own image of himself. *Not our boy*.

'That clarifies things,' I tell Greg, relieved. 'Simon wouldn't touch anything to do with drugs. You should report these people to the police.'

Greg gazes at me for a long time without speaking and I

have the feeling there's something I'm not getting that I ought to be, some understanding I ought to possess but don't.

'Don't be naive, Selina.' His voice sounds rusty, as if it needs oiling. 'Simon didn't have to approve of drugs to profit from them. It's amazing how persuasive a hundred grand or so can be when it comes to silencing the odd inconvenient scruple.'

A hundred thousand pounds? Somehow hearing him say the amount out loud makes the whole thing more possible.

'That's why it's so important,' he says, 'for you to find that secret account.'

'I don't know anything about that other account,' I tell him, my voice sharp.

He leans back, taking his hand away from mine. Something between us has snapped.

'Of course,' he says. 'No reason why you should.'

Abruptly, he changes the subject, switching back to his normal voice as smoothly as changing the channels on a remote. Now he's talking about Lottie. My stomach tightens. I don't want to talk about her. Hettie says I shouldn't feel guilty, but I do. If I hadn't told her about Caroline Howard, would she have done what she did, or at least tried to do?

'Terrible business,' says Greg, tutting like an old woman.

Again I get a fleeting glimpse of another Greg, one I'm not sure I altogether like.

It's amazing that they were ever friends, him and Simon. Such totally different characters. But then I've always been mystified by the nature of men's friendships. It was intriguing watching the children grow up and seeing how

Flora over-invested emotionally in trying to forge emotional bonds with her classmates, while the boys acquired friends on no deeper a basis than who had the best toys or the widest selection of PlayStation games. Simon had tons of friends, of course, but most of his friendships were based on shared interests – a passion for test cricket, a mutual enjoyment of that all-you-can-eat buffet at the Indian restaurant round the corner where the waiters greeted them by name and brought their Kingfisher beers without being asked. All that was quite sufficient. No need for emotional unburdening or sharing.

Now, looking at Greg, I'm wondering what type of friendship can be sustained by nothing more than comparing test scores or passing comment on a particularly tasty Madras. I've spent my adult life colluding in the Myth of Simon Busfield, but now I'm wondering whether my husband, my late husband, might have been just a little *shallow*.

An image pops into my head of my mother, before Simon and I were married, complaining – most unlike her to talk like that – that she could never seem to get to the next layer of Simon. 'I keep feeling that if I carry on digging long enough, sooner or later I'll get through the surface to what's underneath, the *meat* of him,' she said. 'But I never do.'

I laughed at the time, but now that digging analogy comes back to me. Might Simon have been nothing but topsoil?

The bottle of Sauvignon Blanc is drunk, along with a couple of large brandies. Greg is looking at me. *Those grey eyes.* And I know what he is thinking. But he's wrong. I absolutely, definitely am not going to sleep with him again.

*

His finger, one of those thick, powerful fingers, is gently stroking the curve of my hip as I lie on my side.

I close my eyes. If I can't see him, he can't see me and I'm not really here. Again my children's toddler hide-and-seek logic comes back to me through the mists of time.

My head is throbbing and I've reached that stage of a post-boozy-lunch afternoon where the effects of the alcohol are fading in inverse proportion to the creeping awareness of having done something rather regrettable.

'We're so similar, you and I,' says Greg. His finger is still stroking, stroking, stroking.

No. I'm not similar to him. Not similar at all.

'Really? I don't see it.' I fall on to my back so his hand is left hovering in the air, mid stroke.

'We're romantics, but also realists,' Greg persists. He has taken his hand away and rested it on his own beefy thigh where it emerges, dotted with coils of dark hair, from his unbuttoned shirt. In the grey afternoon light, Greg's post-lunch flush seems like a dirty stain spreading across his face. When we had sex earlier, he'd given a running commentary on what was happening, the crude words erecting a barrier between my mind and my body so that I observed, rather than felt, as things went in and out, and up and down.

'Don't get me wrong,' he continues. 'I value security and loyalty, but I couldn't live without adventure and spontaneity, could you? The joy of the new. What would life be without it?'

I lie on my back and try to see myself through his eyes – this spontaneous woman seeking out the next challenge, the next thrill. Is that who I want to be now?

It's true that when I look back on those twenty-eight years with Simon, I'm amazed at the things that seemed so important to the Selina I used to be. Did I really spend months, years even, checking out schools for the children, comparing science facilities, league-table results, pastoral care, even Oxbridge entry numbers. Why didn't anyone tell me that children will be themselves no matter how much you might wish otherwise? I think of the effort I poured into the endless rounds of home improvements – the mood boards, the interiors magazines, the trade shows, the sleepless nights wondering if the Parma Grey had been just a step too far. And for what? To build a home out of lies and air?

And yet surely I'm not this person either, the one Greg seems to think I am, thriving on opportunistic fun?

'I must go,' I say, turning to him and noticing how the skin on his face puckers where it rests on his arm and how the hair on his chest is starting to turn white. All of a sudden, I can't wait to be out of here, away from this stranger with his wedding ring around his neck and his travel-sized deodorant he keeps in his briefcase.

Sitting up, I feel ridiculous and self-conscious of my fifty-one-year-old body on this seedy hotel bed. My bra and knickers are twisted up in the sheet. When I liberate them, I notice they look faintly grey in the glaring light of the bedside lamp. Impossible to believe I used to wash my whites with special detergent I ordered off the internet that makes them come out looking like new. How long has it been since I bothered with that?

'I'm not this person,' I say out loud, fumbling with my bra clasp, and instantly regret it.

Idiot! He'll think I'm quite mad. But Greg looks pensive.

'We're none of us *these people*,' he says. For a change, there's no trace of a smile on his face. 'We just became them by mistake.'

The cramped hotel lift in which, just a couple of hours ago, Greg and I kissed like teenagers, is garishly lit and panelled in plastic laminate made to look like wood. The hotel lobby is full of foreign students, sleeping on their luggage. We are jarringly old and well-dressed. *They all know*, I think to myself. *They all know what we've been doing upstairs.*

I say goodbye to Greg outside on the pavement in the fading light. He tries to kiss me on the lips but I turn at the last minute so his lips land, *smack*, on my ear. I have the strangest feeling, suddenly, that someone is watching us. I peer along the street, but don't see anyone.

'I'll call you,' says Greg. I hope that he doesn't.

My car is on a meter around the corner. Am I OK to drive? I've never felt so sober in my life. In the driving seat I check my mirror, out of habit. *Oh, it's me. There I am.* For some reason I thought that, like an over-exposed photograph, I might not show up at all.

When I turn on my phone I have fifteen missed calls. More loan companies, I expect. I listen to the messages, cutting each off abruptly when I hear the unfamiliar voice saying, 'Mrs Busfield?' Finally, number nine, a voice I recognize.

'Selina? It's Petra here. I know this might sound odd, but I wonder if we could meet? For a chat?'

Meet Petra for a chat? What a bizarre idea! What on earth would we find to say? I try to remember any occasion in the three years she's been seeing Felix when we've met up on our own or even chatted over the phone, but there is none. Well, we've never exactly been close. 'You're jealous of her,' Simon accused me once. Preposterous idea. She's perfectly nice, and obviously very beautiful, just not terribly *sparky*. I always thought Felix would go out with someone with more substance, some-one with something more about her. Although is that actually true? When I try to picture this ideal daughter-in-law of my imagination, my mind is resoundingly blank.

I click off my phone. Again that feeling of being watched. There's a brightly lit noodle bar on the other side of the street. A row of lone diners sit on high stools against the counter at the front, shovelling food into their mouths with chopsticks. Can that really be pleasurable, that kind of solo refuelling? None of them seems interested in me.

The journey home is endless. God, the traffic! I could explode! Cars are backed up all along the Mall, coming to a standstill around Victoria. Young people drift past the car in small groups, hoods up against the cold. Some wear badges and trail placards. Up ahead, a police van blocks the road, diverting cars away from the river and from Millbank and Westminster. Oh God, I long to be home. A group of girls walk past with long hair and tiny skirts, their slender legs encased in black tights. They must be freezing! One of them is wearing a homemade badge saying FUCK FEES in glaring red letters. For goodness' sake! 'What have you got to protest about?' I say to their retreating backs and their glossy, swinging ponytails. 'Life is spread out in front of you like a picnic.'

*

I'm hoping to have the house to myself, but when I arrive back, Josh is home, sitting in the den, half swallowed by a soft leather beanbag, wearing headphones with a mouthpiece attached and clutching a PlayStation controller. 'Die,' he says into the mouthpiece as I walk in. 'Die, you pussy!'

'Charming,' I say.

Josh pauses the game. 'Wanna cup of tea?' he asks.

I stare at him. Hooded sweatshirt, bare feet, shorts (for heaven's sake!) although outside it has started snowing again. I notice the fuzz of black hair on his calves – *my baby boy* – and I want to cry.

'What's wrong?' I ask him. 'Why are you offering me tea?'

His eyes – beautiful hazel eyes, thick black lashes – widen in mock affront, then drop to the floor. 'I met her today,' he says, fiddling with the wire of his controller. 'Sadie.'

'Josh, I told you . . . Her mother said . . .'

'Fuck's sake, Mum.' Josh rarely gets cross, but now his face is scarlet. 'We just went to Maccy D's. It's no big deal.'

I'm over-reacting. It's natural he should want to find out more about the girl. She's his half-sister, after all. That woman, with her soap-star mentality, has got us all over-dramatizing.

'Anyway, she had some news about her mum I think you should probably know.'

I breathe in deeply – *Let's Pran*, the Germanic yoga instructor used to say – and breathe out. Whatever it is, this new drama that's been plastered on top of the existing one like a fresh billboard ad, I don't want to hear it. I'm tired of emotion. I'd give anything, *anything*, for things to be normal and boring again.

'What now?' I ask Josh. 'Not another suicide attempt, please God.'

He shakes his head. That silly, swept-to-the-side hair they all have now.

'She . . . I mean, the mum . . . Lottie . . . Well . . . she's pregnant.'

A rushing inside. Blood whooshing around.

A baby. Simon's baby.

She wins, then. He may have loved me first, but he loved her last. Her body proves it.

I won't have more babies.

I won't have another husband.

She wins.

I keep asking why, why, why? I thought we were happy. I thought we had a good marriage. Friends used to hold us up as an example of the perfect relationship. How did he turn his back on that? What made him decide to step over the boundaries? When I ask him how he could do this to me after fifteen years, he looks at me like I'm crazy and says, 'It wasn't about you, it was about me, and her.' How does he think that makes me feel? Knowing he took this step that would destroy my life, and I didn't even feature?

I'm reading BetrayalHurts' post on the infidelity forum and something inside me is breaking apart. The truth is we all need to think we're central to the story, even if it means accepting betrayal as a deliberate act of violence against us. But I know that the first time Simon decided to step outside of our marriage, with Lottie or Caroline Howard or maybe someone else whose name I'll never even know, I never crossed his mind. Like BetrayalHurts, I'm finding it's the not counting that's the hardest to bear – my casual omission from the pivotal moment of my own life.

As I sit at the kitchen table voyeuristically scrolling through the posts from the betrayed and the cuckolded, the crazed and the heartbroken, my phone rings.

'Mrs Busfield?'

I recognize the hollow, scooped-out voice and am immediately alert.

'DI Bowles here. I wonder if you'd like to pop in. There's something I'd like you to take a look at.'

LOTTIE

Lying in bed at home, I have the weirdest sense that some-one has been here. I'm looking at the chest of drawers with the gilt-framed mirror we bought in a junk shop in Holloway, festooned as always with colourful scarves and jewellery, like a Bollywood wedding. One of the scarves – a red chiffon one – has been draped studiedly across the top of the mirror like theatre-set curtains. That definitely wasn't me. Maybe Jules then, at the same time as she stripped the vomitty sheets and scrubbed the sheepskin rug (just the slightest yellowy stain – you wouldn't even notice unless you were looking) and opened the window to let out the acrid smell of someone giving up.

Nearly forty years old and my sisters are still cleaning up after me.

I lie back against my pillows and study the carefully arranged scarf. Not like Jules to position anything just so. If I half close my eyes, it looks like a smile.

SELINA

The figures in the highlighted circle on the screen are grey and grainy and move as jerkily as puppets through a misted landscape. Only the width of the taller figure's chest, and the thrust of his hands in his jacket pockets and the tilt of his jaw, reveals this to be Simon.

The CCTV footage of Southwark Street on a rainy night in September emerged 'out of the blue', according to the police. The main cameras in the area where Simon was last seen had been checked, but this one was assumed to be out of order.

Though the quality is poor, there's something truly terrible about seeing someone walking around, knowing that in just a few hours he'll be dead. 'Stop!' I long to shout at the oblivious Simon. 'Turn back! Run!'

'Is there anything about this person you recognize?' asks DI Bowles, pointing at the second figure, slightly shorter and squatter than Simon, dressed in what appears to be a bulky dark coat with some kind of hood or hat pulled well down over his face. Dark trousers, dark shoes. No face visible, no identifying features. Even the walk is disguised by the camera's jerky frames.

'I don't recognize him,' I say.

'Or her.'

I glance over sharply. The policeman doesn't seem to be joking, although he has one of those unfortunate faces that make it difficult to tell. I haven't seen him since right after the funeral. The memory of the state I was in at that time sits awkwardly between us like an uninvited third person. It's like trying to do business with someone who's seen you naked. Can the figure really be a woman? I peer at the screen, willing it to come into focus, but the images remain infuriatingly blurred.

'We've traced those three women behind them,' says DI Bowles, pointing out three indistinct shapes walking close together. 'They didn't notice anything. We have yet to track down him,' he indicated a man in a pale raincoat, 'or them.' He pointed to a couple laden with shopping bags.

'And no one has come forward to say they were with him the night he died?' I ask. I suspect the police investigations have been largely half-hearted, that they've been privately convinced all along that Simon killed himself, unable to take the strain of his double life. There's no CCTV footage for the pub Simon was reported to be in, or for the section of the riverfront where he was thought to be seen.

DI Bowles shrugs. 'When you divide up your life into strict compartments, some people are bound to fall through the gaps in between,' he says. 'Your husband seems to have had some friends for one life and some for the other. Maybe he needed to keep a few that overlapped with neither, just to stay sane?'

I realize now that I don't like this policeman. I don't like that he saw me at my most raw, I don't like what he thinks he knows about me and about Simon, when actually he knows nothing. I want to hear him say he was wrong. I want him to admit he doesn't know us after all.

'But surely this proves he didn't kill himself,' I persevere. 'There was someone else with him. Surely anyone who didn't have something to hide would come forward?'

DI Bowles looks at me, then looks away.

'I'm sure I don't need to tell you, Mrs Busfield, that

everyone has secrets, and there could be any number of reasons why someone would want to keep quiet about where they were that night. But yes, I can confirm we are including the possibility of murder among our several lines of inquiry.'

Part Four

DEPRESSION

18

LOTTIE

I'm back in the hospital. It seems like only minutes ago I was discharged and now here I am again. Same hospital, same sickly green-coloured walls in the waiting room, different ward. Antenatal. Two weeks on, and it's still as much of a shock as the first time I heard it. A baby – *his* baby. I'm not ready for this.

Look at the other women here. How much older am I than them? Years? Decades? The woman opposite has the biggest belly I've ever seen, I swear to God. Impossible to imagine my own body distended like that, puffed up like I've swallowed an enormous pouffe.

Where does all that extra skin come from? It takes an awful lot of human skin to cover even an average-sized pouffe, no joke. How will I have time to grow so much skin over the next six months? Maybe they'll have to grow some for me in a lab with the aid of one of those white mice with a human ear grafted on to its back.

The woman opposite shifts in the uncomfortable plastic chair, manually heaving her mammoth belly over to one side.

'What 'ave I told you abaat 'itting?' she says to the

bigger of the two small children who are sitting on the floor at her feet, fighting over a board book. ''Itting is wrong. You 'it her one more time and I'll bloody well wallop ya!'

The little boy glares at her sullenly, digging around in his nose with his finger. Which he then wipes on the book.

'Mrs Busfield?' the nurse calls in a broad West Indian accent.

'I prefer Ms, actually,' I say, following her into a consulting room. Now that I'm a Not-Wife, a Not-Widow, I don't feel comfortable being a Mrs.

The nurse raises her eyebrows. 'We call all da ladies Mrs. Easier. Y'know?'

I ought to protest. But the nurse is holding out her hand. 'You're in?'

What on earth is the woman on about?

'I'm in . . . the antenatal department?' I hazard.

The nurse closes her eyes. 'No. *You*'re in. You're in! *Wee*, dear! Where's your bottle of pee-pee?'

Oh. Urine.

Mortified, I reach down into my bag and produce a specimen jar. The nurse snatches it impatiently. Now she's wheeling out a huge tray of empty test-tubes and a newly unwrapped syringe.

Oh dear God. I've forgotten about this bit. The endless poking and prodding of pregnancy. The way your body is no longer your own.

'This won't take a minute, dear,' the nurse says, yanking the sleeve of my red jumper out of the way. 'Some ladies like to look away.'

Obediently, I look at the wall, where someone has stuck a poster advising women who speak only Swahili, Turkish,

Urdu or any number of other languages how to go about finding an interpreter. I look down at the floor, where a box of brightly coloured plastic toys stands out against the institutional grey of the carpet tiles. I look at the bed running along one wall, covered in a layer of kitchen roll. And all the time I'm looking away, the nurse is jabbing my arm with the syringe.

'Can't find da vein,' she complains. 'Some ladies, dey got big veins just pop up like sausages. But some ladies, dey got little biddy veins so small you can't find dem at all.'

It's my fault. I'm to blame for having mean, anorexic veins. I'm too old to be having this baby. Too unmarried, too unwidowed, too betrayed, too poor, too ill-equipped.

I stare at the wall and try not to cry as the nurse jabs away furiously in the crook of my left arm, before letting it fall and repeating the whole procedure on the right.

At the bus stop, there's a young mother with a buggy waiting in stony-faced silence. Her child gazes up at me, solemn and huge-eyed behind the heavy clear plastic of the buggy's rain cover, and instinctively I put my hand over my belly. Is there really a baby in there, quietly swelling like one of those sea monkeys Sadie once got given for her birthday?

Back home, I crawl miserably into bed.

Jules comes and stands in the doorway. After the thing I did, my sisters have put me back on Lottie Watch, taking it in turns to come and stay. I feel terrible for what I put them through. What was I thinking?

'Are you sure they said everything's OK?' Jules wants to know. She still thinks I ought to have let her come to the

247

hospital, even though she'll probably get the sack if she takes any more time off work.

'Everything's fine,' I tell her.

I don't tell her that sometimes now I'm filled with hate for what Simon did, and dream of digging the baby out with a rusty spoon. How big will it be now? The size of a gallstone? A small cyst? I've always wondered about how people describe tumours in grocery terms – as big as a grapefruit, the size of a small melon. As if danger can be quantified in fruit, in pulp and flesh and skin and juice. The baby will be the size of a large grape, I imagine. Or a shrivelled plum left too long in the fruit bowl – the kind that splits horribly apart when you reach for it, leaving a pool of sticky orange juice and a cloud of fruit flies.

How fluid, in the end, is the line between love and hate. You keep riding the crest higher and higher and then, *pffff*, you're plunged into a black sea where nothing exists except you and your hatred.

There was such love when Sadie was born. An ocean of love. Simon and I lying in cool white sheets, away from the glare of the Dubai sun, gazing at our daughter while she slept. *How beautiful she is ... We've made the most beautiful baby in the world.* How will it be for this poor grape baby? No money, no father, basketcase mother.

My phone cuts through my self-pity. That jaunty little ringtone – legacy of a much happier time.

Emma, the caller display informs me.

'All fine,' I tell her before she can speak.

I love my sisters, but, oh please God, they have to give me space. It's so tempting to let them take me over, not to have to think, but to do that I have to surrender Simon, the Simon I still love, even while I hate him. They won't

248

allow love. Not after everything. I'm dreading telling them about Christmas. *I want Sadie and me to be on our own . . . Just a small Christmas this year, I think . . .* No matter how much I rehearse it, I still can't say the words.

Emma is in a hurry.

'Good, but I'm not phoning about that. I'm phoning about money.' My middle sister has taken on the thankless job of trying to deal with my finances – my debts, more accurately.

'Em, I'm really not in the mood to hear this . . .'

'I think you will be. It seems someone has paid your mortgage.'

I'm not hearing her properly. What rubbish she talks sometimes.

'Lots, are you there? Someone has paid your mortgage, all ninety-five thousand pounds of it, and no one seems to be able to tell me who.'

SELINA and LOTTIE

SELINA: Hello?

LOTTIE: It's me. Lottie.

(*Pause.*)

SELINA: Oh.

(*Pause.*)

SELINA: If you're ringing so I can congratulate you—

LOTTIE: Was it you?

SELINA: Pardon?

LOTTIE: It has to be you. Who else would it be?

SELINA: I haven't the foggiest idea what you're—

LOTTIE: Paying my mortgage. It was you, wasn't it?

SELINA: Pffffffff!

LOTTIE (*over the top of Selina*): *Somebody* paid it. It didn't just pay itself.

SELINA: Why on earth would I pay your mortgage?

LOTTIE: Oh, let's see. Because if I lose my home, you'll lose yours? Because it suits you to have me in your debt? Because you can afford to, as you've been creaming money off Simon into a mystery offshore bank account? Because someone finally waved the 'nice' stick over you while you slept . . .

SELINA (*again*): Pfffff! Sorry to disabuse you, but it wasn't me. In case you haven't noticed, *my husband* left me financially embarrassed. All his accounts are frozen anyway, because of Probate, and even if I could get my hands on them, they're empty. In fact, they're in minus figures, thanks to you.

LOTTIE (*riled*): Hey, lady, I'm not the one who lives in a fucking mansion and stays home all day painting my nails. I bloody well go out and earn a living. I pay my way. You need to find out who those payments were going to. That's the one who bankrupted everyone.

SELINA: I've told you before. I have no clue where the sodding money went.

(*Pause.*)

LOTTIE: *Disabuse?*

SELINA: Pardon?

LOTTIE: Who says disabuse?

SELINA: Me, clearly. Anyway, while you're on the line, there's something I've been meaning to ask you . . .

19

SELINA

❧

If anyone had told me last Christmas that in a year's time I'd not only be a widow, but also preparing to play host to my husband's pregnant mistress (*wife?*) and their love child, I'd have thought them completely barking mad. Nevertheless they'd have been right. Ridiculous, isn't it? Preposterous, ludicrous, laughable, absurd, outlandish, not on your nelly, have you taken leave of your senses? Of all the . . . that takes the biscuit, bizarre, unfathomable, are you quite sure? Have you thought it through? Mad, crazy.

Oh God.

It was all Flora's idea.

Or Josh's.

One or the other.

It was dinner time last week and Flora and Felix were here again. They seem to be here all the time at the moment. Are they doing it for me or for them, I wonder, all these visits home?

'Gonna be weird, innit?' said Josh, as we sat around the kitchen table eating an indifferent meatloaf.

We all stared, waiting for enlightenment.

251

'Christmas this year. Gonna be weird.'

We had to agree it was indeed going to be weird. How could it not be? With Simon dead and money worries hanging over our heads like a comic-book weight.

We could invite people, I suggested – *other* people (the phrase 'normal people' was left unsaid). We often have house guests at Christmas. Hettie and Ian will come, obviously, as their daughter Hannah is spending Christmas with her new boyfriend's family. We could have a houseful, make a party.

The children looked at me as if I was crazy, of course.

'Some party that would be,' said Felix, as usual playing with his food rather than eating it. 'Everyone looking at us like we're animals in a zoo. We're not like *other people* any more, Madre. Or haven't you noticed? We're a species apart.'

He was right, of course. *Genus Completely Buggeredatus.*

I didn't tell my children that I wouldn't mind if Christmas didn't exist at all this year, if the days followed seamlessly from 24th December to 26th. I didn't tell them that I wouldn't mind if I didn't exist at all. I didn't tell them that grief and anger have eroded me like a cliff.

'The only people who are the same as us are *them*,' said Flora.

She was wearing a pink polo-necked jumper. *Pink!* With her colouring! Her eyes were dark-ringed and sad. She's lost weight, I noticed suddenly. That famous Misery Diet.

'Sadie and Lottie, I mean,' she added unnecessarily. We all knew who *them* was. 'I think we should invite them here for Christmas. I mean, they're not going to go away, are they? So we might as well get to know them a bit.'

All of us staring, staring, staring at her. Has she gone utterly mad?

'Well, you're always telling us to do things for other people at Christmas,' she said defensively.

'Oh, I've changed my mind about that,' I replied. 'Other people can rot in hell as far as I'm concerned.'

Felix, agitated, picked up his fork and started jabbing it in the air. 'I can't believe you're seriously suggesting it,' he told his sister, his narrow face all sharp lines and scooped-out hollows. 'After what that girl did to you.'

What that girl did? What did that girl do?

It all came out then. Josh, it seems, isn't the only one who's been rendezvousing with his new sibling. Flora also engineered a meeting.

'I thought I ought . . .' Flora tried to explain to me, her blue eyes swimming. 'A link to Dad . . .'

Ryan had been against it, of course. Flora's *grubby* family. But Flora had gone ahead anyway. In spite of myself, I felt a flicker of pride.

They met in an upmarket patisserie in Soho in the middle of a weekday afternoon. The girl, Sadie, told Flora she had study leave and Flora thought she'd put her foot in it by saying, 'I'm quite sure we never had study leave when I was at school. Mind you, it might be different in the State system.'

'Is that bad?' she appealed to us at the dinner table. 'Is "State" one of those words like "handicapped" that suddenly turn out to have become mysteriously offensive?'

Flora tried, it seems, to draw the girl out, the cardboard sister come to life. But it was like wading through treacle (her words). 'She just didn't want to talk. So I ended up talking twice as much as I should have,' she said. We all nodded. It was too easy to imagine. When the girl announced abruptly, 'I've brought something for you,' Flora had been plunged into turmoil.

'I thought she'd brought some kind of gift,' she told us, angst written across her face. 'And I was kicking myself for not having bought *her* something, but when I said that, she sort of sniggered and said, "It's not a *present*!" Of course it wouldn't be a present, I'm such a *moron*!'

It was a letter, apparently, from Simon to his daughter – *his other daughter, mustn't forget* – to Sadie. Actually, a whole bundle of letters. By the time Flora realized that far from being a peace offering between sisters, they were clearly meant to hurt her, it was too late. She picked one at random.

'I didn't even recognize the writing!' she exclaimed. 'Why would I? He never wrote letters to *me*.'

The letter was typical Simon, it seems. Overblown hyperbole. *Warrior princess*, he called his daughter (*his other daughter*). He would! Pompous ass! He wrote about meeting her from school, standing in the playground waiting for her to appear and about reading her bedtime stories.

'Did he ever come to meet *me* from school?' Flora wanted to know.

I remembered then how I used to stand in the playground waiting for her, armed usually with a clipboard to coerce the other mothers into being on some school committee or other, or supporting a fundraising initiative. I'd watch her emerge from the classroom with her hair coming loose from a carefully constructed plait, or a smudge of blue paint across her school jumper. No Simon, of course. Never Simon.

Flora read it all in my face.

'No,' she said. 'I didn't think so. I've been trying to think of a time when he read to me at night, but I can't. All I remember is lying in bed and telling you I was giving him a goodnight kiss in my head.'

'He called her Darling Lady Sadie,' said Flora suddenly. 'I wish he'd had a special name for me. Silly Old Sausage, he'd say occasionally. And there was a time when I was young when he'd sit me on his knee and call me Pudding – until you put a stop to it.'

Of course I stopped it. It would have given her a complex. At her age! Such a rotund little thing!

'The thing is though, Mum.' Flora looked at me. Such blue eyes. So much hurt. 'I didn't mind Pudding. At least it was something. At least it was mine. I know they were silly names – Sausage and Pudding. I know you all used to laugh at me a bit, but that was my role. That's the thing, isn't it, about families? The roles are how you know you belong.'

Was that really how it was? The way Flora describes it? I try to think back, but more and more I'm doubting my own memories. My joint history with Simon, obviously, has been copiously scribbled over with the red pen of hindsight. When I look back now, as I do relentlessly, I question every decision, every motive. It's exhausting, this constant rewriting of the past.

'People always say you can't change the past, but that's rubbish,' I said to Hettie a couple of nights ago.

But I didn't explain myself very well. What I wanted to say was that the past isn't the sum of its facts, as I've always believed. It isn't something that's done and can't therefore be undone. It's a mirage, a house built on quicksand that changes shape with the tide. Simon's duplicity has taken memories I'd thought were set in stone and bled them of meaning until they are empty sacs flapping uselessly in my mind's eye.

And yet this is how Flora remembers it, and her hurt is clearly real. Guilt set in then, drying in my veins like concrete. Did I really do this? Deny my daughter the link to her father she craved? Poor Flora. Poor Pudding.

I felt so awful after that, I'd probably have agreed to anything. Children can do that, can't they? Leave you massively over-compensating for their imagined slights, all perspective lost. If she'd asked me to cut my own head off, I'd probably have agreed. Which is why I found myself saying yes to her inviting Sadie and Lottie for Christmas. Not that I thought for a moment they'd accept. What about the sisters? Surely a festive season in the bosom of her family would be on the cards after the drama of these last three months?

Felix went ballistic, of course. He said we'd have to lock up all the silver if the parasites were coming. He had a go at Flora and then at Josh when he refused to see anything wrong in this bizarre festive invitation. Normally the two of them would have caved in under the pressure of Felix's disapproval. That's the way it's always been – dominant older child, easily manipulated and eager-to-please younger ones. As children, Flora and Josh vied for Felix's attention and were rendered speechless with joy if they were allowed to play with him – always a game of his choosing, of course, and frequently involving rules known only to him – only to be heartbroken when he abandoned them for some more interesting pursuit. Even now, they still bend to his whims and moods, but amazingly this time they stood their ground. Felix went upstairs in a huff, leaving his dinner largely untouched. I worried that would be an end of it, that Felix would flounce home, calling a premature halt to the evening. 'It's my ball and I'm taking it home,' the young Felix would say when a game wasn't going his way. So I was relieved when he came down again, having had a change of heart.

'Why not?' he said, pacing around the table. 'Why not play happy families? It could be fun.'

Later, when Flora had gone home and Josh had disappeared up to his room (to revise, he said, which made Felix snort and say, 'to smoke a spliff out of the window, more like'), Felix and I sat at the kitchen table, awkward suddenly at finding ourselves on our own.

'How are you really, Felix?' I asked my oldest son, leaning forwards on impulse to take one of his hands in both of mine. I gazed at his fingers, so much like his father's – long and elegant, the type of fingers made to scissor around a cigarette, although, thankfully, neither of them smoked.

For a moment, the two of us watched our conjoined hands on the table between us as if they might at any moment spring independently to life and perform some kind of interpretive dance.

'Not good, Madre,' said Felix eventually. His voice was unsteady.

'You miss him. That's natural.'

'No, I don't. That's just it. How can you miss someone who's been absent for most of your life? But I miss . . . the idea of him, the phantom father I built up in my mind.'

'And are you sure you're OK with having those two here at Christmas?'

I know Felix. Of all three, he's the one who likes things to be as they always have been, sulking about changes, anxious about what has been lost or left behind.

'Sure,' he said. And his voice was back to normal. 'I seem to be the only one who hasn't been taking part in the great love-in with Sister Sadie. This will give me the chance to make amends!'

I glanced at him sharply, remembering how he used to be when the other two had something he didn't, how competitive he could get about things or other people's attention. Might he set out to befriend Sadie just to get one over on his siblings, just as, when they were children, he had to better whatever they did – jumping higher, getting a bigger laugh – just to show them he could?

It wasn't too great a stretch of the imagination and for a moment I felt sorry for the girl. Felix has a habit of picking people up at random, like items plucked from the supermarket shelves, only to be tossed out of the trolley when something else catches his fancy.

'Felix,' I said, 'you must remember she's very young.'

Suddenly his face folded in on itself like origami, revealing underneath a flash of his childhood face, and my heart spasmed painfully.

'Oh Madre Mia,' he said, removing his hand from underneath mine. 'Since when did we make allowances for youth in our family?'

So I invited her, Lottie. Well, how was I to know she'd say yes? What's wrong with the woman? Surely she could tell from my voice on the phone that it wasn't a *real* invitation, that I was just going through the motions?

Ryan's right. We are grubby now. Shopping in the cheapest supermarkets. Two for one, meal deal, money off, buy one get one free, every little helps. We used to be a unit, but now Simon has gone and this girl and her mother have been stapled on to our lives like a misplaced invoice.

I'm so tired of it all. So sick and tired of it.

Why did she say 'yes'? What on earth was she thinking?

LOTTIE

'What on earth were you thinking?'

My sisters are both here on my lap. A conference video call on Skype. Two little boxes on my computer screen, two faces and both of them angry.

The coven, Simon used to call them. Us. *A coven convention?* he'd ask, when I sat at our glass-topped dining table in Dubai trying to organize the next Skype conflab.

'What on earth were you thinking?' Emma wants to know.

What can I say? That I don't know what I was thinking? That I wasn't really thinking at all? That I haven't really thought since all this started?

Dumbfounded is what I was when she asked me over the phone. Spend Christmas with Simon's *other* family? What a ridiculous, preposterous idea. I almost died on the spot when she said it, I swear to God. We'd been having an argument about money. I can't believe I actually thought she'd paid off my mortgage. What a moron I am sometimes. Once I'd really thought about it I realized there's only one real possibility – Simon. That mystery

259

account. It must be a fund for me and Sadie. He knows how hopeless I am with money, so he has appointed someone else to oversee it, doling out money when it's needed. It makes total sense, but I'm not going to say anything. I don't want *her* to get her hands on it.

So when she suddenly threw in an invite for Christmas, I was completely wrong-footed. I said I'd discuss it with Sadie, just because I was so flustered.

I was amazed when Sadie didn't react with immediate horror.

'Who'll be there?' she wanted to know.

'Her. Selina. And the children . . .'

'All the children?'

'I expect so. The first Christmas without—'

'Yes. Let's go. Better than staying here on our own.'

I regretted it then, having told her I wanted a Christmas without my sisters for once, just the two of us. No wonder she leapt at the first offer of something else.

'If that's what's worrying you, I'll change my mind,' I told her. 'We'll go to Emma's, like we always do.'

But Sadie had decided. And when Sadie is decided on something . . .

'No point in doing what we *always* do. This isn't always. It'll never be *always* again.'

Try explaining that to my sisters! Needless to say, they haven't taken it well.

'Babe, don't you think you might be self-sabotaging?' Jules, of course. 'You're subconsciously punishing yourself for allowing yourself to be put in this position.'

Emma, for once, agrees.

'It's fucking masochistic, Lots,' she says. She's sitting at her kitchen table in Derby and I can see Ben in the background, stirring something in a saucepan. *That! I want that! That domesticity. I want it back.*

Emma feels personally affronted that I won't be staying at her house as usual.

'We always spend Christmas together,' she says. 'Ever since Mum died . . .'

'It'll never be *always* again,' I tell them, parroting Sadie. Two pairs of eyes glare at me from my laptop screen as if I've taken leave of my senses. I wish I could explain it to them. *It's not that I don't love you*, I could say, *but these people, his other family, are linked to us in a way I can't even describe*. Impossible. How could you understand that, unless it had happened to you?

'You're being selfish,' says Emma. When she's hurt, Emma's default position is always attack. 'Sadie needs her family around her right now. And after what you put her through . . .'

She's referring to the pills, of course. *My poor daughter.*

'It's about time you started thinking of other people for a change.'

And just like that we're back in those family roles. Jules is bossy, Emma priggish. I'm the baby who's always been spoilt, wafting this way and that as her emotions lead her. Alliances are made and broken and made again. The old allegiances of childhood.

Sometimes I wonder what it would take to be able to shed the younger me like a snake's skin and reinvent myself, like other people seem to be able to do. Surely I should be allowed to outgrow my childhood self? Yet no matter how I try to break free of the mould, when I'm with my sisters I find myself inexorably drawn back into the me I keep thinking I've left behind.

'You never try to see things from my point of view,' I say now, hating my own whiny voice. *You always . . . You never . . .* the hyperbole of family rows. 'We can't do the things we've always done, because things are so different now. *We* are so different now.'

Signing off from Skype, I'm agitated. I shouldn't let my sisters wind me up like that. I notice there's an application open, the icon clearly visible on the bottom bar. Further investigation reveals it to be Sadie's Facebook page. She's been using my laptop since her own started making a noise like a combustion engine every time she turns it on. I double click on the icon. Amazing! It's still logged in! Normally Sadie guards her Facebook page like a winning Lottery ticket. Of course, I'm not going to read it, just a cursory glance while I find the 'log off' option. Why is Facebook always moving things?

I frown, noticing there's a chatbox open in the bottom right-hand corner where Sadie has been talking to her friend Gabi. I've never warmed to Gabi. She's one of those bright-eyed, tinny-voiced teenage girls who ply you with compliments – 'I love your hair like that!', 'great shoes!' – while oozing insincerity from every over-made-up pore. Cruelty is threaded through her like a drawstring. But Sadie claims Gabi makes her laugh, and of course my antipathy just makes her more attractive, so I try to hide it. Without thinking, I start reading the visible section of chat, looking for evidence to reinforce my dislike.

GABI: OMG!
SADIE: I know. Crazeh eh?

262

My frown deepens, seeing how Sadie is trying to emulate her friend's way of talking.

GABI: An he jus chopped outta line right there in the bog?

Wham! My heart slams into my ribcage. A line? Surely they're not talking about—

SADIE: Yeah, I was well freaked out!!!
GABI: Awww! An did ya . . .
SADIE: Yeh. I didn dare breathe in case I blew it all over the place. KWIM?

My breath is coming out in shallow gasps and I'm finding it hard to focus. There's a sickening image in my mind of my daughter's head bent over a toilet seat, a hand holding her glossy hair back behind her head.

GABI: hahahahaha! Shit, gotta go. Sposed 2 be revisin. Laters xxx

Heart racing, I scroll back up through their chat, desperate to find the name of the person who has been giving Class A drugs to my baby. Just a few months ago, I was refusing to let her get her nose pierced because I couldn't bear the idea of someone scarring her perfect skin, and now someone has let her put the hard, scuzzy edge of a rolled-up note in her nose and inhale God knows what into her system. But the brief conversation prior to what I'd read revealed no clue towards the identity of whoever was corrupting my daughter, only that he also kissed her.

GABI: On the lips?

SADIE: Yeh, I guess so. Weird, yeh?

My thoughts surge violently this way and that. Who is this boy who is kissing my daughter and giving her drugs in toilets? Surely not Josh? He's the one I was concerned about, but he doesn't seem capable of this. And where was I when all this was going on? Swallowing down pills like a naughty child? Lying in a hospital bed watching daytime TV? I shouldn't have brought her here. I thought London would expand her horizons, but not like this. Simon was right, we should have stayed in Dubai. I should have wrapped her up in insulating felt and bound her to me by the shared experience of being foreign (despite the accident of her UAE birth) in a place where we'd always be 'other'.

Snapping shut the laptop, I slump back against my pillows. How should I deal with this? If she knows I've read her sacred Facebook page, Sadie will never forgive me. But *cocaine*? A good mother would know what to do. A good mother wouldn't wriggle underneath the covers and pull the duvet over her head and pretend to be someone else.

What's the worst thing that can happen when the worst thing that can happen has already happened?

20

SELINA

~

'You really can't tell this isn't the real stuff.'

Petra is holding her glass up appreciatively. Her long black hair is tied back in a glossy knot at the nape of her neck, secured with a pencil-type stick, and her olive skin looks more than usually exotic in the dishwater-grey winter light. Oh Lord, I've just remembered I never returned her message. Didn't she want a chat about something? So unlike me to forget. But my head's all over the place. Surely she'll understand . . .

'This Cava is very good,' Petra adds for good measure.

Is it just me or does her voice sound forcedly bright? As if she's trying extra hard.

'Ca-va,' my mother repeats slowly, staring at her own glass as if it contains something highly experimental. 'Is it foreign?'

She's in her customary seat, one of the matching pair of armchairs by the French doors to the rear of the kitchen-diner. Why is she alone already wearing a paper hat? Pink and zig-zagged, it perches on the top of her immaculately coiffured hair, making her look like an imposter Queen. My heart tears a little at the sight of her, remembering

265

the Christmases of my childhood where she stage-managed proceedings with effortless proficiency, wafting around the house in a cloud of graciousness and Chanel No. 5.

'Don't be ridiculous.' Felix is scowling at Petra. 'It's budget fizz, anyone can see that. Standards in this house have slipped, Madre.'

Oh, that's just what I need today – Felix in one of his devil's advocate moods.

'Yes well, needs must,' I say.

'Needs must what?'

'Needs must . . . oh, for goodness' sake, Felix, stop being so pedantic, will you?'

As if Christmas Day isn't going to be difficult enough without him playing up.

'Your overflow is dripping,' Ian remarks. He has possession of the second armchair, next to my mother. 'You'll be wanting to get that seen to before it gets much worse.'

Breathe in . . . that's it . . . plenty of Pran . . . and out again. I'm standing in front of the cooking island that separates the kitchen from the diner bit. Chopping swedes. I have no idea what I'm doing standing here chopping swedes for a bunch of people who probably don't even like swedes. I don't want my house to be full of these people. I don't want to look across my kitchen and see Ryan hunched over a beer, his skin the colour of old white pants. I don't want to see the difference a year has made to the faces of my children, the distance from last Christmas to this one mapped out in hollows and shadows and a certain wariness around the eyes. I don't want to feel the crushing weight of Simon's absence, or look in the eyes of a woman

I hardly know and know she feels it too. I don't want to see the beautiful girl my husband produced with someone else, or think about his baby growing in that other woman's womb while my own shrivels up like a prune inside me. I want to go back to a year ago, yet how can I want that when a year ago it was all a lie? The woman who dressed the tree last year (a purple theme, if I remember) and picked up the turkey from the butcher on the high street (twenty-four pounds!) and baked trays of mince pies for the annual Christmas drinks with the neighbours isn't me any more, if indeed she ever was.

I mustn't make my life before into a fairytale, mustn't rewrite the past. I must remember the bad things as well as the good, the things that used to make me scream with frustration.

Remember that Christmas? How many years ago now? Four? Five? Opening up Simon's beautifully shop-wrapped gift – a dress I'd picked out from that boutique on the King's Road and set aside for him to pick up – and that dull thud of disappointment.

'It is the one you wanted, isn't it, darling?' Simon said, noticing my expression. 'The woman in the shop insisted it was.'

I looked down at the wisp of silk that I knew cost nearly four hundred pounds and felt an overwhelming wave of revulsion. Was that what Christmas had turned into? Opening overpriced presents I had chosen myself. I remember looking at Simon then, really looking at him in that way you don't when you've been married twenty-odd years. *Who are you?* I thought. *Who is this man who's lived with me for all these years yet still gives me gifts like a stranger?*

'Next time I wouldn't mind something with a bit more thought,' I said. Mrs Prim and Proper.

'Thought?' He looked at me as if awaiting a translation.

'Look, this is lovely. Well, of course it is – I chose it myself, so it jolly well ought to be! It's just that sometimes it would be nice to know you've thought about me, even just for the half an hour it'd take to choose something I'd like. Just thirty minutes of thought, that's all.'

'But darling, I think about you all the time, you know that. And you know what you're like to buy presents for. You have such set ideas about what you do and don't like.'

He was right, of course. The attic is still stuffed with wedding presents I've never allowed to be taken out of their boxes – monstrous vases in garish colours, electronic gadgets made from moulded white plastic, a sofa throw in a wild paisley print. I had a wedding list, naturally, but some people will insist in going off-piste. '*We think it's so much nicer to buy something a bit more personal.*' Pressing into my hand a carving of a pendulous-breasted African woman, or a piece of ghastly pottery. '*Lovely,*' I said, inside vowing it'd never see the light of day in my house.

So it wasn't without merit, Simon's accusation. Yet still it grated.

'I suppose my husband used to buy you lovely presents for Christmas,' I say to Lottie. I'm pleased with my light and conversational tone. I could be enquiring about the weather.

Lottie gives me a wary look. 'Of course. But don't worry, he never spent much, if that's what's bothering you.'

So far we've managed to be surprisingly civil, the two of

268

us, but our politeness is like a pair of borrowed shoes we're itching to kick off.

I should stop there. Josh has that 'please, Mum, leave it' expression. But my fingers are clutched tight around the knife chopping the swede. *Chop, chop, chop.*

'What kind of things? What did he get you last year, for example?'

She's sitting very upright now, sizing up the situation. Her hair is in two loose plaits. Plaits! At her age! And she's wearing a dress that looks not unlike the sack the man delivers the organic potatoes in. Patterned tights and those black clumpy boots complete the look. She's pretty! I realize it for the first time. But there are violet shadows like bruises under her eyes.

'If you must know – and to be honest I don't think it's any of your business – last year he bought me a painting.'

My mind freezes. A painting? It doesn't seem conceivable – something he picked himself, something that didn't arrive already gift-wrapped from an online store?

'He bought it from an artist friend of ours in Dubai. It's of a woman's back, just one curved line really. He said it reminded him of me.'

It reminded him of me. She didn't have to say that bit. She could have left that out. *An artist friend of ours* was enough. The rest is just overkill.

I mustn't lose it. I must keep going. *Keep calm and carry on*, like on that tea-towel Flora bought me a couple of years ago. That's the way. *Chop, chop, chop.*

A thin layer of resentment settles like mildew over us, turning us sour and ill-tempered. Outside the window the promised White Christmas fails to materialize. There's still a smattering of greying snow on the grass from the big fall on Monday, and the air temperature is freezing, as it has been for weeks, but the sky is flat and empty.

There's a small commotion around the table. Lottie has spotted some marks on Petra's arm and suddenly everyone is glad to have something to focus on.

'I burned myself,' Petra explains, 'taking a pizza out of the oven.'

Hettie is all sympathy. 'So easy to do,' she agrees. 'I did it last month, didn't I, Ian, with that apple crumble?'

Ian concurs that she did indeed suffer a crumble injury.

'Extreme Baking,' says Josh. 'It could catch on.'

He is trying to make a joke, to lighten the atmosphere, but no one seems in the mood to find things funny.

Who are they, these people sitting in my kitchen talking such nonsense?

'I think we should have a toast,' says Petra merrily. 'To absent friends.'

Everyone looks at her in surprise. It's only two twenty-five. Can she be drunk already?

'Don't be such a tit, Petra.' Felix's voice is soft and low, a sign he's getting angry. *Oh God, don't have an argument here, you two. Not today.*

'Well, I think a toast is a nice idea,' says Hettie, stepping in as peacekeeper. 'To absent friends!'

But Petra is already pushing past her out of the door. Well!

I glance over at Felix. His has his head bent over the table so his dirty-blond hair hides his face.

'Is everything all right, darling?' That's right. Breezy, upbeat. That's the ticket! *Where did that expression come from? I sound a hundred and ten years old!*

'Yes,' snaps Felix. 'I mean, no . . . Fuck it, I know I

probably shouldn't say anything, but Petra is pretty much losing it at the moment.'

'Losing it?' I say.

'You know – happy pills, tantrums, all the typical loony-tunes stuff. Those marks on her arm aren't burns, you know, they're self-inflicted.'

There's an audible collective intake of breath. *What?* Perfect Petra. Not possible, surely. I feel guilty all over again for not phoning her back. Then cross with her for making me feel guilty. Then cross with myself for being cross with her. *Maybe they'll split up.* Now I feel guilty about that thought as well, and about the little lift it gave me. True, Petra and I have never really got beneath the surface of each other. But this? Making marks on her own skin?

As the others exclaim in dismay, the dismalness of it weighs down on me.

What hope is there for us all, if Felix's beautiful, poised, good-hearted girlfriend with her little satin ballet pumps and her model-agency job and everything ahead of her can find life so impossible that she has to do that? Are we all just presenting façades to the world, behind which we crack and crumble like the cellars of Victorian houses?

Oh, now Petra is back. *Everyone look busy.* Lottie begins a conversation with Hettie about *Downton Abbey*, Josh hunts for a charger for his phone in the Everything Drawer, Felix materializes by my elbow to help with the chopping, while Flora and Ian suggest answers to an end-of-year quiz Ryan is reading from yesterday's paper.

Marooned on a high stool on the other side of the cooking island, her long legs wrapped around the stool's chrome legs, Sadie blazes with quiet misery.

Beep! My phone. *Overspent at Christmas? We can have £500 couriered to your doorstep right now.*

'Another loan company,' I remark to no one in particular.

'Why are loan companies texting you on Christmas Day?' Felix wants to know.

'Oh, it's not just loan companies,' I assure him. 'Mortgage advisers, travel companies, VD clinics. They can't get enough of me.'

Ryan is doing something. He has already consumed four of the six cans of Red Stripe he brought with him. In a Tesco carrier bag! How festive! He has reached that stage of inebriation where he clearly considers himself rather witty and believes others secretly share this view. The result is that he's performing an imitation of Flora progressing along their local high street.

'She's walking so slowly, she's practically going backwards,' he says, moving his skinny, etiolated limbs in an exaggerated slow-motion fashion. 'And her eyes are swivelling around like this.' He flicks his eyeballs, crablike, from left to right and back again.

I look at my daughter. She has a 'good sport' expression plastered to her face, but she is rigid with embarrassment.

'I only did it the once,' she says. 'I never should have told you . . .'

Flora, it seems, made the mistake of confiding in Ryan that sometimes, when she walks down a busy street, she scans the passing crowds so that in the event of there being a crime committed and witnesses sought she'll be able to provide a thorough description.

'One too many episodes of *Crimewatch*, I expect,' says Hettie sympathetically.

Flora nods, mute with misery. *Don't put up with it*, I

want to tell her. *He shouldn't do that to you. Someone who loves you shouldn't try to make you look silly.*

'Knob,' Felix whispers under his breath.

Sadie looks up, catches his eye and looks away. The back of her neck is livid red.

I notice Josh has also witnessed this exchange. His hazel eyes flick from Sadie to Felix and then back again. I remember what Felix said about getting to know Sister Sadie, and wonder if Josh is thinking along similar lines. He's had plenty of experience of how it feels to be cast aside by his older brother . . .

Now Flora has got to her feet and is rummaging around in a huge carrier bag. Presents. Oh dear God.

The first one out of the bag is for Ryan.

'Hope you haven't gone mad, doll,' he says, accepting his gift warily, as if it might explode at any moment. 'You know we're saving for a new bathroom.'

Idiot!

Inside the layers of tissue paper is a suit. Dark grey and lined with purple silk. I look at the label. Crikey!

'It's lovely and all that, doll,' says Ryan, stroking the material greedily. 'But can we really afford . . .?'

Don't finish that sentence, I urge. *Just tell her you love it.*

Now he's fishing a rather soggy package out of the Tesco carrier bag which still holds his other two beers.

'It's not much.' He's clearly embarrassed. 'We did say we wouldn't . . . with the bathroom and everything . . .'

'I don't care if it's not much, silly!' *Oh, Flora!* She makes a big show of prodding the poorly wrapped gift and holding it up to her ear to rattle it. 'Soft and squidgy!' she says, clearly delighted to be able to rule out the *Little Britain* box set she got last year.

My heart constricts as she tears into the wrapping. *Please, please, please, let it be nice, let him have chosen with care.*

'Oh, how lovely!' she says, before she's even properly opened it.

Ryan's frown uncreases slightly. 'I thought you'd like it,' he says. 'You're always complaining about the cold.'

Now Flora is gazing in silence down at her present. A matching woolly hat, scarf and gloves set. Dear God.

'It's brown,' Ryan points out unnecessarily. 'You like brown.'

She might well like brown, you cretin. Brown leather sofas, brown eyes, brown skin. But not a bloody brown angora-mix hat, scarf and gloves set. Or rather she might like it, in its place, but not as a present from her fiancé on Christmas morning. *Does he love her even?* I ask myself suddenly, and remember Flora saying once she thought Ryan might believe there are actually *four* little words rather than three, so seldom does he say 'I love you' without adding a 'but' on the end.

'Oh, that's . . . useful,' says Hettie, trying to help.

'Is it some sort of animal?' my mother wants to know, eyeing the fluffy brown heap with suspicion.

Flora is quiet. Something inside me tightens at the sight of her blue eyes gazing down on that ghastly hat. *I must go to her. I must hold her. Make the hurt go away. That's what Simon would have done.* Oh God, Simon. To think he'll never be here again. I'll never again experience that warm glow of relief at seeing my husband comforting my daughter. It's all up to me now. I must be all things to my children. It's too much responsibility. Too great a burden. Simply too much.

LOTTIE

Such an embarrassing present. The poor girl looks shattered. And look at the mother, blanching potatoes, completely oblivious. Ice in her veins, my mum would have said.

Oh, now Flora is distributing presents to everyone. Peach body scrub. Thoughtful of her. Was that tin of chocolates we brought enough? Ought we to have bought individual gifts? Ha! As if there's the money for that!

Thank God Sadie and I exchanged our presents in private this morning. I think I was more excited than she was when she opened the silver necklace. I know she liked it – I'd seen her coveting it in the jeweller's window – though all she said was 'Thanks, I thought we were broke.'

Still punishing me, I suppose, for reading her Facebook page. We had a huge row about it – just as I'd thought we would. She accused me of snooping, of spying, of invading her privacy. I said I'm her mother and have a right to know what's going on. I asked her about the cocaine. At first she refused to answer, but when I threatened to call Gabi, she admitted she'd had that one line. That was the first time she's tried it, she swore, and she'll never do it again, she said, complaining it had burnt the inside of her nose. She refused to give me the name of the boy – denied flat out it was Josh. She said it was someone from college that she wouldn't be seeing again, and when I tried to pressurize her she told me I was trying to ruin her life, just like I'd ruined my own.

I shouldn't have been disappointed about her present to

me. It's not as if I was expecting anything much, but a *goat*?

'It'll keep a family in Africa going for years,' she told me. And of course, I don't want to begrudge a family in Africa anything, but it did feel a bit like more punishment, that goat.

Look at her now, my beautiful daughter, sitting there so awkwardly on that stool. This was a mistake. We should have gone to Emma's. I thought coming here might be good for us and bring us closer to him, but instead it just reminds me how much about him I didn't know. The Simon I knew would never have been happy here in this Sunday-supplement house. All these gadgets – there's even one of those extendable chrome shower attachments next to the kitchen sink – all this money, all this *stuff*. And that woman, blanching potatoes. I bet no one ever bought *her* a goat!

SELINA

All this fuss about presents. As if any of it matters.

It's funny to think how much effort I used to put into them – giving each person a theme and scouring the shops for months beforehand for gifts, large and small, that fitted in with what I'd chosen. *Who was that woman?* The year Felix went travelling in South America, his presents were all based on a Latin theme; the year Flora moved out she had her 'Survival Kit', with everything a newly independent girl could possibly need.

But this year, I looked at shop windows heaped with

consumer goods – electronic devices, clothes, cushions, things to cook with, things to fish with, things to sit on, things to slather on your skin or run in your bath, scarves, jewellery, make-up that comes in heavy glass pots or tiny glossy black cardboard boxes embossed with gold writing – and I felt disgusted, in the same way one feels disgusted at the sight of rich food after a heavy meal. It's not even about not having money. Well, not just about not having money. Why didn't I ever notice before how much waste there is, how much gluttonous excess, how it leaves one feeling queasy and flabby around the edges? All that glitter! All that oozing, slimy velvet and silk! Too much.

Now I hand out my stack of identical envelopes.

'Are these M&S vouchers?' queries Felix, tearing his envelope open. 'Push the boat out, Madre!'

I turn my back to him. I'm tired of it all. Everyone wanting so much from me, pulling me this way and that, stretching me between them like fine pizza dough.

Now there's someone behind my back, strong arms clasping me tight, a chin resting on my shoulder.

'Poor Madre,' coos Felix's voice in my ear. 'Poor, poor Madre.'

LOTTIE

Oh, but look. How would that feel, I wonder, to have that young, handsome version of Simon putting his arms around you, loving you?

But isn't there something just a little *creepy* about it? Standing so close together, almost swaying, the mother with her eyes closed, the son with his face in her neck?

Now Selina has pulled away.

'The cabbage won't prepare itself!'

Chop, chop, chop.

SELINA

I want them all to leave.

That hug from Felix, such a sharp reminder of the human touch I miss. Not Greg, not him, not that. What I mean is the physical intimacy of being with someone you know so well (*thought you knew so well*), the million little gestures you don't even notice. Simon's hand resting like a warm compress on my thigh when I sit in the passenger seat as he drives, his arm round my shoulders when we emerge from the theatre on brisk winter evenings, his fingers stroking my toes through my tights as we watch television, my feet on his lap. The warmth of skin upon skin.

I glance at Lottie's arm where it rests on the table. So small, like a child's arm really.

When I thought he was in meetings, on building sites, sweltering under the desert sun, instead he was with her, their skin touching. Skin upon skin.

Ah, there it is! The now familiar lurch of betrayal. I wait for the nausea to come . . . No, nothing. The feeling subsides just as quickly as it arose. Emotions are too wearing, I realize now. I am emptied out like a rusty can. So he loved that other woman, with her silly hair and her soap-opera melodramas. Does it really matter? Do any of us really, in the end, have a monopoly on each other? I'm so sick of it all suddenly. Simon, Lottie, Greg. The sordidness of my life. My grief-damaged children.

My family have become like the cheap baubles on the token Christmas tree Josh dragged home at the last minute a couple of days ago – garish and over-coloured on the outside and hollow and empty on the inside, liable to shatter into a thousand pieces under the slightest pressure, each one sharp enough to draw blood.

How I wish they would all just go away.

LOTTIE

We've been summoned for lunch. The Royal Summons. I'm looking for Sadie and Josh to call them in. Flora offered to find them but I was already on my feet. Any excuse to get out of there for a few minutes. To be honest, I didn't even notice them leaving, Josh and Sadie, they just melted away while I was making small-talk with Hettie about whether it's worth paying extra for supermarket mince pies with a picture of a celebrity chef on the box.

I can hear voices coming from a room I haven't been in before, on the opposite side of the hallway from that hideous mausoleum of a living room we went in the first time we were here. Josh's low bass tones are difficult to make out behind the closed door, but just as I'm about to go in, I hear Sadie.

'Great Christmas this is – broke and soon to be homeless.'

Josh murmurs something, to which Sadie replies, 'You

wait. We'll go first, then you. It'll be like a house of cards. The house that Simon built.'

I freeze. When did my daughter get so cynical? My own stupid fault for not talking to her more about what's been going on. I thought I was protecting her, but now I see she's been gathering choice snippets of information from here and there like a magpie – piecing it all together in a patchwork approximation of the truth.

There's a lull now, but still I hover outside the door with my hand poised in the act of reaching for the handle.

Now Sadie resumes speaking. 'Did you like him? Dad, I mean?'

The word 'Dad' feels like a stone in my stomach. For all these years it has belonged to Sadie exclusively – only she had the right to say 'Dad' and for it to mean Simon, with his squidgy left knee, the legacy of a teenage skiing accident, and the mole on his shoulder he kept under anxious observation. ('Do you think it's changed shape?' he'd ask. 'Is it darker than it was?') Now she tosses it out for Josh to share as carelessly as an old tennis ball. I'm astonished how much I mind.

The question clearly embarrasses Josh – even through the solid door I sense his discomfort as he replies, 'Yeah, he was all right, I s'pose.'

Sadie murmurs in what sounds like agreement.

'Yeah, he was better than my mum anyway,' she says. The hurt is instant, vicious. Stupidly, my eyes blur with tears. 'But sometimes,' she continues, 'I used to feel as if I had to, I dunno, entertain him or something.'

To my surprise, Josh laughs.

'I thought that was just me!' he says. 'Sometimes I used to rehearse what I was going to say to him in my head –

d'you know what I mean? – to make sure it was interesting enough.'

I'm shocked to hear Simon's youngest son voicing what
I never admitted even to myself, that I'd occasionally run
through a story in my mind before telling it to Simon,
polishing it up to make it more worth listening to.

From the kitchen comes the sound of someone shouting,
'Going cold!' Hettie perhaps, or maybe Petra.

Josh and Sadie instantly fall silent and I grab the handle
and push open the door.

SELINA

When I look down the table at all the half-eaten food,
glistening under the downlighters – a clot of mashed swede
in an earthenware container, overcooked Brussels sprouts
with chestnuts that leave a slimy trail of greeny-brown
across the plates, the desiccated carcass of the turkey, one
uneaten leg pointing grotesquely at the ceiling – I feel
sickened by it all. All this excess. All this waste.

Lottie has hardly touched her food, just pushed it
around her plate with her fork. She probably has an eating
disorder. She seems like the type. Anything to make herself
seem more interesting. She thinks I don't know what she
was doing when she disappeared off earlier. She said she
went to get Josh and Sadie – as if it really takes that long
to walk down the hall! *Had a good poke about, did you?*
I want to say, but I don't. I'm supposed to be nice because
of the thing she did with the sleeping pills, because she's
pregnant, because I'm older. But I'm sick of being the

bigger person. I'm sick of holding it together. I want to scoop up the uneaten food from her plate and smash it right into her face. I want to curl up in the middle of the table, amid the leftover roast potatoes in their puddle of congealing fat and the gravy with its thick wrinkled skin, and scream until I can't scream any more.

Instead, I purse my lips together, so the bad thoughts can't come out.

'It's amazing about your mortgage being paid,' I say through my tightly pressed lips, the words emerging thin and flattened. 'You must be sitting pretty now.'

I don't mention the secret account, but she knows that's what I'm thinking of. No mortgage on her flat, a nice little nest-egg in an offshore bank. No wonder she's looking so smug – rubbing her neat little bump under the table with a Madonna-style smirk on her face.

'I wouldn't exactly say that,' she says.

'Oh, come on.' I keep my voice light, sifting the hard lumps of bile from it before letting it out. 'You've done pretty well for yourself out of all this, surely? Ironic really that your mortgage has been paid off thanks to this "anonymous benefactor"' – I make exaggerated quote marks in the air when I say this – 'while I'm still saddled with the one Simon took out to pay for your flat!'

'Mum!' Josh's voice is raw with embarrassment.

'It's OK, Josh. I'm not criticizing, merely stating fact. And you've got no idea who this "anonymous benefactor" is?'

I've turned back to Lottie to ask the question, and I say it with a slight smile. It occurs to me suddenly that there's only one possibility, as far as I can see – another lover somewhere in the wings. She's waiting until all the fuss over Simon's death dies down to introduce him. Probably the baby isn't even Simon's.

I allow myself to be carried away by this fantasy until she speaks.

'Actually, we're not "sitting pretty"' – *oh, so she can work the quote-mark gesture too* – 'as you call it at all.' She does an ugly thing with her mouth when she says 'sitting pretty', pulling her lips back like a snarling dog. 'I had a phone call from Greg Ronaldson yesterday morning.'

The heat rushes to my face. Am I blushing? Does she know?

'He's been talking to Simon's solicitor. Apparently, because I wasn't legally married to Simon, I'm not exempt from inheritance tax. If I can't come up with thirty-six thousand pounds, I'll lose my home.'

LOTTIE

We shouldn't have come.

After that nightmare lunch (*'anonymous benefactor'* – surely everyone can guess it's Simon), we're all being so polite, on our best behaviour. I want to put my head in my hands and howl like a wolf, I swear to God.

A layer of torpor lies over us like fake snow. How long before we can leave?

The girlfriend Petra is trying so hard. A lovely girl. If I had any sympathy left inside me, I'd feel quite sorry for her. What was he saying, the son, about self-harming? You never know, do you, what goes on behind closed doors?

'I know,' she says. 'Let's play horse/currant bun. We played it at the agency the other week.'

She works in a modelling agency, I think. It figures.

'Basically everyone in the world falls into one of two categories. They're either horses, or they're currant buns.'

I don't know what she's talking about, but that's nothing new at the moment.

'How can people be horses or currant buns?' The old lady, Selina's mother, looks puzzled, and who can blame her? 'Do you mean they look like a horse, or sound like one?'

'It's not about physical resemblance,' says Petra. 'It's more a general sense of horse-ness or currant-bun-ness. You know it immediately. Go on, think of someone. Think of Obama.'

'Oh that's easy,' says Hettie. 'Horse!' She's all right actually, Hettie. I thought she'd be a bitch, being Selina's best friend and everything, but you can tell she's making a real effort. Best foot forward, stiff upper lip – she's that type.

'Exactly!' You can sense Petra's gratitude a mile off.

'I don't understand.' Flora is shaking her head. 'Why is President Obama a horse?'

'He just is,' says Petra. 'OK, here's an easy one. James Corden.'

'Currant bun!' we all chorus dutifully.

There's a sense of relief now, flowering amongst us all. Such an awkward situation, but look how we're making it work! See us all laughing together! *Howling inside, though.*

'Oh, I see.' Flora is smiling. 'It's about being fat. Fat people are currant buns and thin people are horses.'

No, no, that's not it.

'I've got it now!' Flora continues, excited like a puppy. 'Simon Cowell?'

'Currant bun!' we all shout, at exactly the same moment as Flora shouts, 'Horse!'

Oh dear. Oh how awkward.

'It's not a question of physique, doll.' Flora's boyfriend is talking now. He sounds so patronizing. 'It's just something indescribable. Take Posh and Becks.'

Ah, Posh and Becks. Now that's an easy one.

'Now Becks is unquestionably . . .'

'. . . a horse!' we chorus.

'Whereas Posh is – well, I think anyway – a currant bun.'

'Oh, come on,' the older son, Felix, interjects, looking cross. 'I don't think that's true. You're stretching the point.'

Petra is clearly keen to avoid arguments. This is her game, after all. Her responsibility. 'I think Posh may have horse pretensions,' she says. 'But deep down she's a currant bun.'

'I assume by currant bun you mean something like a tea cake?' Selina's mother is still trying to work out what's going on. 'Marks and – oh you know, what's the name? – *Sausages* do a very good one.'

Now everyone is going around the room saying what each of us is. *That's it – keep the game going. Our relentless goodwill will force the situation to work.* Felix is a horse, Sadie, my baby, undoubtedly a horse. Weasly-faced Ryan, also a horse. Flora, plain currant bun.

'But I don't want to be a currant bun,' she wails. 'All the least attractive people you've mentioned have been currant bun. It's not fair. I want to be a horse!'

SELINA

Oh, poor Flora. It isn't fair.

And my poor mother, sitting there with her silly paper hat. She used to be so glamorous. She was always rushing out of the door to some event or other while I tried to hold her back. Where does it go, the time?

I'm worried about my children. Josh is laughing now, but I fear he is stashing his feelings away inside him the way he used to smuggle sweets from the sweet cupboard in his trouser pockets when he thought I wasn't looking. I've seen the way he looks at Sadie. Or rather, the way he *doesn't* look at her. Such a giveaway. My poor boy.

Felix has gone upstairs after that little spat with Petra about that silly game. Will they split up? It's none of my business, but even so . . . Mightn't it be for the best?

Ah, here he comes. Sniffing again.

'You really must take more care of yourself,' I tell him. 'You've got a perpetual cold.'

For some reason, Josh seems to find this wildly funny. So weird sometimes, my sons. So *other*.

They feel it very strongly, I think, boys. The sins of the father. How will Simon's actions affect how my sons are in the world, what they become? The newspapers here have been full of that disgraced American financier recently – what's his name? – and his middle-aged son who committed suicide, unable to cope with it all. So much to worry about.

Josh will be all right in the end, I think. He's definitely the more emotionally robust of the two. He has more sense of himself, which surely makes him more able to see

Simon as a separate entity whose failings were entirely his own. But Felix?

I remember an occasion. How old was Felix then? Four? Five? He is playing in a garishly coloured plastic car in the garden, twisting the steering wheel this way and that, pretending to be his father driving whatever flash car Simon had at the time.

Simon appears at the French windows in his suit, his case already packed on the floor behind him.

'I'm off,' he says to me. I'm lying on a lounger, I recall. One of a set of stripy ones I was very fond of.

Simon squats down in front of his son, blocking his path.

'You look after your mother,' he says, his tone mock-serious. 'You're the man of the house now.'

Felix looked up at him with a face full of . . . what? Worry? Pride? Triumph? It was always a power struggle between those two, a locking of horns. When one moved one way, the other would move the other way to compensate. No sense of separation. Where does that leave Felix? The boy who grew up defining himself in terms of what his father was not?

We stayed in the garden that day, Felix and I, watching Simon turn his back and leave. The sun was glorious, as it always is in memories, and the flowerbeds hummed lazily with the sound of summer.

Or did they? Now I'm not so sure. Suddenly I'm doubting.

Were we, in fact, inside the house when that scene occurred, with Felix crashing around in his car from room to room while rain rendered the garden out of bounds? Rather than gaily waving Simon off, did I instead glare pointedly at his packed case, brooding with the resentment of the house-bound parent?

That's the problem with memory, isn't it? You're always so convinced you're right, that the way you remember it is exactly the way it happened, until a completely different version of reality presents itself, and then suddenly you're convinced about that too.

Anyway, whichever version is correct, I'm sure about what happened next, after Simon went.

'Don't worry, Mummy,' said Felix. I can still see his little face looking up at me through the years and the decades that have passed since then. 'You don't need Daddy. You've got me.'

21

SELINA

A job.

Seriously?

When Hettie first rang and told me that the junior department of Josh's school needs a new teaching assistant, I dismissed it out of hand. Whenever I've thought about my triumphant return to the world of work, I've always envisaged something in PR, or journalism maybe. Not a teaching assistant. But Hettie didn't waste any time in setting me right. She didn't actually use the phrase 'beggars can't be choosers'. She didn't have to. Much as I love Hettie, there was something vaguely unseemly about her zeal as she urged me to apply. I've noticed there are few things that make a woman more impassioned than advocating on behalf of someone else something she'd rather die than do herself.

But lying awake the night before the start of the new school term, fretting about money, or the lack of it, moving it around in my head from current account to unpaid bill to credit card in a ghastly choreographed dance, I realized I didn't have much choice. A job at the school would give me an income *and* a sizeable discount on Josh's fees.

The funny thing is, I always meant to have a career somewhere down the line. I remember, very early on, going to a party where a woman with bright-pink lipstick asked me what I did and laughed out loud when I said, 'I'm a homemaker.' When Simon and I got home I was livid. Felix was still very small. 'Of course I'll get a job once he's old enough,' I said. But then came Flora, followed by Josh. We'd bought the house in Barnes, which needed a total overhaul, and then the place in Tuscany, and there never seemed like a right time. 'Do you miss it?' Simon asked just once. 'Having something outside of the family, something that's just yours?'

At the time I was defensive, feeling judged by him. 'My family and my home are what's mine,' I bristled. 'I'll come into my own when the children are grown, don't worry.' But of course, I didn't. There was always another project ... and then another ... And now here I am at fifty-one, without any marketable skills and potentially broke.

The truth is I'm not really doing poverty very well.

It's the humiliation of it that affects me most, the way everyone has to know about it. Like Josh's head teacher when I went to see her before Christmas. We share (*used to share*) a hair-stylist, so we've always had a sort of bond, and I suppose she was as understanding as she could be in the circumstances, agreeing that I could pay this term's fees at the end of the term rather than the beginning. But she made it crystal clear she could do no more.

'We're in the midst of a recession,' she said solemnly, gazing at me through the vase of calla lilies on her desk. 'Many of our parents work in the City and have been greatly damaged by what has happened there. I'd love to make an exception for you, Mrs Busfield. I do sympathize immensely with your . . . predicament.' She looked away when she said that word, 'predicament', as if it were something indelicate. 'But the fact is that if I made an exception for you, I'd be setting a precedent for all those other parents in similar positions of financial stress, and, much as I'd like to, we simply cannot afford to let the school run at a loss or standards would suffer. You can appreciate that, I'm sure.'

I could indeed appreciate it. Just as I appreciate that my Chelsea gym can't allow me to go into arrears in membership fees and that my private healthcare insurance has lapsed now that Simon is no longer paying his premiums. I appreciate, too, that I can no longer nip into the little boutique in the village to pre-order a few key items from the forthcoming season's catalogue. 'Hello, stranger,' Maria, the boutique manager, said the last time I gave in to temptation and popped my head inside. Immediately I knew it to be a mistake. The clothes with those monstrous price tags. Another world, another era. 'Sorry,' I told her, backing out of the door. 'I'm just so busy these days.'

The fact is that the chasm that opened up in my life when Simon died has sucked everything into it – marriage, status, the lifestyle I took for granted, all the trappings that define who I am.

It's funny how I never used to think of myself as well off, just comfortable. Only now can I see how much I took for granted. Did I really buy packets of freshly ground coffee from the deli for £7.90? Did I book flights to Florence without bothering to shop around for cheap deals, often changing them at the last minute at vast expense when other things got in the way? Now it seems absurd that I used to go to bed night after night with nothing more to worry about than whether I should, after all, have plumped for the stalls rather than the circle, or bought the mocha coat as well as the ivory.

Where is that other profligate Selina now? She isn't here. She isn't me.

The real Selina, the current, impecunious Selina, is sitting in the office of Briony North, the head of the lower school, who, even though I've never met her before today, clearly regards the Saving of Selina Busfield as her new mission in life.

'How have you been coping?' she whispers, standing so close behind my chair I can feel her breath on my neck, and laying a hand on my shoulder.

This is what I hate – the way perfect strangers feel they have the right to come into my personal space because they know things about my life. What Simon did has turned me into public property.

I fidget with the clear plastic folder in my hand which contains the bullet-pointed list I made of my 'skills set' (I've been Googling it – the jargon of the job market) and excerpts from scientific studies which purport to show how running a household equates to experience in the workplace. I came prepared for everything. Except pity.

'Oh, you know,' I say. 'Bearing up.'

Oh dear God. I have turned into the kind of woman who says *bearing up*.

Briony North nods violently above my head, and her grip on my shoulder tightens.

'Of course you are,' she murmurs.

'I've brought along a CV,' I say, desperate to change the subject.

'Why don't we just have a little chat to start with,' she says, pulling up a chair so close to mine she's practically sitting on my lap. 'I just want you to know how much I – well, all of us really – have been feeling for you and what you've been going through.'

My knuckles are white, as I clutch the folder. *Please make her stop.*

'Thank you, I appreciate that. Which is why getting a job is so important to me. I'm sure you understand.'

At the word 'understand' Briony is nodding again – clearly a Pavlovian response. She has reddish-brown curls that bob up and down as she nods, revealing coral earrings shaped like sea horses.

'Of course, of course.'

I remember now Josh talking about her once. Didn't one of his friends' dads find her profile on Guardian Soulmates? Listed as something like 'DreamsDoComeTrue'? Yes, I'm sure it was Briony. 'Separated, 37, looking for fellow dreamer, must love cats.'

Businesslike now, Briony reaches behind her and plucks a ring-binder from her desk. 'Teaching Assistant Position' reads the self-important label attached to the front with clear plastic tape.

She opens it and leafs briskly through, wetting the fore-finger of her right hand as she turns the pages. It's a habit I've always hated. She stops on one page and runs her eyes along the print before marking her place with a well-manicured finger. I brace myself for the serious questioning to start.

Pausing, finger poised at the relevant point, Briony North looks at me.

'And how is Josh *bearing up*?' she asks.

LOTTIE

So I survived Christmas without my sisters.

I should get it printed on a T-shirt, or a bumper sticker.

It wasn't much fun. All right, it was hideous. But we survived. And Jules and Emma survived too. Happily, *gallingly*, they seem even to have thrived. Jules spent Christmas Day having a curry with friends, followed by a waifs and strays party where they played charades and forced each other to drink eggnog, while Emma and Ben had a cosy family Christmas for once, which, I suspect, is what he's been wanting for years. And Jules admits that when she went up on Boxing Day, without me there, she and Emma had far fewer rows than usual. Strange how family dynamics shift, depending on who's around.

All good then. So why do I feel so awful?

Hmmm . . . let's think about that one. My husband who wasn't my husband is dead. My home is at risk. My daughter is lost.

Oh yes, and I'm pregnant.

Pregnant. It still seems so unlikely. I mean, Simon and I weren't exactly taking precautions, but we hadn't been bothered with that for years, not minding if another baby came along. I'd just assumed it wouldn't happen now. I certainly wasn't trying. But while my head is in denial, my body isn't in any doubt. The sickness has already started, waves of nausea whenever I change position. Coming home from work the other day, I had to make an emergency dash off the Tube and stand with my back against the platform wall and my hands on my knees, fighting an urge to vomit. How long has it been since there were bins on Underground platforms? Why have I never noticed the lack of them before?

At home I lurch from one horizontal position to another – bed to sofa to bath to bed – lugging my body around like a bumper sack of lentils from the cash 'n' carry. I have no energy, no get-up-and-go. I am turning into Slug Woman.

Jules has bought me a CD of Yoga for Pregnancy and I've forced myself to try it out. I'm sitting cross-legged on the living-room rug, waiting for it to start.

'Concentrate on your breathing,' commands the low, calm voice. Strange how when you're not thinking about it, breathing is so effortless, but once you focus on it, you almost forget how to do it, your breath emerging in self-conscious, uneven gasps.

'Imagine you're a plant,' says the voice. 'Imagine your body is the stem, and your head is the flower, delicately balancing on the top. Wobble your flower a bit.'

I wobble my flower. Not bad. I wobble again, more confidently. Mid-wobble, my phone goes. Thank God, I've been trying to get hold of Sadie for ages. But it's just Jules, ringing to check up on me.

'What are you doing?' she asks.

'Wobbling my flower,' I reply.

I tell her I've been back from work an hour and Sadie still isn't home.

'She's sixteen,' says Jules. 'She's spreading her wings.'

It's all right for Jules, she hasn't got any children. She

thinks an hour is just an hour. She doesn't understand that tightness in your ribcage when you think of all the terrible things that can happen to a sixteen-year-old girl in the space of sixty minutes. I tell her I don't want Sadie to have any wings, I tell her I want my daughter to have useless decorative wings like an ostrich.

'You're sounding better,' says Jules. 'More like your old self.'

For some reason that makes me feel worse. Why would I want to be like my old self, when my old self was a naive, blind, trusting fool who people pretended to marry and then left impregnated and alone?

After the call, I give up on the CD and crawl into bed. Sometimes I think I should move into my bed permanently. I spend most of my life in here as it is. I actually think I could almost be happy if I knew I never had to get out of bed again. My sketchbook is open on the duvet next to me. I'm on to S now. Sad, Stupid, Self-deluded.

It's so hard to concentrate when my mind is all over the place. Though it's not yet dinner time, it's pitch black outside my window. I must get up and pull the curtains. I feel so exposed in here with the light on. The studio out in the dark garden looms up like something huge and monstrous.

Sadie really ought to be home by now. I pick up my phone and press her number. It goes straight to voicemail, as it did the last two times I tried – so infuriating!

'Sadie, remember our agreement!' I say crossly, when her voice tells me to 'Leave a message, yeah?' 'I pay your phone bill but you *have* to pick up. We agreed!'

My voice becomes shrill at the end and grates even on my own ears.

Where is she?

I never used to be a worried parent. Dubai was a bubble anyway, where kids were ferried around from international school to pool to shopping mall. But even back here I was relaxed at first. Simon and I used to argue about it, how much freedom I gave Sadie. 'She's finding her feet,' I'd tell him when he challenged me about letting her roam the streets aimlessly with her friends. 'It's a shock to her system. She's just trying to fit in.'

I never fussed. Until what happened to Simon happened.

What's the worst thing that could happen?

Now I see danger lurking everywhere. Her phone will make her a target for muggers. No phone means she'll be cornered in an alley without being able to summon help. Or she'll lose her way, take a wrong turn somewhere. It's a foreign country for her, really, here. Opportunists will spot her and lure her away. She'll look the wrong way when she crosses the road (*how many times did I do that myself, in the early days?*), she'll get in with the wrong crowd (*that Facebook chat with Gabi – Sadie's head bent over a toilet seat*), won't feel able to say 'no'. Drugs, binge drinking bullies, self-harming (*surely not Petra – she didn't seem the type*). I've watched the way Sadie eats her food, dividing it on the plate into different food groups, making sure none of them touch. Is she anorexic? OCD? When she goes to the loo I listen out for sounds of vomiting or muffled crying. Has she got low self-esteem? Is she lonely? Does she visit suicide websites on the net or strike up online friendships with paedophiles pretending to be teenagers?

Even the house isn't safe. I swear to God I hear footsteps pacing and breathing in the night. In the morning I hunt for prints in the soil outside her bedroom window.

So many things that could go wrong. I can't bear it.

She's always secretive these days, Sadie. Always disappearing into her room with her phone, or staying out without telling me where she's been.

Who will protect her, my baby, now that Simon has gone? I close my ears against the voice in my head that points out there's only me.

SELINA

'I told you!'

Hettie is exultant. Something has gone right at last, a reason to celebrate. (Maybe I'm finally turning back into the Selina she knew.)

'I knew you'd get it. The school is far more interested in your ability to do the job than the murky details of your private life.'

I smile, but the word 'murky' lodges in my throat like a fish bone.

'So that's the job sorted. How are you getting on with the other thing?' Hettie wants to know.

I look down at the sheaf of papers in my hand. Property particulars. Can I really be thinking of selling the house? Our family home? It doesn't seem real somehow.

'Don't think of it as downsizing,' says Hettie now. 'Think of it as a lifestyle change.'

Easy for her to say. She's not the one changing lifestyles.

The estate agent's in which I'm sitting while on the phone to Hettie looks like the inside of an Ikea showroom – all bright-red furnishings, bright-green painted walls and smooth wood-laminated floors.

Everything is Bright! Fresh! Stylish!

To take my mind off all the properties that are Small! Pokey! Bland!

Saying goodbye to Hettie, I turn my attention to the first one in the pile. Peach-coloured living room and a built-in walnut television cabinet? What possesses people? The second has a nicely designed kitchen but hardly any garden. The third is better, but only has three bedrooms. Could I? Could we? I squint at the wide-angled colour photograph that squashes an armchair into a squat low-slung sofa, all oak flooring and bespoke bookshelves, and try to imagine all my prints and photographs hanging in the cramped living space.

But I do have to sell the house. That much is clear. Once Probate is finally settled, I'll have to start paying interest on the mortgage my husband so thoughtfully bequeathed me – unless the inquest rules out suicide, but the police have already hinted that's unlikely. I'm trying to be practical about it, not to think about the pencil-markings on the door-frame to the garage mapping the children's growth over the years, or the way you could scrape off the paint in the boys' bedrooms and reveal layer upon layer of their childhood selves, from sailboat-print wallpaper to black teen rebellion (Felix) to current neutrals. I must just train myself not to see my house as a home any longer. The half of it that hasn't been mortgaged (*my half!*) will buy a reasonable flat, or a much smaller house somewhere else. Yes, it's the place where my children grew up, but the family life we lived there was a lie, all my memories of it now tainted.

Was anything real – all those dinner parties, kids' birthdays, Sunday lunches that spread like butter across lazy afternoons?

Funny, the only memories I trust now are of arguments. And there weren't many of those. Simon and I were never really ones for rows.

A memory comes to mind suddenly of one quarrel we once had. We were sitting in the den, on the sofa. I can't remember what started it. I think it might have been about one of the children. Felix, mostly probably. Simon thought he got his own way too much, at the expense of the other two. Things got heated, that much I do remember. I stomped off to bed, expecting him to follow on straight after to apologize, as he usually did. In the event, I lay there alone for hours, staring up into the darkness and bristling with resentment. Much later he slipped in beside me. For a while we lay rigidly side by side, like railway sleepers. Then he turned to me.

'Do you ever wonder if you might be happier with someone else?'

Well!

The shock of it!

But after the shock died down, there was a split-second when I thought about what he'd said – starting afresh with someone who was actually *there*, not forever missing. Building a life around a presence rather than an absence. I'd never asked to be this person who shopped, entertained, nagged, held the fort. Was there a chance that, aligned to a different man, I could become someone else?

Then – clang! Just like that, the doors of fantasy slammed shut. If you started thinking that way, where would it end?

'No,' I told him. And my voice was terse and dry as toast. 'I never think like that. Do you?'

He was aggravatingly silent after that, turning away, his back broad as a shield, until I couldn't help myself.

'I don't know what you expect me to say to something like that! What were you hoping to hear?'

'It doesn't matter,' he said. 'I'm very tired.'

Afterwards I lay awake, listening to his breathing and trying not to think of what it meant, what *he* meant. I'm surprised our bedroom ceiling doesn't still bear the imprint of my glare from that night – that'd flummox the surveyors when they come round!

LOTTIE

It's not snooping, looking through her room. It's being concerned. It's what Good Mothers do. She's only sixteen, for God's sake, and if she won't tell me where it is she keeps disappearing to, what else am I supposed to do? We had such a row the other night when she came home and went straight to her room and wouldn't tell me where she'd been. 'Out,' she says. As if that should be enough.

Her phone isn't here, of course, it's surgically attached to her like a colostomy bag or something. But there's a padded notebook under her bed. I recognize it instantly from my own teenage notebooks – full of song lyrics, bits of poetry, doodles of flowers and huge weeping eyes, a few comments in other handwriting – from her friends, pre-sumably (the language they use now!). I sit on her bed and leaf through the notebook, which belongs to someone young and hopeful and funny and dreamy – the part of herself Sadie now keeps hidden from me, like a museum that locks its most precious exhibits out of public sight. And then I reach a page near the back.

'I love him,' she's written, in a violet-coloured pen. 'I love him. I love him.'

22

SELINA

It's a mistake.

I knew it from the moment I walked in, shaking off my umbrella from the sudden downpour outside, and saw him sitting here. I've never seen Greg wearing anything but a suit before, and his long-sleeved, mushroom-coloured polo shirt and precise jeans come as a shock. Some men aren't cut out for casual-wear.

Already the idea that I was ever naked with him, this stranger, seems preposterous. I look back on those three months after the funeral and it's like a sickness. It wasn't me. That woman in the hotel rooms doing those things. Yet another Selina, to add to all those other imposters. What do I know about this Greg, after all? That he has an 'understanding' wife tucked away somewhere? That he knew my husband? That he gasps, 'Do it, do it, DO IT!' when he climaxes and digs his fingers into the top of my arms and stares into my eyes as if he has no idea who I am?

The Festival Hall lobby bar on a weekday evening in February is busy but not packed. There's a string quartet playing Gershwin tunes in a corner, the violinist twisting her torso from the waist as she plays like a puppet. Greg is sitting on one of the red leather sofas when I come in, and he's already ordered me a glass of white wine. I feel a prickle of irritation. *How presumptuous! What makes him think he knows what I want?*

Incredible to think that at the beginning I thought him quite urbane. Now he shifts around in his seat, clearly ill at ease, and taps his feet in their ugly grey suede trainers. When I sit down next to him he puts his hand briefly on my knee, then looks at my face and removes it again without speaking. We both know that whatever it was, it isn't any more. It's over.

'You look lovely as ever,' he says, although his eyes slide right off me. 'Nice to see you dressed down for a change.'

Me, dressed down! I glance down at my clothes in surprise. A long cashmere jumper, narrow jeans, boots. Casual, sure, but not dressed down, surely not slobby? It's my hair, I expect, longer, less styled. Or maybe a general loosening. I don't spend quite as much time in front of the mirror now I no longer care quite so much. But still, 'dressed down' is going too far.

'Are you sure this is OK?' Greg asks. 'Us meeting here, I mean. Not too many awful associations?'

He's talking about being on the South Bank, so near to Southwark, the last place Simon was seen alive.

'It's fine,' I say. 'I had to face it some time.'

We talk about my finances. Or rather my lack of finances. Greg has news on the Italian house, which he's been trying to sell on behalf of Simon's estate.

'The Italian agent thought we might have trouble, but a buyer has come forward almost straight away,' he says. 'We'll have to wait for Probate, of course, and there won't

DEPRESSION

be much money left over, not after the bank has been paid and all the various property taxes. But at least it's one less thing to worry about. That place was a financial liability.'

I'm sure he thinks I should be relieved, but the loss of the house in Tuscany feels like a physical wound. Looking back, I think it's the place where I've been happiest . . . as well as unhappiest.

'Have you had any luck, Selina,' Greg wants to know, 'with tracing that bank account?'

Who am I, Sherlock bloody Holmes?

Greg is looking awful. His skin is blotchy, his eyes hooded. He looks like someone who hasn't been sleeping well, like someone keeping secrets.

'You're involved, aren't you?' I ask. It hits me yet again. *Of course!* 'In whatever Simon was up to. Those back-handers you were talking about. You're involved in it too.'

Greg's faces sags suddenly and I see a flash of the old man he will be. I'm sorry for him, I realize. It's not his fault, all this. He never pretended to be anything he wasn't. I just saw what I wanted at the time. I sewed my expectations on to him like sequins.

His eyes are on mine, grey and sad, and I have a sudden urge to lean forward and give him a hug, just because he looks so alone and defeated. But I don't want him to get the wrong idea.

'I don't know what you're talking about, Selina,' he says, looking away.

'You're hiding things, Greg,' I say.

He looks up at me wearily. *Such tired eyes.*

'Selina, darling, we're all hiding things. Haven't you learned that by now?'

He's impatient now, anger peeling away his usual mask

305

of insouciance, and for the first time I get a glimpse of the real face underneath. It takes me a second to put a name to the expression etched into each pore and crevice, each line and purple shadow. Then it comes to me: disappointment. Whatever Greg Ronaldson once thought he might be, it's a long way from the person he's become.

'What are you scared of?' I ask him, noting how the disappointment is tinged also with fear.

'There have been a couple of strange texts,' he says, giggling abruptly, as if what he is about to say will sound ridiculous. 'Quite threatening ones.'

'From those people you think Simon was involved with?' I'm floundering, struggling to make sense of this new, unfamiliar world, where right and wrong seem to dance around like the reflections of the sun on a dark wood floor, impossible to pin down.

'Presumably,' says Greg. 'They didn't give much away, just said they were "friends" of Simon's. They want their money, Selina.'

'Have you called the p—'

Greg raises a hand to cut me off mid-sentence, and as he does so, he slides the mask back on, obscuring the face where disappointment and fear have become like extra features in addition to the usual nose and eyes and mouth.

'Let's not talk about this boring stuff,' he says. 'Let's talk about you and me and nice things.'

We both know it's just a line. There is no him and me. The nice things, if indeed that's what they were, are in the past. Yet still he feels he must play on, spinning his lines, even though neither of us believes them any more. It occurs to me that Greg Ronaldson probably doesn't know a different way, that this – the easy flattery, the hand on the thigh – is the only form of interaction he has.

'Shall I get us a bottle of wine?' he asks, while behind him the violinist contorts her body and tosses her hair.

'I don't think so,' I say, getting up to leave.

Now I'm pushing out through the swing doors and on to the riverside. Despite the rain there's a man busking with a guitar, his fingers swaddled in fingerless gloves, singing a maudlin song about how everyone he knows goes away in the end. He's right, of course. Everyone does go away in the end. And then what does it count for? All the hard work and the emotional investment, all the early mornings and long nights, the tears, the boredom, the dashes to the late-night chemist when the other one is ill, the disillusionment, the compromises, the endless negotiations. 'I've settled for you,' said the woman in Felix's film. Maybe in the end we all settle, just to be left with nothing.

I leave the throngs of tourists behind on the brightly lit embankment, and pick my way through the puddles round the back to the road which runs behind the Festival Hall and the Hayward Gallery, where I've parked my car. It's semi-deserted and feels desolate and gloomy after the buzz of the riverbank. Hurrying towards my Fiat, I notice a pale shape on the windscreen. *Fuck. Just what I need. A parking ticket.* Getting closer, I notice it's actually a piece of paper that has been carefully placed under one of the wipers. A flyer then. That's a relief. It's very cold and I can't wait to get home.

But it isn't a flyer. The paper, I see when I take it out, is a lined page, smooth and heavy and slightly creamy and glistening with rain. It looks as if it has been torn from a notebook – it's neatly folded, the crease needle-sharp. I glance around. There's no one here. Just the odd deserted car and the shadows of the bins lining the pavement on the far side – London lurking in the dark, as it does sometimes.

When I open it up, the writing inside is also neat and perfectly centred. Using blue ink now starting to blur in the rain, someone has written in completely even capital letters: HE ISN'T WORTH IT.

Someone. Here. Watching. Following.

I stand by the car, reading over and over. As if repetition might unlock some clue.

Heart. Thumping. Pulse. Racing.

Was it always this dark here? The windowless, hulking backs of buildings, sacks of rubbish crouching in the shadows.

A couple come lurching out of the darkness, arguing.

'You never organize anything,' the woman complains, her voice shrill in the still, damp air. 'If it was left to you, we'd have no social life at all.'

'Good,' says the man. 'Our social life is shit.'

As they pass, they glare at me, as if I'm a voyeur who has chosen to listen in to their squabble rather than have it foisted on me. I fumble in my bag for my keys and they resume their argument.

'If it's that shit, you should just stay home,' the woman says.

In the car, I lock the doors.

'Shit,' I say to myself out loud, just to hear the sound of my own voice. 'Shit, shit, shit.'

Now that I'm safely locked inside my car, I start to doubt. There must be some mistake, surely. I must have misinterpreted the note. I switch on the inside light and take out the paper again, then smooth it out on my lap. The same blue writing. The same vaguely threatening words.

Someone watched me park my car. Someone followed me inside. Did they see Greg's hand on my knee? Did they hear what we said?

Driving west through London, I can feel the note burning through the denim of my jeans. I turn on the radio to mask the pounding of my own blood in my ears. There's a programme on Radio Four about Love Poetry. *Not Valentine's yet, surely?*

'I gave myself to him like a present,' a woman reads in a soft, West Country accent. 'And afterwards he said/ Did you keep the receipt?'

It doesn't sound very romantic to me. But then, what do I know about romance?

Next up is a man who sounds as if he is reading a sermon rather than a poem.

'I carry my phone in my breast pocket/ set to vibrate,' he intones solemnly. 'When you call, it feels like/ my heart is humming.'

How does that feel, I wonder, being that much in love? I try to imagine it, but I can't. Maybe I just don't have the gene for love. Not love like that. An image flashes into my head of Lottie, sitting on the edge of her bed, feeding pills into her mouth. Is that what true love is? Feeling like you can't exist because the other person doesn't exist, that you cannot possibly remain without them? I try to think of a time when I felt like that about Simon, but nothing comes. Even at the beginning, I was very much me, and he was very much him. We complemented each other, but we didn't feed off each other in that way. So maybe we did 'settle', like the couple in Felix's film. Sometimes when I look back on our married life together it seems like one compromise after another – I picture them all lined up in a row like squares on a board game. But what's the alternative? That destructive, overpowering force that sweeps everything in front of it and makes a grown woman eat sleeping pills like Tic Tacs? I'm better off as I am. I'm tired of feelings, tired of passion. I long for peace, I long for order, for lists and diaries and on-screen reminders. No more notes on cars, no more seedy hotel rooms, no more feeling like everything is galloping away from my control.

HE ISN'T WORTH IT.

Oh God, please make it all just go away.

23

LOTTIE

Sadie's fury is like a physical force-field around her, like that old breakfast-cereal ad where the kid walks around all day wrapped in an invisible thermal layer.

I focus on the road in front and on remembering how to drive. *Clutch, shift, second – no that's fourth!* Simon was always the one who drove. I'd never in a million years have ventured out on the roads in Dubai. You take your life in your hands there just travelling in a car, let alone driving one. And in London, I've never really needed one. We bought this one, a second-hand VW Golf, just for Simon to get around in whenever he was here, but even he didn't use it much. He loathed it really. 'It's so not me,' he used to rage, as if a car could define you. But now that I'm Knocked Up, I'm trying to get used to being behind the wheel again. 'It could save your life, hun,' Jules told me. 'Who knows when you might have to make an emergency dash to hospital.' Looking on the bright side as ever! *What's the worst thing that could happen?*

It's fair to say the parents' evening didn't go well.

'We have some, um, concerns about Sadie,' said her form tutor, also her English teacher, who looked like he

311

wasn't old enough to shave, let alone discuss the finer points of *The Merchant of Venice*, or *Wuthering Heights,* or any of the other texts I've only just discovered they're supposed to be covering. Why didn't she tell me she needed to buy the books? How embarrassing to find out she's been coming to class completely unequipped. She ought to have said!

We were in the dining hall, which was rammed with laminate tables where teachers sat, frozen with fear, behind cardboard name signs, like exhibits in a zoo, while parents queued and jostled and pushed and tried not to look like they were eavesdropping on each other's consultations.

Sadie glared down at her lap, not meeting anyone's eyes. She was still angry because I wouldn't change my dress before we came out. 'I'm sorry if I embarrass you, but it's an academic review, not a fashion show,' I said, not wanting her to see I was hurt by her criticism of my clothes. What's wrong with this dress, for God's sake? I glance down at it now – deep red, with a black panel up the middle, stretching over the gentle curve of my belly.

'Obviously we understand things have been very tough for her – for you both, of course,' continued the teacher, his chubby face – *still spotted with acne, just how young is he?* – flushing deep pink. His baby-soft hands plucked at the ring-binder in front of him.

I didn't want to talk about how tough things have been. Not there, not with him.

'Concerns?' I queried.

He looked uncomfortable. 'Sadie's academic work has suffered, but then that's only to be expected.' *Nice of him to acknowledge her father dying might have had an effect.*

'But it's the, um, attendance issues that are worrying us most of all.'

Attendance issues. What attendance issues?

'I don't understand,' I said. 'Sadie leaves for school every morning at eight o'clock. She doesn't get home until tea time, sometimes later if she's gone to the library.'

I glanced at Sadie. Her eyes were burning into the table, her mouth set. Oh God.

'I'm afraid, Mrs Busfield, that several of Sadie's teachers have complained about her missing lessons.'

Breathe, breathe. That's it. Nice and slow.

'Sadie,' I said, trying not to choke, trying to remain calm and reasonable. 'Can you explain?'

She looked at me then, shrugged, and looked away. 'Sometimes I don't feel like going,' she said.

Sadie's parents' evenings have always been fraught. At her little International School in Dubai, she had a reputation among the staff for being stubborn – 'unteachable', that one French teacher said. 'Sadie, she listen only to 'er own 'eart,' the woman told us. 'She believe no one else 'ave anything she can learn from.' Simon was delighted, of course. Afterwards he slipped Sadie 150 dirhams.

But now it's just me, I don't want to have to deal with exasperated teachers. I want things to be easy, straight-forward. Sitting there in the school dining room, I gazed at my daughter – so closed off, so uncompromising – and I felt the beginning of a surge of anger.

'But where have you been going?' My voice grew ominously shriller. 'You've been meeting up with that boy, haven't you? The one you and Gabi were talking about.'

That image came back into my head – Sadie's head

bent over a toilet seat – and I fought a surge of nausea.

'It's none of your business what I do! You made this mess. You and Dad and that woman. You're pathetic! What right do you have to tell me how to live my life when you've made such a fuck-up of your own?'

Oh, that was a shock! To see how much vitriol there was in her. I knew she was upset. Of course I did – how could she be anything else with all that's happened to her? *My poor girl*. But such anger! Directed at me! Where has she been going, when she's not at school? Who does she see? How am I to cope with a new baby when my old baby is running wild and there's nothing I can do about it?

I tried to breathe, I tried to keep control, but the tears came from nowhere, as they so often do these days. *All those haywire hormones. It's only to be expected.* And suddenly I was sobbing at this boy-teacher's table in the middle of the dining hall while all around us other parents and teenagers gawped and whispered and teachers at other tables exchanged raised-eyebrowed looks and tried to remember what they'd been saying.

'Please don't get upset, Mrs Busfield.' That poor teacher, his hand hovering uncertainly in the air between us, unsure whether to risk a touch to the arm, not yet used to dealing with emotional women. Emotional *pregnant* women. 'I'm sure Sadie will find her way,' he added lamely.

And Sadie, face burning, stood up so abruptly her whole chair tipped backwards, clattering on to the tiled floor, and stormed out. I followed her out without a word, a tissue clamped to my face.

'I'm sorry,' I say now, as we wait at a red light and I try to find the balance between the clutch and the accelerator.

I must have said sorry a million times already, but she's refusing to talk.

I've embarrassed her, I know, in front of all those people. It's so hard being a teenager, even more so when you've spent most of your life in a different country. Trying to make new friends, learning a new way of speaking, trying to understand how things work. And now this. A dead father. A suicidal mother. A home at risk of repossession. A new family who aren't really your family. A world built on lies.

No wonder she skips biology and history. No wonder she looks at me like I'm the enemy. I've let her down. *I'm sorry, I'm sorry, I'm sorry.* I've taken my eye off the ball. I've been self-absorbed. I've fallen apart. I've failed her. I've been blind. I've been selfish.

And now I've stalled.

As I park the car on the road outside our house (*three attempts at backing into that space and still a good foot from the kerb. How embarrassing*), Sadie is out of the door before I've even switched off the engine. Getting out I notice, for the first time, that the bump of my belly is pushing out under my dress. It has been very discreet up until now, as if it knew it wasn't really wanted and was trying to make itself scarce. But now it's unavoidable.

'Mum. MUUUUUUM!'

Talk about extremes – one moment she's mute and now my daughter's yelling her head off!

'Coming,' I say, starting to feel uneasy. Why is she screaming?

'*Mum!*'

I'm rushing now, unsure what's happening. I don't like the panic in my daughter's voice. My heart is hammering, my palms are sweaty.

When I arrive in the communal hallway, the door to our flat is wide and obscenely open. I can sense immediately that something is wrong. There's a change in the smell of the place, an alertness in the air, a sense of things disturbed. I push through past the stairwell and into our hallway.

Sadie is standing in the doorway of the living room.

'Someone's been here,' she says, and her voice is small and achingly young.

The place is trashed. Books all over the rug, cushions ripped and leaking entrails of white foam, a family photograph of Simon, Sadie and me lying on the floor, glass smashed.

My breath won't come. *Breathe, breathe*. I rush to my bedroom for my inhaler, but stop just inside the door. Carnage here too. Drawers pulled open, all my things – *my knickers, for Christ's sake* – spilled out on to the carpet, the wardrobe door open, Simon's clothes in a multi-coloured heap. Oh God, ripped up. All of them. His favourite suit, the slightly tweedy one with the faint purple thread, lying in pieces on the floor. Dismembered.

Grab the inhaler from next to the bed, quick. At least that's untouched. Press and gulp, press and gulp. Breathe breathe.

Someone has been in here, going through my house, through my private things, running grubby fingers over silk and lace and the things I wear next to my skin.

Sadie appears next to me, her lovely green eyes frozen with fright.

I must pull myself together. I must be strong for her. I'm all that she has now.

There is only me.

SELINA

It has to be a coincidence.

I won't let myself think of what else it could mean, won't add two and two together to make five or ten, pondering the significance of the note on my windscreen last week, and now this.

'In pieces on the floor!' Lottie is saying on the other end of the phone. I haven't spoken to her since the dismal failure of Christmas (well really, what did we expect?) and she sounds like a clockwork toy that has been wound up just a little too far. 'Simon's favourite suit. You know, the tweedy one?'

I recognize it from her description, the one he had made for a wedding weekend in Scotland years ago, but can't remember the last time I saw it. How ridiculous I've been, I see now, imagining he must have had it in his wardrobe in Dubai. *Tweed! In that heat!* And now it's lying in pieces on her bedroom floor.

'I don't understand,' she wails. 'Who would have done that?'

Should I tell her? About the note? I don't want to scare-monger, but at the same time . . .

I tell her. I don't go into details about Greg, of course. There are some things she doesn't need to know – we're not friends, after all. Far from it. But I tell her about the note, and the way I felt watched.

'Me too!' she shrieks.

The sudden, awkward solidarity jars.

She describes hearing footsteps and breathing noises. She's clearly highly strung, a touch neurotic even, but still . . .

'Do you see him?' she wants to know now. 'Do you see Simon? I see him everywhere. Lying on the sofa, pouring himself a glass of wine in the kitchen, on the hammock in the garden.'

Oh, so she is mad after all, inventing things that aren't there. Ghosts in her imagination, whispering in her sleep.

I don't believe in ghosts. I think they're cheap solace for people who aren't strong enough to face reality. Of course, I've lost people in the past – my dad twelve years ago, an old friend who recently died quietly and unshowily from ovarian cancer, insisting to the end it was a nasty bout of flu. I loved them both, but I've never felt compelled to wonder where they are. And though I once thought I saw Simon queuing in the local deli, deep down I knew it wasn't really him, just some other fair-haired, broad-shouldered, middle-aged man buying focaccia wrapped in greasy brown paper on a Saturday morning.

A ghost wouldn't trash Lottie's flat, a ghost wouldn't rip Simon's clothes to shreds.

'Where do you think he was, that last night?'

I don't know where this question comes from, but once I've asked it I'm glad I have. I realize it's been sitting heavily in my subconscious, like last night's stodgy lasagne.

'He wasn't in Dubai,' I continue. 'He wasn't with you, he wasn't due back with me until the next day. Oh, I know he was somewhere in Southwark.' *Seen in a bar. Seen by the bridge.* 'But who was he with? And why?'

She's quiet then. Makes a change!

So I tell her about what Greg said, about the back-handers and the 'unpleasant' people. And I remind her about the CCTV footage and the mystery account.

318

'I thought it was you,' we both say at once, then laugh over-brightly. *It still could be her*, says a voice in my head. *You don't know what she's capable of.*

'So you think he was involved in something dodgy,' she says when the laughter stops. 'Not surprising if he had to support that great big house of yours, with you not working and everything.'

There's no rancour in her words now. It's as if she's just saying them for the sake of it.

'Give it a rest,' I say.

When I come off the phone, Flora wants to know who I've been talking to. She's sitting at the kitchen table with her laptop open. By my reckoning this is her third day staying here in Barnes, although time seems recently to have lost all meaning, the days bleeding into each other like a watercolour painting.

'I've come to keep you company,' she said when she first arrived. But really, I know she's come to escape.

I tell her about Lottie and the break-in. Immediately she wants to know if they're all right, if they need anything – such a huge heart my daughter has, why did I never realize before how that can be a gift rather than a handicap? Only now is it beginning to occur to me – after all these years – how much easier it is when you accept your children for who they are, rather than holding them up against who you thought they'd be, like a pair of spot-the-difference pictures.

'What are you doing?' I ask her.

She sighs. 'Tweeting,' she says. 'Or trying to. Last night I had seventy-nine followers and this morning only seventy-six. I've got to think of something witty to say so I don't lose any more, but nothing I say sounds right. Why

319

on earth would people be interested in my life. *I'm* not even interested in my life and I'm the one living it!'

I sit down opposite her and look at her unruly brown hair where it has escaped from its ponytail, and at the soft round curve of her cheek and the pink tip of her tongue poking out between her lips as she concentrates on her screen, just as it did when she was a child working on her homework, and something inside me tears apart like a worn rag.

'Flora? Why are you still here?'

I say it gently but she looks up, shocked. Her mouth opens. Then closes again.

'I don't know, Mummy,' she says finally.

'Don't know about what?'

'About anything. I don't know about anything.'

We gaze at each other for a moment, across the blond-wood table. Then I reach out my hand to stroke her face.

Her eyes widen with surprise. Mine too. When was the last time I was so spontaneously affectionate with my daughter? For a moment, self-consciousness freezes my hand in the act of stroking, turning my fingers briefly to stone. But I push through it.

I don't know what is going on with her and Ryan, but I can see things aren't as they should be. From what Flora has said, it seems Ryan has been stacking up our family's faults like dirty dishes next to the sink. It ought to make me happy, this division. *Perhaps they'll split up!* But I worry about Flora. She never had any boyfriends when she was younger, and she was so excited when she met Ryan, so pleased that now she'd have someone. Like everyone else.

'You have choices, Flo.'

I've never used the diminutive of her name before, but somehow it just slips out. She looks so gratified my heart constricts. It's such a small thing, to make her feel special, to make us feel bonded to each other.

'You don't have to stay with Ryan if he isn't what you want.'

A wariness creeps into her eyes now. I realize she suspects my motives.

'I love Ryan.' She's defensive suddenly, her shoulders hunched against the suspected slight. 'Anyway, I've always known I wouldn't end up with someone larger than life and Bear Grylls-ish like Dad. I'm not like you.'

'Fat lot of good it's done me.'

'What?'

'Being me.'

Flora blinks. We don't have talks like this, she and I. Neither of us are quite sure of the form. We have veered off piste without any clear idea how to navigate our way safely down. She opens her mouth, clearly wanting to keep chatting.

'I know Ryan's not exactly Alpha Male, not like Dad and Felix,' she says. 'And I know you've always kind of looked down on him for that, but then I'm not exactly Alpha Female like you either, in case you hadn't noticed.'

Alpha Female. Is that what she thinks? That I'm some sort of Amazonian superwoman? After all that's happened? After all I've let happen? A lump forms in my throat.

'It doesn't have to be an either/or choice, you know,' I say, my voice croaky with unshed tears.

Flora stares at me. Her expression is puzzled.

'You mean,' she is talking slowly, as if thinking out loud, 'Eeyore, as in always moaning?'

'Pardon?'

'The Eeyore choice? The donkey in *Winnie the Pooh*. Always moaning.'

What on earth?

'Not Eeyore,' I manage eventually, as realization dawns. '*Either/or*. As in one or the other.'

We gaze at each other, mute. *Please don't let this be yet another example of my failure to communicate with my daughter . . .*

But now Flora is laughing. And I'm laughing too. *It's funny! Of course it's funny. It's hilarious! Thank God!*

'I thought . . .' splutters Flora

'Eeyore!' I exclaim. 'Of all things!'

Now the laughter is dying down and awkwardness sets in.

'What I mean,' I try to explain, 'is that it doesn't have to be a choice between Ryan or your father. There are millions of other men out there who aren't like either of them. And anyway, being married to an Alpha Male isn't something I'd necessarily advise. They feel it too much, you know, the passing of time. They can't bear to see their opportunities narrowing.'

It's something I've never really thought about before, but when Flora goes up for a bath and I have time to reflect, I can see it's true. Simon bought right into the myth of himself as this huge, unstoppable force of nature. It was the frame through which he chose to see the world, and to be seen by it. So how must he have felt about getting older, about losing his power?

I remember the fuss he made about getting reading

glasses. He hung on right until the last minute, until he couldn't even read the menu in restaurants any more and used to hold it out at arm's length, angling it this way and that in the dim candlelight. He couldn't bear to admit he was ageing. There was that time he came home from a rare walk with Walter in a filthy temper.

'I've lost my new glasses,' he said. Three hundred pounds they'd cost him, just weeks before, and they'd fallen out of his pocket somewhere on the Common. He insisted I come with him to retrace his steps.

'But why do I have to come?' I asked, cross at the interruption to my orderly routine, although goodness knows I couldn't have been doing anything *that* important.

'Because how on earth will I be able to spot my glasses, without my glasses on?' he retorted, livid with irritation, and I realized, for the first time, just how blind he was without them.

'What I don't understand is why you took them with you in the first place,' I complained as we tramped, out of sorts, through the muddy grass. 'Who needs glasses to walk the dog?'

'I need them to read texts,' he answered, even though, as far as I knew then, he'd never sent a text in his life.

Now I suppose he'd been texting her, Lottie. Or else Sadie. How little I knew of his inner life, of how he felt about getting older. Was his hatred of glasses pure vanity (he was always so proud of his green eyes) or just fear of the impending mortality they represented? How is it that I never asked him those things? What on earth did we talk about, the two of us?

Of course, I know the answer to that. We talked about

the children, and the house in Tuscany, and whether Hettie's facelift that no one was supposed to know about was just a little too tight, and if Walter's back leg was dragging slightly. We talked about Josh's lack of motivation and the crowns on Felix's back teeth. We worried about Flora's self-esteem and whether she'd ever get a boyfriend and then, when she did, whether she'd ever get rid of him. We talked about converting the loft space into a teenagers' den, and papering one wall of our bedroom in a contrasting print to the paintwork. We talked about the little things. But about the big things, I suddenly realize, we didn't talk at all. What did he fear? What motivated him? I have no idea. And now I don't suppose I ever will. 'I've settled for you,' said the couple in Felix's incomprehensible film. Did Simon settle for me? For a married life lived along parallel but not intersecting lines? Is that what he found in Lottie? Someone to intersect with? The phrase comes back to me that the policewoman used when I went to identify Simon's body – did Simon feel he was stuck in the trapping point of our marriage?

Perhaps that's what he was trying to explain that afternoon on the terrace in Tuscany all those years ago, against the noisy backtrack of the cicadas and my own heart thudding in my ears. The clink of the wineglass on the table. *We need to talk*. No, I'm not going to think about that now. It was all so long ago. Time mends things, doesn't it, growing new skin over the hurts of the past so it's as if they never existed?

Hettie calls round and I tell her about Lottie's break-in.

'Oh my God, Selina! What is happening to your life? Who needs soap operas, hey?'

Hettie is worried about me. I know this because she's

my oldest friend and because she keeps telling me so. Again and again. At length.

'I can't believe you didn't go to the police about that note,' she says now. 'I'm so worried about you.'

I wish I hadn't told her about the note now. I left out the Greg bit, of course, but she still doesn't understand why I just want to pretend it never happened.

'The thing is . . .' I say. But what exactly is the thing, when you come down to it? 'The thing is, what's the point in going to the police? It wasn't overtly a threat.'

'No, but . . .'

But Hettie still lives in a world where right is right and wrong is wrong, where the police always help you and the people you love don't hurt you.

'The thing is . . .' I say a third time. 'I don't know about anything any more. I used to be so sure about things, but now . . .'

'You're bound to feel like that, Selina, after all you've been through.' Hettie pulls her chair up close so her earnest brown eyes are just inches from mine – any closer and we'd be rubbing noses like Eskimos. 'But you mustn't let what's happened destroy your faith in people. Not everyone will let you down. Look at me and Ian, for instance. I know Ian would rather die than hurt me.'

I gaze at her, incredulous. Can she really be that naive, after everything that's happened? To believe she knows what's going on inside Ian's head? Clearly she is.

'Look, Sel,' she says, 'I know Simon behaved like a complete dickhead, but there are good people out there, you just have to believe it. Ian worships me. You've said so yourself, many times.'

'Simon worshipped me too,' I say, more sharply than I

intended. 'He adored me, he said. It didn't stop him cheating on me for thirty years. I'm not saying Ian doesn't love you, Hets, I'm just saying that love isn't . . . all that.'

Felix's expression comes back to me unexpectedly.

'All that what?'

'Just all that. Love isn't all that.'

Hettie doesn't want to hear this, I can tell.

'I still don't understand what all this has to do with you not going to the police,' she says crossly, leaning back in her chair now, away from me, as if doubt were catching. 'You have to protect yourself – and your family.'

But I know what Hettie doesn't know. That it's impossible to protect yourself when the greatest dangers lie on the inside, not the outside, and the very people you turn to for protection turn out to be the people you need protecting from. I know how you can think you know someone, *really* know someone, only to find the person you thought you knew turns out to be a hollow timber structure with someone entirely different inside – a plastic wheelie bin of a someone. I know about love and I know about loss and how at any minute the solid ground can give way beneath your feet, revealing the chasm that's been there all along, waiting to suck you in.

What can you do, when you come down to it, except cling on to the sides and try not to look down?

LOTTIE

Such a mess! Not just the broken things and the ripped things and the shattered and smashed things, but the dirt the police left behind when they came to take prints, and the half-full mugs, and the muddy footprints from where they trekked out to check the garden. The smashed window at the back has now been boarded up and there are shavings of wood everywhere.

Not to mention the mess my life is in.

Next door I can hear Sadie crying in her bedroom, muffled sobs she doesn't want me to hear.

'I miss him, Mum,' she said earlier, her face streaky with tears, when the police finally left. 'I miss my dad.'

I sat cuddling her on the sofa for ages, so happy to be allowed to put my arms around her. *My poor baby.* I should have left it at that, just enjoyed the novelty of being close to her and comforting her, but instead I tried to take advantage of this moment of intimacy to push her about the absences from school, about the boy in the toilet cubicle, about what she's doing. Unsurprisingly, she snapped right shut.

'What do you care?' she said eventually, running from the room after one question too many. 'You'll have a new baby soon. You won't have to worry about me any more.'

And now the door's locked and she won't let me in.

'I'm sorry,' I say from outside, leaning my forehead against the cool wood of the door. 'I'm so sorry.'

Since reading her notebook, I've realized how little I know about my daughter. Who are her friends these days? What is she reading? What music does she like? She has become an enigma to me, and I've been so preoccupied I've allowed it to happen. Is it too late to claw her back?

I should call my sisters and let them know what's happening. But I don't.

My sisters will worry.

My sisters will fuss and insist on coming here.

My sisters will make it their problem, when it has to be my problem.

That's why I called her instead. Selina. I had to talk to someone, so I talked to her.

But now she's gone and it's just me again, and a wooden board on the kitchen window. I long to take an anti-anxiety pill and drink whiskey from the bottle, but because of the baby I can't. Someone has been in my home. Someone has been through my things. *Grubby fingers on satin. Grubby fingers on lace.*

I'm sitting in bed, looking at the remains of Simon's suit still heaped on the floor, and listening to our daughter crying through the wall.

I could fall apart. *No one would blame me.* But I know I can't. I house the cluster of cells that will one day be a baby. I am all my daughter has.

I pick up my sketchbook.

T for 'Twat'.

24

SELINA

∽

'I just *love* the original features.'

The estate agent can't be much older than Josh. So far she has just *loved* the location, the sliding cupboard in the kitchen, the finish on the floorboards, and the view from the roof terrace over the neighbouring gardens.

'It *is* nicely done,' I allow. 'What a shame there's no second bathroom.'

'But *so* easy to knock out that built-in wardrobe in the master-bed and pop in a little en suite!'

('*You're a little en suite*,' says Josh's voice in my head.)

This is the fourth flat I've viewed and easily the best. Small, obviously, compared to the house, and more Mortlake than Barnes, but I could buy it outright with the money from my half of the house and still have a little left over. And when my job starts next school term (God, how weird that sounds), I should just about be able to manage. The prospect of sleeping through the night instead of lying awake moving money around in my head, unable to find a safe place for my thoughts to rest, is intoxicating.

Walking out to my car with the agent, I tell her I'll be in touch.

'Lovely,' she says, smiling brightly. 'Is this yours? I just *love* Fiat 500s!'

It's only a short journey back home, but it takes ages because of the traffic. Stop. Start. Stop. Start. Stuck for ages at a junction, I lock the car doors. Ever since the incident with the note, I've felt exposed even in my car. Someone could come in through the passenger door, hold a knife to my ribs and force me to drive somewhere. You hear of such things. For all these years I've inhabited my life largely without fear, knowing that bad things happen, just not to me and mine. But what was outside has come in. What Simon did has made a crack through which anything can get in – car-jackings, teenage stabbings, murders in suburban cul-de-sacs where neighbours shake their heads in disbelief and say, 'But they were such a nice family.' Nothing is now out of bounds.

After learning of Lottie's break-in the night before last, I haven't even liked being at home alone, so I'm relieved when I pull into the driveway to see the lit-up windows, signalling that Josh is in. I know I'll have to get used to the idea of being on my own sooner or later. He is seventeen, after all, reacting to the news of our move with a shrug of the shoulders and a flippant 'Can we get somewhere within walking distance of a KFC this time?' But right now I'm just glad he's here. Slamming the car door, I flip the switch on the key fob. The lock lights wink once, as if saying goodnight.

The front door is slightly ajar. *That boy! Always in a rush. So oblivious to consequences. Anything could have happened!* But inside the hall, I hesitate. Something isn't right. Nothing looks out of place but there's a definite sense of disarrangement.

Boom, boom, boom! My heart thuds loudly in the suddenly still air. I try to make my mind blank. As long as I believe in the power of the normal, of the expected, of the safe, all will be well.

I nudge open the door of Simon's study. *And exhale.* Everything is just as I remember it – a clutch of Probate letters still spread out across his desk, the safe untouched.

How paranoid I've become.

Reassured, I stroll into the kitchen.

Oh!

My hand flies to my mouth as I survey the room.

Such devastation! Such destruction!

It looks as if a tornado has found its way into my home, opening up cupboards, violently strewing tins, pasta, glasses and crockery over flat surfaces. It has whisked the tops off bottles of ketchup and jars of jam and splattered the contents around the walls so that my kitchen resembles an abbatoir, where blood drips thick and sweet from the ceiling. It has ripped apart boxes of cereal so that Rice Krispies pile on the floor like snow drifts. It has wrecked and torn and soiled and ruined.

Oh God, someone has done this!

Oh God, what if they're still here?

My mobile phone is in my handbag, which I dropped as I came through the front door. Without it I feel unmanned and horribly vulnerable. *I must stay still, I mustn't panic.* The fine hairs on my arms prickle as I listen for noises, imagining that the person who did this is still here, breathing out into the same air as me so that our breath intermingles in the stillness of the house. The thought of such unwanted intimacy is too much.

I creep back out into the hallway and peer through the open door of the living room.

Sick. I feel sick.

My stomach churns as I survey the dark plum paint sprayed over the butter-yellow and grey Persian rug that I fell in love with all those years ago in Paris. When Simon and I rang the bell of the antiques shop where it was displayed in the window, the man who came to the door told us off, I remember. 'I was sleeping,' he said, as if it was beyond selfish of us to come to his door in the middle of the afternoon wanting to spend thousands of pounds on one of his carpets. Now, looking at the bleeding gashes of paint criss-crossing the rug, a blade of pain slices through me, clean and sharp. It cost us a fortune to get that carpet home. I remember being breathless with excitement the day it arrived and watching Simon unroll it in the empty living room. 'I told you, didn't I?' I crowed, dancing around the edges of the room to survey the new acquisition from every angle. 'I told you it'd be perfect.'

A house full of valuable objects that have turned out to be worthless. I thought I was building a home, piece by expensive piece, but it turns out that it was no different from that antiques shop in Paris – a big empty space filled with beautiful things.

And now ruined.

I'm looking at the paint daubed on the walls, drying darker than on the carpet, like an old scab. I recognize the colour, of course. Didn't I spend weeks scouring the paint charts of south-west London until I found just the right shade, and then further weeks bulldozing Simon into dropping his objections?

Someone has been in the garage, where the old tins of excess paint are stored on shelves in case touch-ups are required. I imagine him, this intruder, standing in front of the piled-up cans, weighing up which will inflict the most damage.

How dare he! Suddenly it's as if my anger might drown me. But now I sense something – not so much a noise as a presence, a sense of displaced air and hot stranger's breath.

He is still here! My mouth is dry; the noise of my own swallowing deafens me.

If I crane forward a little, I can see my handbag across the hall, but reaching it means exposing myself to view from the upper landing.

My heart thumps wildly in my chest, my pulse is charging. Fear burns a path up through my throat and out of my mouth, becoming a presence so tangible I'm sure the intruder must sense it.

What's the alternative? Wait here in terror until he leaves? But what if he comes back in here to survey his handiwork? What if – *oh dear God* – there's more than one of them?

My breathing sounds so loud. I must keep calm. But panic is snapping at my ankles like an angry pit bull.

Simon, Simon, Simon.

Click! The sound of a key in the front door and Josh bursts into the hallway. *No! Quiet! Shhhhh!*

'All right, Mum?' His booming voice is thunderous in the still house. He glances over but seems not to notice that his mother is plastered to the wall of the living room as if stuck fast with Velcro.

'There's someone here, Josh.' My whisper reverberates thunderously through the expectant house.

I mean it as a warning, but Josh seems to take it as a call to action.

'No!' I exclaim uselessly, watching his feet in their enormous, high-top trainers pound up the stairs and along the landing at the top. 'I didn't mean—'

My boy, my boy, my boy. I hear the thud of his footsteps on the upstairs carpet, each thud producing an echoing lurch in my stomach.

Then: 'Oh *shit*!'

He sounds neither angry nor frightened.

Still frozen, I wait for a reaction from the intruder – shouting, arguing, shooting (*God forbid*). But there is none. Slowly I peel myself off the wall, hearing Josh speak again.

'What the *fuck*?'

I climb the stairs, my legs wobbly, as if I'm using them for the first time after a lengthy illness.

Josh is framed in the second doorway along the corridor, Felix's old bedroom. He looks like a freakishly tall child, standing there so awkwardly, shifting his weight from side to side.

'What the fuck have you done?' he repeats, but his voice is still curiously free from anger.

I don't understand. What is happening now?

Coming up behind Josh, I peer through the open doorway. *Oh my God. Is it snowing?* The air is full of white flakes and I have the strangest feeling of looking into a snow-globe. No, not flakes, feathers. The air is full of tiny white feathers, seemingly suspended in space. And at the centre of the feathers, doggedly chopping up Felix's duck-down duvet with an enormous pair of secateurs that usually live in the garage, is Sadie.

334

What the hell?

Sadie is muttering to herself. 'Doesn't matter,' she is saying, her shiny head bent intently over her task. *Chop, chop, chop.* 'Doesn't matter a fuck.'

Her voice is thick and lumpy and there's a nearly-empty bottle of vodka on the floor next to her. She's drunk, that young girl – totally, paralytically, disgustingly drunk!

Now there's a rush of something in my ears. Anger, relief, alarm. My legs are shaking properly now that the adrenaline is fading. I need to sit down.

Josh crosses the room and crouches down next to the girl, putting an arm around her shoulders. He's so gentle, my boy, as if she's a small child.

'It's OK,' he murmurs, easing the secateurs from Sadie's hands and casting them aside. 'It's OK now.'

'No it's bloody well not OK!' My voice comes back to me now, bursting with pent-up fury and fear. 'What the *hell* do you think you're doing?' I'm looking down at the girl's bowed head. 'Do you have any idea how much damage you've done?'

Josh's eyes are pleading. 'Mum! Calm down!'

'Calm down? Go downstairs and take a look at the kitchen and the living room, then tell me to calm down!'

The girl is looking at me now, black rings of mascara smudged around her green eyes. *Simon's eyes.*

''S OK,' she tells me. As if she's trying to reassure me! 'Doesn't matter.'

The nerve of her!

'I'm calling the police.'

I turn around to go back downstairs for my phone, but Josh cuts me off on the landing.

'No, Mum.'

His hand grips the top of my arm so I have to stop.

'Don't be ridiculous, Josh. She's caused thousands and thousands of pounds' worth of damage. Do you really expect me to do nothing? How did she get in anyway? You left the alarm off again, didn't you? What about the insurance?'

Josh's face is hardening now like plaster. 'Who gives a *fuck* about the insurance?'

Oh, really! This is too much!

He's looking at me now, carefully. 'She's probably got her reasons,' he says.

Fury shoots through me. 'Yes – jealousy, pettiness, spite . . .'

Josh's fingers tighten on my arm. 'Felix,' he says. And his boy-man's voice is croaky.

I don't understand.

So now Josh tells me about coming home a couple of days ago and seeing coats hanging over the banister. Felix's pork-pie hat, the one he always wears. Then Sadie, coming down the stairs, her face burning, refusing to meet his eyes.

'I was just using the bathroom,' she told Josh.

Oh yeah, right! thought Josh.

And Felix appearing on the upstairs landing in just a pair of jeans. Bare chest, bare feet. Whistling. Sadie snatching up her coat and picking up Felix's keys from the hall table. *How angry he was later when he couldn't find them,* Josh said. *Turning the place upside-down.*

'Gotta go,' Sadie told Josh.

Looking ashamed, said Josh. *Looking like she wanted to cry.*

'So you see . . .' he says.

But I don't. I don't see anything. Felix is twenty-six. He's a man. He has a girlfriend, a life. I can see how Josh might get the wrong idea or how an impressionable sixteen-year-old girl might have misconstrued things, but I don't see anything else. I don't see why this is happening to me. Why is there a strange broken girl in my son's bedroom, why is my house in tatters, why is my life out of control? What has happened to all the people I love? To Simon? To Josh? Why is my baby boy standing in front of me with the world-weary face of an adult who has seen too much?

I'm so tired of it all, tired of thinking about it.

'Even so,' I say to Josh, not looking at him, 'there have to be consequences.'

He lets go of my arm.

'Whatever,' he says, holding his hands up and turning away.

I continue along the landing, but halfway down the stairs I stop. How heavy my legs feel. I'm too exhausted to go on. I sink down on the step behind me and rest my head against the newel post. That's better. The varnished wood feels reassuringly solid against my skin.

From the bedroom above I can hear Josh's low voice murmuring soothingly, and now – *horrible* – the lowing sound of a young girl keening to herself.

What a mess. What an ugly, tragic mess.

I heave myself to my feet and carry on down the stairs, my legs leaden. Retrieving my mobile from my bag, I call up a number.

'Hello,' says Lottie.

'Your daughter is here,' I say. 'She needs you.'

LOTTIE

Clutch, shift, first. That's right. I can do it. Nothing to it. I won't panic. I won't think about what will happen if I get lost in the middle of London and end up driving endlessly around Hyde Park Corner, causing hold-ups with drivers hooting behind me.

My daughter needs me.

Oh God, I don't know the way!

Head for Hammersmith, that's the best thing. No need to panic, just follow the signs. Don't think about any of that other stuff now, concentrate on the road. Don't think about Sadie, drunk, Felix, bedroom, red paint across walls, feathers floating in air.

I shouldn't have driven!

No. I can do this. I need to drive. To bring my daughter safely back home.

So many cars. So much traffic. Headlights coming so fast. So many lanes. Wrong turn. Fuckity fuck. Can't U-turn. Too many cars. Must keep going. Do a left then another left. That'll put me straight. Can't go wrong if I head for Hammersmith.

My daughter needs me.

SELINA

Back upstairs, I hover in the doorway of Josh's room, where he has installed Sadie after half-dragging, half-carrying her from the wreckage of Felix's room.

She lies curled up in his bed in the foetal position, moaning faintly. There's a bucket on the floor by her head, freshly washed out. Her hair is plastered to her head with sweat, and flecks of vomit lodge in the strands around her mouth. Her skin is clammy like sweaty cheese and there's a long ladder in the left leg of her black tights. Her clothes are splattered with specks of paint and sick. The room stinks of the nasty things bodies do that no one likes to think about.

Josh sits on the end of the bed with his back against the wall, watching her.

'You don't have to stay in here,' I tell him. 'She's not your responsibility.'

He looks up at me and shrugs.

'Josh,' I say, weighing up my words. 'There's nothing between you . . . ? What I mean is, you do know she's your *sister*?'

He nods.

'I know,' he says. 'And that makes her my responsibility.'

An overwhelming rush of love sweeps over me now. *Such a good person, my son. Such a kind person.*

'Even when,' he adds, eyeing the sick bucket and the clammy figure in the bed, 'she's proper minging.'

In my own room, I take out my phone. *I don't want to do this. Please God, don't let me have to do this.*

'Felix?' I say. 'I need to talk to you.'

LOTTIE

I'm here! *Thank God!* I recognize the street – the line of plane trees studding the pavement, the wide driveways, the detached houses.

I pull into the kerb, next to that little Fiat. W*ho put a fucking wheelie bin there?* Just missed it. *Clutch, neutral, off.*

For a second I sit gazing up at the house. What on earth is Sadie doing here? So far from home.

She comes to the door. Selina. Her face gives nothing away – the advantages of all that Botox!

'Before you go upstairs,' she says, 'I'll show you your daughter's handiwork.'

I follow her, obediently, even though I just want to see my baby and take her home.

Oh my God! The living room is graffitied with shocking-red paint. The kitchen looks like a bombsite. Selina watches my face carefully, monitoring my reactions. I think my obvious shock gratifies her, because she starts to lead the way upstairs now. Halfway up I pause in front of a framed photo of Simon and Selina and their children. They're in the garden with lots of other people, all dressed up to the nines, and there's a big cake in front of Simon with '50' written on it in red icing. The air goes out of my stomach as I remember the huge fiftieth party I organized for him at a beach club in Dubai, with all our friends, an Abba tribute band and silliness and dancing. Two parties, two wives, two lives. How? How? How? Was there something inside him, some switch, that made him able to pass from one life to the other without ever forgetting who he

340

was? I'm about to ask Selina what she thinks, but stop myself. What's the point now? We'll never know. Instead I follow her upstairs to the second doorway off the landing and look into a wrecked room where feathers and red paint clot together, making it look like the scene of a brutal cockfight.

'Obviously it's going to take a lot of money to put right,' I say, finally, because I have to say something.

'Ha! You don't know the half of it,' she barks. 'Just the living-room carpet alone—'

'I'm very sorry,' I interrupt, wanting her to stop. 'She's never done anything like this before.'

'I should bloody well hope not!'

We move away now and into another room.

There she is! Oh Sadie!

I hurl myself down next to the bed.

'Sadie? Poppet?'

There's a movement at the end of the bed and I'm suddenly aware that Josh is here too. I don't care. Let him be embarrassed.

Sadie opens one eye, then closes it again.

'Don't need you,' she slurs. 'Goway.'

She does though. She does need me. I'm all she has.

I stroke her forehead, pushing back the damp hair from her face. There's a clump of something nasty by her ear. I won't look, just carry on stroking. *There, there. That's right. There, there.*

I'm here now. *I'm here.*

341

SELINA

For a moment or two, I continue watching from the door-way. Then I turn on my heel, throwing my hands up in disgust. I give up! Downstairs in the living room, I sink on to one of the mink sofas, which has, miraculously, escaped the carnage, and put my head in my hands. I have no idea any more what I should think.

In my mind I run through the phone call with Felix. He was in a restaurant, he said, having a work meeting. (*At nine thirty at night?*) He really couldn't talk.

'It's important,' I said. 'It's about Sadie.'

I told him what had happened. And what Josh had told me.

'I need to know,' I said. 'Did you . . . ? Have you . . . ?'

Felix's outrage spluttered down the phone like something living. 'Do you really think . . . ?' he said. 'With my half-sister? That's sick!'

Sitting on the sofa now, I rub my eyes, trying to clear my mind.

Felix is right, of course. I should never even have mentioned it to him. It's been so hard for the children, all of this. No wonder they're all making approaches towards one another, trying to work all this out. I remember what Flora said, about meeting up with Sadie in a patisserie. That's what it'll be, this thing with Sadie and Felix. Just trying to suss each other out, trying to negotiate these strange new relationships.

And it would make sense, wouldn't it, for a young girl – *so impressionable at that age* – who has just lost her father to become fixated on her father's adult son? *That poor girl.* The flash of sympathy takes me by surprise.

Now I can hear noises on the stairs. I go out into the hallway and see that Josh and Lottie are bringing Sadie down, one on each side of her. The girl's head droops forward, her face is bloodless. There's a tiny feather matted into her hair at the back. I think of what she's done to my house and the damage I'll never be able to fully put right. So senseless! I'm glad she's going home. It's for the best.

I hold the front door open and they make their way outside to where Lottie's car is parked practically on top of the wheelie bin.

They lie her down on the back seat. That's it. Wait! I run up and fetch a blanket and the bucket to put in with her. There. Better safe than sorry.

We're all sorry. And none of us is safe.

LOTTIE

Driving home, I do indeed get lost and end up driving around Hyde Park Corner several times but I don't panic, just keep on driving round until I pick the most likely exit. That's the one. Sorted. See? Nobody died. *What's the worst thing that could happen?*

Pulling up outside our flat, I manage to park only a short jump away from the kerb and open the back door. Sadie is lying across the seat, wrapped in a blanket, with that bloody bucket on the floor next to her.

'Sadie? Poppet?'

At first, she's unresponsive when I try to shake her awake, then hostile. Finally she allows herself to be led indoors. I take her into her room and she climbs into bed in all her clothes. *That's OK. At least she's safe. Stinky but safe.*

I don't bring up the subject of the break-in or the vandalism. I don't ask her what she was doing in Barnes. I don't mention Selina or Simon or Josh. I don't have a clue what just happened tonight. All I know is that an awful lot has been going on in my sixteen-year-old daughter's life.

And I haven't been aware of any of it.

Part Five

ACCEPTANCE

25

SELINA

There are people hanging around by the bicycle racks outside the main hospital entrance, either singly or in small groups, all wearing pyjamas and slippers or hospital-issue gowns, and smoking cigarettes. Some have plaster casts on their arms or legs, a couple are pushing drips in front of them. One is in a wheelchair with a metal brace drilled into his head. They look at me when I hurry past as if *I'm* the odd one, in my coat and my tights and my suede knee-length boots.

What am I doing here?

I've been asking myself the same question again and again during the interminable drive to Archway. Bloody roadworks. Bloody Olympics. All these months and years of misery so London can present itself all shiny and new, a poor girl wearing a designer dress she can ill afford and hoping her tatty bag and shoes won't give her away.

The phone call took me by surprise, that's the truth of it. I didn't have time to think about how to react. Such a shock. I wasn't thinking straight.

'Is that Selina Busfield?' A woman's voice. A stranger.

'Ye-es.' My response was slow. After everything that's

happened to me, I'm wary now of voices I don't recognize, nervous of the news they might bring.

'My name is Maggie Ronaldson. I'm Greg Ronaldson's wife.'

Oh.

The truth is, I haven't really thought about Greg's wife at all. Since the exposure of Simon's double life ripped out my moral framework by its roots, I've convinced myself there's no such thing as commitment, monogamy, exclusivity, and that whatever I used to think about what people in relationships should and shouldn't do was clearly all wrong. Greg's wife – largely abstract apart from the one Facebook photo – belonged to this new post-Lottie reality where people hop from marital bed to hotel bed without a backward glance and no one expects anything less. So I didn't give her much thought. Until there she was this morning. On the other end of the phone.

'I'm sorry—' I started to say, but she cut me off.

'Something's happened,' she told me, and her voice sounded strained but not angry. 'Greg has been attacked. He's in the hospital. The nurses gave me his phone. That's why I'm ringing you. Your number was in there, and . . . some text messages.'

Instantly, I was overcome with shame, remembering the texts Greg and I had exchanged at the beginning of our affair (*tawdry, tawdry word*), when I'd only just discovered how focusing on the physical could take one's mind off emotional pain, if only temporarily. It was my first experience of writing down the kind of words I'd never before even said out loud. Simon and I never developed a sexual vocabulary, preferring to communicate in a range of small gestures, our own sexual sign language. The texts I sent to Greg had left me feeling shocked and strangely empowered.

'What do you mean, *attacked*?' I asked her, fighting the urge to apologize all over again. 'By whom? Is he OK?'

'Beaten up,' she said briskly. 'Not far from our house. I've no idea who did it. He's stable but unconscious. I was wondering if you could come in.'

What?

'To the hospital. I'm here by myself. I could do with the company. And we could . . . chat.'

Why did I agree? Some kind of self-flagellation, I expect. I should have said no, of course. What on earth will I chat to her about? She'll be wanting a scene, presumably, her pound of flesh. Except she didn't sound angry.

And Greg? Poor Greg, in his ghastly polo shirt. But *attacked*?

So here I am, heading into the main entrance of the hospital. I walk past an old woman standing outside the automatic hospital door, wearing a pink dressing gown and slippers, her lumpy, veiny, purple and white legs shockingly bare in the February chill.

'Got a spare fag?' she asks me hopefully. Her mouth is a black cave, containing just two yellow teeth, looming like tombstones out of the void. I shake my head and continue inside, then make my way up to the third floor as Maggie Ronaldson instructed.

I could still change my mind.

I allow myself to imagine turning around, making my way back along the bleach-infused corridors, back through the automatic door, past the gurning woman in her pink dressing gown, into my car, across the river. Home.

But instead I keep going. *Good old Selina Busfield,*

349

always does what she's told, what's expected. It's more than that, though. Whatever it is that Maggie Ronaldson wants to do or say to me, it's what I deserve. I believe in punishment. I believe in consequences. This has to be endured.

She is sitting in a small waiting room off a long corridor, just as she said. There is a vending machine in the corner and a couple of peeling posters on the wall, and five or six orange moulded-plastic chairs.

'Selina?' She gets to her feet, offering her hand, her eyes openly appraising me. 'I know this must strike you as very odd.' She's talking as if I'm any old person she's just met. Not her husband's lover. Ex-lover. *Oh God.* 'The thing is, I wanted to talk to you, to help me get a few things straight. I hope you don't mind.'

I find myself shaking my head and sitting down in the chair she indicates. I glance at her face. It's a kind face, a tired face. Toffee-coloured eyes with laughter lines around them. But she's not laughing now.

'Is Greg OK?' I ask.

Immediately I wish I hadn't. *Please don't let her mistake my concern for something more.*

'He's got a couple of broken ribs,' she says. 'And a sprained wrist. But it's the head wound that's most worrying. His skull is fractured – probably where he hit his head on the ground after being punched, the doctors said. They've put him into an artificial coma, to give the swelling on his brain time to go down. They don't want to risk him moving around.'

She recites this litany of injuries almost matter-of-factly, as if she's reading from a menu. *How very odd. She's talking to me as if she's glad I'm here.*

While she explains about what happened to Greg, I study her more carefully. Early forties, I'd say. Long brown wavy hair, threaded with faded orangey highlights and the odd strand of grey. A purple jumper, a patterned knee-length skirt, low-heeled brown boots. The kind of look that comes from a certain type of mail-order catalogue, modelled by women walking through muddy fields in Scotland with laughing children in brightly coloured wellies.

'I'm so sorry . . .' I try again. 'About the messages and . . . everything.' *And everything? For pity's sake!* 'My husband died, you see. I wasn't myself. I just went a little crazy. I feel terribly ashamed.'

She smiles a sad little smile.

'Don't be,' she says. 'You didn't make any vows to me. He did. He's the one who should be ashamed. He's the one who spent his time thinking up elaborate lies to fool the person he was supposed to love.'

'I just wanted to see you,' she goes on. 'To find out what you were like, and how long it was going on.'

So I tell her what she wants to know. I don't leave anything out – not the meeting at his office, not the shower curtain, or the last painful drink. It's a relief, really, to talk about it at last, although embarrassing too. She nods a lot, and at the part where he told me how understanding his wife was, she even laughs.

'I'm leaving him,' she says abruptly, when I've finished. *Because of me!*

'You mustn't!' I tell her. 'It wasn't anything. *I* wasn't anything.'

She laughs again now and her face becomes quite beautiful.

'Oh, not because of you. Well, not *just* because of you. There were others, of course. Many others, who came before you.'

It shouldn't be a surprise, but even so, there's a slight pang of . . . what? Surely not jealousy?

'It's a pathological thing with him,' she says. 'The cheating. And the worst thing is I know he does love me, he just doesn't know any other way to be.'

'And do you love him?'

Even as I ask the question, I'm wondering what gives me the right – *marriage-wrecker* – but she doesn't seem to mind.

'Not any more,' she says. 'I used to, but it's as though he's taken all the feelings that were there and squeezed them and squeezed them until there's nothing left. You know, I used to love looking at him, when we were first married. But recently I can't stand the sight of his weak face, or the noise he makes in the back of his mouth when he eats. Even here at the hospital, instead of worrying about how he is, I've been thinking about all the time I'll never get back and all the men I could have been happy with.'

She gets up and stands by the vending machine, as if deciding what to have, but I can tell from the way her eyes dart along the shelves without really seeing that she hasn't finished saying all the things she's been storing up throughout her solo hospital vigil.

Sure enough: 'It's not altogether his fault though,' she continues, still staring into the machine. 'He told me from the beginning that he was scum. The trouble is, I thought it was just one of those things people say to make themselves sound more interesting. I thought there was something worthwhile in there, if only I could reach it. But now I see that he was right all along. He was scum all the way through, like a stick of rock.'

For a while I don't say anything. What is there to say? I scour my purse for coins and buy two cappuccinos from the machine – disgusting, chemical-tasting drinks that arrive in little plastic cups so hot I have to wrap them in paper serviettes just so we can hold them. *Should I tell her about Simon now? A quid pro quo confessional?* No, I don't think so. This is her moment, her crisis.

'It's low self-esteem that's behind it,' she says now, glancing at me sideways to see how this goes down. 'I bet you thought Greg was Mr Confidence, but really he isn't. That's why he has to keep trying to prove things to himself.'

'By seeing other women?'

'Yes, that. And the business stuff.'

Business stuff? I take a swig of my cappuccino and wish I hadn't as the scalding liquid burns the roof of my mouth.

Maggie Ronaldson looks at me, as if she's deciding whether to tell me something.

'He and your husband were involved in something,' she says at last. 'I don't know exactly what, but I know they took money from some very shady people to invest in property overseas. Your husband needed the cash, from what I can gather, but Greg just liked the idea of being a player. He liked the image. Until your husband died, and he found out the money had gone.'

It's what I suspected. But hearing it spelt out feels surreal, like dialogue from a bad film.

'Do you think that's who attacked him?' I ask. 'Those shady people?'

She shrugs. 'Maybe, or maybe it was completely random, which is what I told the police.'

I stare at her, and something comes into my mind, a shadow idea taking shape, growing bigger. *If that's what happened to Greg . . .*

'Do you think the same thing might have happened to Simon?' I blurt out. 'Maybe he didn't fall or jump, but someone pushed him?'

Maggie shrugs again, disinterested, and I can see I've reached her emotional limit. Her husband is in a coma. Her marriage is over. She has no patience left for other people's dramas, other people's lives.

But my thoughts run wild. The note on the windscreen. The endless spam. Is it all a warning? And if Simon was pushed, it means he didn't choose to die. *Maybe I'm not such a failure as a wife, if my husband didn't choose to leave me.*

'Would you like to see him?' Maggie Ronaldson asks abruptly. 'Would you like to see Greg?'

I'd rather eat my own arm.

'He's just down the corridor,' she continues. 'I'll take you.'

I follow her out. Well, what choice do I have? The hospital floor is grey, but specks of green sparkle in it like crystals.

Greg is in a high bed in the middle of the room. I know it's Greg because she tells me so, not because I recognize him. He is covered in tubes, his head encased in a metal frame. He looks like something not human.

Oh dear God. To think I . . . With him . . .

There's a nurse in the room who smiles broadly when we enter.

'You've brought a friend with you, Mrs Ronaldson,' she says in a lilting Irish accent. 'That's lovely.'

I am soaked through with shame. Not a friend. If she only knew.

'We're doing very well this afternoon, aren't we, Greg?' says the nurse, smiling down at Tube Man as if he is a baby. 'We'll be back in that pub in no time.'

Maggie Ronaldson stands by the side of the bed, looking down at her husband, and her face gives nothing away. *When did we all get so good at hiding things?*

'I should leave you in peace,' I say to her, putting on my coat. 'Will you be all right?'

'Oh yes,' she says. 'I expect so.'

'I *know* so!' the nurse chimes in.

I place a hand on her shoulder. 'I really am sorry,' I say.

'We're all sorry,' she says.

All of us sorry. None of us safe.

26

LOTTIE

'Was it very bad?'

Fresh from the shower, her wet hair combed back from her newly scrubbed face, Sadie could be ten years old again.

'Oh, you're wearing . . .'

'Yeah, there wasn't anything else clean. It's OK, isn't it?'

No, it isn't OK, her standing there in her father's favourite sweatshirt, her long legs bare and horribly thin. She has lots of clean clothes. I should know, I do the washing. But I understand. She wants something of his. She wants to feel close to him. Why wouldn't she? *Not that sweatshirt though. I was saving it. The last one with his smell . . .*

'It's fine,' I say.

'Was it very bad?' she repeats, dropping on to the sofa next to me.

I don't pretend not to know what she's talking about.

'Yes. It was bad.'

'A lot of damage?'

'Yes.'

'That rug?'

'Yes.'

'Shit. I bet it cost a fortune.'

I nod. Then add, 'Hideous though it was.'

She looks at me and smiles as if smiling hurts. But it's something.

Nearly twenty-four hours after her vandalism spree, Sadie is finally feeling well enough to be out of bed. We sit side by side on the sofa, under my duvet that I've brought in from my bedroom.

'Want to tell me what happened?' I ask.

She shakes her head. 'I don't want to talk about it,' she says.

We carry on sitting in silence. There's a television programme on where a man has three weeks to arrange his own wedding without consulting his fiancée.

'This is all I ever dreamt about since I was a girl,' sobs the would-be bride. 'And now it's all out of my hands.'

'I'm never getting married,' Sadie says.

I start to protest, then remember I'm not married either. *A Not-Wife, a Not-Widow.*

'No,' I say. 'I don't blame you.'

My phone rings. Selina's name flashes up on the screen. *Oh shit. Not tonight. I can't face it tonight.*

'Don't answer it.' Sadie has also seen who's calling. '*Please*, Mum.'

I let it go to voicemail.

'Is the front door double locked?' Sadie wants to know.

I nod. 'All sorted,' I assure her.

We're both jittery. So many strange things are happening at the moment. Nothing feels as it should.

SELINA

Lying in bed, amidst the wreckage of my once beautiful home, I listen to the noises the night is making. It's funny to think that I was once comforted by the sounds of my hundred-and-ten-year-old house creaking its way through until dawn. Now I jump at every fresh disturbance, every click and groan of the pipes. *Things used to feel safe.* But everything I once thought solid has turned out not to be so – my marriage, my home, all my things. Even the man I shared my life with turned out to be someone else entirely and died wearing a stranger's wedding ring.

The events of the day roll through my mind like one of Felix's films. Greg (*surrounded by tubes*), his wife ('*a friend . . . that's lovely,*' *said the nurse*). Beaten up, attacked. The world has gone quite mad and yet somehow I keep going, readjusting to each new impossible reality. How are human beings so resilient?

The visit to the hospital wrung every emotion from me. When I reached home I crawled, depleted, from the car and headed straight upstairs, pausing only to set the alarm and lock the doors, even though it's Friday night and Josh doubtless has something planned. Though it's still early evening, my body craves sleep, but my idiot mind won't rest, hearing ghosts in the walls.

Thank God Josh is here. I can hear the low bass from his iPod speakers even from two rooms away. Normally it drives me bonkers, but now I'm grateful. We must talk about it all, I realize that, my children and I. We must sit down and talk about everything that has happened, and about how we go on from here. Josh and Felix must thrash it out – what Josh thinks he saw, what Felix insists is the truth. But not now. Not yet.

I must sleep. Let me sleep.

But it's no good. I imagine danger everywhere. Even with my eyes heavy with tiredness, I hear ghost footsteps on the stairs and the muffled thud of doors softly closing. Fear lodges in my throat like glass, making it hard to swallow.

LOTTIE

The doorbell startles us both, even though Sadie and I have been expecting Jules.

Try keeping anything from my sisters. They sniff out my problems like pigs with truffles. *Pigs with truffles! I must remember to tell them that. Who are you calling pigs?* They know about the break-in, and about Sadie's spree of destruction.

'Emma wants a conference call,' says Jules as she comes in, shaking off her leopard-print coat and slinging it on to the sofa arm.

I shake my head. *Not en masse. I can't cope with them en masse.*

'OK,' says Jules. 'I don't blame you. She can take over, can't she?'

She? She's not even being ironic!

Jules squeezes herself in next to Sadie on the sofa and puts an arm around her. 'I've been chanting,' she says glumly. 'To find the best way forward.'

'Was it helpful?' I snort.

'Was it fuck!'

I notice Jules's bright-red tote bag for the first time, on the chair where she dropped it. It's suspiciously full.

'What's in there? You're not staying, you know.'

She looks at me over the top of Sadie's head.

'Come on, hun. Stop trying to do this on your own. I'm worried about you. We're all worried about you. There's some really bad energy around at the moment. You're not safe.'

'*Bad energy?*' queries Sadie. 'Oh pu-lease!'

We carry on watching the television. The bride is upset because she's just seen the dress her fiancé picked out for her.

'I never would have chosen something like this,' she sniffs. 'Three years together and it's like he doesn't know me at all.'

'I've got a date on Saturday,' Jules announces.

'Another one off the internet?' I ask. 'Let's hope he's an improvement on the last.'

'He wasn't *that* bad?'

'He *dribbled*!'

'Only when he got animated. Anyway, this isn't from the internet. This is a real live actual see-each-other-across-the-room kind of date. My friend Finn introduced him to me in the pub after work last Friday.'

I glance across. My sister is looking decidedly pink.

'Anyway, I don't want to jinx it by talking about it. He's bound to be a loser who lives with his mother and irons his pants. Let's talk about you, and what's going on. I'm worried about you, babe. We're *all* worried about you. If you won't let me stay, why don't you and Sades come to mine for the night? It'll be like a sleepover. Like in *Grease*.'

360

Sadie groans theatrically. 'You are so sad,' she says.

For a moment I allow myself to picture it. To picture us, away from this flat, with all its memories and the boarded-up window and the scraps of Simon's ruined clothes still piled up on the surfaces. Being looked after by Jules. Not having to make decisions for myself. It's tempting, I swear to God.

But I'm thirty-eight years old.

I'm five months pregnant.

My daughter needs boundaries and routine.

I have to find a way to manage on my own.

I shake my head.

'Fuck off then,' says Jules, resigned.

SELINA

The noise wakes me from a vivid dream in which I was chasing around after Simon but he was always ahead, receding into the distance, growing smaller and smaller. Greg was in my dream too, trailing blood that looked like the paint on the living-room walls.

Immediately I'm alert. Ever since that first phone call from the police – *'Mrs Busfield, we're outside your house. Can you let us in?'* – sleep is no longer a warm, comfortable bath I immerse myself in, but something treacherous from which I wake abruptly, drenched in fear.

The sound which woke me came from downstairs, and is followed by total silence. But it's the kind of silence that watches and waits.

I get up out of bed and ease open my bedroom door. I

creep along the landing to Josh's room and nudge open the door, my heart pounding.

Oh thank God!

Josh's bed is empty. So it's him downstairs, after all. How jumpy I've become!

'Josh,' I call, fetching my dressing gown from my room and padding down the stairs. 'What are you doing? Have you had dinner?'

The house beneath me is steeped in darkness. Waiting. Expectant.

At the bottom of the stairs, I hesitate. *Something is weird. Something's not right.*

No lights. That's what it is. No red winking light to show me the alarm is on. But I set the alarm. I know I did.

But already my certainty is fading. Did I? Can I be sure?

I switch on the light in the hallway, and am shocked all over again by the desecration of my home – I glimpse the living-room walls, through the open doorway, viciously daubed with red.

Such violence. Such hatred. Where did it come from?

I move onward, in search of Josh.

I'm at the door to Simon's study now. But something is different. I look inside, peering into the darkness. Flicking the light switch, the room is suddenly over-bright and I blink, trying to adjust.

The desk is just as it was. Still the same Probate paper-work spread out. *Oh dear God, don't remind me.* The sight of his black sheepskin slippers still lying under the desk gives me an unexpected jolt to the heart. *How he hated to be the kind of middle-aged man who wears slippers around the house. But still, everyone needs to be comfortable . . .*

My eyes travel across the room. The door of the cupboard at the back is ajar, revealing the safe gaping open.

Someone is here, in my home. As if Sadie wasn't enough! But perhaps it is Sadie again, back to finish what she started.

But the safe? What would she want with the safe?

Isn't it funny how you can know two conflicting things at the same time, and yet they still don't rule each other out?

My rational mind knows it's not right that the safe door is open and the alarm is off, but part of me still believes, despite everything, that living in Barnes and ordering a weekly Ocado shop and having a direct debit to sponsor a child in the developing world inures me to serious harm, and that nothing untoward has happened – that the sound I heard was just Josh and there's a perfectly good explanation for everything.

It's always been this way – the two Selinas fighting it out inside me. The sensible Selina who made plans and lists and arranged project after project, each overlapping with the next, so she'd never have a chance to fall through the cracks; and the other Selina who knew deep down that all of it was a sham, a charade.

Back out in the hallway, I take a deep breath. *And let's Pran*, says the Germanic yoga instructor in my head. This is my house. I am in control within my own house. Nothing happens here unless I allow it.

I head towards the only door I haven't yet tried. The kitchen. *There was a thud. But it's OK. It's Josh. It's Sadie. It's OK.*

I give the dimmer-switch a slight turn, mindful of the shock of the desecration I know I'll find. A subdued half-light suffuses the room. Eyes blinking, I scan the softly lit carnage. *What's that?* Something on the floor, a dark shape hulking against the Chinese black slate tiles. *No, please . . .* I turn the switch on full now so the room is drenched in white light.

Oh my God!

LOTTIE

After Jules has left, Sadie and I continue watching television, but a loud sniff makes me turn and I'm shocked to see tears coursing down my daughter's face.

'Sadie?'

'I can't stand it, Mum.'

Her voice is thick with whatever it is she cannot stand, and I move closer to her on the sofa so I can put my arms around her, feeling her ribs under her sweatshirt like a set of knives. How thin my daughter has become!

'What is it, Sadie? What's the matter?'

I won't blow it this time. I won't push it.

'I've been so fucking stupid, Mum.'

My own eyes fill with tears now in sympathy for hers, but I force myself to wait for her to continue.

'You remember when you snooped on my Facebook chat with Gabi?'

'I didn't . . . Never mind. Go on.'

'The guy in the toilet with the cocaine was . . . Oh God, I'm such an idiot!'

'Was what, Sadie? Come on, you'll feel better once you've told me.'

I'm not at all sure that's true.

Sadie puts her hand to her mouth and turns her head away, biting her lip, before sniffing loudly and taking a deep breath. 'Was Felix! The guy was Felix!'

'Felix!'

Astonishment makes the word explode from my mouth and I turn to face Sadie fully, horror and disbelief rendering me momentarily mute.

'But he's . . .'

'Old?' she suggests.

'Your *brother*!' I say. 'He gave you *drugs*!'

'It was just one line – I was too nervous to say no. I didn't like it, it burned.'

'And you *kissed* him?'

For a split second, Sadie looks at me, her green eyes so stricken it hurts to see them. Something occurs to me then, something horrible. I shake my head.

'Oh Sadie, no. Please say you didn't . . .'

In one violent movement, she wrests herself from my grasp and buries her face in the cushion at the other end of the sofa.

'I know it was wrong, but he was so . . . I *loved* him! Oh God, I'm so stupid!'

She's crying properly now, taking great heaving gulps. A damp patch is spreading on the cushion from contact with her mouth.

My thoughts race uncontrollably in every direction and my head is filled with images I can't bear to confront. Meanwhile the sofa throbs with my daughter's misery.

'What did he do? What did he make you do?'

'He didn't make me. I wanted to. I thought . . .' And again the sobs.

'I'm phoning Selina right now,' I say.

The reaction is instant.

'No, you can't! You mustn't! It's finished. Over. Promise me you won't say anything.'

'But she needs to—'

'Promise!'

Sadie's face is wild with worry. What else can I do but make the promise?

'I won't call her tonight. But we'll talk about this tomorrow and I'll decide what to do.'

SELINA

I can see from here that Walter is dead.

His woolly grey legs, with their four white socks, are stiff, and his pink tongue protrudes slightly.

Oh, Walter.

Impossible to believe it's fifteen years since I bowed to family pressure and agreed to get a dog. Simon and Felix had been the most vociferous, over-ruling my objections. *The mess ... The commitment ... What about our foreign holidays ...? No prizes who'll end up walking him ...* Now I wonder whether it was a guilt thing with Simon, wanting me to have someone at home with me, while he was out there in Dubai with *her*.

We all went to the breeder to pick him up, a tiny bundle of grey and white fur all going in different directions like Josh's hair used to do when he was little. Fluffy white patches on his ears.

The children fought in the back seat for a turn to hold

him. Felix, in the middle, had tears streaming down his face. He cradled the quivering creature as if he was scared he might break him and, looking down into his face said, 'I'm going to love you even more than my mum.'

So much family history built around one little dog.

And me? A goner, of course, from the moment he fixed me with his bright black eyes and cocked his tiny, tufty head, raising one ear as if challenging me not to love him.

I remember sleeping on the sofa when we were trying to get him used to being downstairs at night, then trying to close my ears to his plaintive cries when I finally moved back up to our bedroom. There were mornings when I'd get up to find Josh curled up in Walter's basket alongside the sleeping dog, and long school holidays when one or other of the children would take out a book on dog training from the library and, armed with a packet of dog biscuits, try to coax an intransigent Walter into rolling over on command.

Poor Walter.

I remember how keen Simon was for us to get another puppy, how he nagged me in the months leading up to his death. Another conscience-salving gesture, I suppose. With Josh only having a year left at school, he'd have been worrying about me rattling around this huge house on my own.

So he was planning to leave me then, after all? It comes to me, just like that. He'd made his decision, was paving the way for an exit. The mystery account must have been a fund to buy himself out of his marriage.

The idea creates a dull ache in my stomach. All those times he sat next to me on the sofa, his arm slung loosely behind me, his fingers absently stroking my shoulder; all the times he lay on our bed while I stretched out in the bath of our en suite, the door open between us as we swapped notes on our respective days; all those moments when intimacy looped around us both like a silken cord, binding us loosely together; throughout all that, he was planning to leave me, thinking of the money that would buy him a different future. Of all the things he did, that illusion of intimacy is the hardest to bear.

We argued about the puppy quite recently. 'Walter's on his last legs,' Simon said. 'He won't last much longer. A puppy will be a distraction. It'll be company for you.'

'That's not the kind of company I want!' *Snappy*. 'I want normal, adult, human company. A full-time husband, for example.'

He was cross then, sullen. Defensive.

'You know my work is there. We've been through this a million times.'

And me, bulldozing through.

'Yes, but it won't always be. You're fifty-three. You'll be retiring soon. We'll have time then to go travelling, to see the world. We won't be able to do that with a new dog.'

Over the distance of time I try to force myself back into the memory, to see Simon's face, his expression. What was it? Cornered? Anxious? Terrified?

The truth is, I have no idea. We'd long passed the point of really looking at each other.

I sink to my knees next to my poor, stiff dog and stroke his head, imagining for a moment that I can bring him back to life just by loving him enough. Idiot! When was love ever enough?

There's a bare patch on Walter's side where he had that operation last year to remove a non-cancerous lump and the fur never grew back. I remember bringing him home from the vet, barely conscious, and carrying him in from the car, sitting down on the sofa in the den and holding him in my lap for hours, until Josh came home and didn't know whether to be more shocked at the state of Walter or at the fact that I was allowing him on the furniture.

He was so woven into the fabric of our family life.

I wish someone else was here. Josh. Suddenly I'm remembering the switched-off alarm, the safe door flapping open. *Nothing in the safe though, just . . .*

Where *is* Josh? He ought to be here.

I'm so tired. Just so tired.

I rest my head on Walter's unyielding body and wail like a banshee for all the things that I have lost.

LOTTIE

Only later, when Sadie has gone to bed, and I've checked all the locks a thousand times – (*that's all I need – late-onset OCD*), do I remember to check the message from Selina. I grit my teeth before playing it back, knowing her voice will make me think of Felix and what he did. Immediately nausea overwhelms me as the images take over – my daughter in a toilet cubicle, glossy hair trailing in toxic white powder; my daughter in bed with— But no, that's a step too far. I can't go there and my mind clangs shut. My hatred for Felix takes me by surprise, clotting inside me. I know I will have to deal with it, but not tonight. I promised my daughter.

When I play Selina's message I'm half-expecting her to

give me an inventory of everything Sadie ruined or broke. That's the type of thing she'd do – send me a spreadsheet, with links so I can see how much replacements cost.

Her voice, when it comes on, is louder than usual, and she sounds breathless.

'I'm in the car, on my handsfree,' she says. She *would* be. 'On the way back from the hospital.'

Hospital?

'Lottie, it sounds as if Simon was mixed up in something . . .' Her voice goes crackly at this point and is impossible to hear. Then suddenly she's back. 'I really think he might have been murdered.'

SELINA

It's after midnight when Josh finally comes in. I'm sitting on the floor in the den, next to Walter's basket, where I've moved him. The curtains are undrawn and in the soft grey light, with his tartan blanket laid over him, he looks just like he's sleeping.

Josh stands in the hallway, looking in.

How very peculiar!

He's wearing a black wool coat of Simon's that seems to be coated with grey grit and dust, and by his side is the large black holdall, complete with handle and wheels, that's usually stored in the garage.

'What are you . . . ?' Both of us are speaking at once.

We smile slightly, embarrassed.

Josh steps into the den. He looks so tired, his hazel eyes smudged around the edges with shadows.

'Why are you . . .?' he asks, stopping when he draws closer to Walter. 'Oh God, he's not . . .?'

A lump forms in my throat and I nod, not trusting myself to speak for fear that if I open my mouth I won't be able to control what comes out of it. I worry that if I start to cry, I might never be able to stop.

Josh flings himself down next to me on the floor and strokes Walter's ears. A single tear runs down the gentle curve of his cheek.

'He was old, darling,' I say now.

Josh nods, but I know what he's thinking. It's not really about how old Walter was and who he was, it's about the ending of things. Walter has been around as long as Josh can remember. His death is also, in a sense, despite everything that has happened recently, the end of Josh's childhood. I imagine the adult Josh in years to come, telling his own children (*what a wonderful father he will make, this son of mine*) about his first pet, and am shocked by the jolt of pain that goes through me at the thought of my son building a separate family folklore with his own children, in which, at best, I'll be peripheral.

Now that Josh is so close to me, I have a clearer view of the grey clumps of dust all over his coat, or rather all over Simon's coat. From this near I can see it's not actually grit or gravel, it's more like . . .

'Josh, where have you been?' My voice is sharp now, worried.

He wouldn't have . . .

He couldn't have . . .

My son leans forward and presses his face into Walter's furry ears. Then he faces me. 'I should never have had that whisky,' he says.

Oh!

'After you'd gone to bed last night, I sat in the kitchen, admiring Sadie's artwork, and I thought it wouldn't hurt to have a little whisky. Just a tiny glass,' Josh continues.

'Josh!' I break in, voice lumpen with warning.

'I know, I know,' he says. 'But it has been very stressful around here recently.'

That's one way of putting it.

'Then I was on my way to bed, and I just thought I'd have a little sit down in Dad's office.'

'Why?'

Josh shrugs, looking embarrassed. 'I dunno. I go there sometimes.'

Of course he does. He's lost his father. How easy it is to forget that! Looking at Josh, this child in a man's body, I feel something delicate bend and quiver inside me, threatening to break. Somehow in my head I've been imagining him fully grown and complete, my work quite done, my influence minimal at best, but now I see how he is still partly unformed. Suddenly I'm reminded of the soft spot on my babies' heads during their first weeks of life and how horrified I was when Felix was born that there was something still unfinished about him, something that left him exposed to harm. Each day I anxiously felt the alarmingly yielding flesh, praying for the bones to hurry up and fuse together to make him safe.

But Josh is speaking again. I must concentrate.

'Then I was thinking about all the shit that's been going on, and I got this mad idea that it was because of Dad not being . . . you know . . . sorted.'

I blink at him. 'Sorted?'

'You know, peaceful.'

Don't tell me Josh is getting spiritual?

'So then I thought, what I should do is do something with the ashes.'

Josh says this as though it's entirely obvious and for a second I nod. Then it sinks in . . .

'Your father's ashes? You've disposed of your father's ashes without consulting anyone else?'

He looks at me, sheepish. 'Sorry,' he says.

He opened the safe, he tells me, remembering that the new combination was our wedding anniversary, and took out the box, deciding to get the holdall from the garage when he realized how heavy it would be to carry. He also took his father's coat from the cupboard in the hall.

'And then I went,' he says.

'Went where?'

Along the river, comes the answer. My son strolled out into the night, wheeling the ashes of his dead father all the way to Putney Bridge.

And the madness keeps on coming!

I can picture him so clearly, still warmed by the effects of the whisky (*was there also a spliff involved? I wouldn't be surprised. I've been such a negligent mother, thinking only of myself*), reaching into the box and opening up the plastic urn.

'It was a plastic flowerpot, for fuck's sake,' says Josh, suddenly angry. 'No wonder Dad hated it in there.'

He tipped out the ashes, standing in the middle of the bridge, and watched them fall into the water, wondering where they'd end up. A rogue gust of wind blew some of the finer particles back at him and they settled like dandruff on his coat. *Literally wearing his father on his back.*

My anger at what he's done drains out of me. Somehow it doesn't seem wrong after all, this private little ceremony.

'Did you say anything?' I want to know.

God knows why it seems important. What is there to say, for goodness' sake? And yet . . .

Josh looks embarrassed. 'I dunno. I guess so,' he says.

He clearly doesn't want to talk about it, but I press him. It suddenly seems burningly important to me that Simon had some sort of send-off, lying bastard though he was.

Josh looks at my face. Gives in.

'I told him he really bollocksed things up, but he wasn't a bad person. I said he was my dad and I loved him and I miss him.'

Josh stares fixedly at Walter's basket, obviously mortified to have made such an admission out loud. We both gaze in rigid silence at the small blanket-covered body.

The sob comes from nowhere, ripped out of him like something he has absolutely no control over. And suddenly he's once again the cheeky, good-natured, warm-hearted toddler he once was, albeit one who reeks of whisky. How impossibly long seem the decade and a half that separate the person I am now from the woman I was then, who kissed his chubby hand when he fell over and crawled out of his room at night on my knees in case he woke. It's a whole lifetime, and yet, looking at my sad, grief-drained boy, it seems like no time at all.

I move towards him, my arms open, and suddenly we're hugging each other quite as if the world might be about to end.

27

LOTTIE

I am up well before it's light, having lain awake most of the night, my stomach churning with a mixture of panic and dread, knowing I have to confront what Sadie told me last night. I don't want to talk to my daughter about the things she's done with that boy, that *man*. Everything in me wants to shy away from it, pretend it didn't happen. Yet I must, because if not me, then who? I steel myself to bring it up over breakfast. Sadie is already closed off after last night's blurted confidences. She doesn't want to talk.

'I need to know,' I tell her, my voice sounding unnaturally loud. 'Did it go . . . all the way?'

All the way? I've turned into a 1950s housewife! But we don't have the language for this kind of conversation, Sadie and I. It's all so new.

Sadie snorts with laughter. '*All the way*?' she parrots, but her face is burning.

'It's important, Sadie. Did you use . . . ?'

She makes an 'ugh' sound and turns away, embarrassed. 'It's OK,' she says, to the wall. 'I'm not *completely* stupid, you know?'

I expect her to storm off to her room at this point, as she

usually does, but to my surprise she stays, spooning cereal into her mouth.

'And afterwards?' I venture. 'What happened then?'

Her face droops and I long to get a straw and suck all the sadness away from her.

'I never heard from him,' she says. Again, I feel a rush of hatred for the boy that is Simon's son.

'I must tell Selina,' I say. 'She needs to know.'

Sadie glances at me, then away. She doesn't speak.

SELINA

I awake to the beeping of my phone, announcing a text message.

Greg out of coma, it reads. *Not yet fully conscious but all looks promising.*

I'd forgotten about Greg!

I stare at the screen, trying to assess my own reaction. Guilt tugs at me like a small child at my hem. Obviously I'm happy to hear he's going to be all right, but I ought to have been more concerned, oughtn't I? I oughtn't to have pushed him from my mind so easily. I ought definitely to have given him as much thought as a dead dog. This is someone I was intimate with ... Or was I? Does 'intimacy' really describe the relationship I had with Greg Ronaldson? Come to think of it, does 'relationship' really describe it? Wasn't it just sex, when you come down to it?

Even so, I shouldn't have had to be reminded that he had been injured. In spite of everything that has happened, and that keeps happening, I should have responded from the heart, shouldn't I?

Should. Ought. The bricks from which my life has been built.

In the cold light of a grey, late-February day, the crazy theories that ran through my head after finding out about Greg's attack seem ludicrously far-fetched. The grief-stricken widow grasping at straws to prove her husband didn't choose to die.

I lie in the big white bed, allowing my thoughts to settle. Daylight seeps in through the opaque ivory curtains, turning our bedroom, *my* bedroom into something resembling an empty gallery – all white walls and white floorboards on which deep-pile white rugs settle like snow.

'What this room needs is a bit of colour,' Simon was forever saying. But I find it soothing, the purity of white on white. It's strange to think I'll soon be waking up in a different room. Once the house is on the market, the agents expect it to go very quickly – well, as soon as we've cleared up after Sadie's little spree. Apparently there's a waiting list of people desperate to move into these roads. I try to imagine myself in that other bedroom in the Mortlake flat. Will I still be me, I wonder, in that new, unknown room that Simon will never see? Is the me without Simon still the same person as the me who chose that distressed-white-painted chest of drawers over there, or the painting of a Cornwall cove that hangs over the bed?

From downstairs comes the sound of a woman laughing. What is the time anyway? I glance at my phone screen. Twelve thirty-five! How can I have slept so late?

Heading downstairs, I try to make out the voices I hear.

Flora definitely, and I think Hettie. Oh, and Josh is already up!

Glancing out of the window on the turn of the stairs, I see Felix's vintage Merc parked in the driveway alongside Hettie's convertible VW Beetle. Some kind of convention. What on earth is going on?

Flora is upon me even before I reach the bottom of the stairs.

'God, Mum,' she mumbles into my neck, her arms locked solid around my waist. 'Poor Walter. I can't believe it!'

I pat her on the back and mutter something about it being his time. At times like this, it doesn't really matter what you say, I always think, it's all about the way you say it. Pulling away, I glance at the curious jumper Flora has on. An appliqué animal of some sort. And why not, for heaven's sake? *Good for her.* Flora's eyes are puffy, as if she's been crying, but she seems to be holding herself together remarkably well.

'What's Ryan up to?' I ask her casually. It's a Saturday, after all. Shouldn't he be here, playing the supportive fiancé?

She shrugs and examines the ends of her hair. 'I don't know,' she says. 'I didn't really ask him.'

Josh has appeared, red-eyed, in the hallway. 'We're going to give him a proper funeral,' he says. 'We've been waiting ages.'

I make my way to the kitchen, Flora Velcroed to my side, and find Hettie and Felix sitting at the table. Between them stands an empty cafetière of coffee and a wooden board heaped with leftover croissant flakes. Petra is curled up in one of the armchairs by the French windows, gazing out at the uninspiring grey day. My stomach lurches at the sight of her. She's lost weight, and her normally gleaming hair looks dull and lank. Guilt at never returning her call makes me unable to meet her eyes, my gaze sliding right over the surface of her.

'So sorry, Sel,' says Hettie, jumping up to give me a kiss.

Sorry for what? For my husband being dead? For being married to a bigamist? For losing my home? My life is a shop-window display of sorry.

'Thanks,' I say.

'How are you, Madre?' asks Felix, getting slowly to his feet to give me a hug. 'I'm loving the new décor.'

I glance around the room. Already I'm so used to the damage wrought by Sadie the other night that I hardly notice it. Anyway, it looks as if someone has been clearing up. Hettie, I imagine, or Petra.

I pull away, looking more closely at Felix. His eyes are sunk into his face, a sure sign that he's not sleeping well. I'm not going to talk to him again about that business with Josh and Sadie, not in front of Hettie and certainly not Petra, but sooner or later we'll have to have a proper chat about it, establish some boundaries. I don't relish it.

'I'm fine,' I say, dropping into one of the dining chairs. 'Well, still alive anyway.'

To my surprise, I notice my mother is here too, sitting in her usual armchair by the window. 'I went to pick her up,' explains Felix. 'I know how Granny loves a good funeral.'

'Come and see Walter,' says Flora, waving her hand in the direction of a large cardboard box in the corner of the room. 'We've made him so comfy.'

I allow myself to be pulled to my feet and escorted the length of the room.

Walter is lying in state in a nest of blankets taken from his basket. Something catches in my throat when I see the threadbare toy seal he unaccountably took a liking to many years ago, which is tucked up next to his head. I remember Felix winning that seal at a fairground stall when he was young, bringing it proudly home like a hunter with the evening meal.

'Your oldest son has been manfully wielding a shovel,' says Hettie. 'He's been digging a hole in the garden under the willow tree.'

I nod. Why not?

'I'd better go and finish it,' says Felix, disappearing through the French doors into the garden. His back is a curve of sadness.

We make a strange group of mourners, crowded under the willow tree in the grey drizzle, branches draped over our shoulders, leaves trailing over our backs. Flora sniffs as Josh staggers out through the French doors with the makeshift coffin, and I lean across to grab my daughter's hand. At first it feels strange, but the longer I force myself to keep hold of it, the more natural it becomes.

The children have decided they'll each say a brief eulogy for the dog who has, faithfully and without fuss, patrolled the perimeters of their lives for fifteen years.

Flora starts by remembering how Walter came to us as a puppy.

'Remember how I used to wrap him up in my T-shirt and carry him around in that Easter Egg basket?' she says. 'This little ball of fluff. And remember, Fee, how you held him on your lap in the car when we first brought him home and said,' – here everyone joins in the well-worn phrase that has long since been absorbed into family folklore – ' "I'm going to love you more than my mum"?'

Josh's contribution is short and to the point.

'Walter was the crappest guard dog that ever lived.' A murmur of assent from the assembled company. 'But when it came to getting in the way so you tripped over him or chasing squirrels in his sleep, he was champion.'

Now Felix. How ill at ease he looks, with his red-rimmed eyes and his fingers always fidgeting at his leg.

'Dearly beloved, and everyone I can't stand the sight of,' he begins. 'We are here to commend the soul of our dear departed Walter – the best, if not the brightest dog in the history of the world.'

Now he stops.

'Walter was . . .' he tries. 'Walter was . . .'

Everyone stares.

Felix is crying!

He didn't cry for his father, but here he is with tears silently running down his face, crying for his dog. *Poor Felix. Poor boy.*

'Oh my God, Fee, are you all right?' Flora asks. Her own eyes are surprisingly dry, as if her older brother's tears have soaked up her own.

'He didn't deserve to die,' Felix blurts out, and my heart contracts for him. Nearly twenty-six but still such an emotional baby – still thinking of death as something merited, rather than something meted out willy-nilly.

'Well!' My mother is looking around as if she can't quite believe her eyes. 'All this fuss over a dog. You want to try getting to my age. Death is just another thing that happens, you know. Like supper.'

As we all fall into contemplative silence, I look around

at the family Simon and I made together, and for the first time since his funeral, I feel a sense of, if not peace, then at least acceptance. In my mind the burial of our Walter merges with Simon's death, and it feels almost as if I'm laying something to rest between us. In the end, I think there are as many versions of Simon as there are people gathered around the willow tree. More, when you consider how our perceptions of him have changed since he died. Alive, Simon was infuriating and bombastic and funny and inconsiderate and suddenly, unexpectedly kind. Dead Simon is cloudy with secrets. His secrets were rocks in his pockets, weighing him down.

I feel an overwhelming urge to come up with a message for Simon now, something that will give some meaning to this occasion. I could find a million things to say about our life and about how I feel, but in the end, my message comes down to just three words.

I forgive you.

LOTTIE

It has a name, this thing that has happened to my daughter. Genetic Sexual Attraction. I've been Googling it all afternoon, propped up in bed, while Sadie's music thumps through the walls and I put off calling Selina Busfield. Apparently it's not uncommon where family members have been separated and then find each other later in life. It happens with sisters and brothers who were adopted, even mothers and sons and fathers and daughters. This scientific provenance ought to make it easier to bear, yet it doesn't.

I can't put it off any longer. I steel myself to call Selina, not even knowing what I'll say. When the phone goes straight to voicemail, I feel at first relieved and then deflated. The dread that kept me awake last night won't leave. I need to speak to someone about what's been happening, but at the same time I don't want to tell my sisters. I need to handle this myself. This is about my daughter, my family.

I fire up the laptop again to read more about Genetic Sexual Attraction. Opening up the History bar to find the site I was on, I am confronted by a whole list of sites I've never heard of before, obviously ones Sadie has been visiting while using my computer. *What on earth?* My mind races as I go down the column – debt sites, loan sites, no-win-no-fee solicitors, dating sites, STD clinics. I click on a few at random, trying to work out what my daughter could possibly have been looking for. Finally I call up a website inviting me to register for an immediate cash payment, despite my poor credit rating. *Your registration is incomplete*, it says. When I click on the link, there's a form which is empty apart from the name of the person being registered: Selina Busfield.

SELINA

After the burial ceremony, the afternoon limps slowly and bad-temperedly on towards evening. My mother (*why can I never think of her as Mum, even now, always my mother?*) is still impatient with what she sees as our self-indulgent grief over Walter.

383

'All this fuss,' she keeps repeating. 'For a dog!'

The children, who don't yet understand how age can make you tired of feelings, are hurt by her lack of sympathy.

'He was part of the family, Grandma,' Flora tries to explain.

'What does that mean?' sniffs my mother. 'My sister Milly was part of the family and I didn't speak to her for forty-five years.'

In the end Felix says he'll take her back to her residential home. She spends ages hobbling painfully around collecting her scarf and gloves and coat, refusing offers of help.

Before she leaves, she reappears in the doorway of the den.

'I expect you all think I'm a bit harsh,' she says, and there's a suspicion of pink in the whites of her blue eyes. 'I just meant . . . it's not the end all and be all . . . death, I'm talking about. It's just . . . something else we live with. Because there's no other choice.'

I get up and give her a hug. *She's so tiny now. How long before she shrinks clear away?*

After they've gone, I go into the kitchen to make tea. As I'm filling the kettle at the sink, Petra materializes by my side. Her lovely olive skin is stretched so tight over the delicate bones of her face, it looks as if it could snap.

I was wondering if we could meet for a chat, said her message. The one I ignored. Once again I'm flushed through with guilt.

'I've been trying to talk to you,' says Petra.

'I know. I'm so sorry, dear. I've been so distracted, you know how it's been . . .'

I've been so distracted? For goodness' sake, how lame I sound! But Petra nods. She even has the grace to look concerned. Simon was right – she *is* a nice girl. Why haven't I realized that until now? I wish she didn't look so unhappy though. I'm so tired. Too tired to hear whatever it is she wants to say.

'It's about Felix,' she says, her cheeks flushing slightly. Three years we've known each other, Petra and I, but intimacy feels as awkward as if we were strangers making small talk in a lift. 'Have you noticed anything strange lately, about his behaviour?'

I think about Felix, and how thin he's become.

'He's not . . . anorexic, is he?' I ask.

Well, you hear of such things, men suffering eating disorders. But Petra seems to find the idea funny.

'No,' she says, giggling in a way that seems not to contain any mirth at all. 'He's—'

'Ah, there you are.'

Felix appears in the kitchen. Surprisingly, while the rest of us seem to have wilted as the day has progressed, Felix appears brighter and more alert, as if his earlier graveside collapse has invigorated him somehow. He slings an arm around Petra and I instinctively glance away. *Oh, to have that again, the casual arm around the shoulders.*

'You're needed,' says Felix. 'Flora is trying to force us to watch *The Only Way is Orange*.'

'Essex,' Petra says in a voice that's impossible to read. '*The Only Way is Essex*.'

'Exactly,' says Felix, steering her out of the kitchen. 'So you must come and outvote her.'

'But I was just talking to your mum . . .'

'You go,' I tell her, as Felix eyes us both with curiosity. 'We'll finish our chat later.'

For a moment after they've gone I am charged with guilt. I should have listened, should have asked more. I know there's a conversation coming that I'm not going to like. Something about Felix. Not anorexia then, but something. Surely nothing to do with Sadie? We sorted that . . . it's done. But then I lean against the worktop and feel myself sag with relief.

In the back of my head, I register that my phone is ringing. I close my eyes, only opening them again when it stops. Glancing at the screen, I see it was Maggie Ronaldson calling. There's a message: *Greg's conscious and talking about what happened to him. It's really important you call me as soon as you get this.*

But I can't face calling her now. I will, just not now.

There's also a message from Lottie, asking me to call her back urgently. She sounds very stressed. I definitely can't deal with that neurotic woman today.

Just let me have tonight. Please. This one last evening to empty my mind and lose myself in the luxury of thinking of nothing. I'll have this tea – *herbal, I think* – then run a bath. I'll light candles that smell like new beginnings and close my eyes and think of pine trees in the rain and fields of fresh flowers.

I will not think about Simon and the secrets that multiplied inside him like tumours.

I will not think about Greg.

I will not think about poor dead Walter or my wrecked house or my children who, though grown, nevertheless wind themselves like bindweed around my tired heart.

Everyone reaches a tipping point, don't they? And this, I suspect, is mine.

LOTTIE

The discovery that it's Sadie who's behind all Selina's spam has sent my anxiety levels rocketing – I can hear the music blaring out from her room, but I can't face another confrontation with her, so soon after this morning's breakfast scene. Equally I'm too restless to stay in bed. My stomach feels tight and I keep stroking my bump to try to soothe myself. My daughter is so lost. How have I allowed it to happen? After a night without sleep, my nerves are on edge, and as I go into the kitchen to make a cup of tea, I can't shake the feeling that there's something wrong, something amiss.

Filling the kettle, I glance around. The same mess as always. This morning's breakfast things still out on the table, next to a teetering pile of laundry waiting to be sorted. Sadie's English books dumped on a chair from when she emptied her schoolbag two days ago. But something is different. I can feel it.

Taking out a teabag from the tin inside the cupboard, I look around again, my eye finally falling on the back door, which, now I look closer, seems to be fractionally ajar. Well, how weird. I don't remember—

The scream comes from everywhere and nowhere at the same time. Fear surges through me, white hot. *Sadie. I must protect Sadie.* I start towards her room at the same time as the hall cupboard bursts open.

SELINA

The phone is ringing. That's what's woken me. I feel so groggy, I can't tell if my eyes are open or shut. Shut, I think. Everything is dark. I shouldn't have taken that sleeping pill.

'Mrs Busfield? This is Detective Inspector Bowles.'

The sense of déjà vu combines with the sleeping-pill grogginess, plunging me into the deepest confusion. Is this real, or have I somehow gone back in time?

'Is your son there, Mrs Busfield?'

'Josh? I'm not sure, I—'

'Not Josh. Your oldest son. Felix.'

I'm trying my best to follow, but my thoughts are flabby and gelatinous, impossible to wade through. Why Felix?

'He's not here,' I manage eventually. 'He went home. What's the matter? Why do you want him?' My voice sounds thick and floury.

'I've been watching the CCTV again, Mrs Busfield.' The policeman sounds excited, as if he's about to tell me the punchline of the most enormous joke. 'You know, all this time we've been scrutinizing your husband and his companion on that footage, together with the people immediately behind and in front of them. Well, earlier on my attention was caught by a woman who was coming towards your husband. She was wearing one of those shapeless padded coats, you know the kind I mean, and I found myself wondering why women wear those things.' The policeman seems to be too excited by his own cleverness to pay much attention to what he's saying. 'So I kept the footage rolling even after your husband and his companion exited the screen on the right, following her as she disappeared into the darkness at the end of the street. And that's when I saw it. Just a flash, mind, before the screen closed off as the lab technicians cut the film short like they'd been told to.'

I'm not following at all. I don't understand why he's telling me this.

'Saw what?' I break in, rudely.

'A figure coming towards the camera, still a bit of a distant blur, mind – but wearing a very distinctive pork-pie hat.'

LOTTIE

'Chris!'

My cry seems to have its own echo, and my hands shoot over to cover my belly, instinctively protecting it. I've seen the expression on Chris Griffiths' face, and I know there's nothing I can do to stop him doing whatever he's been hiding in the cupboard to do. I just want to keep him from Sadie, that's all. I just want her to be safe.

I close my eyes, but the anticipated attack never comes. Instead I feel a blast of freezing air from behind me, so shockingly unexpected that for a second I think I must have been shot.

'Chris!'

Two things strike me immediately about this second cry. First, that it's calmer than the first, and second, that it isn't coming from me.

Opening my eyes, I see that Chris's wife Karen, who has

just come in through the back door, has intercepted her husband and is standing between him and me.

Chris stops, his breath coming out in sobs, his expression confused.

'Karen?' he says, and his voice, just a few moments ago twisted into that inhuman scream, now sounds almost childlike. For a split second no one speaks, and then Chris's face caves in on itself like flour.

'It's all right,' says Karen, putting her arms around her husband's heaving shoulders. 'It's OK.'

Standing in my kitchen, my heart pounding painfully against my ribcage, I feel like a voyeur, like I'm witnessing something that ought to be private.

'He hasn't been taking his medication.' Karen doesn't turn around, so it takes a while to realize she's talking to me. 'Normally we're very happy. He never even thinks about you.'

I remember the noises in the night, the sense of things having been moved around in my bedroom, the footsteps outside, and I feel sick.

'I don't understand,' I say. But now it's coming back to me. Those first months after Simon and I got together, we were so happy in our little bubble – except for my ex-boyfriend, Chris.

'*I can't accept it's over. I won't accept it's over.*'

In vain I attempted to explain that for me it had never really begun.

'*It's all about money, isn't it? Because he's a flash git and I'm not!*'

An avalanche of dreadful self-penned songs followed, recorded on to cassettes and arriving hand-delivered through my letterbox or warbled down the phone in late-night calls, anthems to heartbreak. Then, when he passed into the angry stage, furious letters replaced the songs, words scratched across the paper in red biro. All those weeks where sleep was punctuated by bitter, incoherent phone calls until Simon finally snapped and tore the phone out of the wall. That awful scene where Chris arrived on the doorstep of my old flat in the early hours and curled up in a ball under the dining table, refusing to move.

Some kind of a breakdown. Historic mental-health issues.

I hadn't been taking my medication, said his brief letter of explanation – the last time I heard from him. *I'm completely fine now.*

Then nothing . . . until that phone call about Simon.

Egg leaking out between my fingers. Egg pooling on the floor.

'I've come here a few times,' says Chris now, and his voice is totally flat. 'To make sure you were safe.'

So that was him? The footsteps on the path outside, the breathing in the night.

Not Simon at all. Not Simon looking out for us.

Anger surges through me. How dare he? Coming here to my home, lurking in the shadows, making me believe in ghosts.

'It was you, wasn't it?' I yell. 'Breaking in, trashing the place. It was you!'

He looks at his wife, looks at me, looks away again.

'Sorry 'bout that,' he mumbles. As if it was a slight error – a misunderstanding over meeting times, dry cleaning he forgot to pick up.

'It's just that the funeral brought it all back,' he says,

and I notice his eyes for the first time. Dead fish eyes. 'And all that . . . *unpleasantness* with the other family. You should have listened to me – about Simon Busfield. I did try to warn you.'

I don't believe what I'm hearing. It's like a horrible dream.

'Did you know he'd been following me?' I ask Karen Griffiths, who remains locked in a swaying embrace with her husband in the middle of my kitchen.

She shakes her head. 'I only noticed tonight that he'd stopped taking his lithium,' she says. 'That's why I came after him. He wouldn't . . . He's not dangerous.'

Hunched over, with his face buried in her neck, Chris gives out a low moan. 'Sorry,' he says. 'Sorry, sorry, sorry.'

'It's all right, sweetheart,' says Karen. 'You're not in any trouble.'

'No trouble?' I shout. 'Do you have any idea what he's put me through? I should call the police. He scared me to death. Not to mention all the damage . . .'

My words tail off as I remember the damage my own daughter caused not much more than twenty-four hours ago.

'Please don't. I'll make sure he takes his meds from now on. He's always fine when he's doing that.' Karen is talking to me, but all her attention is focused on him and I'm hit by a shocking realization.

She loves him!

This quiet, plain, uncommunicative woman is totally in love with her husband, even though he's clearly barking mad.

Who'd have thought it?

For a few moments I watch them, trying to make sense of it all.

What on earth is this thing called love that makes people hide themselves away in cupboards? 'Love is about wanting more,' Simon said once. 'Wanting more of someone, more for someone, more life, more love. More everything.'

But watching Karen Griffiths standing in the home of her husband's ex-girlfriend, wearing her oversized fleece with a rugby shirt underneath it, the collar turned stiffly up, and her ludicrous red shoes (*Kickers, for Christ's sake!*), loving her man, it occurs to me that maybe we got it wrong, Simon and I. Maybe love isn't about excess, after all. Maybe all the time I've been lying in my bed, weeping and thrashing about and wanting to die, real love was quietly and sensibly dressing itself in its husband's fleece and following him to another woman's house, watching over him and waiting for the moment to step in and take him home.

My anger is draining out of me, and now I'm thinking about Sadie, still in her room playing her music. Can she really not have heard anything?

I slip out of the kitchen and along the hallway to Sadie's room, where something with a lot of drum and bass is making the door shake. Out of habit I look at my watch – eleven fifteen. The neighbours will be getting cross.

'Yeah?' she says, looking up, startled, as I come in. 'What's the matter?'

I look down at my daughter, lying in bed, writing in her secret notebook with a pink felt-pen, and I'm flooded with love and relief. I make a silent promise to take better care of her. I know I can't protect her from the Felixes of the future, but I can at least show her that when you're let down, it's possible to get up again and to keep getting up, even when everything in you feels you'll never get up again.

'Nothing,' I say. 'Nothing at all.'

When the worst that can happen has already happened, what can you do but start again?

SELINA

My phone is still in my hand. I stare at it, willing it to make sense of what the policeman just told me, but my pharmaceutically dulled thoughts are sinking like sediment to the bottom of my mind. I lean back against the pillows and shut my eyes.

All of a sudden, I'm awake again, conscious of warmth in the bed next to me.

'Simon?'

His arms around me, comforting. His words soft and soothing. *It's all right. Everything's all right now.*

I want to drift off again, but something is nagging at me, something not right . . .

'Felix?'

I turn to face him.

His eyes are wide and staring. 'Don't be frightened, Madre. It's only me.'

I sit up in bed, shock chasing away the sleeping pill's lingering effects, but Felix puts his hand on my shoulder, firmly pushing me back down.

'What?' I say wildly. 'What's happened?'

That maddening smile. 'Chillax, Madre. Nothing's the matter.'

There's something disturbing about the way he's looking at me, and his limbs seem to be moving of their own accord, jerky and persistent, softly thudding against the mattress.

'The police rang me,' I say. 'They said you were there, Felix, on the night your dad died. What's going on?' Too late, I think about Petra and her face when she asked if I'd noticed anything different about Felix.

'Please tell me this isn't anything to do with Sadie?' My voice is sour with disgust. 'You know she's a child, Felix. Not to mention your sister.'

'Don't fret,' he says, as if I'm a baby. 'You know what sixteen-year-old girls are like. They make stuff up.'

But I'm looking at him in disbelief, thinking about the marks on Petra's arm at Christmas – how unhappy would you have to be to do that?

'No wonder Petra looks so terrible,' I say. 'No wonder she's doing such horrible things to herself.'

Felix lets out a loud, high-pitched giggle. 'Oh yes, I forgot,' he says. 'The self-harming.'

Now something nasty and bitter is coming into my mouth as a horrible thought forms. He wouldn't . . . he couldn't . . .

'She didn't make those marks on her arm, did she, Felix? It was you.'

Again the grin, but his face is so thin and sunken in the semi-darkness, it is more like a grimace.

'You see, the thing is, Madre, things aren't too great.'

One of his arms is around me, like a clamp, but I can feel his other hand drumming against his leg.

Oh Felix. Oh my boy. What have you done?

'Let me sit up now, Felix. You're scaring me.'

'Oh, we mustn't have that.' His voice is mocking as always, but lacking its usual lightness, grating in my ears like fingernails down a blackboard.

'He wasn't worthy, Madre. You could have done so much better.'

What's he talking about now? The sudden change of subject takes me by surprise. *He isn't worth it.* A connection stirs in the back of my still-sluggish mind.

'Don't say that, Felix. Whatever he did, he was your father.'

Again that horrible squealing giggle.

'Not *him*,' he splutters. 'The other one. Greg Ronaldson.'

And now a scream rises in my throat like bile.

'What are you saying, Felix? What do you know about Greg? What have you done?'

The memories crowd into my head now like ants and I bat them off, one after the other. Felix as a toddler biting his little playmate on the arm – '*Wasn't me*' – and me believing him because of his wide outraged eyes, despite the raised red welt on the other boy's plump skin. Then at four or five, coming out of Flora's nursery. '*Baby sleeping*,' he said, but something in his smile gave him away, and I flew in to find a pillow dropped in Flora's cot, all but smothering her tiny head. And then in secondary school, the allegations of bullying from that awful American boy. '*I didn't do it!*' Felix grabbing my hand in the headmaster's office, willing me to believe him. '*He's lying. You know he is.*'

At the time I separated these incidents off from each other, refusing to see a pattern, although occasionally Simon would express doubts. *Felix can be highly strung*, I told him, *we all know that*. And sometimes we had to walk on eggshells around him, when he was in one of his moods. But he was so funny as well, and so clever and so loving. I remember waking up one morning when he'd only just made the transition from cot to bed, and finding him standing by me, his forehead pressed tightly up against mine as if he wanted to push his way right into my skull. 'Wake up, Mummy!' he demanded. 'Wake up and be with me and not with you.'

The memories mass around me, blocking my nostrils and mouth, making it hard to breathe.

'Please tell me it wasn't you who attacked Greg. He could have *died*, for God's sake.'

That note on my windscreen. HE ISN'T WORTH IT. Of course.

But Felix doesn't want to talk about Greg.

'I knew, you know,' he says suddenly, conversationally. 'About Dad and Lottie.'

I force myself up to a sitting position to stare at him, the words of the policeman echoing in my head.

'Yes, I found out when I was about fourteen. He had a photograph on his computer of the three of them lying on a beach, with a picnic. The little girl was eating a red ice lolly and it looked like her mouth was bleeding.'

'Felix, you should have—'

'Told you? What would I have said, Madre mia?'

With a sudden violent motion, Felix jumps out of bed and begins pacing around the room, picking up objects randomly and studying them in the thin moonlight without really looking at them, and then discarding them.

'So you never confronted him?'

'Not then. no. I realized pretty quickly that a secret is a

valuable commodity. And you know how much Dad liked valuable things. Almost as much, it turned out, as he liked secrets.'

I'm looking at my son, but I'm not seeing him. This isn't him. It's someone else. His eyes are wide and staring, not like Felix's eyes.

'You blackmailed him?'

I realize I'm hoping that he'll be appalled, that this will be one accusation too far. But Felix continues as if he hasn't noticed the subject matter, as if this is a perfectly normal conversation.

'Not at first. For the first few years I just waited for him to stop. I waited for him to leave them, but when I realized he wasn't going to, I wanted to make him pay. By then I had lots more evidence to hold over him – it was so easy to find once you went looking for it. At first I didn't ask for much, a few hundred here and there, but as I got older I got greedier. I am my father's son, after all.'

'And he never knew it was you?'

Felix shakes his head, laughing. As though this is a game.

'I kept upping the ante. Well, I had a lifestyle to support by that stage, films to make. You know how it is?'

I'm still staring at him, the sick feeling corroding me inside like acid.

'He became a criminal because of you,' I say. 'You know that, don't you? Whatever corruption he was involved in over in Dubai – he did that because of you.'

Felix giggles again, an uncontrollable sound that seems to belong to someone else. Only now does it really sink in that my son is completely off his head.

Drugs. That's what Petra was trying to tell me.

'What are you taking?' I ask wildly. 'What are you on?'
But he doesn't hear. He wants to continue talking.

'No, Madre,' he says excitedly. 'He didn't do it because
of me. He did it because of *him*. All because of him,
because he couldn't bear to give anything up.'

And now I'm thinking ahead, following the narrative
along its natural, inescapable trajectory. 'You were with
him on the night he died! That was you, on the police
camera.'

Felix is nodding and smiling, as if he's pleased with
himself.

'I was bored with it, you see. The secrecy, I mean. I went
to meet him, to see how he'd react. He could be so dis-
missive, you know, Madre. I wanted him to see that I was
someone of . . . consequence.'

I can't take it in. I won't take it in.

'He wasn't alone when I first arrived. He was with the
other one. Your *boyfriend*.' A horrible peal of giggles
follows this pronouncement.

Greg. And now I make myself confront what I think I
knew all along – that it was Greg with Simon on the
CCTV footage of that night. My head is throbbing. So
Greg was involved in Simon's death? But why is Felix calling him my boyfriend? Nothing is making sense.

'I think he assumed the blackmailer was one of the less
than savoury people he'd been doing business with. That's
why he brought loverboy along. Because they were both in
it together.'

When he says *loverboy*, Felix's mouth twists in distaste.

'They waited a while, but when they realized no one was
going to show, the other one left,' Felix goes on. 'Then I
stepped up to make myself known to Pa. He was horrified

at first. Ashamed, as you would be. We had a few drinks – more than a few drinks really. He cried a bit, as he always did. But after a while I think he started to convince himself that he was in the right, that he hadn't done anything terribly wrong. Do you know, Madre, I honestly think he expected me to come round to his way of thinking in the end. I think he thought he could make an ally of me.'

An ally! It makes sense. But . . .

'He was a textbook narcissist,' adds Felix breezily. 'You knew that, surely?'

I'm looking at him, but my head is pounding, my brain thumping against my skull. Can this be real? Can this be happening?

'After a while,' Felix continues, 'we went out and walked along the river. He was begging, pleading, saying he couldn't bear to lose either of his two families. Can you imagine him saying that to me? His *families*? As if we were both equal, as if they were the same as us? That's when I lost it. Well, anyone would have.'

Thumping, thumping in my head. This isn't happening. It isn't real.

'You didn't . . . ?' I try. Then again, 'Tell me you didn't . . . ?'

Felix is off again, moving jerkily around the room.

'The thing is though, Madre, I didn't mean to do it. That's what's so funny about it. I'd climbed up to sit on the railings by the river, just to be by myself. We were drunk, I told you. And then, of course, Dad had to climb up too, just to prove he still could.'

I can imagine it so clearly – Simon still thinking he could win his son around, just like he did everyone else, refusing to be left behind on the ground like some old man.

'When he said that thing about losing his families, he tried to put his arm around me and I hit out,' says Felix chattily. 'I just wanted to stop him touching me, that's all. But he was drunk. He overbalanced. It was an accident.'

I'm looking at him as if I don't believe him, yet at the same time I see it as if it's happening right in front of my eyes.

'And you did all that for money, Felix?'

Now he looks at me as if I'm the one who's crazy.

'Not for money, Madre. For you. Didn't I pay off Pa's BabyMother's mortgage so you wouldn't lose your house?'

'*You* paid Lottie's mortgage?'

'Oh yes. And I'm buying back the house in Tuscany.'

Shock makes my mouth slack. 'The buyer is you?'

Felix nods vigorously.

'You see now?' he says. 'How it's all been for you? I thought I'd set you free. I thought you'd finally find your-self. But instead you found Greg Ronaldson.'

He is looking right at me, but not seeing me. He is sniff-ing, and wiping the underneath of his nose with his hand.

'After everything I did for you, Madre. You did that!'

Oh dear God, he's a monster. But he's not a monster. He's my son. And what he's done, he's done for me. And now it comes to me, clear and stark. It's all my fault.

And again, there comes into my mind that scene on the terrace in Tuscany, the vines overhead sagging grotesquely with swollen, overripe fruit and throwing dappled shadows over Simon's face as he looked at me. His expression for once serious and fiercely intent as he put his wineglass down on the table. *Thud.* 'I've got something to tell you,' he said, and I knew right then, right there, that I didn't want to hear it, whatever it was, that I wanted to seize the cork from the corkscrew on the table and stopper him right up so he couldn't say what he was going to say.

'I've met someone,' he said.

My insides disintegrating in the Italian heat.

'I'd do anything not to hurt you,' he continued, 'but I can't live a lie. We've had a good marriage, Sel,' his voice sagging with sincerity like the vine above our heads. 'We've produced two wonderful children. I thought that's what happiness was until I met her. But now that I have – met her, I mean – what we have just isn't enough any more. Now I know that happiness isn't about sipping fine chianti while the sun sets over the hills. It's something else, something *visceral*.' And he pointed to a spot in his gut, and I felt my own stomach clench in misery.

'That isn't love,' I shouted at him, when I was finally able to speak. 'That's infatuation. It's teenage stuff. It'll blow itself out in weeks. You can't give up your family for that!'

And his expression, almost zealous, as he tried to make me see what he was seeing. 'You're wrong,' he said. 'I can't explain. I feel known by her. I feel like me.'

'And you don't feel like that with me?'

'No.'

'You're saying I stop you being who you are?'

'Sel—'

'You're wrong!' My voice was sharp and ugly in the soft amber light of the afternoon sun. 'I give you the stability to go off into the world and be who you are. Stability is the thing – not love.'

'Selina, I don't expect you to understand.'

'That's big of you.'

'But I *am* leaving you.'

The words fell hard as stones on the terracotta tiles between us.

'You can't.'

'I'll make sure you're well provided for. Your lifestyle won't change. You can keep the house, this villa. We can be the most tremendous friends, Sel, I know we can. Better than lovers. You can—'

'You can't, because I'm pregnant!'

That shut him up. He was quiet then, shocked, his mouth opening and closing without a sound like a silent movie.

'Pregnant?' he repeated at length.

'Yes.' My voice was steady now. Sure of itself. 'So you can't leave me.'

He stayed looking at me for a long time, while I tried not to see the regret that fell over him like a net.

'No,' he said at length. 'Of course not.'

He came over to me then to hold me in his arms. *Oh, the relief!* Knowing it would be all right, after all.

But now, looking at my oldest child's wild face, I realize what I've done, what I set into motion with that split second of deception. Because it was all of it a lie. I wasn't pregnant then, when I watched his desperation to do the right thing shrivel up and die under the glare of the Tuscan sun.

Perhaps it happened later that night when he held me in bed and cried and said he was sorry and I turned to him and wrapped my leg around him like one of the terrace vines and told him not to mention it again. Or perhaps any time during the rest of that holiday, where I allowed him to treat me like someone made from egg-shells and tried

403

not to mind when he spent long afternoons lying on his own in one of the spare bedrooms, the shutters drawn against the intrusive light of day.

All I know is that the next month, when my period was due, it didn't arrive, as I knew it wouldn't.

Only once afterwards did we speak of it.

'It is all over now, isn't it?' I forced myself to ask, as we rode home in a taxi from the airport.

'Yes.' His head turned to look out of the window. 'It's over.'

I almost said it then, almost told him, quite spontaneously, that I loved him, but still I judged it better to hold back, to keep it in reserve. I thought love should be meted out sparingly like sweeties.

Only now, with Felix pacing the room, do I see how much that deception has cost my family. The husband too weak to leave me but too in love to let the other one go. The son who took the weight of his father's weakness on his own too-narrow shoulders, the daughter who grew up in the shadow of a sister she didn't even know existed. And Josh, the child I brought into existence to save my relationship, the Elastoplast baby made to plaster over the great big crack down the centre of my marriage.

For one fleeting, noble moment in Tuscany, Simon tried to do the right thing and set us all free, but I didn't let him. How different would all our lives have been if I had?

I turn to my son, whose glassy eyes don't see me. His jaw is moving though he's not saying anything.

'I'm sorry, Felix,' I say.

For a moment confusion blurs his features, softening them into those of his long-gone boy-self.

He flops down on the bed next to me.

'It doesn't matter, Madre,' he says, and his voice weighs a thousand tons. 'None of it matters any more.'

He puts his hand – *such long, elegant fingers* – up to my face, gently stroking. Then he wraps his arms around me. Tight, so tight. So hard to breathe.

'It's all over now,' he says.

Epilogue

Hope Busfield was born on a May morning that was shiny as a new penny, to a father who was a ghost and an elder half-brother who was criminally insane.

It didn't matter to her. She watched the world with eyes that were full of wonder, and thought it the most beautiful thing ever – the lights and shapes crossing over each other to make patterns of magic.

When her mother was in the bathroom, her sister Sadie picked her up and took her to the hospital window to show her how the aeroplanes painted pure white lines of cloud across the blue sky.

'It's not so bad, really,' Sadie whispered to her. 'Being alive.'

Sadie had long hair that shone bright like the sun, but her mother had lots of dark curly hair that made Hope want to reach out and touch it, and big brown eyes that drank her daughter in like a glass of water on a scorching day.

'My Hopey hun,' she said, in a way that would at some stage become annoying but for now was just fine. 'I'll never let anything bad happen to you.'

And Hope didn't for a moment doubt that was true.

Hope met a lot of people who were related to her in ways she wouldn't fully understand for a long time – long enough for it not to matter any more.

Josh was big and tall and he gave her a soft elephant in lots of different colours that made her feel happy just to look at it, and held her awkwardly as if she was made of china and could break into little pieces. Hope loved him instantly and completely. Flora had lots of hair, like Hope's mum, but it was coarse like a brush and tickled Hope's nose and made her sneeze.

'Do you miss him? Ryan, I mean?' asked her mother, who was lying back against the pillows and smiling to herself.

Flora was quiet for a moment. 'Sometimes I miss being with someone,' she said in a way that told Hope she was not someone who much liked to be alone. 'But no, I'm glad I kicked him out really. He was a twat.'

The word made Hope giggle inside. Twat, she repeated to herself. Twat, twat, twat.

Jules and Emma were loud and argued a lot, which made Hope's ears hurt, and when her mother was asleep they talked about her in whispers (that were louder than anything) and wondered if she could cope.

'I'll be fine,' said Hope's mother, who wasn't really asleep. 'Especially now the kids' books have taken off and I don't have to work at the hotel any more.'

Jules took Hope for a walk down the hospital corridor and muttered some kind of prayer over her. It had the words 'goddess' and 'brave' in it, and Hope didn't mind. When they got back, her mother smiled a smile that contained the world.

'You'd better go,' she told Jules, stretching out her arms for Hope. 'Your boyfriend will be waiting.'

There was another person called Selina, who came one evening wearing a face that was as sad as the saddest thing ever, but when she saw Hope it lit up like one of the night-lights someone had given her mother to plug into the wall.

Selina told her mother about her job. When she talked about the children she worked with, her voice was as soft and warm as the cashmere blanket the woman called Hettie had knitted for her mother to wrap her in.

She talked a bit about someone called Felix, who lived in another hospital somewhere, just like Hope, then her voice became tighter and harder, as if someone had varnished it. The doctors were very hopeful, Selina said, and Hope liked that because it was like her name. He was doing fine, Selina told her mother. Well, without the drugs he was a different person.

Hope wondered about being a different person. She hadn't yet had a chance to become the person she was, let alone someone different. Selina talked about her new flat. She said it 'took some getting used to'. But she didn't say it in a bad way and Hope felt she might not mind too much about getting used to it.

'I still feel bad that you had to move while I've kept my flat,' said Hope's mother.

'Don't be silly.' Hope liked that word. Silly. It sounded like a tickle. 'The endowment paid up as soon as the inquest ruled out suicide, and it was right for you to have the money. After what happened with Felix and Sadie . . .'

Hope's mother looked sad then, as if she was folding in on herself.

'He didn't force her. She was lost at that time. I had allowed her to be lost.'

The two women sat in silence and Hope wondered a bit about being lost, and hoped her mother wouldn't allow *her* to be lost.

Selina leaned over Hope's incubator and held out a finger, which Hope grasped with delight.

'Anyway,' she said, looking at Hope as if she was talking to her rather than her mother, 'it was my fault, all of it. I should have let Simon go when he asked me.'

Behind Selina's head, Hope watched her mother's face sag like the balloon Sadie had brought her when all the air went out of it.

Again there was a silence, and Hope realized for the first time how much silences could say.

'What would have happened if Josh hadn't come in, that last night?' her mother asked suddenly, as if it was something she'd been wanting to ask for a long time. 'Do you think Felix would have . . . ?'

Selina shook her head, and as she did her hair parted and Hope was transfixed by the streaks of grey she could see under the yellow. 'I try not to think about what ifs,' she told her mother. 'I just think about what is. Besides, I know Felix wouldn't have hurt me. He was just lost, that's all, like Sadie.'

'And the new man?'

Selina's face turned as pink as the rosebuds on the Baby-gro Hope was wearing.

'Early days,' she said, and her voice suddenly sounded as if she'd borrowed it from someone much younger.

When it was night and the room was empty of visitors and her mother was asleep, Hope's father came to see her. He wasn't like the others, with a face to smile at her and hands to pick her up and stroke her head. He wasn't in one place, he was everywhere, like specks of glitter in the air, catching the moonlight.

He talked to her about responsibility and about regret

and about how sometimes you can have too much of both, or else not enough, and how difficult it is to get the balance right when life has you by the hand and is pulling you along so quickly your feet don't touch the ground and you feel like you're flying. He talked about lies and secrets and how it's possible to tuck things away into little pockets inside yourself so you don't see them or think about them. Until it's too late.

Above all, he talked about love. The shape of it, the feel of it, the way you could let it trickle over your hands like water, the way it swelled you up like a balloon and sent you soaring, the way you could never ever love someone too much, only not enough. 'In the end you can forgive anything,' he told her, 'if it was done for love.'

Hope lay on her back and watched the glitter shimmer and listened to the gentle hum of her father's voice, and though she didn't know it yet, some of what he said would stay with her, and some of it wouldn't, and some of it would be proved to be right, and some of it wouldn't. She was the product of all of these people and all of their expectations, but she was also just herself and she would learn her own truths about love and about life and regret and about everything in between.

For now, she was content to be who she was and where she was and to wait for her future to unfurl ahead of her like an endless magic carpet.

She was in no rush.

ACKNOWLEDGEMENTS

People aren't joking when they talk about Second Novel Syndrome (think Second Album Syndrome but without the bonus of five months' thumb-twiddling in a Bahamian recording studio waiting for inspiration to strike). It has been a uniquely challenging experience, and I wouldn't have survived it without the help and support of many talented people.

First and foremost, my wonderful editor at Doubleday, Marianne Velmans, who encouraged me throughout and said the tough things that needed saying in the nicest of ways. This book wouldn't have been possible without her. A massive thank-you also to her assistant, Suzanne Bridson, who gave invaluable suggestions and read all the different drafts more times than was probably good for her sanity. Thanks also to the entire team at Transworld, especially Lynsey Dalladay, Kate Samano and Larry Finlay, and to Janine Giovanni for her perfectly timed vote of confidence. And a special mention to Claire Ward, the genius behind the gorgeous cover design.

Felicity Blunt, my lovely agent, has stuck with me and with this book throughout very exciting times in her own life. Thanks to her and to Katie McGowan and everyone else at Curtis Brown for their continued support.

I'd like to thank Detective Chief Superintendent Mary Doyle for answering various police-related questions, and Nicky Stewart for advice on legal details. In both areas, any misakes that remain are entirely my own.

When a book goes through several incarnations, as this one did, it takes an exceptionally loyal friend to read every one of them, which is why I'm so grateful to the supremely generous and patient Rikki Finegold. Thanks also to old pal and early reader Mel Amos for her insight.

Finally, I'd like to thank Michael for putting up with a lot while this book has been in gestation and my three fantastic children, who, much as they occasionally drive me mad, also without doubt keep me sane.

The Mistress's Revenge
Tamar Cohen

You think you are rid of me.

You think you have drawn a line under the whole affair.

You are so, so wrong.

For five years, Sally and Clive have been lost in a passionate affair. Now he has dumped her, to devote himself to his wife and family, and Sally is left in freefall.

It starts with a casual stroll past his house, and popping into the brasserie where his son works. Then Sally befriends Clive's wife and daughter on Facebook. But that's all right isn't it? I mean they are perfectly normal things to do. Aren't they?

Not since *Fatal Attraction* has the fallout from an illicit affair been exposed in such a sharp, darkly funny and disturbing way. After all, who doesn't know a normal, perfectly sane woman who has gone a little crazy when her heart was broken?

'With a twist, will grip you from beginning to end'
PRIMA

'Gasp in recognition at this cracking tale, narrated by a woman scorned . . . Sister, we've all been there'
GRAZIA

The Light Between Oceans
M L Stedman

A boat washes up on the shore of a remote lighthouse keeper's island.

It holds a dead man and a crying baby.

The only two islanders, Tom and his wife Izzy, are about to make a devastating decision.

They break the rules and follow their hearts. What happens next will break yours.

'Mesmerising'
WOMEN'S WEEKLY

'Compelling'
DAILY EXPRESS

'Tender'
SUNDAY TIMES

'Moving'
WOMAN AND HOME

Unforgettable'
GUARDIAN

'Gripping'
GRAZIA

The Mistress of My Fate

Hallie Rubenhold

THE CONFESSIONS OF HENRIETTA LIGHTFOOT
There is much to be learned from a woman of her sort . . .

England, 1789. The Bastille has fallen, King George is mad, and Henrietta Lightfoot flees her home at Melmouth Park after a suspicious death, for which she is blamed. She has no life experience, little money and only her true love, Lord Allenham, to whom she can turn . . .

When he suddenly goes missing, Henrietta embarks on a journey through London's debauched and glittering underworld in the hope of finding him, but discovers more about herself and her mysterious past than she imagined. With the assistance of a sisterhood of courtesans, her skills at the card table and on the stage, the unstoppable Henrietta is ready to become mistress of her fate.

'A remarkable picture of a fascinating age'
DAILY EXPRESS

'A full-blooded historical romp'
INDEPENDENT

'Ricochets with energy, witty observation and rollicking pace'
EASY LIVING

Someone Else's Wedding

Tamar Cohen

Mr & Mrs Max Irving request the company of:

Mrs Fran Friedman, mourning her empty nest, the galloping years, and a disastrous haircut.

Mr Saul Friedman, runner of marathons, and increasingly distant husband.

The two Misses Friedman, Pip and Katy, one pining over the man she can't have, the other shaking off the man she no longer wants.

At the marriage of their son **James,** forbidden object of troubling desire.

For thirty-six hours of secrets and lies, painted-on-smiles and potential ruin. And drinks, plenty of drinks.

There's nothing like a wedding for stirring up the past. As Fran negotiates her way from Saturday morning to Sunday evening she is forced to confront things she's long thought buried, sending shockwaves through her family, and to make decisions about the future that will have far-reaching consequences for them all.